STEPPING

INTO

tomorrow

A. M. KUSI

Published by A. M. Kusi 2022

amkusinovels@gmail.com

Visit our website at www.amkusi.com

Editor: Lauren Clarke of CREATING ink

Sensitivity Edit: Renita McKinney of A Book A Day

Proofreader: Judy's Proofreading

Cover Design: Regina Wamba of ReginaWamba.com

OTHER BOOKS BY A. M. KUSI

A Fallen Star (eBook FREE on all retailers)

(Book 1 in The Shattered Cove Series)

Glass Secrets

(Book 2 in The Shattered Cove Series)

Defying Gravity

(Book 3 in The Shattered Cove Series)

The Lighthouse Inn

(Book 4 in The Shattered Cove series)

His True North

(Book 5 in The Shattered Cove series)

In The Grey

(Book 6 in The Shattered Cove series)

Brave Love

(Book 7 in The Shattered Cove series)

Hope Between Us

(Book 8 in The Shattered Cove series)

Beautiful Collision

(A Shattered Cove Novel)

One Holiday Kiss (eBook FREE on all retailers)

(A Shattered Cove Short Story)

The Orchard Inn Series

(Our first complete steamy romance series.)

For a complete list of all our books, visit:

WWW.AMKUSI.COM/BOOKS

This book is dedicated to the grumpy hero lovers out there who like their fictional men a little bit gruff and a whole lot sexy.

"People speak of hope as if it is this delicate, ephemeral thing made of whispers and spiders' webs. It's not. Hope has dirt on her face, blood on her knuckles, the grit of the cobblestones in her hair, and just spat out a tooth as she rises for another go."
— Mathew @CrowsFault

"For a seed to achieve its greatest expression, it must come completely undone. The shell cracks, its insides come out, and everything changes. To someone who doesn't understand growth, it would look like complete destruction."
— Cynthia Occelli

GET A FREE SHORT NOVEL

Join our newsletter to get a FREE short novel that's not available on any retailer. Plus updates about new releases, giveaways, pre-orders, sneak peeks, and more.

Visit the website below to join now.

WWW.AMKUSI.COM/NEWSLETTER

TABLE OF CONTENTS

PLAYLIST

"Healing" by Fletcher
"Dirty Mind" by Boy Epic
"Broken" by Seether featuring Amy Lee
"Popular Monster" by Falling in Reverse
"Unsteady" by X Ambassadors
"I'll be Good" by Jaymes Young
"Empty Space" by James Arthur
"Is There Somewhere" by Halsey
"Keep On" by Sasha Sloan
"Hurt" by Oliver Tree
"Little Do You Know" by Alex & Sierra
"2012" by Chris Brown
"Be Here For You" by Sam Tinnesz

1

ISABELLA

Inhaling a shaky breath, Isabella cupped some of the cool water from under the tap and splashed it on the back of her neck. The icy water grounded her. She would have put it on her cheeks, but she'd actually done her makeup and dressed up for the first time in a few years—except for Robert's funeral. But that was six months ago.

Isabella dried her hands quickly and left the bathroom, her gaze sweeping over the tent that was bustling with wedding activity under the soft Edison bulb lighting.

"Whiskey, double," a deep bass voice carried over the upbeat music playing through the venue. His shoulders hunched over as he sat at the bar to her right, so only one side was visible to her.

Tingles spiraled over her skull. Her lungs seized. Tufts of wild curls stuck out of the top of his hair like the wild break of a crashing wave. Sharp cheekbones slashed towards a wide, strong nose. Serious, thick eyebrows slanted together with a deep crease between them as if he perpetually frowned.

His wide shoulders flexed as he moved to accept the drink

the bartender slid across to him. Two long, thick umber fingers wrapped around the glass before he tipped it to his full brown lips, his pink tongue darting out as if savoring every drop. The move shouldn't have been sexy, but Isabella's blood turned molten just the same.

Her gaze roamed over his veined, tattooed forearms to the white dress shirt rolled up at his elbows and farther to the material stretched taut across his broad shoulders, tapering in at his waist. Black dress pants wrapped around his thick thighs. The man looked as if Poseidon himself had crafted him from the depths of the sea in his image.

Isabella tried to swallow, but her mouth had gone dry. *Wow.*

Someone bumped into her, drawing her out of her lust-induced daze.

"Sorry," they apologized.

She shook her head, forcing herself towards the table with her waiting friends. She'd never been affected that way by someone—had her very breath stolen and held captive.

Isabella weaved around a few people, grabbing a fresh glass of champagne from a passing server, eyes zoned in on the table her close friend Tessa sat at.

"Did you get cake yet?" She flopped into the seat next to Tessa before taking a gulp of the bubbly beverage.

"Not yet."

"*Dios*, there was a long line to use the restroom."

Tessa chuckled. "Isn't there always?"

"True."

"So . . . how is it being back in your hometown?" Tessa asked, picking up her glass and taking a sip.

Isabella sighed. "Honestly, it's good to be back. I feel like I've made the right decision. Eli is having a blast with his grandparents. I think it will be good for him—for us."

Tessa's eyes flashed with sympathy. "So you're gonna go with one of the apartments we looked at this weekend?"

Isabella shook her head. "No, I'll move back in with Mom and Dad and see what I can find later around here. I think they need more help at the marina than they're letting on, and it's not like I have much to occupy my time with right now anyways."

Tessa gasped. "Now? I thought you weren't leaving me in Colorado until the end of May. I'm supposed to get another month with you at the shop."

Isabella pulled her into a hug, not sure how she'd be able to start over without her one constant—her best friend. "I don't mean right now. I'm sticking around for a little while. Same plan. I still have to finish going through Robert's things." Her eyes stung with the reminder.

Tessa took Isabella's hand in hers. "Do you need help?"

Isabella shook her head. "No. We had most of it done before things got too bad—as he insisted. But it's the second to last thing on his list for me to do."

"What's the last item?"

Isabella's cheeks flushed. "To move on with someone new . . . actually, he specifically said a one-night stand. It's crazy that even in death, he was trying to take care of me."

Tessa's eyes widened. "Seriously? That sounds like Robert. He wanted you to be happy. It makes sense that despite his ALS, he made sure you had this last gift to give you a sort of compass while everything was so . . . hard."

Isabella nodded, a soft smile turning her lips up as memories of the man who was once her best friend flitted through her mind.

"Do you think you're ready for that?" Tessa asked, her voice soft and free of judgment. If anyone knew how to seize the day, it was Tessa.

Her reaction to the stranger at the bar was still thrumming through her veins. "I . . . do. For something fun—definitely not something serious. A one-night stand . . . well, that has potential." *Not that I've ever had one.* But maybe the new Isabella could do it. The Isabella who was moving halfway across the country. She lifted her drink to her lips.

"A wedding is the perfect place to find that." Tessa scanned the room. "Anyone caught your eye?"

Isabella pressed a cool hand to one of her flushed cheeks. "I did see a man by the bar when I went to the bathrooms. He was alone and . . . I don't know, he looked . . . well, hotter than Hades, actually." *And just as mysterious too.*

Tessa's attention focused on the bar. "Him?"

Bella turned to look in the same direction, her attention catching on the isolated man in question. *What made him so sullen at a wedding?* "Yeah. There's just something about him . . ." The people around him gave him a wide berth, as if afraid whatever weight he carried on those broad shoulders would rub off on them.

"Go for it," Tessa said.

Isabella spun back to her, chewing on her bottom lip. "I don't know. It's been so long since I had to do something like this."

"You don't have to have sex with the guy if you don't want. But you could try and talk to him. Ease yourself into it," Tessa pushed.

Am I really ready for this? It's just a conversation—just one small step into the new me. And the new Isabella is confident. Fake it 'til you make it, right? "If I do, will you finally ask Roy about doing that tattoo you've wanted?"

Panic flashed through her friend's gaze before she turned her focus to the very man they were speaking of. He wasn't hard to find, with his blue-tipped hair and several face piercings. He was down on one knee, speaking to Joshua, the bride's son.

"I—"

"Come on. What are you so worried about?" Tessa and Roy had been dancing around each other for so long.

Tessa shrugged.

"You ask him for the tattoo and I'll go talk to the man at the bar. Deal?" Isabella asked, holding out her pinky finger and trying to act like the idea didn't terrify her.

"Deal." Tessa hooked her pinky finger in Bella's.

"What are you two troublemakers up to now?" Roy's voice lilted with his Irish accent. Isabella smiled to herself as her best friend tried to make it seem like she wasn't affected by the man, but her shiver gave her away.

"Cold?" he asked Tessa.

"A little." She reached for her sweater, but he'd already picked it up off the chair and held it out for her arms, anticipating her needs.

Isabella wanted someone to do that for her. To have a man look at her like she was the sun and moon as Roy did to Tessa. She hadn't found it with Robert, but maybe someday she would discover it with someone else.

Though Robert was a great man, and best friend, he had not been her person. The next time she agreed to marry, it would be because she'd found the kind of love that she'd only read about in books or witnessed in a few lucky friends. But she'd learned her lesson. Isabella would never settle for less again.

"Well, wish me luck." Bella stood, smoothing her glittering gold dress over her plentiful curves. "I'm so nervous."

"'Bout what?" Roy asked.

"Stepping into tomorrow." Isabella took a deep breath.

Using the phrase she and Robert had shared bolstered her confidence.

"Do I look okay?" Bella plucked the fabric from her belly and rolled her shoulders back.

"You look grand," Roy assured her.

Bella smiled and turned to Tessa, nodding towards Roy. "Well?"

"Well, what?" Roy asked.

Isabella cut her friend a warning look. They'd made a deal, after all.

Tessa stood abruptly. "I wanted to know if you'd dance with me?"

"Of course. That'd make me right delira."

Tessa's eyebrows drew together. "Delira?"

He smiled. "Deliriously happy, as you Americans say."

Isabella laughed.

Tessa slipped her hand in Roy's before focusing on Isabella. "A deal's a deal. Get your cute ass over there and say hello."

Nerves swirled in Isabella's stomach. She bit her lip and nodded. Her chest rose as she took one last deep breath. "Don't wait up for me." She spun around and walked towards the bar with her head held high.

Legs trembling, Isabella moved to the empty seat next to the intimidating man. The energy around him shifted as she got closer like he was a whirlpool, ready to swallow up anything and anyone around him. A slow song drifted through the speakers as the bartender moved to the opposite end of the drinks station, filling orders. *I should have downed my champagne before coming over.*

She turned to her right, putting on her friendliest smile. "So, are you here for the groom or the bride?"

It wasn't the best icebreaker, but she thought she'd at least get a response. Instead, awkward silence pressed between them like stagnant air.

Her belly squeezed. His only reaction was a subtle tightening of his shoulders as if he could make himself smaller and stay invisible. The thought was ludicrous, not just because of his sheer size but because he was so handsome. Something about him made her want to crack him open and see what lay inside.

"What can I get you?" the bartender asked, wiping down the space in front of her.

"Tequila, please."

He got to work, filling a shot glass and plating a lime before setting the salt shaker beside her drink in front of her.

"Are you from around here?" the bartender asked. At least someone was talking to her.

She sipped the tequila, savoring the flavor on her tongue. "I flew in from Colorado."

His eyes widened with interest. "That's cool. Always wanted to go skiing there."

"You should do it, then."

"Someday." He smiled before moving to the other end of the bar to help another guest.

Isabella took another sip of her drink before picking up the salt and shaking it over the lime wedge. She set down the shaker and retrieved her drink, savoring another small sip before sucking on the end of the salty fruit. A burst of citrus flooded her mouth, the tang mixing with the salt and liquor, warming her.

"I believe the salt is supposed to come before the liquor, then the lime." The mystery man's voice was as deep and rich as the whiskey he drank.

She turned to him, her breath stuttering. "So he speaks."

The corner of his lips twitched before they flattened back

into a thin line. He grunted. "You here for the groom or the bride?"

A small puff of air left his nose, a subtle scoff. "Not too many here for the bride. She has a history. The fact that you don't know that makes me think you're a plus-one."

"Subtle."

"Hmm?"

"Trying to see if I'm here alone and single?" she added, just a little bit hopeful.

"Was I right?" He ran a massive hand over his neatly trimmed beard.

"My friend Roy is Maddy's cousin. I came with him and my best friend, Tessa." She turned, finding the very couple mentioned on the dance floor, moving close to each other.

"Third wheel, huh?" the man asked.

She shrugged. "I'm used to it."

Isabella turned away from the couples moving on the dance floor to the man next to her and gasped. Two dark eyes stared at her, fathomless and magnetic. Something akin to sympathy flashed in his gaze before it was gone, hiding behind the shadows of secrets kept in those eclipsed orbs. She recognized the pain though—this man was grieving. That was the weight he carried.

Her lungs strained with the need to breathe. Isabella sucked in a ragged breath, her heart racing.

"I made a deal with my friend that she would do something she'd been too scared to do, and so would I."

His eyes flashed as he leaned closer. The whiskey scent on his breath wrapped around her like silk ties binding her in place.

"What is it you had to do?" He cocked his head to the side.

"I had to come talk to you."

He grunted, but still, his attention burned her flesh.

"Why do I scare you?" he asked.

"You don't. Not like that. Just talking to a man, putting myself out there for the first time." Heat burned her skin. *Good Lord. Does he think I mean I'm a virgin?* The liquor loosened her tongue. "First time in a long time, I mean."

"So why do it at all?" he pressed.

She sighed. "Because sometimes to move forward you have to do something scary and uncomfortable. And I need to do something different. Because what I've been doing has led me to a place I don't want to be in anymore."

He blinked as if she'd surprised him. Silence passed as the wedding guests laughed and spoke around them. It was as if they were in their own little bubble, separate from everyone else. She was held in the trance of his perceptive gaze.

Maybe it was the mixture of champagne and tequila. Or maybe it was the fact that after today, she'd most likely never see this man again. But for once, her inhibitions were lowered. What did she have to lose?

"I'm ready to get out of here." She left the invitation hanging in the air, hoping he'd make a move.

His jaw tensed, his eyes clouding over as if fighting a war with himself—to accept her invitation or not.

She was already committed to this—what was one more step? One last try?

If she'd learned anything during the last twelve years, it was that her pride could take a hit and she'd survive. Still, her stomach tipped and her hands grew clammy with sweat as she readied herself to ask the question. *Here goes nothing.* "You want to join me?"

2

ISABELLA

Several emotions flitted through those midnight pools. Desire. Fear. Guilt. And finally, resolve. "Don't think that's a good idea." His voice was raw, like he'd swallowed a bucket of saltwater—his rejection just as bitter.

"Oh. Okay." She tried to not react to the sting. Here she was, offering a night of no-strings fun, and she'd been turned down. Wasn't that what most guys wanted?

Just not with her apparently.

Stop. I am good enough. There is someone out there for me. And I'll find him someday.

"Well, you have a good night." She spun off the seat and moved towards the restrooms once more, hoping to hide the burn of her humiliation. She rushed inside, heading straight for the sink to run her hands under the cold water once more. She peeked at the mirror. Her tan cheeks were flushed from a mixture of tequila and embarrassment.

The door opened and a young woman rushed in, barely giving Isabella a second glance before she rushed to one of the stalls.

Isabella gave one last look at her reflection, brushing back her dark hair and the curls that Tessa had helped her do. She pulled out the red lipstick from her clutch and applied a fresh coat, finishing up as the young woman sidled up to the counter near her to wash her hands.

Isabella smoothed her hand down her stomach self-consciously, as if she could hide some of her cellulite that way.

"I love that dress," the young woman next to her said.

Isabella smiled, meeting her gaze in the mirror. "Thank you." Familiarity prickled at the base of her skull. "Nova?"

Nova dried her hands on a paper towel. "Yes?"

"It's me, Isabella Noveas." She introduced herself using her maiden name.

Nova's eyes widened. "Oh my goodness. It's so great to see you. Are you just in town for the wedding?"

"Yes—well, at least for now. I'm moving back in a couple months with my son, Eli."

"Wow, how many years has it been?" Nova asked.

"Twelve or so."

"You look great. I heard you got married and moved out west."

Isabella nodded. "Yes, Colorado actually."

The door opened and a frazzled-looking server leaned in, relief painting her face as soon as she spotted Nova. "We can't find the extra champagne."

"I'll show you where we keep it," Nova answered before turning back to Isabella. "I'd love to catch up once you're in town for good."

"Me too," Isabella agreed, following the two women out of the bathroom into the soft-lit tent. She pointedly avoided gazing at the bar, focusing instead at the couples dancing and laughing through the tent to the night beyond. Tessa and Roy weren't dancing anymore, and their seats were empty. Had they left? She steered towards the back of the tent, walking out to the darkness. Nova chatted animatedly with one of the servers on the corner. It would be good for her to have a friend here. What had little Nova Emerson been up to since Isabella had been gone?

Hopefully, her life had been easier than Isabella's.

Isabella gave one more scan of the room for her friends, but it seemed she was alone. *Good for Tessa.*

"Do you want another?" The bartender's voice drew her attention back to the handsome stranger shaking his head.

What was I thinking asking him out?

Isabella turned and headed out of the back of the tent into the night. Her head tipped towards the sky lit up by a million stars. She moved farther from the tent, letting the cool spring air compete with the heat of humiliation still scalding her cheeks. Her heels sunk into the wet long grass, and the voices of the guests blurred with the peeping sound of the frogs.

"At least I took a chance. I tried, Robert," Isabella whispered, continuing to walk down a path by the fence posts. Her heartbeat returned to normal.

A tiny meow drew her attention to the ground ahead of her. She narrowed her eyes in search of the noise. Another little meow sounded just ahead. She bent low to find a little kitten writhing on the ground. A piece of white string highlighted by the moonlight was wrapped around its paw.

"Are you stuck, sweetheart?" Isabella reached out carefully to grab the kitten and find the knot. "How did you get so twisted up in this, huh?"

After a little maneuvering, the kitten was freed. She tucked it against her chest and petted it while it meowed and nuzzled against her.

"You're welcome." She set it down and the little black thing scampered off into the tall grass.

"You still want to get out of here?" the deep bass from behind her asked.

Isabella jumped and spun around, her hand on her heart. The mystery man from the bar stood with his hands in his pockets just a few feet away. How had she not heard him approach? He was stealthy for a lumberjack of a man, and God, so much taller than she'd thought. She searched the area around them, gauging how far away everyone else was. Would anyone be able to hear what they were talking about?

"What did you have in mind?" Her voice was all breath.

For the first time, his lips parted, curving up into a smile so sexy it was almost sinister. "Ever been fishin' on the ocean?"

Isabella blinked. That had honestly been the last thing she'd expected to come out of his mouth. But somehow, it fit her mystery man—unexpected and a little bit risky.

"I got rods we can use," he continued.

Was he . . . was that a euphemism? Was that how dating went nowadays?

"Rods?"

"And a boat at the marina."

He was serious. He wanted to take her fishing? She must be more rusty than she'd thought if he'd confused her offer for a midnight fishing trip.

She laughed, free and uninhibited for the first time since . . . she didn't know when. It was bittersweet knowing she'd been so lost in the sadness of grief for so long.

He was looking at her like she'd had one tequila too many. Maybe she had. Because she was going to go fishing with a stranger in a sparkly gold cocktail gown. "I've been fishing once or twice."

"So is that a yes?"

"Okay, but first, I need to know your name."

"Nash."

She held out her hand to him. "Nice to meet you, Nash. I'm Bella."

He hesitated and then took her hand. His palm enveloped hers, big and rough with calluses. *How would they feel on my skin? Brushing over my breasts, or dipping between my thighs . . .* She shivered.

He dropped his arm and stepped back, his mouth set in a grim line. "I'll pull the truck around."

"I'll just grab my purse and meet you out front."

He nodded and turned around, walking towards the gravel parking lot, filled with cars.

Isabella tipped her head back to the sky. "Okay, I'm doing it. I'm stepping into tomorrow."

Maybe then she would be able to figure out what the hell to do next.

3

NASH

Nash opened the door to his truck as the chilly ocean breeze blew over him. The marina always smelled like brine, what had fast become one of his favorite smells. The fact that it cleaned his senses of the sweet rose hip blossoms the woman in his passenger seat wore was a bonus. *How long has it been since someone made me look twice?*

It was that lost look in her eyes that pulled at something familiar inside him. Nothing and no one evoked so much of a spark of emotion in him these days—and that was just the way he liked it. Simple. Clean. No attachments.

The passenger-side door opened and she climbed out, her sexy heels clicking on the pavement as she shivered in the salty air. He took his time, studying her while her focus was preoccupied by their surroundings. Her toned calves led up her long legs to the shimmering dress that hugged her curves. His mouth watered. God, he wanted to get his hands under that fabric and see if she was just as juicy as she looked. Wide hips and an ass he'd only ever dreamed about sashayed as she walked. But she didn't seem to be conscious of just how fucking sexy she was, which made her all the more enticing.

"So, this is where your boat is?" she asked.

His focus drifted up her stomach to her ample breasts and farther until he met her electric gaze. "Yup."

A few strands of dark brown hair blew over her round face as she scanned the marina again, starting with the bait and tackle shop behind them and moving back to the docks. Her pert little nose crinkled and those full red lips that begged him to bite pursed. Bella tucked her arms against herself, shivering slightly.

"You still want to do this?"

Her attention shot to him as she rubbed her hands over the too-thin sweater covering her arms. "Of course." Her voice cracked, the only tell that she wasn't as confident as she seemed.

He locked the truck and headed towards the boat. The floodlight outside the store flashed on, temporarily blinding him as they headed for the docks.

Bella gasped and ducked, moving closer to his side, but not touching him.

"It's motion-activated."

"Right." She sighed.

His boat was farther down, inky-black water lapping at the floating docks as he walked just a little slower than normal for his guest.

Bella stumbled. His hand shot out to grab her before she ended up in the bay. He tugged her against his side, his hand firmly planted on her lower back. Energy pulsed between them. Her chest heaved as her liquid amber eyes—the color of his favorite whiskey—flicked to him, wide and unsure.

"Be more careful." His voice came out much gruffer than he'd intended.

She gave him a curt nod, but relaxed against him as he gently ushered her to the boat. He grabbed the edge, pulling it closer to the dock, and slid a leg over until he was safely on board. There was no way she was going to make it in that sexy-as-fuck dress. He was half tempted to let her try, just to see if her cheeks got pink.

She clasped her hands on the metal railing on the side of his boat, determination lighting her expression. He slipped his hands under her arms. She gave a surprised squeak as he lifted her onto the boat and deposited her in front of him.

She swallowed. "Th-thank you."

He grumbled and headed for the door leading below deck to the small kitchen/bedroom. Grabbing a sweatshirt from the hook, he smelled it to make sure it wasn't too fishy. Thankfully, it wasn't. He grabbed a pair of extra rubber boots and returned to the top deck. Bella had turned towards the full moon, her whispers floating on the wind, but he couldn't be sure what she was saying. Was she talking to herself?

"Here." He handed over the sweatshirt. She'd probably swim in it, but it would keep her warm.

She swiveled around, blinking at the material in his hands before tentatively reaching for it. A small appreciative smile curved her lips upwards. Some of the ice around his heart melted.

"Thank you." She pulled it on and zipped it up. "What about you?" She motioned to his thin dress shirt.

"I'll be fine. You'll be safer in these." He held out the waterproof shoes to her.

She looked down to her heels and then back to him. "I guess I'm not really wearing the right footwear for fishing, am I?" She giggled and accepted the shoes, leaning against the side of the boat for support while she changed them out.

There was something about the sight of Bella in his clothes that made his rib cage squeeze tight.

He grabbed a life vest from the storage under one of the seats. "Put this on and we're ready to go."

Her brows drew together. "Is that really necessary? I can swim."

"Captain's rules." Safety was the number one priority.

"If you insist." She pulled it on, trying to zip it up and failing. Her breasts were too big for the vest he usually reserved for his teenage help, Anthony.

"Here." He loosened the straps on the side, pulled it together with one hand, and zipped it with the other. The movement jerked her closer so that her scent melded with the sea air in a way that became intoxicating. His abs clenched as his blood heated. It had been a long time since he'd been with a woman. He'd only indulged in quick fucks once in a while. He'd not spent this much time with someone he was attracted to since . . .

"Nash?" A hand just as soft as the voice that had spoken landed on his arm. "You okay?"

He pulled away, unhooking the ropes from the dock. "Fine. You ready to go?"

"As ready as I'll ever be."

He headed towards the cabin and the steering wheel. She followed close behind.

Nash pointed to the seat on the other side of the walkway that led down to the cabin. "You can sit there."

He started the engine, waiting until she was settled before guiding them through the no-wake zone out of the marina, through the bay, and into open water. The wind wasn't strong, but the sea wasn't calm either. The up and down of the waves lulled him as it always did.

He turned to his guest, her head tipped towards the

window, pointed towards the blackness of the night. The moon glinted off the water, their only source of light save for the few dim lights on the boat. He kept the cabin illuminated enough to see, but not too bright. Her skin glowed under the soft bulbs. A few stray curls of her hair danced in the sea air.

"Do you do this often?" she asked, turning to face him.

"Take women I've just met night fishing? Never." *Not even Ana.*

Guilt weighed down his shoulders. He was used to the burden. He deserved it.

"Well, I meant night fishing, but that's nice to know too," Bella said.

"Sometimes when I can't sleep, I come out here." Offering that personal information was like removing an infected sliver —painful and yet necessary.

"Is this a hobby or a profession?"

He slowed the boat before cutting the engine. "Both I suppose."

"Why did you change your mind?" Her voice wavered.

Because I'm trying to move on—little by little. Nash leveled his gaze on her, repeating the same words she'd used at the wedding. "Because sometimes to move forward you have to do something scary and uncomfortable. And I need to do something different. Because what I've been doing has led me to a place I don't want to be anymore."

She blinked studying him closely.

Nash stood, flicking the bright light on that aimed towards the back of the thirty-foot boat, making the once black water turn green under its illumination.

He set up the first rod in silence under her perceptive gaze. The satisfying whine of the line releasing was his reward for casting it as far as he could. He picked up the second pole.

"Can I bait it?" she asked.

He stopped short. She wanted to get her hands dirty? Bella didn't stop surprising him. "If you want."

She smiled triumphantly, rolling up one of the sleeves on the oversized jacket before dunking her hand in the bait tank. Her pink tongue darted out as she concentrated on catching one of the smaller fish. She pulled her arm out, water splashing onto the deck.

"Got it!" She laughed, and it shot straight through his frigid heart. The joy that lit her face was magnetic, pulling him in until he wanted to make her release that throaty expression of giddiness again and again. He couldn't be happy, but tonight, he could live vicariously through her.

"Here's the hook," he said.

She wrapped her hand around the metal and looped the bait on before rinsing her hand off in the water.

"You've done this before," he noted.

She shrugged with a shy grin. "A time or two. Been a while though."

"Ready to cast?" he asked.

She glanced around the boat nervously. "Okay, I'll be honest. I enjoy fishing. I don't mind touching fish or worms. But I suck at casting. And I usually get the hook stuck in a tree, power lines, or on a piece of the boat. One time I even got it in my dad's ear." She winced. "After that, I was forbidden to do my own casting." She chuckled.

His mouth twitched as he fought the urge to smile. It was the most unnatural feeling. "Sounds like it's better if you sit this one out, then."

He cast the line on the other side of the boat and set it into the rod mount.

"Now we wait?" she asked.

He grunted his agreement.

There was no sound out here except for the waves lapping

at the boat. The silence was one reason why he loved the sea. It was calming. Bella's presence didn't seem to change that.

"If you could have anything in the world, what would you want?" Bella asked.

He turned his attention towards her, the moonlight shining in her eyes. There was something about those whiskey orbs that sucked him in and made him throw his usual caution to the wind.

"A second chance." *To make things right.*

She nodded as if understanding, but that was impossible. Still, it loosened some of the pressure in his chest.

"What about you?" he asked.

She chewed on her bottom lip. Nash got the urge to reach out and pluck it from her mouth. He fisted his hands by his sides instead.

"Honestly, I want to figure out who I am, and then . . . find my own happily ever after."

He didn't mean for the sound rumbling in his chest to come out, half scoff, half grumble.

She tipped her head to the side studying him, eyes narrowed. "Too cliché for you?"

"It isn't that."

She crossed her arms over her chest as if that would somehow protect her from his cynicism. "What is it, then?"

"Nothing. A woman like you? You deserve to find that happiness."

"But you don't?" She hit the nail on the head, seeing more than he'd intended.

He sucked in a gulp of fresh sea-laced air and focused back on the water. "I had my shot and blew it." Understatement of the century.

"Oh." Something a lot like sympathy edged her voice.

He didn't want her pity.

The rod whined as something tugged on the line, bowing the pole.

"We got a bite." He picked up the rod, swiftly shoving it into Bella's unsuspecting hands.

She gasped, clinging to the pole as he moved behind her, his front to her back, and yanked the rod.

"Oh my God!" she exclaimed, reeling it in.

The fish tugged the line, but Nash held on. His hands kept the pole from slipping through Bella's small palms.

Her ass rubbed against his groin as she wiggled in excitement, making his cock stiffen. He tried to not be a dick and give her some space, but it was impossible to hold on to the rod around her voluptuous curves without getting up close and personal. That was one of the things that had drawn him to her when he'd first turned to her, second to those amber eyes. Nash was a big man; he needed a woman with something to grip. A woman he wouldn't be afraid to break as he fucked her three ways to Sunday.

There was another hard tug and then the line snapped, sending them both careening backwards. Nash would have been able to stabilize himself if not for the fact that Bella lost her balance and fell on top of him.

He dropped the pole in favor of wrapping his arms tighter around her to soften her fall.

"Oomf." He grunted as they hit the deck.

She spun around in his arms, her hair kissing his chest. "*Dios*, are you okay?"

The Spanish falling off her lips was like an aphrodisiac. Shadows of the night played on her soft skin, highlighting her beautiful round face. She bit those red full lips he wanted to taste. Her thighs spread over his, the heat of her pussy hovering over his cock.

"Fuck," he breathed.

"Where are you hurt?" she asked, lines of concern marring her brows.

"Not that kinda ache."

She blinked and then, as if realizing that the hardness under her was not in fact a flashlight in his pocket, her eyes widened, her mouth forming an *O*.

"Oh. I . . . you . . . you like me?"

A hoarse bark of the closest sound he'd made to laughter in years escaped his throat. "I wouldn't have invited you on my boat if I didn't."

She smiled. "So this was all a plan to lure me away so you could, what? Have your wicked way with me?"

"If you want that," Nash said. It was scary, taking a risk like this, but she wasn't a local, so there would be no harm done. He could take this one small step, and then maybe someday he'd fully be able to move on—as long as she wanted this as well. "If not, you still got your night of fun, fishing under the moonlight."

Her expression softened, her voice a hoarse whisper. "And if I do want more?"

"Then you'll get your one night of fun with me. I'll make you come at least twice, and then we'll go our separate ways." There, he'd laid out his rules. One night. No future.

"One night," she confirmed.

"One nigh—"

Bella's lips slanted over his. Colors and sensations burst in his mind's eye. He groaned, running one hand up her spine to cup the back of her neck, the other settling on her lower back as he rolled them so that she was below him. He sucked her bottom lip into his mouth and tugged with his teeth. A tiny mewl escaped her, shooting straight to his cock. Want blinded him. Desire rocketed through his body, sending all his blood rushing south. She tasted so good—like sweet rose hips and champagne.

Nash stood, taking her with him, not breaking the kiss. His tongue slid into her welcoming mouth, tasting, seeking, conquering. Each stroke only made him crave more. He reached for the zipper on her life vest, removing it and tossing it onto the deck. Her small hand fisted his dress shirt as she leaned in, rubbing herself against him, stoking the fire raging within him. God, he wanted to feel her everywhere. Strip her down until every inch was laid bare.

"I have a bed in the cabin below deck."

Her lips, swollen from his kiss, glistened under the moon. "What about the other fishing pole?"

"Forget it." Nash took her hand and tugged her down the walkway to the cabin. He hadn't felt this alive in so long. He stepped down into the small space, turning back to her. Bella's chest rose and fell almost as rapidly as his. Heart drumming in his chest, he checked one more time with her. "You sure you want this?"

Her heated gaze never wavered from his. "It's the only thing I'm sure about right now."

His self-control snapped. His lips crashed against hers as his hands worked to remove his sweatshirt from her body. His mind reeled, overcome with her scent and feel under his hands. She felt like goddamned heaven. And he was the devil who would consume her light under the shadows until the sun came up.

4

ISABELLA

Goose bumps prickled Isabella's flesh as the sweatshirt fell to the ground. Hot sweet lips delved between hers, feeding the wildfire blazing through her bloodstream. Calloused, working man's hands slid over her shoulders, forcing her thin sweater to the floor. Her head spun from his touch, his taste, and his sea and cedar scent, spinning her up on already unsteady feet. Knees weak, she leaned against him. The boat rocked in the waves, but Nash was immoveable. Like he commanded the very sea. Her Poseidon.

She gripped the buttons on his shirt, undoing them as his teeth raked over her lip, a bite of pain only melding with her excitement. Her skin flashed with heat. Her dress was too tight and suffocating all of a sudden.

She opened his shirt, placing her hands on his abs. Good God, was any part of this man not perfection?

A warm chuckle rumbled in his chest. Had she said that aloud?

"Turn around." His deep voice made her thighs clench.

She obeyed, facing the door. Deft fingers pulled her hair off her neck and over one shoulder before the scrape of his beard tickled her nape. He pressed open-mouthed kisses behind her ear, trailing down to her shoulder. She closed her eyes, a small moan leaving her lips. Had she ever been this savored before? Were all one-night stands like this?

The sound of the zipper sent a rush of self-consciousness crashing through her. She tensed as he pushed the dress to her feet revealing the spandex hip-and-tummy-control garment she was wearing.

Dios, this is probably the least sexy thing I could have worn.

Nash placed two big hands on her shoulders, shifting her to face him. She licked her lips nervously, flicking her attention to him as nerves skittered through her body.

The lust in his dark eyes made her gasp.

"Take it off," he commanded, his hands fisting at his sides as if he was barely in control.

She slipped the boots off first. Then she fumbled with the elastic waist, pulling the spandex from her skin, which wasn't easy in a rocking boat. She stood before him in her black lace bra and matching panties, glad she'd chosen something to make her feel sexy, even though she hadn't expected anyone to see it. She took a deep breath as he studied her. Isabella was a plus-size woman. Standing in front of Nash, with his open, untucked dress shirt, showing off his barrel chest and muscles, she couldn't help but feel self-conscious. But the way his heated gaze worshiped her flesh filled her with a heady sense of sensual power.

"You're so fucking beautiful."

His compliment warmed her, snuffing out most of her insecurities. She wasn't thin by any stretch of the imagination.

"Take the rest off." Nash raised his shirt up and over his head, showing off the tattoo sleeves on both arms.

She unhooked her bra, tossing it to the ground before pushing her fingers under the elastic of her panties and shimmying them down her legs, holding the small table to her left for balance.

The clink of his belt seemed magnified in the small cabin. It hung undone as he unzipped his pants, his focus never leaving her.

Stepping out of his pants, he reached for her once again. His fingers threaded through her hair as he brought his mouth to hers. He devoured her mouth as his palms skated down to cup her breasts.

"I've been thinking of tasting every inch of this body since I laid eyes on you," he confessed.

"Is it . . . I mean . . . I hope it's what you wanted." She bit her lip.

Nash pulled back, his penetrating gaze leveled on hers. All that power directed at her made her knees wobble. "You seriously have no idea, do you?"

Her brows drew together in question.

"Do you own a mirror?"

She nodded.

"Has no one told you how fucking perfect you are?"

She shook her head.

"That's a tragedy." He pinched her nipple.

"Ah."

His hot mouth closed around the other, sucking and licking before he dragged his teeth over the peak. His other hand massaged the other breast, spilling from his giant palms.

"These tits have me so spellbound I'm not sure whether to lick, bite, or fuck them."

"Oh, *Dios*." She blinked lazily, arousal pooling in her pussy. A steady throb of need built deep within her.

He bent on his knee, wet kisses trailing down her soft stomach, paying special attention to the stretch marks.

"So soft." He rubbed his beard over her sensitive flesh, pouring gasoline onto her already blazing inferno.

"Nash," she pleaded.

"And these thick juicy thighs. I knew they'd be gorgeous, hidden under that dress." He cupped the back of her calves and nipped her inner leg.

"Oh!" He'd bitten her. And she'd liked it.

"Now bend over that table, sweetness." He got to his feet and pointed to her left.

Isabella turned, anticipation winding through her, the tension in the air making it hard to breathe. She placed two shaking palms over the built-in table. Her heart thudded, and her ears rang. What was he going to—

"Ahhh," she moaned as his thick fingers parted her folds.

Slap!

"Nash!"

"Fuck, this ass is incredible." He kneaded the sore spot with bruising fingers while his other hand cupped her pussy.

Her legs trembled. The ache built like the returning tide.

"Please," she said.

"You even beg so pretty."

"Gah, Nash. I need—"

"Need what, sweetness?" He slid a finger inside her, stealing her breath.

"More. You." She was unable to form sentences as his digit worked her, curling and hitting a sensitive spot inside her. She clenched her inner walls.

"You're so wet. Need to taste this gorgeous cunt." Wide palms stretched her thighs farther apart as he licked through her folds.

"Ahhhhh! Fuck. *Santa mierda de mierda!*" She squeezed her

eyes closed, every muscle in her body tensing. Need unfurled in her womb. Pressure exploded through her until she was at the brink of orgasm.

Nash added another finger as he lapped at her clit. She'd never experienced this before. And now she knew what she'd been missing. She rocked her hips shamelessly against his mouth.

"I'm gonna—"

"That's it, sweetness. Come for me. Come on my tongue."

"Naaash!" She screamed as her orgasm shattered through her. Black spots filled her vision as everything inside her tensed and pulsed. Warm, soul-deep pleasure crashed over her like a rogue wave, more powerful than she'd ever experienced.

With her chest heaving, she tried to catch her breath as he pulled his hands out of her with one last lick to her already sensitive nub. She hissed.

"Come here," he said.

She pushed off the table, turning to face him. Her knees gave out, but his strong arms were there to catch her.

"Lie on the bed." He ushered her to the full-size mattress that took up most of the space in the small cabin.

She crawled onto the bed, lying on her back. Nash slipped off his black briefs, his long, thick cock slightly curved towards his belly. The tip gleamed with pre-cum. She licked her lips.

Nash reached for his discarded pants, pulled a condom from his pocket. He ripped it open and slid it onto his shaft.

"You don't want me to suck—" She pointed towards his groin.

"Oh, I very much want those red lips wrapped around my cock. But I'm so close to coming already, and I want to feel that pussy clench my dick like it did my fingers."

"Oh."

He crawled over her, settling his weight on his arms

pinned on either side of her. For the first time in her life, she felt small with a man. She couldn't help but roam her hands over his inked muscles. Her mouth was dry and her pussy, aching for him.

He kissed her, hungry and yet gentle. "You okay?"

"Mmmmm." She nodded, kissing under his jaw.

"You want to keep going?"

She pulled back to look in his eyes. "Do you?"

"Abso-fuckin'-lutely."

Isabella smiled. "Then yes. But you should know . . . it's been a while for me."

"Me too."

Her eyes widened.

Nash's lips slanted across hers as his tattooed hips settled between her thighs. She widened them to accommodate him.

The tip of his cock slid in the first couple of inches. She closed her eyes and hissed from the stretch.

His thumb brushed her cheek as he stilled. "Does it hurt?"

She opened her eyes. "Just a little uncomfortable. I think I need you to move."

He kissed her lips. "Tell me to stop if it's too much."

She nodded.

He rocked his hips in and out. Her fingers dug into his shoulders. There was some pain, but pleasure soon took over.

"Yes," she encouraged him.

He thrust harder, spinning her up in desire once again.

"You feel so good." Her voice came out breathless.

He grunted. "This pussy was made for me. So wet and tight."

"Nash, I'm so close. Harder." She'd never had multiple orgasms—not unless they were self-induced with a vibrator. It seemed tonight could be a night of many firsts.

"That's it, baby. God, you're so fucking sexy like this, laid out under me." His gaze never left hers as Nash slammed his cock deeper and faster into her. His palm splayed over her breast, plucking the nipple and pinching it between his fingers.

Her ears rang, pleasure raking through her. A surge of bliss rammed through her as she soared over the cliff into her second orgasm. She dug her nails into his broad shoulders, her eyes wide, her senses sharpening. A keening cry left her lips as his expression morphed into one of carnal ecstasy. His heated gaze flashed. As his cock pulsed and emptied inside her, he roared. All his walls crashed down for one brief flicker.

His hips slowed. His chest rose and fell against hers as he stared down at her in a half-lidded haze.

She gave him a satisfied smile. "That was amazing." The best sex of her life actually. *I guess that's what happens when you sleep with a man who's actually attracted to women.*

The open expression on Nash's face flashed with fear before quickly morphing into stone. The boat lurched, and Bella gripped the sturdy wall. He got up, pulled out of her, and turned away. He slipped the condom off, wrapped it in tissue paper from the small kitchenette, and threw it in a trash can.

Was it not as good for him? *Am I really a bad lover after all?*

He pulled on his clothes as if the cabin were on fire, not even turning to look at her. It stung. How could the man who'd worshipped her body only moments ago be so cold and shut off now?

Embarrassment flooded her cheeks. But this was how one-night stands went. And technically, she'd gotten what she'd come out here for.

"I'll get us ready to go back to the docks," he grumbled before heading up to the top deck, shutting the door behind him, effectively dismissing her.

Isabella rushed to her clothes, slipping them on as she

tried to ignore the growing ache in her chest. Her pussy was sore in the best of ways, some of her arousal dripping down her thigh. She grabbed another tissue and cleaned herself up before finishing getting dressed. She couldn't quite get the zipper up all the way on the dress, but there was no way she was going to ask Nash. She slipped her sweater on, and the sweater he'd given her.

A thump from above sounded. Isabella drew in a deep breath and let it out. Her night of fun had come to an end.

One thing was for sure. She'd never forget Nash, the mostly quiet, broody grump who'd played her body like it was made for him. If only the end didn't have to come so soon.

5

NASH

Nash ran a hand over his face in frustration as he pulled his truck onto the main road.

"I had fun tonight," Bella said in the passenger seat beside him.

His stomach hardened as guilt slashed through his chest. He clenched the steering wheel and stepped a little harder on the gas. The sooner he could get her to The Lighthouse Inn, the sooner he could put this night behind him.

"Thanks for taking me fishing . . . and uh, well, for everything." She tried again.

Nash didn't respond. It was better this way. He'd made the mistake of being friendly with one of his hookups and she'd thought they had a future because of it, despite him being clear before they'd fucked that it was a one-time thing. That was why his hookups were rare.

He'd never met anyone like Bella before. It was a good thing she didn't live nearby. He'd be tempted to break his one-time-only rule. But that would muddy the waters. And Nash couldn't do complicated.

I just fucked Bella on a boat named after my fiancée. God, he was a bastard. The last time he'd seen Ana five years ago was burned into his memory. The hurt—the anger. All of it directed at him. His shoulders hunched as his stomach burned with bile.

Thankfully, Bella had given up on conversation, instead opting to stare out the window, her arms tucked tightly against her chest.

The lights from the white Victorian-style inn came into view. He slowed and slipped into one of the parking spaces.

Bella unzipped his sweatshirt and left it on the seat between them. She opened her door but turned to face him.

"I . . ." She hesitated, her expression glimmering as if she were fighting a war within herself. She chewed on her lip, now free of lipstick.

"You should get inside," he said.

She swallowed, her focus darting nervously around the cab of the truck, the seat—anywhere but him. "I just . . . I have one question. And I want honesty, even if you think it will hurt my feelings."

Shit. She was going to ask to see him again. He tensed.

"Am I a bad lover?" Her voice was so quiet he questioned whether he'd heard her right.

He jerked his attention towards her. Insecurities shone in her big brown eyes. Someone sure had done a number on her.

Anger welled in his chest that his actions had made her doubt herself. "Not at all, sweetness. And anyone who told you different is a lying dick."

Her shoulders lowered and she let out a sigh seemingly in relief. A small smile curved her lips before she nodded. "Thanks. Uh, you have a good . . . life." She laughed awkwardly and stepped out of the cab. She shut the door with a click and walked towards the inn. She didn't turn back once.

He waited until she was safely inside before putting his truck in reverse, backing out onto the road, and heading home. It felt as though he'd left something behind. Rather than turn around, he stepped harder on the gas pedal, putting as much distance as he could between himself and Bella. Nash was better off alone. And Bella didn't even live on the same side of the country. The possibility of running into her again was slim to none. A woman like that deserved everything. And he was a man who knew nothing but guilt and failure.

If you could have anything in the world, what would you want?

Bella's words flitted through his mind. He shook his head. Men like him didn't get second chances.

Nash had too much to atone for. It was better he kept his distance—that way he couldn't let anyone else down.

6

ISABELLA

Three Weeks Later

Isabella stared at the cup of tea in front of her, idly running her finger over the rays of sunlight streaming through the window onto the handle as she counted the days since she'd been on that boat again. Ugh, what was the point. She knew the answer already. She just didn't know what to do about it.

"Mom?"

She blinked out of her daze, looking over to her son, Eli, who looked so much like his father. Same blue eyes and square chin. His dark hair and tan skin were the only things he'd inherited from her.

"Yes, sweetheart?"

"Is something wrong?" His attentive and too perceptive gaze focused on her. The last thing she wanted was her twelve-year-old son to worry about her on top of grieving his dad.

She smiled. "No. Just lost in my thoughts."

"Do you want me to take the load in the garage to Goodwill?" Phillip, her late husband's boyfriend, asked.

Their family was not traditional in the least. Not since Robert had come out as gay to her. It had been a shock but also a relief. For so long, she'd tried everything she could to be the perfect desirable wife. Turned out that was never the issue. They'd been planning to get divorced, and then he was diagnosed with ALS.

"I would appreciate that." She turned to Phillip. "You sure you're okay to hang out with Eli until I get back from my girls' night?"

"Of course." Phillip ruffled Eli's hair. "He's gonna do all the heavy lifting and save this old man's back." He laughed.

Eli shrugged his hand away. "Uncle Phillip, don't mess up my hair."

"Sorry, kid." Phillip held his hands out, placating. "How about we get pizza afterwards?"

Eli's eyes lit up. "Yeah!"

"Okay, I should be home by nine." Isabella stood, taking her still full tea with her and setting it in the sink.

She stared out the window leading to the backyard she and Robert had walked through when they'd decided to buy the house. They'd planned barbecues and birthday parties for Eli there. It was a life they'd done their best to fit into with a marriage that never should have been more than a friendship.

She exhaled. At least Robert had found some happiness before he passed.

"What's on your mind?" Phillip asked, leaning against the counter next to her. He was taller than Robert had been, thin and fit. She could see why Robert had been so taken with him.

She turned to check the table. Eli was nowhere to be seen.

"He went upstairs to fix his hair," Phillip supplied.

She turned back to him. "Just have a lot to do before our

move." It was a half-truth. She wasn't ready to voice what had her so out of sorts today.

"You know I'm here to help. Anything you need."

She nodded, emotion clogging her throat. "I appreciate it. I know this can't be easy for you either."

Phillip's eyes grew glassy before he cleared his throat. "I made a promise to him that I'd do what I could to help you both out. I'll always be here if you need anything. And I'd like to stay in Eli's life as an honorary uncle if you're comfortable with that."

She swallowed. "I know Eli could use a man to talk to. And I know you didn't get much time with Robert, but I saw how much he loved you. You gave him what he needed most."

"You are an amazing woman, Isabella. Truly exceptional," Phillip said.

She shrugged and forced a laugh. "Someday I hope to find a straight man that thinks the same." *Although that will have to wait seeing as I may have much bigger things to worry about first—like a possible baby.*

He gave her a wink. "You will."

Isabella walked up the stairs to Tessa's apartment on shaky legs. All she wanted to do was crawl into bed and sleep, just shut the whole world out for a little while. But she didn't have that luxury. Her son was counting on her. *And maybe one more.* Her throat closed with the rising panic spiraling through her.

She shook her head, trying to rid the thoughts. It was girls' night. One of her last before she moved. Tonight, she wanted to focus on enjoying time with Tessa.

Isabella stepped in front of her friend's apartment and

drew in a deep breath, forcing a smile she hoped was believable on her face before she knocked.

The rumble of Roy's voice sounded behind the door. After quite the epic show in the tattoo shop last week, Tessa had left almost in tears and Roy had closed the shop to chase after her. Now, it seemed they were inseparable. She was a little jealous of her friends, but happy for them just the same.

Isabella knocked again. A girlish squeal came from behind the door before Tessa opened it.

Her friend's smile was bright as the sparkle in her eyes. "Hey, chica, I just need to grab my bag." Tessa's eyes narrowed, brows marring with concern as she grabbed Isabella's arm and pulled her into the apartment. "Are you okay?"

Guess my fake smile isn't as convincing as I'd hoped.

Bella glanced at Roy who was eagerly devouring what looked like a grilled cheese sandwich by the counter.

"Just pretend I'm not here." He turned his back on them, heading towards the fridge.

Tessa closed the door and focused on her. "Is it Eli?"

Bella shook her head. "No, Eli's fine. Nothing's wrong. I'm just tired. Haven't been sleeping well."

Because I can't stop thinking about the what-if.

"You still feel like going out for drinks? We can stay in and order food, watch a sappy movie."

Isabella grimaced. "I don't think drinks are a great idea."

"Is something wrong, or is it from the challenge of packing Robert's things?"

Isabella chewed on her lip and dipped her head. Tessa was the one person she could tell and know she wouldn't be judged. But admitting it out loud was almost as terrifying as thinking about it. "I'm late. Really late."

"You're . . . oh." Tessa's eyes widened to saucers. "Oh! Shit. Did you take a test?"

Bella shook her head. "I've been too chicken. But I made a doctor's appointment for tomorrow. If it isn't that, maybe something else is going on. Probably better to just get some bloodwork done."

"Right . . . Would it be the guy from the wedding?"

Bella nodded. Tears burned her eyes. She sniffed. "It has to be. Nash is the only one I've been with—but we used a condom."

Tessa pulled her into her arms. The physical support of her friend brought a wave of comfort to Isabella.

"Condoms aren't bulletproof. But maybe it's just stress?" Tessa offered.

Isabella shrugged and pulled away. "I've never been late other than when I was pregnant with Eli. Maybe. I'll find out tomorrow."

"Do you want me to go with you? Or we can go right now to the pharmacy and get a test."

"I . . . I want to put it off. I just . . . I'm not ready quite yet. You're probably right and it's just stress with the move and managing a grieving autistic preteen. I'm making a big deal out of nothing. I'll be fine." Bella sniffed and nodded, her voice steady.

"Well, I'm here. Say the word and I'll come over with ice cream, chocolate, and wine—even if I have to drink it all myself," Tessa teased before giving her another hug. "Whatever happens, you're not alone. I'll be the best long-distance auntie. And you'll have your parents nearby this time . . . You could always stay here, too."

Bella laughed and then quickly sobered. "I haven't done the test yet. There's still a chance I'm sick or something."

"You say that like it's a good thing." Tessa gave her one last squeeze before pulling away. "I'm here for you."

"Thank you. I just . . . I don't think I'm going to be very good company tonight. Maybe I should head home."

"Nonsense. We'll send this guy to the store for lots of ice cream, and order some Chinese. You pick—comedy or crying movie?"

Bella's gaze flicked to Roy.

He offered her a smile. "What kind of ice cream?"

"Mint chocolate chip. And double-chocolate cookie dough if they have it," Bella answered. Go big or go home, right? If she was going to wallow, best to do it properly.

"Done. Call your order in and I'll pick it up too." Roy grabbed the keys from the bowl on the counter before he made his way over to kiss Tessa on her cheek.

"Thank you." Tessa met his gaze.

"Anytin' for you, a stór."

Isabella choked back tears at the affection those two shared in such a short amount of time. *If I can't have that, I don't want anything at all. I won't settle again.*

Roy nodded towards Bella before he left the apartment.

"And to think you almost didn't give him a shot." Bella chuckled, relaxing onto the couch.

Tessa smiled, joining her. "I guess I have you to thank for helping me see the light."

"You just needed a little push." Isabella ran her fingers over the tassels on one of Tessa's colorful pillows.

Tessa was quiet for a few moments before she asked, "You okay?"

Isabella sighed. "You mean because I'm most likely pregnant by a man I only know the first name of? The fact that in less than a week I'm traveling halfway across the country to move back in with my parents, newly widowed at thirty years of age?"

"Stupid question."

Bella snuggled against her. Sometimes a girl just needed to snuggle. "I don't want to think about it tonight. Let's watch some stupid comedy so I can laugh and forget everything for a little while longer."

Tessa picked up the remote and looped her arm around her friend. "Whatever you need."

The movie played while Isabella tried not to think about her absent period. Surely it was just stress. *I can't be pregnant.* Wouldn't it be too soon to tell? Could she really do this? Begin all over with a baby while raising a teenager? This was supposed to be her fresh start. Mixed emotions swirled inside. Fear. Excitement. Trepidation.

So much for moving on. Looked like she might be back to the beginning.

7

ISABELLA

sabella sat still as a statue, her eyes glued to the doctor's lips. No sound reached her ears—not since "you're pregnant" had fallen from her mouth. Isabella's chest tightened as her breaths came more rapidly. A riot of emotions swirled in her belly. Terror. Excitement. Disbelief. Hope.

A soft, cold hand touched hers, sound returning as she met the doctor's sympathetic gaze.

"How are you feeling?"

Lost. "Shocked. I . . . the only person I had sex with—it was only once and we used a condom."

"They're not foolproof, as many can attest. It's possible it broke and you didn't realize."

Isabella closed her eyes, picturing that night. Nash's face shutting down, growing cold and emotionless as he pulled out of her. She'd needed to clean up after, but it wasn't a lot. She'd thought it was her fluids. Had Nash realized and not said anything? Was that why he'd grown distant?

The doctor tucked her brown curls behind her ear before

she pulled up her tablet and tapped on it. "It looks like you were fertile on the date you gave me."

Fuck. She'd wanted another baby for so long, but her husband had barely had sex with her. And then she'd found out why. But having a baby now? This was not ideal. *What am I going to tell Eli? Can I do this alone?* Raising an autistic preteen presented its own challenges. *Will Eli not get the support he needs from me if I have another baby? And do I really want to do this again?*

"Would you like to talk about your options?" the doctor asked, obviously sensing Isabella's inner turmoil.

Isabella closed her eyes, picturing her life if she kept the baby. Her body growing with life once again. The adjustments they'd need to make. The changes to their routine that would be challenging to Eli. It would mean juggling more. Facing her son and explaining things. It would mean he'd get a little sister or brother. And that they could find a new normal.

She wiped the scene of Eli holding a little bundle from her mind and imagined her life without carrying to term. Returning to Shattered Cove with just Eli, going on with her plans to start fresh. It would be easier in all respects.

The question was, what did she want? Which path was right for her where she was in her life? She didn't have a job, but Robert had made sure they were taken care of even after his death. Between his life insurance policy and selling their house, she had the rare privilege of taking this year off work —even more if she was careful. She wouldn't take that for granted.

Isabella opened her eyes, placing a hand on her belly where the tiniest cells were replicating, changing her body even this very second.

"I think we're gonna do this—*I'm* going to do this." *I'll find a way to explain to Eli.*

"Okay. You still have time to think about it. You came in

quite early. For now, I'll write you a prescription for prenatal vitamins and make an appointment in another six weeks or so and we can do an ultrasound to get a look."

"Alright. Thank you. Um, I won't need that appointment. I'm moving to New Hampshire."

The doctor offered her a warm smile. "No problem. Good luck on your move. Did you want a copy of the test results for the father?"

Isabella's eyes widened as a lump formed in her throat. God, she hadn't even thought about telling Nash. She would have to though. He deserved to know, and decide for himself what kind of relationship he wanted with their child. "No, thank you. That won't be necessary."

"Alright. I'll have the nurse come back with your discharge paperwork and information. Have a great day."

"You too." Isabella waited until the doctor left, and shifted on the table. Paper crinkled under her. She blew out a breath, sliding her hands over her face as she sighed.

"How am I going to tell Nash? Maybe just rip the Band-Aid off? 'Hey, uh remember the fun time we had on the boat? Well, you left behind a little something. *Surprise.*'" She shook her head. Tipping her chin up, she stared at the white ceiling. "Is this what I get for following your advice, Robert?"

Isabella laughed—it was that or cry. She'd do that when she was alone in her bed. She'd tell Eli this week. She'd move to Shattered Cove and face her parents. And then she'd find Nash and give him the news. She'd figure this out. One day at a time.

One step at a time.

8

———

ISABELLA

Two Weeks Later

Isabella stretched her arms over her head. It had taken a full week to drive from Colorado to New Hampshire, four days longer than she'd anticipated, because Eli had needed more breaks to move around. As much as she'd tried to prepare him for the change in schedule, her son had a hard time with it. The sheets had been too scratchy, so she'd unpacked the trunk only to find his blankets had accidentally been packed with the moving crate that was set to be delivered to storage sometime this month. She'd found a bedding store and picked him out a new one. There had been a plethora of sensory triggers all along the way. Isabella did what any parent wishing to hold on to their sanity and help their child would do—she accommodated him as best as she could.

Isabella hefted the last box of her things from the trunk, watching her step as she headed towards the stairs leading to her parents' flat above the marina. Her father led the way, a few paces ahead. She followed him into the home she'd grown up in. It was small—but cozy. With her and Eli's things, it was cramped. They couldn't stay here long, that was clear. She'd look for places tomorrow. Isabella passed through the open space serving as the living room, dining area, and kitchen all in one.

"Oh, *mija*, have you heard who else is back in town?" her mother asked, stepping in front of her, wiping her hands on her apron.

Isabella opened her mouth to reply but her mother, always eager to share gossip, spoke before she could.

"Luis Salvador. Remember him? I think he was a grade ahead of you. Well, Nancy Plotts told me that she heard from Sue that he's back in town after a divorce."

"Por favor, Mama? I just got into town. I am in no way looking to be set up."

Her mother scoffed and waved a hand. "You're not getting any younger, *chica*. Besides, Eli needs a man in his life, and you need someone to take care of you."

"Thanks for the vote of confidence. Can you at least let me finish moving in before you try to marry me off?"

"Oh, of course. Put that away. Dinner is almost ready. I made your favorite—mole poblano." Her mother smiled.

"You shouldn't be carrying something that heavy," Eli scolded, pulling the box from her hands.

"It wasn't too heavy," she said, wiping the sweat from her brow.

After she'd told him about the baby last week, he'd gotten quiet, and then asked her a million questions. He'd stayed glued to his tablet after that. A quick peek over his shoulder revealed his research was all about the do's and don'ts during pregnancy. Since then, he'd been overprotective of her, going as far as hiding the caffeinated coffee and throwing out their lunch meat. People with Autism could get hyper-focused on specific interests. For as long as she could remember, Eli had been obsessed with boats and fishing. *I hope his interest with pregnancy is just a phase because of the baby.*

"Can you make sure the chicken is cooked all the way, Abuela?" Eli asked.

Her mother's brows pinched together. Oh, dear. If there was one thing Catherine Noveas was sensitive about, it was her cooking.

"Of course it will be cooked properly. Have I ever let you down before?"

"We'll break out some of my good tequila tonight to celebrate your return to us," her father announced, walking back into the room and going for his liquor cupboard.

"Mom can't drink," Eli insisted.

This wasn't how she'd wanted to do this.

Her parents turned to her, question in their eyes.

"Why not? Is there something wrong? Are you sick?" her mother asked.

Eli turned to her. She'd asked him to promise to let her tell them. But it was unfair to have him shoulder such a burden for long.

"I'm pregnant."

Silence blanketed the room. The only sound came from the slow bubbling of her mother's mole sauce simmering in the pan.

"I'm gonna go put this away," Eli mumbled, carrying the box down the hall to the closet-sized room he'd be sleeping in for the near future.

"Robert . . . but you . . . you don't look *that* pregnant," her mother said, obviously trying to make sense of the situation. Because it would never cross her innocent mind that Isabella would have sex with someone so soon after her husband's death.

"It's not Robert's."

"Dios, *mija*." Her mother clutched the fabric at her neck.

Tears burned the back of Isabella's eyes as she braced herself for her parents' disappointment. They hadn't known about Robert's struggles before his ALS diagnosis. They'd thought she and Robert had been happily married all these years.

Two strong arms enveloped her as her papi hugged her close. She melted into him, soaking in the love and support as her mother spouted her disbelief in a string of Spanish.

Papi kissed her forehead. "Are you okay, *mija?*"

"I will be. I want this baby. And I know it will be hard for a while, but I also know I can do this."

"Of course you can. You're Isabella Noveas. You can do anything." He squeezed her tighter.

When he released her, her mama had poured herself a shot of tequila. She tossed it back before she shook her head. "Who is the father? When do we meet him?"

Here was the hard part. "I don't want to say until I've had the chance to talk to him."

"He doesn't even know?" her mother cried. "Tell me this is a man you're serious about."

Were they judging her for being intimate with a man only six months after her husband passed? It wasn't their fault. If they knew the truth, they would understand—maybe. But she couldn't bear to ruin Robert's reputation with them, even if he was dead. Robert was a great man. *He just couldn't love me the way either of us wished.*

Isabella swallowed, her hands trembling as a wave of shame tumbled over her. "I haven't gotten the chance to tell him. I just found out recently. And no, Mama, it wasn't serious."

"Ay, Christos. I thought you would have learned your

lesson the first time you went through with this, Isabella Maria." Her mother chastised her like she was eighteen, coming home from her first semester of college to tell her parents of her unexpected pregnancy all over again.

"Mama—"

"You better hope that man marries you."

Isabella saw red. "This is not the nineteen fifties, Mama. I don't need a man to take care of me. I can raise both of my children by myself if that's what I want to do." *And I'll never marry a man again unless it's for the right reason—love. I won't settle.*

Her mother's mouth dropped open, her cheeks flushing red, a signal she was well and truly upset.

Isabella softened her voice, some of the anger dissipating, instead replaced with determination. "I'm not a scared teenager this time, Mama. I'm an adult who made a decision. And now I will also deal with the consequences of that decision. I chose to keep this baby. Try to find a way to be happy for me. Because as much as this was unexpected and unplanned, this was also a gift."

"Of course. Every child is a gift." Her mother's eyes watered. She blinked, tears dripping down her cheeks. "I just worry about you. You have so much you're already dealing with."

Isabella's heart ached. She opened her arms and hugged her mother. "I know, Mama. *Te quero.* And I appreciate all you are doing for us."

"It will all work out," her father added.

"I'm going to take a shower and change before dinner," Isabella said.

"Hurry, it will be ready in twenty minutes," her mother said.

Isabella turned and headed down the hall, past Eli's room.

God, she needed to find a place. Not even an hour back home and she was ready to leave.

She opened the door to her childhood bedroom. A few boxes were stacked in the corner.

She sat on the bed, her shoulders sinking as she let out a sigh. At least that part was over. Her phone vibrated in her pocket. She pulled it out.

Tessa: *Are you safe and sound, all settled in?*

She scoffed.

Isabella: *Boxes are carried in. Does that count?*

Tessa: *Wish Roy and I could have driven over to help!*

Isabella: *There isn't much room to turn around in this tiny room. You may not have fit! I don't know how I made it eighteen years in this place without going insane.*

Tessa: *Well, if you want to move back, you can totally have your job again. This new chick doesn't know her ass from her elbow.*

Isabella: *LOL. I just need to find a place to rent. I don't have the energy to look for a place to buy just yet.*

Tessa: *When are you gonna tell him?*

Her stomach flipped.

Isabella: *Soon.*

Tessa: *I'm here if you need to talk.*

Isabella: *I appreciate it. I better go. Mama's making my favorite and I don't want to be late for dinner.*

Tessa: *Tell Eli I love him.*

Tessa: *You got this, babe. Don't doubt yourself. You're one of the strongest women I know. I understand your life is chaos right now, and you never expected half the shit you're dealing with. But I know you'll get through it. You're a badass bitch, and don't you forget it. I'll even tattoo it on you next time I see you if I have to.*

Isabella sniffled, trying to stave off the tears.

Isabella: *Love you too. Thank you. I needed to hear that.*

She left her phone on the wicker side table and stood.

"You can do this, Bella. You're a badass bitch, even though you don't feel like it right now." She repeated her friend's words. Maybe someday she'd believe them with her whole heart. For now, she needed to get through the rest of this night and then find Nash and tell him the news. Hopefully he would take it better than her mother had.

One could dream, right?

9

———

ISABELLA

Isabella opened the door to The Stardust Café and walked in. The scent of roasted coffee beans and sweets immediately had her mouth watering. Her shoulders lowered with a small sigh as she stepped up to the counter. She was just glad to be out of that small apartment with her well-meaning but smothering mother. It had only been a week, but she was already at her wits end. It didn't help that Nash hadn't been docking there either. Was he even from Shattered Cove or had he just been visiting the area? She could look through the records at the marina, but that felt like an invasion of privacy. If she didn't run into him soon, she might have to. Her hand rubbed over her belly as her lips tilted up in a small smile.

Her phone buzzed in her pocket as she stared up at the chalkboard menu on the wall behind the counter. Isabella pulled her cell out just in case it was Eli.

Mama: *Papi said you were up early today. Are you not sleeping? Where are you? When will you be home?*

Isabella shook her head and typed out a quick reply letting

her mother know she'd be home soon before she slipped the phone into her pocket.

"Can I help you?" a beautiful and vaguely familiar woman behind the counter asked.

"Yes, I'd like a latte, please, with a shot of hazelnut, and two of your mermaid cookies and a lavender scone," Isabella answered.

The woman smiled, grabbing a paper cup and typing the amount into the register. Isabella swiped her debit card while the barista busied herself making the order.

"Are you just passing through?" the woman asked.

"No. Well, returning, more like. Just moved back."

A steaming cup of delicious-smelling coffee was set in front of her, next to the bag of pastries.

"Thank you very much." Isabella picked up the drink, inhaling the blessed caffeinated beverage that had been deemed contraband in her parents' house after Eli had convinced her mother caffeine was harmful to the baby.

The barista chuckled. "I almost feel like I should give you and that latte some alone time."

Isabella laughed and took a small sip. Perfection. "It's been too long since I've had a proper cup of coffee."

"Happy to be of service." She flicked her long braids over her shoulder.

"You look so familiar." Isabella picked up the paper bag with the treats, stepping to the side, even though there weren't any other customers waiting for service.

"Same. I'm Remy Evans. Well, my maiden name was Stone."

Isabella's eyes widened as she took in the woman with recognition. "We went to high school together." She pointed to her chest. "Isabella Noveas."

Remy's smile brightened. "No way. How have you been, girl?"

"It's been . . . an adventure. Is this your place?"

Remy nodded, her gaze roaming over the cozy café. "Yes."

"And Evans . . . did you marry Bently?"

Remy laughed at that, her bright white teeth flashing a contrast to her midnight complexion. "No. I married his younger brother, Mikel. He owns Sea View Construction with my brother, Andre."

Isabella had vague memories of the mostly silent bad boy of Shattered Cove. Hopefully he'd done a lot of growing and changing this last decade. "That's nice. I remember you worked here in high school, didn't you? Back when it was under a different name."

"Yes."

"Well, I love what you've done with the place. Expect to see a lot of me."

"I will. Thanks for stopping in."

"And thank you for making my morning." Isabella took another sip of her drink, savoring her latte.

She turned to leave as Nova Emerson entered the café. Nova's face lit up with surprise. "You're back?"

Isabella nodded. "I'm back."

"Do you have a minute, or do you need to rush out?" Nova asked.

"No rush. I was just going to find a table to drink this." Isabella held up her cup.

"You snag us seats. I'm gonna get some coffee and meet you there." Nova walked past toward a waiting Remy at the counter.

Isabella found a small table by the window overlooking Main Street. The Oyster Bookstore sat opposite, right next to Shattered Cove Records. So many other boutiques and small businesses lined this street. A feeling of nostalgia passed over her.

"Are you all settled in?" Nova asked, sitting across from her.

Isabella gave a sarcastic laugh. "As settled as one can be in a tiny apartment with both parents at thirty years old."

Nova's brows pulled together. "Oh, yeah. I couldn't do it. I love my mother but . . ."

"But sometimes you need your own space so you can get along with her too," Isabella finished for her.

"Absolutely." Nova sipped her coffee. "Are you looking for a place to rent or buy?"

"I'd like to rent first. I had wanted to wait, but I don't think I can stay at my parents' much longer. It isn't fair to make my son sleep in a glorified storage closet either."

"Move in with me."

"What?"

Nova nodded. "I have a big ol' house to myself. It's three bedrooms. How old is your son again?"

"He's twelve."

"He'll have a blast on the farm. My parents do family meetups every weekend with outdoor movies in the summer and dinners, and if he likes animals, we've got plenty of those too," Nova said.

"You . . . you're serious?"

"Of course. I wouldn't offer otherwise."

A flutter of excitement danced in her belly. A chance to get out of her parents' small flat? Space for Eli to explore? It sounded too good to be true. "I couldn't impose. I have Eli and . . . and I'm actually pregnant."

"Oh." Nova's gaze dropped to Isabella's stomach. "Well, that's not a problem for me."

"Nova, are you . . . I don't want to be in the way."

Her friend waved her hand. "Pshhh, you wouldn't be. In all honesty, you'd be getting my mom off my back for a bit. She's always on my case about living alone. I mean, we're all on the same damn property. If you ask her, it's like I'm a hermit, two states away. And don't get me started on her *subtle* hints of dating. Seriously, you would buy me some time."

"Really?"

Nova took another drink and leaned forward, her brown eyes glinting. "Besides, I owe you."

"For what?"

"Back in high school. You protected me from those Barbie bitches."

A foggy memory of stepping between a young freshman Nova and a few nasty juniors solidified in her mind. "Oh, really, you don't owe me for that."

Nova shrugged. "Just the same. Come stay with me. Help me get my mom off my back, give your kid some space, and reclaim your sanity."

Isabella considered it. Her friend's offer was so tempting. It would mean another upheaval for Eli, but the benefits outweighed the struggle. "I'm paying for rent, and pitching in for utilities and groceries. And it would just be for a few months, six max, while I get my shit together and find a house for us to buy. I want to be settled before the baby comes."

"Done!" Nova extended her arm.

Am I really doing this? Isabella shook her hand. "I can't believe it."

"We're gonna have so much fun together. Trust me." Nova winked.

"Oh, I'm sure we will. Thank you." A lightness that wasn't there before lifted her spirit. Some of the weight disappeared from her shoulders. *I guess living at home was more stressful than I realized.*

"When can you move in?" Nova asked.

"The sooner, the better."

"My brothers can help this weekend. Saturday?" Nova offered.

"It's just a few suitcases and boxes. I don't want to trouble anyone."

"Nonsense. You and Eli show up Saturday, and I'll help get you settled."

"Thank you."

Nova winked. "Don't mention it."

Isabella sipped the last of her warm latte.

Coffee. Nova. Eli. This baby. Four things she was thankful for and it was only eight in the morning. Today was already shaping up to be a good day.

10

ISABELLA

Isabella set the bag of cookies on the counter as she searched the marina's back room for any sign of her son.

"You might want to change. I can smell the coffee beans on you," her papi pointed out as he sorted through a box of lures from the desk under the light of a small green lamp.

"I was just buying cookies." She gave him a sly smile, while scanning the *Fish and Game* posters covering the faux wood walls.

He chuckled. "You never were a good liar. Glad to see some things don't change."

She laughed and kneeled on the orange couch against the far wall that was older than she was. She peeked out the large bay window overlooking the marina. "Have you seen Eli? He's got a therapy appointment in half an hour."

"He's on the docks. I taught him how to fill the boats with fuel."

Her son's head bobbed from the end of one of the docks behind a boat. "Thanks." She headed out of the office but paused at the doorway, turning back. "Oh, I uh, I found a place for Eli and me until we find a house. I'm gonna move in this weekend. A friend from high school offered her home to us."

"I'll handle your mother." He answered her unasked question.

She slid behind the desk and hugged him. "Thank you, Papi. I don't know what I'd do without you."

He patted her hand. "You'd be just fine."

"*Te amo.*"

"Love you too."

She straightened and made her way out back. The salty brine of the ocean greeted her. If she could capture the scent of her childhood, it was this.

Isabella walked towards the fueling station, her gaze wandering absently over the docked boats as it had every day since she'd been back. She froze, nearly tripping on the swaying dock.

She'd know that boat anywhere. Nash was here. Isabella's mouth went dry as nerves ratcheted up her spine. Her belly flipped, churning like the sea.

She took a deep breath and let it out. "You can do this, Bella. He deserves to know."

She straightened her shoulders and turned around to make her way closer to his boat. She searched wildly for the man who owned it.

She stepped closer. It didn't seem as if anyone was aboard. Should she wait here? Ask her dad about it?

"Can I help you?" The gruff voice made her jump.

She spun around, eyes wide. Nash stood in front of her looking even better than before if that was possible. His wild hair was still untamed, and now his short beard looked as wild as the mess of curls on the top of his head. He only wore a T-shirt, showing off his tattooed muscular arms. His waist tapered down to a pair of camo shorts that came to just above his knees. She forced her gaze back up in time to catch his jaw tighten as his eyes flared.

"What are you doing here?" His abrupt tone made her flinch.

"I was looking for you. We need to talk—"

A young teen in a hoodie with a backpack walked up behind Nash and climbed onto his boat. "Mornin', Nash."

Nash grunted.

"We have company joining us today?" the kid asked, turning towards Isabella. "I'm Anthony, first mate of The Anastasia."

She offered him a shaky smile. "Nice to meet you."

Nash climbed on board the vessel.

"Nash! I need to talk to you. It's important."

His back remained to her. "Get us untied, Anthony."

"If now's not a good time, I can come back later," she pressed.

Nash's shoulders tensed, rising to his ears. He started the engine as Anthony cast her a questioning look, obediently following his captain's orders.

"We have nothing to discuss," Nash ground out loudly, not even giving her the courtesy of looking at her when he spoke. As soon as Anthony freed the last rope, Nash steered them through the marina and the no-wake zone, heading out to sea.

She blinked a few times. "Did he really just . . . *cabrón!*" *What an asshole!*

Why was he so cold to her? They hadn't parted as best friends, but still. You'd think he'd at least be cordial. She fumed.

She had seen that going somewhat differently in her head.

Of the hundreds of scenarios she'd come up with, behaving like she didn't exist hadn't been one.

He still deserves to know. Something told her he was going to be less than pleased, especially after that reunion. But the gossip would spread around town soon enough. She was surprised her mother hadn't spilled the beans already. She had to give her some credit.

Isabella would never forgive herself if she kept a secret like this from the father of her child just because he didn't like her. He'd been kind to her for most of that night. And he'd been honest with what he could give her. *I'm good enough to fuck but not to love.* Not that she'd entertained such fantasies with the grumpy fisherman. But if he wanted to be in their child's life, they'd have to work something out. They needed to be friends at the very least, pleasant acquaintances.

She placed a hand on her belly. "You deserve more. And I'll do my best to give you everything."

Why did the first man she slept with since Robert have to be so prickly?

"Mom?"

She turned, facing her son, forcing a smile. "Hey, *cariño*. I brought you back some cookies from the café in town."

"How old do you have to be to own a boat?"

"Um, well, I think it depends on the boat. Not sure there is an age limit. But I don't think you're quite ready to go out on your own. Why?"

He scratched his head and shuffled his feet shyly. "Just wondering how soon I can start my own charter business."

Her chest tightened as her son's gaze focused on one of the boats off to the side through his dark eyelashes. Isabella swallowed the emotion that swelled in her throat. His love for boats had been something he'd shared with Robert. They'd made plans for Eli's future, a goal of independence.

"I think we should find out the details, then. Let's go talk to Abuelo." She wrapped her arm around her son, tugging him against her as they walked down the docks towards the shop.

She cast a quick glance over her shoulder at the greenish-gray waters. She'd try again with Nash when he came back—make him listen. She had to.

11

NASH

Nash's hands slid over the wheel, slippery with sweat. Dots of perspiration lined his forehead and none of it had to do with the warm summer weather or being out in the sun all day on the boat. No, it all had to do with the curvy woman who he never thought he'd see again. Why was she back in Shattered Cove? Had she lied about being from Colorado? Was she looking for another hookup? Well, too bad. He was into one and done. No emotions. That was why he'd run as far as fuck away from her as he could after he'd orgasmed. Because she stirred feelings in him. And he had no room for feelings. They were dangerous.

"Nash!" Anthony's voice cried out in alarm.

He jerked his gaze to the front of the boat and immediately corrected the steering and speed so he didn't hit the dock.

"That was close," Anthony commented, tying the boat up.

"Take the catch in to Tomas—all except the ones I need to drop off to Atlantis," Nash said, bounding off the boat. He needed to restock his vessel and get the hell out of there in case Bella came back.

A young boy walked towards him from the other end of the dock. "Do you need fuel for your boat?"

"You work for Tomas?" The kid couldn't be more than twelve or thirteen.

"Yes. I'm the dock manager," he answered in a monotone voice, his gaze focused on Nash's chest.

Nash crooked his head. Was the kid joking? "You know what you're doing?"

"Yes, sir."

"You don't gotta call him sir. He's Nash and I'm Anthony," his one and only employee supplied. "What's your name?"

"Eli. So . . . do you want the fuel?"

"Fill 'er up." Nash nodded.

"Is this your boat?" Eli asked, eyes admiring.

"Yup."

"Is fishing your job, or do you do charters too?" Eli's question surprised him.

"Mostly fish but if the season's slow, I'll do a charter for the right price. Why?"

The kid shrugged. "I'm going to buy my own boat and run my own fishing and charter company. My abuelo said I need to learn how it all works before I get my own boat."

Nash recognized the eagerness. The glint in his blue eyes told him all he needed to know. He was once a kid with a passion that someone once took a chance on too. He grabbed a card from his wallet and handed it to Eli. "Have your parents give me a call, and I'll take you out with me and Anthony one day. But be ready to earn your keep," he added with a wink.

Eli's eyes widened. A beaming smile split his face as his hand flapped excitedly. "Thank you, Nash."

"Don't mention it." He clapped his shoulder and walked past him.

Eli frowned. "How can I tell my mom if I can't mention it?"

Nash hesitated. *Is he serious?* "It's just a saying."

"It doesn't make any sense. Do I tell my mom or no?"

"Yes. You tell your mom." He waved in farewell and headed into the marina shop. Instead of Tomas, his wife, Catherine, leaned over the counter, gossiping with Nancy Plotts. She looked up when he walked in, her eyes narrowing on him as her cohort gave him the same sneering look. The usual welcome he got from many of Shattered Cove's residents. From those who believed he was a monster. The people who'd turned their backs on him and his family because they thought he'd murdered his fiancée. He might as well be seen as a scary motherfucker—people tended to leave him alone that way.

Nash gritted his teeth and walked to the back for a bottle of cold water, grabbing a Coke for Anthony. He had a short list of items he needed to grab and then get out of here.

"Your daughter's pregnant?" Nancy's voice rose in the small store.

I didn't know the Noveas had any children. His lack of knowledge didn't surprise him; Catherine hated him, yet Tomas was a good man. But other than talk of business and the weather, Nash kept to himself. Everyone was safer that way.

"She won't tell us who the father is."

"It's not her husband?" Nancy gasped.

Nash rolled his eyes. The dramatics of these women were unmatched by Hollywood. He grabbed a few of the new lures and browsed the hook section.

"No, she's only two months along. Robert died eight months ago."

Eight months after she became a widow she was already knocked up by another man? Damn. Anastasia had been missing for almost five years and it had taken him three years before he could even look at another woman. But six months? Was the poor bastard even cold in the ground when she fucked someone else?

Everyone grieves differently. But don't you think it's time you move on?

His mother's words echoed in his mind. Nope. He was fine as he was. He'd live his life alone. That way, no one else would be hurt—least of all him.

"Oh, shhh, here she comes. Don't tell her I said anything. Keep this between us," Catherine whisper-yelled.

Nash snorted. Like that was going to happen.

The bell jangled as the front door opened. "I found the supplies you wanted, Mama."

Nash froze, his blood turning to ice. *No. Nononono.* He spun around. Sure enough, Bella walked behind the counter, setting a box in front of her mother.

"Oh, thank you, dear. It's been a lifesaver having you back. You remember Nancy?" Catherine asked.

Bella gave what seemed like a forced smile to the woman. "Of course."

The blood drained from Nash's face. Two months. Sixty days. That meant he might be . . . oh, fuck. *I used a condom. Maybe it could be someone else's?* But she'd said she wanted to talk to him about something.

He ran a hand over his face, pulling his hair out until his scalp screamed in pain. "Fuck!"

Three pairs of eyes jerked towards him. But only one mattered.

Bella's mouth dropped open. She straightened, casting a wary gaze over her mother and the other woman before she announced loudly, "I'm gonna go get some air." She turned towards the door, glaring at him and nodding towards the back door.

Maybe she just wanted to warn him that he might hear she was pregnant but it wasn't his. Wishful thinking had never worked before, but perhaps his luck was about to change.

12

NASH

Nash forced one leaden foot in front of the other, following a small distance behind Bella across the marina parking lot towards the shore. Her arms hugged her body as her feet padded through the rocky sand, carefully maneuvering over the bits of driftwood, washed-up lobster traps, and rope.

His heart thundered in his ears. Waves swept over the tan sand, the tide bringing bits of seaweed in. His stomach churned as his mind raced.

It's not mine. It can't be.

So what else did she want to talk about, then?

His body trembled as terror crept through his veins like ice. He was thrown back in time as memories crashed over him.

"Please don't leave me, Nash. You're all I have in this world." Anastasia's tear-filled face looked up at him, regret shining in her eyes.

"You should have thought about that before," he snapped.

She winced. "You said you'd always be there for me. You'd protect me. You'd love me no matter what."

"Not this, Ana."

"Please," she begged.

He'd remained silent, a mixture of anger and hurt boiling inside him until it tipped him over the edge and he said words he'd never be able to take back. The last words his fiancée heard from him.

"Nash?" Bella's voice brought him back from the flashback like a life buoy to a drowning man.

"What?" he snapped.

She flinched back.

Fuck! He closed his eyes, inhaling the brine-soaked air. Traces of rose hip blossoms kissed the wind, just one more memory of their night together that had his shoulders tensing.

When he opened his eyes, Bella was turned towards the water, her cheeks pink, only the left side of her profile visible. She tucked her arms closer to her body and straightened her spine as if sensing his eyes on her.

Her gaze flicked to his, unsure. Fear and determination flickered in the molasses depths of her eyes. Wisps of her dark hair escaped her bun and blew over her face.

One trembling hand reached up to tuck the unruly strands behind her ear. She was shaking. His gut burned with regret. Nash's hands itched to reach out and pull her into his arms to offer her comfort.

She's not mine. And she would never be. He fisted his hands instead.

"I'm sure you've heard by the way you're glaring at me . . . It was a miracle my mother kept it to herself this long." She let out a self-deprecating laugh. "I tried to talk to you earlier." Her voice shook, but she kept eye contact.

"You're pregnant." The words escaped his throat, rough and raw like he'd swallowed a bucket of saltwater.

She nodded, the toes of her worn Toms digging into the sand to kick over a shell.

"Why are you telling me?" *Please let it not be mine.*

She blinked as if confused. "Because . . . you're the father."

The world spun around him. Father? The roaring of his blood in his ears made it seem like he was in a wind tunnel as the words sunk in, confirming his fears. *I can't be a father. I can't protect the people I love. I failed Ana when she needed me most.* His chest screamed in pain. Unable to get a full breath of air in, he clapped a hand against his rib cage. Panic suffocated him at the image of a vulnerable little baby. *No. They'll be safer without me. I can't . . .*

"Nash? Are you okay?" Bella's voice was soft, concerned.

"We used a condom."

"Did you check to see if it broke?"

His mind raced back to that night. Had he? *No. I was more concerned with getting the fuck away from her and the feelings she stirred up in me.*

"It's impossible. It must be a mistake. Someone else's . . ."

She shook her head. "I haven't been with anyone but you since . . ."

No. This wasn't happening. He'd been so careful. He shoved his fear down, masking it with anger. "Since your husband died only six months before you fucked a perfect stranger in a boat? And I'm supposed to just take your word for it?"

He regretted it the moment the words were out.

Bella's eyes widened. She staggered back a step as if his words had been a physical blow. Color rose in her cheeks.

Her eyes narrowed. "You have no clue who I am or what my life has been like. You have no right to judge me. Did I plan on this? Fuck no. But I'm dealing with it. I thought you deserved to know. That's all this is. I thought I'd give you the courtesy of deciding what role you want to play in his or her life."

Nash coughed, his throat closing up. *A baby. A son or daughter to laugh with, or share his business with.*

No way . . . I can't be the man she and this baby need. I can't protect them. She deserves someone who can give her what she needs—someone who could love her. But . . . that's my baby. A piece of me. I may not be enough, but I'll be damned if I'm not going to try. Fuck, I'm going to be a dad.

Bella kicked the sand, sending it flying over his feet. "You know what? I don't need you. I can do this myself. Just forget it. Forget you ever met me." She stormed past him, running back to the marina.

"Fuck!" he spat. "How the fuck am I going to fix this?"

He'd avoided any and all new attachments, pulling away from everyone since Ana's disappearance. Now he had a baby on the way and his or her mama to worry about. So much for keeping life simple.

I'm going to be a dad. He might suck at it—hell, he was already off to a horrible start. But he'd make this right. He'd take care of his responsibilities. And he'd do everything in his power to keep Bella and their child safe and provided for.

Maybe that would be enough to atone for his sins.

13

ISABELLA

Isabella slid the last drawer closed, her clothing now put away. Her gaze roamed over her new room at Nova's house. It was more spacious than the one at her parents'. White shiplap walls with gold geometric-shaped art and watercolor prints with inspiring quotes adorned the walls. A dreamcatcher with white and grey feathers hung above the queen bed, which was covered in at least ten light jewel-toned pillows.

"All settled?" Nova asked, peeking her head inside the room.

"Yes. I love what you've done with the place." Bella smiled.

Nova stepped inside. "It was a fun distraction. I needed to do something with it. It was my fiancé's gym before . . ." A shadow passed across Nova's expression. "Well, before. Now it's a guest room."

"It's lovely."

"Thanks. Should we go check on Eli?"

"Yes. Can't wait to see his setup."

Nova led the way down the hall to the last bedroom and knocked.

"Come in," Eli called.

Nova walked in, Isabella following, taking a look around the space. The queen bed was against a blue-watercolor-stained accent wall; the others were a muted grey. A giant full moon was the centerpiece of the space, directly above the navy-blue bed frame, adding a pop of white. His sheets and comforter were a soft grey to match the walls and the pillows were a mix of the limited color palette. A few black-and-white photos of starry skies and a large splatter painting finished the decor.

"Wow. Seriously, Nova, you should do interior decorating."

Her friend waved her hand dismissively. "I should have done a great many things. But that's not my passion—getting people high is." She laughed. "Just kidding—kinda. I mean, it's a plus. But getting them the medicinal relief for their symptoms that no other option can, with basically no side effects? Now that is truly fulfilling."

"That makes sense. Must keep the local takeout places in business too." Isabella pulled out her phone, pulling up the app to order from Pirates Pizzeria. "Speaking of, I was thinking of ordering pizza for dinner. How does that sound?"

Nova clapped her hands together. "Oh, actually, my parents do a Sunday dinner every week. We're all invited. You guys don't have to go if you're too tired, but my mama wanted me to invite you along. She is the best cook. Seriously, you guys will thank me later. It's worth the grilling on my lack-luster love life every week, so that should tell you all you need to know."

Isabella chuckled and looked over to Eli. "What do you think, *mijo?*"

"Is there going to be other kids there?" he asked.

"I have a niece who's six. She communicates through sign language, but she can hear you," Nova explained.

"Will you teach me how to say hello to her?" The gesture might have seemed insignificant to some, but for Eli to put in effort for a possible new friend was huge. Social situations could be challenging for him.

Nova beamed. "Absolutely."

"Can I use the hot tub before we go?" he asked.

"Sure, dude. Just remember to take a towel with you. Bathroom closet, middle shelf."

Eli smiled triumphantly and went to his drawer to pull out his swim shorts.

Nova and Isabella left him to change, shutting the door behind them.

"In the mood for a cup of coffee? Or I have tea?" Nova asked.

"Mom can't have coffee!" Eli yelled through the door.

"I have decaf too!" Nova countered.

Isabella chuckled and headed down the stairs to the kitchen. "Tea would be lovely."

Nova pulled out mugs and went to work preparing the drinks as Isabella's phone buzzed in her pocket. Eli jogged past them, heading out the sliding glass doors to the back porch where the jacuzzi was situated.

Isabella pulled out her cell. Phillip's name flashed on the screen.

Phillip: *Hey, gorgeous. I've got some time off soon. I was thinking I'd take a trip to Shattered Cove and come see you and Eli. Up for a visit?*

Isabella: *We'd love to see you. Just text me the dates. I'm staying with a friend, but I can recommend a wonderful inn, and it's right on the beach!*

"Here you go. Do you take milk in your tea?" Nova slid the steaming cup in front of her on the bar.

"Just some honey if you have it?"

"Pshhh. Do I have honey?" Her friend laughed. "Two of my brothers run an apiary. I have so much honey I don't know what to do with it. Good thing it doesn't expire."

"Oh, I forgot they were bee farmers."

"Beekeepers, but yeah." Nova set the jar of honey and a spoon beside her.

Isabella scooped out what she needed and stirred her tea. "I appreciate you letting us stay here. I'm happy to cook and clean in addition to paying rent. I don't have a job yet; Mom and Dad have the marina under control, but they still need some help. I'll be there a few times a week. But other than that, I'm going to look into getting some clients."

"Clients? For what?" Nova asked, sipping her own tea.

"Massage. I had a pretty good base before . . . well, before my husband got so sick."

"Now that I will take you up on. You want to pay your rent in massages? I'm all for it." Nova giggled. "Can you do that when you're pregnant? I mean, like, when you get closer to your due date?"

Isabella sipped her tea, the sweet herbal notes wrapping around her like a warm hug. "Not when I get too far along. My belly will probably get in the way. I don't know, maybe I should wait until after the baby is born. I wouldn't want to get all those clients just to have to take months off."

"And the father? Sorry. If it's none of my business, just tell me to fuck off."

Isabella laughed. "No, it's fine. I can only imagine what

the gossips are spreading now…" She cleared her throat. "It was a one-night stand. I confronted him, told him about the baby, but . . ." Nash's accusation still stung. His silence had told her all she needed to know. She wouldn't be getting any support from him. "Well, he's made it clear he doesn't want to be involved."

"Asshole."

Isabella nodded. "I mean, I didn't plan for this either. But I had hoped he would at least give it a try to be there. I don't know. Maybe when the baby comes he might change his mind?" The brash way he'd treated her after they'd had sex and then again when she'd stood on the dock to talk to him as he ignored her flashed in her mind. Maybe it was better that her child didn't have a father like that. "Or not."

"It's his loss," Nova loyally agreed.

"What about you? Why do you need me here to get your mom off your back?"

Nova rolled her eyes. "Oh, God. Seriously, I know enough about your situation to know you understand a very involved mama." She laughed. "But in all seriousness, I love her to death. She and Daddy saved me from a pretty bad situation. My biological mom couldn't take care of me and I ended up in the system for a little bit. By some miracle, the state found out my mom had a half sister. And the next thing I know, Mama Emerson was pulling up in front of the group home to take me here. She adopted me as soon as the paperwork could be filed. I owe my parents so much. And I know I'm disappointing them, but . . ."

Bella reached across the table and took Nova's hand. "I heard about what happened to your fiancé." She gave her fingers a squeeze. He'd passed away overseas during deployment. "Are you just not ready to move on?"

Nova hesitated, old pain flashing in her gaze before she nodded. "Something like that."

Isabella reached out, covering her friend's hand with hers, hoping to provide comfort. "I get it."

Something told her Nova was hiding the true story—but then again, so was Isabella.

14

NASH

Nash pulled the tumbler to his lips, downing the rest of the whiskey glass. Normally, he'd savor the notes of vanilla and oak, enjoying the whiskey like it should be. But this week wasn't just any week. His world had been rocked off its axis days ago. He needed something to take the edge off. Something to numb the fear vibrating through his veins. Quiet the chaos in his mind.

He sighed and tipped his head back in the chair, staring at the blank ceiling. Heavy metal music screamed from his speaker—"Popular Monster" by Falling in Reverse was a song that spoke to his soul.

His hand held the pen to the worn notebook where he'd just finished pouring out his soul in splashes of ink and lines of words woven together in a way that made him breathe a little easier. Getting it out gave him the smallest reprieve, like he could take a breath after drowning in his pain.

His parents would no doubt be ecstatic to have another grandchild—but first he'd tell Bella.

Bella had wanted to know how involved he wanted to be. The answer was one hundred percent. He'd go to the appointments—fuck, he'd be at every doctor's appointment. And once their child was born, he'd change diapers—thankfully, he'd had practice with his niece. He'd do midnight feedings. *Wait, can the baby even be away from its mom so soon?* They'd find a way to work it out. Co-parent—wasn't that what people called it these days? He'd be there for his child. He'd provide financially, and he'd show up in every way he was capable.

His son would have him there every step of the way. And if he had a daughter? Shit. Well, that thought terrified him even more than the fact that he was going to be a dad. There was just something about a girl, knowing how vulnerable they were. How much shit they'd have to deal with in life because they were born with a vagina. One thing was certain: if he did have a daughter, she'd know how to defend herself. How old did a kid have to be to start learning self-defense?

"Hey, fucker!" a voice shouted over the music.

Nash sat up, tucking the notebook under his thigh as something hard hit his foot. His brother, Roman, grimaced and waved towards the speakers. "Can you turn that shit down?"

Nash grabbed his phone, hitting the control to stop the music. "Ever heard of knocking, asshole?"

Roman grabbed the bottle of whiskey on the coffee table, squinting at the label. "I did. If you didn't have the music so loud, you would know that. Shit, man, I heard it from the driveway. What the hell are you listening to that white-boy noise for?"

Nash grunted.

His brother set the bottle back down. Nash scooped it up and poured himself another two fingers.

"Bad day?" Roman asked, sitting on the arm of the couch.

I found out I'm gonna be a dad this week, so bad? More like fucking life-changing.

"Where's my niece?" Nash leaned forward on his elbows.

"At Mom and Dad's already. I've been sent to fetch you for dinner since you didn't respond to anyone's texts."

Nash picked up his phone, eyes catching on the missed calls and unopened texts. "I've been busy."

"You already drunk? It's barely past six."

"No, I'm not drunk. I was getting a good buzz going until you ruined it." He swirled the amber liquid in the glass.

"You could tell me, you know, if something was bothering you. I'm here for you, bro. We all are."

Nash gritted his teeth. *No one will understand.*

"You and Ricky have a good week?"

Roman hesitated as if he wanted to push. He sighed and nodded. "Yeah, the bees are busy making honey and the yards all look healthy. Inspector is coming by next week."

Nash nodded, eyes unfocused in his sparse living room. He'd begun building this house for him and Ana. They'd talked about it for years. But she wasn't here to see it completed. And when it came to filling it with things . . . nothing felt right. He'd only let Nova add the bare minimum.

"You changing before dinner? You look like shit," his brother helpfully pointed out.

"I'm not up for dinner tonight."

"You missed the last two. Besides, Nova's got a new roommate she's bringing. Mom wants us all there to welcome her."

"I don't do company. You know this."

"No one says you gotta do her." Roman snickered at his own childish joke. "Sorry, channeling Ricky there for a moment. Mom really wants you there."

Nash didn't want to be an even shittier son than he already was. He'd been enough of a disappointment and brought enough shame on their heads by not protecting Ana.

He itched to take the missing poster folded up in his wallet out. It was barely held together from being unfolded and refolded so many times over the years. He needed to carry his burden to remind him exactly why getting involved with someone again was a bad idea. The flyer might still say missing, but his ex was dead. He knew it in his bones. It had been five years. There was no way she'd have survived this long. But not knowing for certain ate him alive as he wondered what had happened to her after she walked out of the Shipwreck after their argument. *I should have been there—gone after her.*

"Nash, tell me what's wrong?" Roman pressed, knocking Nash's foot with his own.

"Nothing. I just wanted to be alone."

"You keep pushing people away. One day, you're gonna look up and realize you've lost everyone who ever cared about your sorry ass . . . but we're family. You can't get rid of us." Roman stood, turning to walk out the door. He swung the front door open and paused. "Mom made upside-down pineapple cake. Said don't be late or you won't get any."

My favorite. She knows I can't resist it.

His younger brother left, shutting the door behind him, leaving Nash alone once more. The silence in his house was deafening.

The phone rang from his lap. Nash checked the caller ID and sighed. He downed the last swig of whiskey, setting the glass on the table before swiping to answer.

"Ro already told me Ma wants me at the house."

"Get your ass over here. We don't want to wait on you to eat," his father ordered.

Didn't matter if Nash was fifteen or thirty-nine; his dad

told him to do something, and he did it. "Yes, sir. Be there in ten."

"See you soon, son."

Nash jogged up to his room and quickly changed into a fresh black T-shirt before he headed out into the summer evening. The sun was low in the sky, bordering the mountains in the distance. Cicadas trilled in the field to his left as he made his way down the gravel driveway towards his parents' house.

Each of the four kids had picked out a plot of land to build a home on their parents' property. Nash had chosen the one tucked away the farthest, bordered on one side by the forest and open fields everywhere else filled with wildflowers and sweet hay.

Nash wandered up the stone path to his parents' home. Laughter spilling out of the open windows made him hesitate on the wraparound porch before going in. They were so happy while he was still barely getting through the day without feeling like he couldn't breathe under the weight of his transgressions. He was an outsider. He didn't deserve this—not when the woman he'd loved was rotting in an unmarked grave somewhere. He couldn't bear the pitying looks from his mom, but this was his life. And now he had a baby counting on him to get his shit together.

Nash straightened his spine and filled his lungs with a fortifying breath before entering his parents' home.

The scent of pineapple and savory dishes hit him as soon as he walked in. The comfort of his childhood home wrapped around him like a warm blanket. Voices came from the dining room. He bypassed the mudroom, heading into the foyer and through the living room with his father's worn recliner sitting to his right. Continuing down the hall, he passed the bathroom, and made his way across scuffed wood floors to the brightly lit dining room where his family gathered most Sundays to share a meal.

"Finally, Nash is here. Can we eat now?" Ricky asked standing up to clap him on the back harder than necessary.

Nash shoved him.

"Enough, boys! No roughhousing. We have guests. Please try and act civilized," his mother scolded.

Nash turned to her to give his mother a quick hug and kiss on the cheek before turning back to the table and froze.

Bella stared at him eyes wide and mouth parted. *What the fuck is she doing here?* His gaze snapped to his mother and father before going back to her. Her eyes dropped to the table, redness staining her tan cheeks. *Did she plan this? Or did she know who I was all along?* Everyone in Shattered Cove knew the Emersons, even before losing Ana had made headlines. They were hardworking people, and they were wealthier than most. *Did I read her all wrong? Was she here for a meal ticket?*

"Nash, come meet my new roommates. This is Isabella and her son, Eli," Nova said.

Bella looked up to him. Her gaze held his with so many emotions flashing in her brown eyes, but one overruled them all: fear. The question was, was it fear of being caught? Or fear of his reaction? After the way they'd left things Friday, he couldn't blame her if it was the latter.

"Hi. It's, um, nice to meet you," she said.

So this was the way she wanted to play it? He'd been an asshole to her, and she deserved the benefit of the doubt. So, he'd sit down in the chair and follow her lead, pretending this was the first time they'd met.

"I met Nash at Abuelo's marina already. He said he'd take me fishing sometime if you say yes. Then he told me not to say anything and then he told me it was okay." Eli waved as Nash took a seat across from them.

"What a coincidence we're all sitting here now." Nash looked pointedly at Bella.

She shifted in her seat before reaching for her glass of water and taking two big gulps.

This dinner was sure going to be interesting.

15

ISABELLA

No. This isn't happening. I am trapped in a nightmare. I'm going to wake any second and this will all be a very bad dream. Isabella squeezed her eyes closed before opening them again. Nope. Nash was still sitting across from her, glowering at her. Her heart raced, and her skin flushed. *Why is it so damn hot in here?*

"Are you alright, dear?" Renita Emerson—or Mama E, as she'd asked them to call her—asked, her eyes crinkling in concern.

All eyes turned towards Isabella.

"I'm fine. Just a little hot."

Nova poured her some more iced herbal tea. It was a tad sweeter than Isabella was used to, but it was delicious.

"Thank you."

James Emerson, the patriarch of the family, nodded to his wife. "Why don't you start, dear? The food's getting cold."

"Of course." Renita grabbed the dish closest to her, pushing her long brown, purple-tipped locs over her shoulder before scooping food on her plate and passing it around the table.

"So, how do you two know each other?" Nash asked, passing a basket of rolls towards Ricky, who'd been cracking jokes since she'd arrived. He was the same age as Roman and adopted much like Nova.

"Oh! Bella and I went to school together. I was a freshman when she was a senior and she saved me that year from the resident bi—I mean, bullies," Nova corrected, her gaze roaming over the kids before she continued. "We ran into each other at Turner and Maddy's wedding and then reconnected once she moved back. She and Eli are my new roomies."

"At least until I find a house. It's just temporary," Isabella said.

"You in the market?" Roman asked, scooping some food onto his daughter's plate. He was handsome and clearly related to Nash. But where Nash was big and bulky, Roman was lean and trimmed, and shorter than his giant of a brother.

"Yes. I mean, I will be soon."

"What brought you *back* to Shattered Cove?" Nash asked.

"She wanted us to be closer to my abuela and abuelo after my dad died," Eli supplied, reaching for a second dinner roll.

Everyone quieted at the table. Ariel's hands moved into intricate patterns, using sign language to communicate. She'd seemed so shy when they'd met her earlier. Eli had signed the few things Nova had shown him and then told her all about the different types of boats he was considering buying someday.

Roman cleared his throat, turning to Eli. When he spoke, his voice was thick. "Ariel wants you to know her mom passed on too. She said, maybe your dad and her mom are in the same place, watching over the two of you."

Eli turned to Ariel, a small smile tilting his lips. "That would be nice. But there is no proof that an afterlife exists. Although there is some research that's been done on reincarnation—"

"Eli, I think that's a topic for another time." Hopefully, Roman didn't hate her for her son's bluntness.

"I'm so sorry, sweetheart," Renita added her sympathies.

"Thank you."

"Well, you have a little brother or sister to look forward to as well, don't you?" Nova asked Eli, obviously trying to change the subject to something more upbeat.

If only she knew how much worse bringing up her pregnancy was.

Isabella didn't dare look at Nash. The macaroni and cheese she swallowed sunk in her belly like a rock. Her skin burned with awareness of Nash's glare.

"Oh? You're expecting?" Renita asked.

Isabella nodded, forcing a polite smile.

"I'm sure things are difficult right now, but you'll be so grateful to have another piece of your husband to remember him by," Renita comforted.

"It's not my dad's," Eli not-so-helpfully supplied.

Isabella shot him a look. If she could be swallowed up by the floor right now, that would be great. She'd have to have a talk with him later about blurting out their life story to strangers.

"And the story thickens," said Ricky. "Don't go breaking my heart and tell me you're already taken."

Nash tensed and finally fixed his glower off her and towards his brother.

"No. He, uh, won't be in the picture," Bella said.

"Yeah, well, you don't need that asshole anyways," Nova encouraged.

Oh, if she only knew that *asshole* was sitting at this very table.

The tension radiating from Nash was palpable. Was he afraid she would expose him as the coward he was to his family? She just wanted this dinner to be over so she could go to bed and forget this night had ever happened.

"Of course you'll be just fine. Besides, you have this young man's help." Renita pointed to Eli.

"Honestly, I know it was a surprise to him. It was to me too. I have a twelve-year-old and I never expected to start all over." She forced a chuckle. "But we'll find our way one day at a time. Anyways, this lamb is so tender and this macaroni and cheese is delicious. Thanks so much for inviting us," Isabella said looking between Renita and James.

"Maybe he just needed a little time to get over the shock." Nash's voice slammed through the room like an electric current. Everyone at the table turned to look at him, but he held her gaze.

Isabella's stomach flipped, nerves skittering up her spine. "Maybe." Her voice cracked. Was he saying he was in this? Could she dare hope?

"So, most of you know I've been put in charge of helping with the town's annual Juneteenth celebration." Nova blessedly changed the subject.

Isabella focused on her friend.

"We celebrate Pride and Lovings Day at the same time. I need some more volunteers since half the rotary club came down with some sort of virus. So consider yourselves all signed up."

"No way. I got a date that day," Ricky objected.

"I'll help. Ariel and I can sell raffle tickets," Roman offered.

Nova smiled at him. "You are my favorite brother for a reason."

"Hey! I thought I was your favorite!" Ricky pouted.

"That was before you chose to be with one of your many women rather than helping out your only sister when she was in dire need. You can bring your date and I'll consider giving you back your spot." Nova winked.

"I think I'll live." Ricky snorted.

Isabella laughed. It was entertaining to see the way the siblings interacted with each other. As an only child, she'd never gotten this experience. Would Eli get a taste of that with the little bean growing inside her? Isabella's hand smoothed over her stomach.

"What about you two?" Nova asked her.

"I'm more than happy to help," Isabella answered.

"Can I have more bread?" Eli asked, shoveling another bite of food from his plate. The boy was a bottomless pit lately. Thankfully, Renita had been understanding of his sensory issues with food after she explained and wanted to know more for next time. These people were so welcoming—well, except for Nash.

"Awesome. Daddy, you're going to help with the grilling, right?" Nova confirmed.

"Of course." His smile softened as James looked at his daughter.

"And I'm bringing some pies and honey for the raffle," Renita said.

The rest of dinner passed without incident. Isabella tried to eat, but her stomach was uneasy under the weight of Nash's gaze. As soon as Eli was finished with his second helping, she excused herself.

"I think we better head back. It's getting late. Thank you

again for a wonderful dinner." Isabella stood and stacked Eli's plate on top of hers, ready to take to the kitchen.

"Of course, you've had a busy day. I remember how tiring the first trimester was. You leave those dishes here. Ricky will take care of them." Renita patted the table.

"It's not a problem—"

"I insist."

Isabella lowered the plates obediently.

"Have you been sick?" Nash asked.

She cast a quick look his way before she shook her head. "No, not really. It's still early yet."

She sighed, placing her hands on Eli's shoulders. "Well, we're gonna go. Thank you again."

She said her goodbyes and led her son outside into the humid summer night. The sun was almost over the mountains. The sky was orange and pink. Her heart fluttered and her stomach churned. Sweat beaded on her forehead. She swallowed, trying to hold it together long enough to get away from the house and back to Nova's.

You can do this. Breathe. In through my nose and out of my mouth. Just one foot in front of the other. One step at a time.

16

NASH

Nash waited behind the giant oak tree that separated his sister's property from their parents'. He raised his hand to block the morning sunlight as his gaze roamed over the pale exterior of Nova's house, up to the windows where the guest bedrooms were.

Jesus, I'm a fucking creeper. But he needed to talk to Bella without Nova butting in to his business. Why hadn't Bella told his family he was the father? *She couldn't have been protecting me . . . could she?*

The front door opened. He jerked back behind the tree as his sister appeared. A moment later, her truck rumbled to life. Nash waited for her to drive down the driveway and disappear over the hill towards her greenhouses.

Nash headed for the front door, his knees unsteady and his heart racing. Should he knock? If it was just Nova home, he probably wouldn't. *I should knock.*

He held up his knuckles and rapped against the door. Shuffling on his feet, he swiped a hand through his beard and took a deep breath, trying to calm the hurricane of emotions swirling in his body.

The door cracked open and Eli looked up at him with big blue eyes. "Nash. Did you come to take me fishing today? My mom hasn't said yes yet."

Nash chuckled. "Not today, bud. I'm here to talk to your mom. Is she available?"

Eli's brows drew together. "Mom isn't feeling good today."

Worry clenched his gut. "Mind if I check on her?"

Eli shrugged and stepped aside. Nash walked in, searching his sister's open-plan home. With no sign of Bella, he headed for the stairs and took them two at a time until he reached the top. He went straight for the first bedroom. Immediately, he was hit with the sweet scent of rose. The bed was unmade and rumpled, but empty.

Retching sounds came from the bathroom. He spun and jogged to the door. Heart racing, he grabbed the handle but forced himself to stop even though everything inside him was screaming at him to bust the door down. *Calm down, idiot, before you scare her.*

Nash knocked.

"I'll be out in a minute, sweetie." Her voice came from inside before the sink ran. She obviously thought he was Eli.

Instead of correcting her, he waited. *Is she okay? Is this because of the baby?*

The door opened. Bella stood there in a pair of tiny shorts that showed off her thick dimpled thighs. The buds of her nipples poked against the loose pink T-shirt she wore. Memories of having them in his mouth, her legs wrapped around him, assaulted him.

Bella wiped her mouth with the back of her hand, her eyes landing on his chest before her head tipped up. With flushed cheeks and wide eyes, she asked, "What are you doing here?"

"Were you throwing up?"

She crossed her arms over her chest. "That's what people do when they have morning sickness. Lucky me, it seems to have started."

"You should be in bed."

"Excuse me?" She huffed.

"You—"

"Because I'm pregnant, now I'm made of glass? And who gave you the right to tell me what I should be doing? Why do you even care?" she growled.

Why did he care? *Because it's my fault you're sick. Because I must have used an ancient condom and didn't think of checking the expiration date. I was too overcome with need for you—too swept up in my goddamned lust.*

Bella scoffed and pushed past him, heading towards her bedroom.

Shit.

He followed her, holding out a hand to block the bedroom door as she tried to close it. Bella whirled around, fuming. "You need to leave."

"We need to talk." He stepped inside.

Her chin tilted up, challenge in her eyes as she crossed her arms once more under her breasts, thrusting them up. His mouth watered.

"I think we've said all we need to say to each other. Or well, I have. You seem to just stand there and glare at me. Still, I'm good at reading body language. You've made your position in this arrangement crystal clear."

He sighed before mumbling, "I'm sorry for ignoring you."

Her eyes widened. "What?"

"I said, I'm sorry for ignoring you at the docks."

"Okay."

Man, this woman was something else. "And for how I reacted when I found out. I didn't . . . It was a shock."

She opened her mouth and then snapped it shut, studying him intently. "Apology accepted."

"Why didn't you tell my family it was me?"

She blinked and looked away, pointing her red-polished toes into the wood floor before returning her focus to him. "It isn't my place to tell them."

His chest squeezed with an ache he hadn't felt in a long time.

"Mom? Are you feeling better?" Eli asked from behind him.

Her unsure expression morphed into a bright smile that didn't quite meet her eyes. "Yes, *mijo*. Much better. I'm going to take a quick shower and get dressed before we head out for the day."

"Eli wanted to go out on my fishing boat sometime."

"Oh, that won't be necessary," Bella said.

Eli's expression dimmed. "But, Mom—"

"I'm sure you're still getting settled. The offer stands, whenever it works for you guys," Nash offered.

A small smile tipped the corner of Eli's mouth as his gaze roamed somewhere in the space beside Nash. Bella and Nash were not going to be able to talk with her son here.

"We'll finish this conversation later." Nash turned his attention back on Bella.

Her brows drew together. "We will?"

"Yes. And you should stay home and rest today."

"Are you still sick?" Eli asked, crossing his fingers, a sign of nervousness.

"I'm fine." She shot daggers at Nash with her eyes.

"Nash says you aren't feeling good and so did you. You should stay in bed, Mom. The article said that morning sickness is common in the first trimester. You need crackers and ginger ale and sometimes sour candies work. I'll go get you some." Eli darted out of the room.

Bella sighed and rubbed a hand over her face. It was the first time Nash had noticed the dark circles under her eyes and the exhaustion in her expression. "Thanks for that." Sarcasm dripped from her voice.

"I'm not wrong. You shouldn't push yourself."

"You know, I'm getting really fucking sick of you telling me what I should or shouldn't be doing. Just because I'm pregnant doesn't mean I've turned into a child overnight with an inability to make choices for myself."

"That's not—"

"Just go. Leave before Eli gets back and you make this worse." She grabbed a pile of clothes from the dresser and rushed past him back to the hall and to the bathroom once more before shutting herself inside.

Nash raked his fingers through his hair, tugged on the curls, and let out a frustrated sigh. He'd come here to clear things up, but it seemed he might have made them worse.

17

ISABELLA

Isabella leaned over Eli's bed to kiss his cheek. She pulled his weighted blanket a little higher and shut off the constellation nightlight he still liked to fall asleep to. Quietly, she crept out of the room and shut the door behind her before making her way downstairs to the kitchen. Nova sat on the back deck around a flickering gas fireplace.

Isabella grabbed a bottle of water and walked onto the back porch, shutting the glass door behind her. Nova sat on a couch, a lit joint in her hand. The cherry on the end glowing red as she inhaled and a puff of smoke left her lips a few moments later, followed by the herbal scent of weed.

"I'd offer you a puff but I have a feeling you'd say no, with you being pregnant and all," Nova said, pinching the end and setting it on the ashtray in front of her. The flames danced in the center of the table, encased in glass on four sides.

Isabella took a seat next to her friend, unscrewed the bottle, and took a drink. "I'm good."

"I make edible cookies once a week for some of my clients.

I'll be sure to keep them away from Eli. I can make a regular batch for him to enjoy," Nova offered.

"That's sweet of you. I can let him know which ones are off-limits."

"As soon as they're cool, I'll package them up and move them out of the house," Nova added.

"Thanks. How did you get into farming cannabis?"

Nova tipped her head back, staring up at the sky. "I had some major anxiety. Trouble sleeping. And my mind wouldn't ever just shut the fuck up, you know? Thanks, ADHD." She laughed. "I smoked in high school but it was shitty stuff for recreation. Later on in life, when . . . well, everything hit the fan, I was spiraling." Nova blinked slowly. "Prescriptions made me numb or worse off. I tried some of a friend's home-grown and it worked immediately. I was sleeping better, functioning better. So, I looked into farming it. Now I can help people with a wealth of issues. Epilepsy, autism, chronic pain, PTSD, autoimmune disease, insomnia, anxiety, cancer—you fucking name it."

"So you wanted to help people find relief like you did?"

"You make me sound so saintly." Nova giggled. "A few years ago, I'd still be considered a drug dealer—or at least a supplier."

"Yeah, well, thankfully, times are changing." They sat in silence for a moment. The sound of crickets and a few bats chirping somewhere off into the distance.

Isabella wiped sweat from her forehead. "It's a little warm for a fire."

"Yeah, but it's pretty."

Isabella took another gulp of the cold water as she stood. She capped it and set it on the table. "I'm gonna take a little walk."

"Holler if you get lost," Nova said motioning to the darkness.

Isabella stepped off the porch and headed down a worn footpath that led up a hill. She walked for several minutes, her focus on the dim path in front of her, only lit by the nearly full moon. A bench sat perched on top of the hill. She climbed the incline and sat, overlooking a giant field. The glow of the moon turned the long grass below a mixture of gold and blue. Little bursts of green flashed as fireflies danced in the breeze. Tipping her head up, she took in the giant sky above her. Millions of stars splattered across the heavens. It was beautiful. The image blurred.

Hot tears dripped down her cheeks. She wiped at her eyes but more came. She sniffed and tried to blink them away, but it was no use. At least she could have some privacy here.

"What the fuck am I doing?"

Nash probably hated her for the unfortunate coincidence that had occurred. She knew his sister and now lived with her temporarily. Had he come over to tell her to leave? *Then why apologize? I wish I could get a better read on that man. He's so hot and cold. If only I could ask Nova.* It wouldn't be fair to put her friend in that position.

Nash probably thought she was pathetic. *I'm thirty years old, a single mom of an autistic tween with a baby on the way, and I don't even have my own place to live.* She missed Robert and she was still angry at him, which only made her feel more guilty.

She took out her phone and pulled up the list he'd made and sent to her.

1. Cry until you can't possibly shed another tear.

2. Laugh. Find something that makes you happy every day and hold on to it.

3. Throw out my tennis shoes you hate so much. You're welcome.

Isabella's laugh burst into a half sob, half cry. She'd hated those over-worn shoes. They were stained green from him using them to mow the lawn and even duct-taped in some areas. She'd loathed those shoes and begged him so many times to get rid of them and buy a new pair. But after Robert had passed, she'd found it a lot harder to throw those sneakers out than she'd imaged.

4. Take a year off.

5. This is a two for one. Don't obsessively watch the video messages I left for Eli. And don't beat yourself up with what I didn't get to share with you two. You gave me a gift, one that I can never thank you for enough—our son. More than that, your friendship. You have always been an amazing wife and mother. I wish I had more time to watch you find a man who will love you the way you should be loved.

A sob tore from her chest. Isabella hugged her arms around her. The warm breeze picked up, brushing against her hot cheeks, drying some of her tears. Sniffing, she skimmed down the list to the note left under the last item.

When everything gets overwhelming and you don't think you can do it by yourself, promise me you'll step into tomorrow.

She tipped her head up towards the far-off constellations. "I miss you, Robert."

The sound of insects and the rustling leaves of the forest behind her were her only replies.

"I wish you were here, but I'm glad you're not suffering anymore." Slipping her phone into her pocket, she continued, "Eli is happy to spend time at the marina with Mama and Papi. He's become even more obsessed with boats and fishing. I think it's his way of trying to stay close to you. His way of remembering all the times you took him on special trips on the lake." She laughed and then shook her head. "I don't know what I'm doing with him. You always had a special way of getting through to him. And I . . . feel so lost." She hiccupped and wiped her face, sniffling.

A twig snapped somewhere in the woods behind her. She jumped to her feet, heart racing. *Is it a bear? A coyote?*

Isabella wasn't going to wait to find out. She scurried back towards Nova's house, giving the sky one last lingering glance before she blew a kiss, and with it, a wish.

18

NASH

The following weekend, Nash closed the smoker, quickly checking the thermometer for the pigs cooking inside. A couple more hours and these hogs would be ready to take to the Juneteenth celebration in Green Park.

A firm slap thumped against his back.

"Hey, big brother. Smells good," Ricky said.

Nash filled his lungs with the scent of hickory and savory meat. "That's 'cause I know what I'm doing—unlike *some* people."

"It was *one* time. It's not my fault no one's let me try again to prove that it was a one-off," Ricky argued, crossing his arms across his wide chest.

Nash chuckled. "You forget that one time ended with four suckling pigs that were black as charcoal on the outside and raw on the inside. Still not sure how you managed that."

Ricky smirked. "It's a talent really."

"What are you two assholes talking about?" Roman asked, coming around the barn.

"Ricky here was offering to help," Nash answered.

"Oh, fuck no. You don't go anywhere near that smoker," Roman said.

Ricky shook his head. "Speaking of smoking, have you seen Nova's new roommate around?"

"Why?" Nash asked, picking up a whetstone and his knife to sharpen, pretending not to be interested.

Ricky rolled his eyes. "Well, Nash, I know you're really taking this grumpy hermit thing to heart, but some of us have eyes. Isabella is a MILF."

Nash's teeth ground together. "Watch how you talk about her."

Ricky's eyes widened before his smirk grew. "If I didn't know better, I'd say someone has a thing for our new guest."

"No, I don't," he snapped.

Ricky's brows rose. "You sure, bro?"

"I thought you had a date. That's why you couldn't volunteer?" Roman asked.

Ricky shrugged. "I'm meeting her for drinks later tonight, so technically, I do have a date."

"Fucker will do anything to get out of helping." Nash shook his head.

"Don't think changing the subject gets you off from answering my question." Ricky narrowed his gaze.

"Was there a question in there? I thought you were just spewing your usual shit," Nash grumbled.

"Fine. If you don't want her, why should I pass up this opportunity?" Ricky eyed Nova's house.

"The last thing a woman like that needs is some idiot like Ricky here trying to stick his dick in her. She's a mom and she's pregnant. She isn't one of his hookups." Nash focused on the task in his hands, sharpening the knife.

His brothers were silent a moment before Ricky laughed.

"What?" he growled.

"You think a woman like that wouldn't be interested in something fun and temporary? And hey, I wouldn't even have to worry about knocking her up," Ricky teased.

Nash saw red. He shoved the tools down and stepped in his brother's space, chest against chest. "Don't fucking talk about her like that. And don't you even dare think about laying a finger on her. You get me?"

Ricky's eyes glimmered with satisfaction. His little brother loved getting a rise out of people. Ricky had baited him and Nash had taken it hook, line, and sinker.

"Fucker," Nash growled and shoved his brother away.

Ricky bit his bottom lip and nodded. "I get you. If you wanted her for yourself, all you had to do was say so. You know I don't poach."

"She's not mine."

Roman eyed him as Ricky stepped further away from Nash. "You sure are protective of her for someone who claims not to care."

"I just don't want this fucker harassing her."

Ricky clasped his hand in front of his heart. "I'm hurt you think I'd dare harass a woman."

Nash grumbled and got back to work organizing the spices on the table by the smoker, just to give him something to do besides wring his brother's neck.

Roman cleared his throat. "You sure you don't care about her?"

Nash's body locked up, his heart racing as his stomach burned with jealousy. Roman was a single dad himself. He hadn't dated since his wife passed years ago, but he wasn't closed off to the possibility of romance like Nash was. His brother deserved to find his happiness. *But not with Bella.*

"She's off-limits as Nova's friend. That's all," he lied.

"Someone is more delusional than usual," Ricky teased.

Nash snapped, swinging his fist, but Ricky was a quick little fucker and ducked in time. Laughing, he took off. "Getting slow in your old age, big brother."

Roman chuckled and shook his head. "I don't think he'll ever grow up."

Nash grunted in agreement.

"You said you don't care about Isabella?" Roman asked it more as a question than a statement.

"Why would I?" Had she said something? Did Roman know?

"I guess you won't care that I happened upon her crying up on the hill Monday night."

What? Was it because of something I said at the house? His guts twisted and his rib cage ached at the thought. The last thing he wanted to do was cause her more hurt. God, the woman was dealing with enough without the added stress of his freak-out. He needed to have a conversation with her and put everything on the table and let her know she wasn't alone in this. He'd make this right.

"I gotta go . . . check on something. Can you watch the pigs?" Nash asked.

Roman nodded, the corner of his mouth quirking up into a smile. "Sure."

Nash headed towards Nova's house.

"Hey, Nash?" Roman called.

He turned to his brother. "Yeah?"

"It's okay, you know."

"What is?"

Roman swallowed. "To move on."

"That's not what this is." *Because I don't deserve to.*

Roman nodded.

Nash spun around, jogging towards Nova's, taking a

shortcut through the woods. He exited the trees as Isabella appeared on the porch, carrying a big box. He increased his pace until he was in front of her, and he took the box from her.

"What the hell are you doing? You shouldn't be carrying shit."

Isabella blinked up at him, redness staining her cheeks as her eyes glowed with anger. "Thanks for your unsolicited advice once again. But I'm fine." She pulled the box back, but he didn't let go.

"Nash? What are you doing here?" Nova asked, shutting her front door while balancing another box on her hip.

Eli walked down the stairs with his iPad balanced on top of a bin. "I can't go fishing today, Nash. My mom is making me help with the Juneteenth fundraiser so I can practice being social," Eli explained, matter-of-fact.

"Not here to take you fishin', bud. I was hoping I could talk to your mom."

Nova emptied her supplies into the back of her truck. "Not you too."

Too? Had Ricky been here? That little asshole.

Bella dropped her hold on the box. "We have to get going or we're gonna be late, right, Nova?"

"Yup. You gonna hold those paper products hostage, bro?" Nova questioned, leaning against her truck.

He set them in the back and lifted Eli's bin before shutting the tailgate. Isabella was already inside the car by the time he'd finished.

Nova studied him. "You got something you need to tell me?"

"She's pregnant. She shouldn't be carrying your shit."

Nova's mouth twitched. "It was paper plates and

compostable utensils. Hardly a concern. Plus, it's her body and her baby. She gets to make that call."

His jaw pulsed. *It's my baby too!*

"See you later," Nova said before climbing into the driver's side.

The engine started with a rumble. His sister drove down the gravel driveway. Bella glanced his way before averting her eyes to the road ahead.

This was ridiculous. They couldn't keep avoiding a conversation. They needed to talk without interruptions. After the event, he'd insist they make time to discuss everything. Because like it or not, he was the father of the child. And he'd be damned if he sat on the sidelines.

19

NASH

Nash walked around the edge of Green Park. Most of the tables with food and wares from local artisans and farmers were set up in the center. Hundreds of people milled about, with families on picnic blankets and children running around the playground. Everyone was laughing and smiling, having a good time. Music filtered into the park from The Sirens, a local band that had made it big. Their usual backlist included rock and alternative songs, but today they played family-friendly covers in a mix of genres.

"Good day for the barbecue," Bently, sheriff of Shattered Cove, and Anthony's foster dad, said.

Nash nodded, halting.

"Didn't think I'd see you here," Bently added.

Nash shrugged. "Figured I'd come check it out for once."

"Anthony is really enjoying working for you. Thanks again for giving him a chance," Bently added.

Nash shrugged. "He's a hard worker and a smart kid." Anthony also didn't mind Nash's silence, or grumbly attitude.

"He is," Bently agreed.

"The other kids nearby?" Nash asked to be polite.

Bently smiled. "Gage is somewhere around here. I'm sure Anthony dragged him away from his book long enough to get some fried Oreos. Amara was by the band with her friend Lyric. That boy is like a shadow to her."

"Sounds like you and Belle have your hands full."

"Definitely. And we might have another placement soon. Someone from the Hope Facility."

"Bent?" his wife called from the picnic tables where the rest of the Stone and Evans family was set up.

"Better go. Enjoy the rest of your day." Bently waved goodbye before he headed off.

Nash headed towards the cluster of activity near the tables for no other reason than he wanted to lay eyes on Bella and see if she was okay. She'd been so sick the other day. Maybe she could use a ginger tea? Or some crackers? Maybe that would work as a peace offering. He bought a bottle of ginger soda from one of the vendors and walked towards the tent his parents had set up. They'd know where she was.

A few people eyed him, gazes full of pity or accusation. This was why he avoided the townsfolk. He'd move if he could, but that would destroy his mother.

The floral scent of flowers wafted over him as he passed Lily's Flower Shop's table. The last time he'd bought a woman flowers was . . . the night he'd proposed to Ana. Nash pushed the memory away. A sick feeling churned in his gut. What if he couldn't protect Bella and the baby? What if something happened? The sheer amount of things that could go wrong that he had no control over spun through his mind. He pushed forward on unsteady feet, keeping his head down as his heart raced.

"Oh, come on! You can do better than that," Bella's voice

teased from his right. His attention darted in the same direction, and he blinked. Surely he was seeing things. That was not the woman carrying his baby in the dunking booth. She wouldn't be that reckless.

Bella sat a good few feet above the water, in a black one-piece swimsuit that pushed her breasts together and showed off her sexy thick thighs. A crowd had gathered around the booth. Some young kid pulled back his arm to throw the ball at the target that would send her plunging into the water below. But what if something malfunctioned and a piece of wood struck her stomach? What if she fell wrong? What if . . .?

He ran over to the dunking booth. His body heated with anger, tense and wired with adrenaline.

"What the hell do you think you're doing?" he boomed.

Bella jerked, mouth thinning as she crossed her arms, which only served to enhance her luscious cleavage. She glared at him. "What I do is none of your business."

"The hell it isn't!" Nash stalked around to the back of the tank and ripped the door open, wrapping his arm carefully around her waist and pulling her out.

"*Bájame, cabrón!*" Bella's small fists hit his back with surprising strength before he set her on her feet.

"Why can't you just listen to me?" Nash growled.

She stood straight, shoving him away, tipping her chin in defiance. "Why can't you stay away from me?"

"Pretty hard to do when you're living with my sister and carrying my goddamned baby!" Nash's chest heaved, his nostrils flaring. Anger radiated through his every cell that she would be so reckless.

Bella's face drained of color as her gaze searched wildly around them.

Fuck. He'd been so overcome with the need to protect her

that he'd forgotten they were in the middle of the town square. Everyone was staring at them. Once again, his emotions had gotten the better of him.

Nova appeared, linking her arm with Bella's as she gave Nash a look of disappointment. "Come on, Bella. Let's get out of here."

Bella's gaze locked on to the grass as his sister led her away from him and the audience he'd garnered. The last thing he wanted was to get this town gossiping about his business again, but what he regretted most was that it would affect Bella too. Nash wiped a hand over his face and shook his head. *How do I keep making this worse?*

He needed to go after her and apologize, but first, he needed to find his parents and own up to everything before the rumor mill notified them that their son had once again brought shame on the family.

When will I learn?

20

ISABELLA

Isabella clutched the towel wrapped around her modest one-piece bathing suit and kept her head down. Her skin burned with embarrassment from the attention of strangers who'd no doubt witnessed the spectacle Nash had made. Now everyone would be talking about poor Isabella Noveas, knocked up and a widow all in less than a year. No doubt some would pity her and others think she was a ho. She shook her head. It didn't matter what people thought. But she needed to find Eli. He had to hear this from her.

Nova hadn't said a word as she guided Isabella away from the crowds towards her truck. Isabella turned to face her friend. "I need to find Eli."

Nova nodded, turning to look back at the people spread out over Green Park. The sun was shining. Birds chirped, people laughed, and kids screamed in glee. Her heart raced and sweat beaded on her skin despite being in her bathing suit and the thin wrap Nova had blessedly grabbed as they'd walked away from the booth.

"Do you know where he is?" Nova asked.

"With my parents."

Nova turned back to her, tipping her head to the side as she studied Isabella. "It all makes sense now."

"What?"

"The interest my usually silent loner brother has in you."

Isabella's shoulders hunched. The back of her eyes burned. She wanted to fall apart, but she couldn't—not here. Not when Eli needed her to be strong. *One foot in front of the other, Bella. Fake it until you make it.*

"I'm sorry, Nova. I'll move out—"

"The hell you will."

Isabella's eyes widened. "What?"

"Why would you move out?" Nova asked.

"Your parents are going to hate me. They're all going to think I lied to them. But I didn't know he was your brother until that family dinner—I swear."

Nova crossed her arms over her chest and shrugged. "It's okay, really. I mean, I wish you would have told me, but I get it. We're just getting to know each other again. And he is my brother. But even I can admit he's been an asshole." She sighed. "The thing about Nash is he has a complicated history. Not that I'm making excuses for him. What he did was cowardly, by not stepping up to the plate. You should know whatever is going on with him, it has to do with his past—not with you."

"What happened in Nash's past?"

Nova swallowed, her lips turning down sympathetically. "Nash lost someone he cared about—his fiancée, Anastasia."

Dios. His boat is named after her. "She passed?"

Nova shook her head. "That's the thing. She's been missing for years. No one ever found her body. Nash blames himself. He just shut himself off from everyone after that. This is the first Juneteenth celebration he's been to since, and I think you might have something to do with it."

"I highly doubt that," Isabella scoffed.

"Don't sell yourself short. I know you said your baby daddy made it clear he didn't want anything to do with the baby, but I've also seen my brother approach you with something weighing on his mind. I'm not telling you what to do, because it's your choice. And I will support you no matter what—girl power and all." Nova laughed. "But as his sister, I have to ask if you'll hear him out when he pulls his head from his ass and comes to talk to you?"

Isabella nodded. "I never intended this to blow up like it did."

"Welcome to the Emerson family, where everything turns into drama and nothing goes according to plan. Sometimes I wonder if we're cursed." Nova laughed again, but this time it sounded hollow. She handed Isabella her keys. "Here. You take my truck and get Eli out of here. I'll get a ride back with Roman or Mom."

Isabella accepted them. "Thank you, Nova." She hugged her. "You've been a real friend."

"That's what Auntie Nova is here for." She winked.

Isabella gave her one last wave before she headed towards her parents' picnic blanket. Eli had his head bowed, looking down at his iPad. Her mother was nowhere to be seen, but her father relaxed next to her son on the blue blanket under the tree.

"Hey, sweetie, can you come with me?" she asked Eli, getting his attention by touching his shoulder gently.

He moved his shoulder out of her reach. "I need to finish this video."

"Everything okay, *mija*?" Papi asked.

"It will be." She forced a smile and peeked over Eli's

shoulder to check the time remaining. Twenty minutes. If she wanted to avoid a meltdown, she needed to be creative.

"Eli, there is something important I need to talk to you about. I'd like you to put the tablet away."

"It's my screen time. Every day, I get my tablet between two and three. It's only two thirty-five. I have twenty-five minutes left," Eli answered in his usual monotone voice.

A few women looked her way over by a food cart before leaning in together and whispering. The downside to small towns was everyone knew everyone else's business. She crouched beside him. "I'll make you a deal. If you come with me now, you'll get thirty extra minutes later today. Deal?"

Eli was silent for a few moments. She was about to give up hope when he tapped the screen to pause the boat tutorial. "Deal."

"Grab your bag and come on."

Eli listened, sliding his backpack over both shoulders before saying goodbye to his abuelo and walking beside Isabella. "Where are we going?"

"To one of my favorite places." She led the way to the truck and climbed in, waiting for him to buckle in before driving through town towards the beach.

She rolled down the windows, letting the warm summer breeze blow over her. She maneuvered through the streets, heading towards a long stretch of highway before pulling off a side road that led to Shattered Cove Beach to the entrance that usually only locals could find. She parked and got out, Eli not too far behind.

She ran her fingers through his blond curls. He shrugged her off. "What did you want to talk about?"

"Let's sit over there on that driftwood." She pointed. She didn't bother telling Eli to take off his shoes. He hated the feel of sand.

He perched on the side, facing the ocean, eyes roaming the waves.

"Can you give me eye contact?" she asked. "I have something really important to tell you."

Eli turned to face her, his eyes going just above hers. If she hadn't known what to look for, she wouldn't have realized he was actually staring at her forehead. Eye contact was difficult for her son, but he'd made such amazing strides from where he started.

"Thank you. I wanted to talk to you. I want you to hear the truth about the baby in my belly's father."

"Okay. But it's not in your belly; it's in your uterus. Inside that is a placenta."

She took a shaky breath and let it out. "Right. Sometimes people say belly or stomach to make it sound more appealing I guess."

"But if the baby was in your stomach it wouldn't survive. You have stomach acid and—"

"I know, honey. Never mind that." She needed to steer this back to the topic at hand. "I wanted you to hear from me that the father is Nash. You may hear people say things about it in town or at the marina. But this changes nothing for you and me. Okay? Do you understand what I'm telling you?"

"Are you and Nash getting married?" Eli asked.

Isabella blinked and shook her head. "No. Nash and I are just . . . friends." *Not even that.*

"You had sex with a friend?"

Dios. Robert, if you're listening, I could use some help to save me from this right about now. "Um, yeah. Listen, sweetie, I love you. And I'm going to love this baby. And we're gonna be a family. Some things might change a little after it's born, but we'll find a new routine and work it out together. How do you feel about that?"

Eli turned back to the waves, silent as several minutes passed. Seagulls cawed overhead. Waves crashed. A few people swam farther down.

"Is Nash going to try and be my dad now too?" Eli's voice was loud, making her flinch.

She shook her head. "No. Not at all. Nash is a friend. No one can ever take your dad's place."

"But he's dead."

She reached out, putting her arm around Eli's stiff body. "But we carry him in our hearts. Your dad will always be with you."

"That is impossible. No one can live in a heart. There isn't any proof—"

"I don't mean literally. It's more like he's in your memories."

"What if I forget him?"

Her heart ached for her son. She squeezed him into a hug with the usual pressure he liked—not too soft or too hard. "Then I'll be here to remind you. And we have pictures and videos."

"Mom?"

"*Sí?*"

"Can I have my iPad now?"

I guess we're done with that conversation. She chuckled. "Let's head home to Nova's. You can use it in the car."

She stood, giving the incoming tide one last glance before she headed to the truck. Later tonight, she'd be confronting Nash. He'd had no right to do what he did today. He couldn't have it both ways. Either he was in or he was out. Fuck this in between.

21

NASH

"You *what?*" Nash's father stared at him in disbelief.

The white flap from the tent they were behind blew in the wind, making a snapping noise.

"Damn, bro. You shoulda said something earlier when we were giving you a hard time," Ricky said.

Nash ran a hand over his face, his shoulders slumped. "I know I should have said something sooner, but I was just trying to get my head wrapped around this myself."

"Why would she think you wanted nothing to do with her and the baby?" his mother asked, watching him closely.

"Oh, yes, do tell. I'd like to hear the answer to this too," Nova said, leaning in to Roman's side.

"I overheard her mom talking about her at the marina. I didn't realize she meant Bella. It was a one-time thing. She said she lived in Colorado. I never thought I'd see her again." It wasn't easy admitting his sexual history aloud to his family. "I saw her again and she told me about the baby and I panicked."

His mother shook her head disappointedly as his father let

out a frustrated exhale. He tore his ball cap off, a sign he was well and truly pissed.

"I know I could have handled it better," Nash said. The scent of cotton candy reached him, completely at odds with the tension of the moment.

"Ya think?" Nova's sarcasm wasn't helping things.

He cut her a glare.

"What are you gonna do now?" Roman asked.

"I have no fucking clue."

"I'd start with talking to your baby mama," Ricky offered.

"You better make this right," his mother said before walking away.

"Yes, ma'am." Nash saluted her retreating back.

"I didn't raise a coward," his father stated, following after his wife.

"No, sir." Once again, he answered the back of his parent.

"Damn, I'm gonna be an uncle." Ricky smiled.

"You're already an uncle, idiot." Roman shoved Ricky towards the festivities, leaving Nash alone with Nova.

"Go ahead. Get whatever you want to say off your chest." *I deserve it.*

"You were an asshole." Nova crossed her arms over her chest.

"Yup."

"And you embarrassed her in front of the whole town."

He grimaced. "I know."

"You better not hurt her again."

"I'll try my best," he promised.

She waited a beat and then asked, "How are you doing with this whole 'becoming a dad' thing?"

"I think I'm off to a pretty spectacular dumpster fire of a beginning, don't you agree?"

Her expression softened before she wrapped her arms around his waist, hugging him close. He patted her back.

"I worry about you, you know?" Nova sighed. "I know you think you don't deserve good things—"

He tried to pull away but she just held on tighter.

"Don't try to deny it. I know you. And what happened to Ana was horrible. You've kept yourself shut off from everyone for so long, and you can't do that with a baby. This might just be the best thing to ever happen to you."

Or it could be the worst.

*　　*　　*

Nash left the keys in the ignition as he bypassed Nova's parked truck and headed to her house. He knocked on the door. Footsteps padded on the other side as a curvy figure approached through the blurry glass window of the door.

"I'm here to talk," he announced.

The door opened and a gorgeous Bella stared back at him, her expression carefully blank. The dark circles under her eyes were deeper, as if the afternoon's events had exhausted her even more. *It's my fault.* And now he was here to make it right —whatever it took. Because whether she liked it or not, Bella, their baby, and Eli were now under his care.

So much for keeping things simple.

"Can I come in for a minute?" he asked.

Bella didn't budge.

"I'm sorry for this afternoon."

Her lips parted as she gripped the doorframe.

"I went off the handle and . . . I overreacted and I shouldn't have blown up like that. I'm sorry that I said everything in front of the town. The last thing I'd want to do is hurt you or make you the center of gossip. I know from experience that's a shitty place to be. I saw you in that tank and . . ." *Imagined all the horrible things that could have happened to you in that ancient contraption.*

Bella swallowed and blinked up at him. "You were scared?"

She saw right through him.

He nodded. "I was worried about what could happen to the baby."

"Why? You didn't even believe it was yours at first. And you certainly made it clear this is the last thing you want."

"I deserve that. But you didn't get pregnant on your own. I'm as much to blame if not more so. I should have checked the expiration date on that condom. Or seen if it had broken before I . . ."

"Ran away?" Bella crossed her arms in front of her as if she could protect herself.

He sighed. "Yeah."

His gaze wandered past her to the living room, where Eli's attention was focused on the tablet in his hands. "I want you to know I plan on doing everything in my power to be as good to our child as my dad was to us. And I'd like to find a way to co-parent with you."

Bella touched her temple, blinking up at him in disbelief. "I don't know what to say."

"Say 'Yes, Nash.'"

She chuckled and it loosened something in his chest, setting it free. "Why couldn't you have been this Nash at the marina?"

"Shock." More like complete terror.

"I guess that's fair. You want to start over?"

"You'd do that?"

She placed her hand on her belly. "It's not about just me

anymore. If you want to do this, your son or daughter deserves the chance to know you too."

Right. "I think we should all get to know each other a little better."

She chewed on her bottom lip. Damn, he remembered just how those tasted—sweet as frosting and rich as champagne.

"I can do that."

Nash flicked a glance at Eli once more and then back to her. "Eli too, if it's alright with you?"

Bella didn't say anything for a moment, her eyes growing glassy before she blinked the emotion away and nodded. "I guess it makes sense. Just let me know when a good time is."

"How about now?" he asked.

"Now?"

"Seems only right, since I ruined our Juneteenth celebration, that I make up for it."

One of her eyebrows rose. "And how do you plan on doing that?"

"I heard Eli wanted to know a little more about fishing and boats. You think your stomach can handle it?"

She smiled and the sight nearly brought him to his knees. "Only one way to find out."

22

ISABELLA

The first thirty minutes on the boat riding out to sea with Nash were awesome. Eli's hands flapped in excitement as he drilled Nash with questions or spouted off maritime facts. Nash steered them past the no-wake zone, out of the bay, and into open water. Isabella sat in the same chair she had the first night she'd met Nash, making room for Eli next to her.

"The ancient Egyptians would use boats with oars and sails. The Austronesian peoples were the first to build boats that were capable of sailing on the ocean. They developed the trade route that would later become known as the Maritime Silk Road," Eli said, his focus moving between Nash's hands on the wheel and the direction they were headed.

"Is that right?" Nash replied. He'd been patient with Eli's commentary since they'd climbed in his truck. "What's your favorite ship?"

Isabella's heart squeezed. It wasn't often Eli had someone who was willing to talk about boats constantly. But to see Nash putting in the effort to take them out and spend time with them showed how much he was trying. Maybe this co-parenting thing would work out after all.

Her stomach rolled. She swallowed and focused on the horizon in front of them, hoping it would help ease the nausea that crept up on her from the swaying ocean.

"The Merchant Royal, an English merchant ship carrying over one hundred thousand pounds of gold—it sunk near Cornwall County, England, in sixteen forty-one, but they discovered the anchor off the coast of the United Kingdom in twenty nineteen."

Isabella smiled. Eli never ceased to surprise her with all the facts stored in that unique mind of his.

"Sounds like I'm in the wrong business. Maybe I should become a treasure hunter," Nash joked.

Eli was quiet a moment. "Maybe I could buy your boat, then. You'll need a bigger ship for hunting treasure like that."

The rumble of Nash's laugh stirred something warm and pleasant in her chest. The boat swayed up and down again over a bigger wave. Isabella grabbed the edge of the seat, holding her breath as she staved off the nausea as best she could.

It will pass. Eli's having too good of a time to turn around now. Sweat dotted her forehead as bile rose in her throat.

"I think I'm too old for a change of careers. Think I'll stick to what I know." Nash added, "Why don't you take the helm?"

"Me?" Eli asked.

"Of course. If you're gonna captain your own boat one day, you'll need to practice."

Eli jumped to his feet and swayed to the right. Isabella reached out to steady him as Nash got up from his seat and offered it to her son. Eli's hand flapped in excitement as he beamed.

"One hand here, and the other there." Nash pointed.

Eli listened, focused intently on the horizon ahead. Nash's hand rested on his shoulder, steadying him.

Another wave of nausea crashed over Isabella. She squinted her eyes closed, but it only made it worse.

"How much farther are we going out?" she asked, trying to keep her voice even.

"Another few miles or so," Nash answered before turning towards her, his head tilting to the side. "You okay? You don't look too good."

"I'm fine." As soon as the lie left her mouth she was scrambling for the edge of the boat. Clasping onto the metal rung, she bent over the edge and vomited her lunch.

The engine switched off and the boat bobbed in the ocean as she threw up again. The sound of the door to the cabin below opened and then shut a moment later. A large warm hand rubbed her lower back.

"Here's some water." Nash handed her a bottle and a paper towel.

She gratefully accepted it, wiping her mouth before rinsing it out. She did that a few times before attempting a few small sips.

"I'm sorry. I've never been seasick before. Must be this baby."

"Nothing to apologize for. But you should have told me you were struggling."

She glanced at Eli who was watching them with wide, worried eyes before focusing back on Nash. "He was having so much fun. This move has upended his whole life. A lot of change for a boy who likes routine. And he's always loved boats so much."

"Come on. Eat these and I'll get us back to the marina. I'll take him out another time if that's alright with you. He can come with me and Anthony." Nash handed her a few ginger candies.

She reached out to grab his arm. "Nash?"

He tensed. Stormy dark eyes moved from where she touched him to meet hers. "Yeah?"

"Thank you."

He nodded and guided her back to her seat, one palm on her lower back, scorching her skin. The pulse of electricity was just as strong as it had been the night they'd spent together on this very boat. She shivered. *Get it together, chica. Because you're never going there again with him. It would be way too complicated.*

Not that Nash would want to. The man had barely started speaking to her.

"Mom?" Eli asked as she settled in the seat.

She smiled. "I'm okay. Just morning sickness."

His fingers uncrossed and his shoulders lowered as if in relief.

"Okay, bud. We're gonna have to head back, but I'll take you out again sometime," Nash offered.

"But we didn't even go fishing," Eli protested. "You said we were going fishing."

Isabella tensed, sensing a meltdown coming on. Maybe she could just manage another hour?

Nash bent to get on her son's level. "I did say that, but your mom isn't feeling well. Sometimes plans have to change when things come up. I promise you we'll go out again soon. You and your mom can pick the day."

"But—"

"And I'll let you pilot the boat back to the marina—how 'bout that?" Nash asked.

Eli's eyes widened. "The whole way?"

Nash nodded. "Yep."

"Okay." Eli turned back to the wheel, gripping it like Nash taught him.

Isabella's lips turned up at the corners in gratitude despite her queasiness. Tears welled in her eyes. *God, he's good with my kid. Nash is going to be a great dad.*

* * *

An hour later, Isabella took Nash's hand and climbed out of his truck. Eli bounded ahead to the door, stopping before he entered as if just remembering something.

He turned to Nash. "Thank you for taking me out in your boat today and letting me steer. I'm ready to go back out as soon as my mom agrees."

"Sounds like a plan," Nash said.

He walked with her to the doorway before she turned to him on the porch, covering her mouth as she yawned. Exhaustion had gotten the better of her. She'd forgotten this part of pregnancy. But it would be worth it.

"Thank you again for this afternoon," she said.

"It was fun. But you look like you need a rest. You should go lie down."

Was that his way of telling her she looked like crap? "Yeah, that sounds like a good idea. I guess I'll see you later?"

"Yup."

She nodded and turned towards Eli, pulling open a magazine off the coffee table. "I'm gonna lie down for a little while. Stay in the house, okay?"

"Okay."

"Can you lock the door on your way out?" she asked Nash.

"Sure."

She headed upstairs on tired legs. It had been a long day.

After stopping in the bathroom to relieve herself and brush her teeth, she crawled into bed and closed her eyes.

* * *

Isabella woke to a dim room. She wiped the drool from her mouth before turning to the clock on the bedside table. *Oh, mierda. I slept for three hours.* She sat up quickly, groaning as her head spun with dizziness. She remained still until it settled and then went downstairs. *Eli probably devoured the snack cupboard for dinner.*

The scent of something savory and delicious filled her nose. *Nova must be cooking.*

Isabella made it to the living room first. Eli was reading a book on the couch. Movement from the kitchen caught her eye. Nash stood with his back to her by the stove.

"I thought you left," she said, walking to the counter.

He turned around, her gaze momentarily dropping to his wide chest, the material of his T-shirt stretched taut across it enhancing the defined muscles she knew from experience were just as delicious as they appeared.

He scanned her face. *Oh Dios, I must look a fright.* She pulled her hair out of the messy bun and scooped it back into her hand, trying to smooth out any bed head in the process.

Nash's attention remained on her. "No. I wanted to make sure you and Eli were okay. We spent some time comparing boats to see which one would be best for him to start with. And then we talked sustainable fishing. He knows his stuff."

Nash had spent three hours with her son? Emotion clogged her throat. "What's all this?" She motioned to the stove behind him.

He ran a hand over the back of his neck, eyeing her sheepishly. "Dinner."

"You cooked?"

He shrugged like it was no big deal. "Back in the early days, my parents both worked the farm, so dinner landed on my shoulders as the oldest. Soup was easiest. And this should help settle your stomach. There's some ginger with the chicken."

Isabella was speechless. How long had it been since someone took care of her like this? And how was this the same man from earlier at the town celebration?

He scooped some of the soup into a bowl, slid in a spoon, and handed it to her. "I already made Eli a grilled cheese. He told me about his food aversions."

"Nash, I . . . thank you."

"It's nothing special," he grumbled, turning his back to her to grab another bowl.

She blinked. With her eyes growing watery, she turned away to look at Eli. She had a feeling that if Nash saw her tears, he would run for the hills.

She hadn't expected him to be this supportive. But maybe it was time she learned all there was to know about the father of her child.

23

NASH

Nash loaded the cooler onto the back of the four-wheeler, securing it on the back before running a hand over his face. The warm summer breeze blew over him, sending the trees swishing nearby. Nerves twisted his stomach as he climbed on and started the engine. It had been a long day of fishing in the sun. He'd come home and showered, then thrown together a few things because the moment he'd anticipated all day long had finally come. Nash hit the gas and steered the ATV away from his property towards his sister's.

It'd been almost a week since he'd laid eyes on Bella. He'd had to get the fishing in while the weather was good and had been out spending long days at sea. With her morning sickness, it wasn't like she could come along. But tonight, they needed to make sure they were on the same page. He'd do whatever it took to make sure she and his child were taken care of—and Eli now fell into that category.

Nova's home came into view along with a car he recognized and two figures that had his stomach sinking and his spine stiffening.

Bella turned, looked over at him as he rounded the house in his four-wheeler. Her parents stood by their SUV behind her. Tomas seemed friendly enough as Nash shut off the engine. His gaze was assessing, as if he was trying to read Nash's intentions for his daughter—Nash couldn't blame him. But Catherine scowled, her cheeks flushed like Bella's were when she was angry. Catherine Noveas had been one of the biggest rumor spreaders after he was taken in for questioning for Ana's disappearance. It must be eating her up that he was the father of her future grandchild.

"Good evening," Nash said. He wasn't usually one to greet anyone, but for Bella, he'd make an effort.

"Nash." Tomas held out his hand to shake. "You had quite the catch today."

Nash released his palm and nodded. "Yes, sir."

"Really, Isabella Marie? You couldn't have picked anyone but this man?" Catherine's words spewed like venom in a string of Spanish as she eyed him with disdain.

It might have been the one time he wished he didn't understand the language. But his brother, Ricky, was half Colombian. The family had all learned to make him feel more comfortable after he was placed with them by the state.

"Mama, *detener.*" *Stop.* Bella turned to him, giving him a shaky smile. "Hey, Nash. My parents were just picking Eli up for the night."

Nash's gaze roamed over the empty porch, the few potted flowers, and the open door, searching for the boy.

"He's just getting his things together. He likes to do a double check to make sure he has everything," Bella supplied.

Nash didn't know what to say, so he remained silent. The

awkwardness of the four of them standing there, all eyes on him but Bella's, made his skin itch.

His jaw tensed. "I know this wasn't what anyone planned, but I want you to know I'm not going anywhere. I'll take care of your daughter and the baby."

The lines of Tomas's tan skin eased as some of the tension seeped from his shoulders. "I appreciate you saying that."

"If he wanted what was best for them, he would leave them alone. Leave this town. You know what they say about him. He's a—"

"Enough, Mama." Isabella cut her mother off in English before switching to Spanish. *"You will not speak about the father of my child that way."*

Her defense of him, though undeserved, brought a tightness to his chest that was uncomfortable. Maybe they would be better off without him. *Maybe I should go.*

Chaos erupted in his body at the thought. *Never.* Maybe it made him selfish, and the exact kind of monster Catherine accused him of, but he couldn't abandon his child—even if it might be the right thing to do.

The front door opened and Eli came out with his bag in hand and a blanket rolled under his arm. His attentive gaze roamed over the adults before he smiled. "Nash!"

"Hey, bud. Looks like you have a fun night ahead."

Eli walked closer. "Yeah. I'm going to spend the night at my abuela and abuelo's every Friday night. And then Abuelo will take me fishing on Saturday."

"As long as the weather is good," Tomas added.

Eli's mouth straightened. "But it will be good tomorrow. I checked the weather and it said only ten percent chance of rain."

Tomas chuckled. "Looks good, then."

Eli's part-smile returned. "When are we going out on your boat again, Nash?"

"I'll talk about it with your mom today, okay?"

"You can't be serious. Tell me you have no intention of this man taking your son on the open sea?" Catherine asked her daughter in Spanish.

"Lo mantendré a salvo. Promesa," Nash replied. *I'll keep him safe. Promise.*

Catherine's eyes widened, no doubt in shock that this monster could understand everything she said.

"Well, looks like you're ready to go. Can I have a hug, Eli?" Bella asked briskly.

"Okay."

She wrapped her son in her arms, squeezing him tight and then releasing him. "Have fun, and don't stay up too late."

"We won't spoil him too much." Her father smiled, his eyes on his daughter with affection as he pulled her into a hug and kissed her forehead. "See you next week, Nash."

Nash nodded.

Catherine spun around and headed for the passenger side of the SUV, waiting for Tomas to open the door for her before she climbed in.

Bella waved as they drove off. As soon as their car disappeared down the road, she released a sigh. She turned to Nash. "I'm sorry for my mom. She's . . . just concerned."

He grunted. Bella had probably heard all the rumors and gossip about him from Catherine as soon as she'd found out he was the father. Did she see him as a monster too? Did she regret that night was with him?

"Nash?" Bella asked, studying him.

"Yeah?"

"Did you want to come inside to talk?"

He glanced at Nova's truck and shook his head. "Actually, I was wondering if you'd come with me somewhere." The last thing he needed was his little sister listening in to their discussion and butting her nose into his business.

"Oh. Sure."

He turned and walked towards the ATV, lifting his leg over and settling on. "Coming?"

She eyed the vehicle, biting her lip. "I've never been on one of these things."

"I'll be gentle." *Shit.* He was not supposed to be flirting with her.

Her whiskey eyes met his. God, she was beautiful. Dark strands of hair blowing in the summer breeze. Her full pink lips, curved with a Cupid's bow at the top directly in the center of a round face that was just as soft as it seemed too. And those curves. His cock hardened, making his seat uncomfortable, but he'd be damned if he shifted and drew attention to it.

"Won't let anything happen to you or the baby," he promised. No one would hurt them. Not as long as he drew breath.

She licked her lips and wiped her hands on her shorts before approaching the vehicle. Nash reached out his hand to help her on. She swung her leg over the back of the seat, climbing on behind him. Her thighs pressed on either side of him, making his cock even harder with memories of those legs wrapped around him while he fucked her and had the most powerful orgasm of his life.

"Um, do you care if I hold on to you?" she asked.

He gave a jerky nod. Maybe they should have taken the truck. Too late now.

Nash started the engine and her palms slid over his abs, linking in front of him. A few inches lower and she'd feel just how affected he was by her touch.

"Hang on," he said before hitting the gas.

Bella held on tighter. He eased the four-wheeler down the road to a path he knew by heart. A few minutes went by, the rumble of the engine the only sound as he cut through the forest towards their destination. The path narrowed ahead with a rock formation. He slowed the ATV. Bella peered over his shoulder before her grip tightened.

His hand dropped to her bare thigh without thinking, electric heat searing up his arm. He squeezed, hoping to convey comfort. "This part gets a little tight. Just hang on and lean how I do."

He maneuvered them past the rocks and back onto the trail. Another few minutes passed until the trees broke and the clearing came into view. He drove through the tall grass straight to the center of the hill where a few flat rocks rested. He shut the engine off.

After climbing down, he pressed a palm to his groin to try and calm the ache before he extended his hand to Bella to help her off. Her knees wobbled as she landed on the ground, grasping both his arms to steady herself.

"You okay?"

She nodded with a smile. "Yeah, the vibration turned my legs into Jell-O I think."

"Do you need a moment?" His voice came out gruff. The longer she touched him, the harder it was to control the arousal that flooded his veins. But crossing that line with her again couldn't happen.

"No, I'm good." She straightened.

"Stay here a moment. I'll get a few things set up." He walked back around to the cooler and unloaded it, carrying it to the flat outcropping in the middle. The ground up here was a mix of rock and moss; farther down, it was more like a meadow. They couldn't farm it, but there were plenty of woods around. A small access road led up here, but it wasn't used much—only to log already fallen trees for heating their houses.

He opened the cooler and laid out the blanket he'd brought on the rock. *Maybe I should have brought a chair for her to be more comfortable? Too late now. Next time.*

If there was a next time.

"You can see the whole farm from up here and beyond," Bella pointed out, looking off into the distance.

He took in the view. The sun was shining, though low in the sky, and there wasn't a cloud in sight. Green rolling hills and trees scattered the space below, his parents' and siblings' houses all within view. On a clear day like today, you could see for miles. This was one of his favorite spots. Where he came to think and write and be alone—without the chance of a well-meaning family member dropping by. It was where he came to forget. And to remember. There was only one other woman he'd brought up here.

Flashes of Ana's red hair dancing in the wind as she pranced around the field below, gathering flowers, assaulted his memory.

"Nash?"

"Hmm?"

"Where'd you go?"

He shook his head. "Sorry."

"It's okay. Look, if this is too much for you, we can wait," she offered, her smile sympathetic, which only served to anger him.

He didn't deserve her sympathy.

"I'm fine," he snapped, harsher than he'd intended.

She flinched and folded her arms over her chest, red rising

to her cheeks. "Okay, well, you don't have to be an asshole about it."

He was so used to people backing down from his gruffness, but Bella stood her ground. It was just one more thing that made her so different than Ana.

He sighed. "You're right. I'm sorry."

Her eyes widened as if she were surprised he'd been so quick to apologize. He might be a burly son of a bitch, but he could admit when he was wrong.

He waved at the blanket at his feet. "Care to sit?"

She approached, eyeing the material on the ground. Her lips curled up at the edges before she situated herself on one side, her bare legs crossed in front of her, hands resting on her knees.

He took the spot next to her and opened the cooler. "Water or lemonade?"

"You brought a picnic?" The surprise in her voice was evident.

He shrugged, his stomach somersaulting with nerves. "No. It's a blanket so you don't sit on the grass and get a bunch of ticks. And you need to stay hydrated and fed for the baby."

Bella blinked, her golden-brown eyes getting glassy as an emotion he didn't recognize flashed in them. "Thank you." She turned her head away, wiping her eyes and sniffling.

Fuck. She was crying. The world shifted with her tears as if they cracked open the earth as they fell, knocking him off his axis. He was tumbling into the dark with nothing to hold on to, and he had no clue what he'd done to cause this. "What did I do wrong?"

She shook her head, turning her watery gaze towards him as she smiled. "I haven't had anyone take care of me in a really long time. I'm usually the one making sure everyone else has what they need." She sniffed. "It's probably just the pregnancy hormones making me extra emotional."

"Well, now you have me."

She froze, her lips parting.

"You're not in this alone. I never intended to let you deal with this by yourself. I just needed a minute to wrap my head around everything. This baby is my responsibility just as much as yours. I should have done better that night—at least checked for a break." He turned towards the view, rubbing a hand over the back of his neck.

"Did you ever want kids?" she asked.

Ana smiled, her blue gaze narrowing on the blueprint he'd laid out in front of her. "Why are there five rooms? That seems a little big for just us."

Nash smirked. "For the four kids we're gonna have of course."

Ana's eyes widened with a flash of fear. "Four kids?"

"I'm open to negotiations. You know I've always wanted to adopt, it's not like I'm expecting you to give birth to that many. Unless you want to. Maybe we could even start now?" He wrapped his arms around her, nuzzling her neck.

She giggled and pushed against his chest. "Nash, I'm serious. That's too many."

"How about three? Or we can space them out?"

"I just never saw myself as a mother," she admitted on a whisper.

"That can change. We can wait until you're ready."

She opened her mouth to say something and then closed it, like she was holding back. She did that a lot. Ana gave him a flirty smile. "How about we do a lot of practicing instead?"

Bella reached into the cooler, grabbing a lemonade out and twisting off the cap before taking a drink. Worry lines appeared on her forehead. "I'll take your silence as a no."

What? Oh, right, did he want kids? "I did once."

"But not anymore?" she pressed.

He sighed. "I'll be honest. I don't have relationships in my life except for my family, because they're stuck with me."

"Oh. I see." She hugged herself, turning her face away from him.

Nash reached out, his palm sliding over the soft skin of her knee.

Her attention snapped to him.

"You're part of my family now."

24

———

ISABELLA

I sabella was more shocked by his words than his touch. *You're part of my family now.*

Nash pulled his hand back, angling his body a little farther away like he needed space after his statement that felt more like a confession. The flash of vulnerability in his dark eyes was like a streak of lightning in a storm—one flicker of a second when all his emotions were illuminated. Fear was the easiest to read. Regret. Grief. Guilt. And anger. But was it because of his past or the pregnancy? Perhaps a bit of both. This was the side of him she'd sensed that night of the wedding. The softness beneath the stone.

"Tell me about yourself," she said.

"What do you want to know?" he asked, pulling out a water for himself and a container of mixed fruit. He peeled the lid and offered it to her.

She picked up a grape. "Why a fisherman?"

"The sea has always called to me. My dad used to take me and my siblings out, charter a boat a couple times a year. It was a blast. I enjoyed farming, but I didn't want to do it full-time. The ocean's different. It . . ."

"It's calming."

He looked at her. "Yeah."

"It's kind of magical too. I mean, it's sort of like staring up at the stars. You realize just how small you are in the scheme of things when you stand by the sea."

"Knowing that the force of nature is unmatched keeps a man humbled," Nash added.

She finished the grape and grabbed a strawberry, the sweetness bursting into her mouth as she bit into it.

"Anyways. I got hooked as a kid and made it a reality a few years ago after . . . well, when I needed some change." His eyes clouded over. "Seems Eli might be even more interested than I was. I think you have a fisherman on your hands."

She chuckled. "It's been his obsession since he was seven. Before that it was dinosaurs."

"Did his dad take him?"

She nodded. "Yeah, Robert loved it. It was one of the ways they connected."

Nash remained silent.

"Thank you for answering all his questions and being so patient with him. I'm sure you noticed Eli has his own way of doing things. He was diagnosed with Autism when he was five."

"He's a good kid. Smart. And persistent." He chuckled.

She smiled. "He is."

"We should plan a day for me to take him out with me. If you're still okay with that."

She winced, remembering what her mother had said. "I didn't know you spoke Spanish."

"There's a lot we don't know about each other," he answered her in her first language.

"True. And I'm okay with him going out with you," she admitted. Nash could be gruff, but he was different with Eli. He was protective and patient, and they had to start somewhere. And if he really was a killer like her mother had inferred, he'd had ample opportunity to murder her the night she was with him alone on a boat.

"Maybe Ariel would want to join us," Nash offered. "Anthony will be with me too."

"I appreciate you doing that."

He ran a hand through his beard. "So, what is it that you do?"

"Well, I went to school to be a nurse, but then I got pregnant with Eli my first semester. I finished the year but had to quit because of complications."

Nash's body tensed. "Complications?"

"I was on bed rest the last two months. And then after he was born, it made more sense for me to stay home while Robert completed his degree." Emotion welled in her eyes. A part of her wondered if she should be talking to him about Robert at all, especially after he'd accused her of betraying Robert by sleeping with him only six months after Robert had passed. But Nash didn't know the whole story.

"Anyways, after Eli started school, I got my certificate to be a massage therapist. It made sense with the flexible hours and Eli's needs. But then Robert was diagnosed with ALS. The disease progressed pretty quickly and he needed extra care, and then with Eli, it was too much."

"I'm sorry."

"Towards the end, I started working at my friend Tessa's tattoo shop as a receptionist part-time to get out of the house."

"Are you planning on getting clients here?"

"Probably. But I think I'll wait until life is a little more settled. Routine is important to Eli, and I've already upended his world twice in the last month. I know he's struggling with his dad being gone too."

"If you need money—"

She shook her head. "Oh, no. I'm—we're fine. Robert always planned ahead, and he had a life insurance policy that will carry us through for as long as I need it." *As long as I'm careful.*

"How old are you?"

"Thirty. Why?"

"You just seem older."

"Gee thanks," she answered sarcastically, trying to hide the flinch of hurt at his words.

"I didn't mean it like that. You're gorgeous."

What?

"Fuck. I just meant, you're a beautiful woman."

"Well, being older doesn't equate with ugliness either," she teased.

His lips flattened. "Every time I talk to you, my foot ends up in my mouth. That isn't what I meant. I just . . . ." He blew out a breath. "Your eyes seem like they've seen a lot more of life than thirty years. Damn, just forget I said anything."

She offered him a smile. "It's okay. I get it. And they probably do. My life hasn't been the easiest."

A moment of comfortable silence passed as she snacked on the fruit and he stared towards the view of farmland below. Sometimes it was nice to just sit in the quiet with someone by your side.

"Have you made a doctor's appointment yet?" he asked.

"Yeah, it's in a few weeks. Do you . . . I mean you don't have to, but—"

"I'd like to be there. If it's okay with you."

"Yeah. Okay."

He turned forward once more, the sun hitting his dark brown skin, highlighting the sharp angles of his face. His full beard was dark and ruffled from him running his hands through it. His arms flexed as if he could feel her gaze. His strong nose was just a little crooked, as if he'd broken it at some point in his life. It was the only thing not symmetrical on his face. He didn't look human but carved from marble like the Greek gods of Olympus. Poseidon, god of the sea, sitting on this green knoll and feeding her fruit and asking her questions.

Two obsidian orbs crashed against hers like a tidal wave, sending her spinning into a riot of emotions before receding and pulling her into their fathomless depths. She found unspoken promises of loyalty and a fierce protection in them. Her belly flipped and fluttered. Nervousness or excitement—maybe a bit of both. It was hard to tell the difference sometimes.

Maybe this wouldn't be so lonely after all.

25

NASH

Weeks later, Nash sat back in the chair of the clinic waiting room. The sides bit into his thick thighs and waist. Apparently, it wasn't built for giants. Bella's attention remained focused on the clipboard in front of her, the pen in her hand moving fluidly across the pages of paperwork asking for her information.

A few other men sat with their partners, most of which were pregnant, or had a newborn in their arms. One dad wrangled a toddler away from the water cooler by the door. A couple of kids played in the corner where there were a few toys and books laid out.

He shifted in the uncomfortable seat. This would be his life now.

"Isabella Bates?" a woman in a white lab coat and purple scrubs called.

Bates? Right, she was married. Noveas was her maiden name. *We still have so much more to learn about each other.*

Bella stood, offering the woman a smile. Nash followed her.

"I'm Karlie, and I'll be doing your ultrasound today. Go ahead into this room." She pointed to her right.

Bella entered and climbed onto the paper-covered bed in the center of the small room. If he'd felt like a giant in the waiting room, he was a goddamned mountain in here. The room was barely bigger than a closet. He pressed himself into yet another small chair across from the tech, Bella lying between them on the table.

Karlie scooted her chair closer, slipping gloves on and starting the ancient-looking computer. "Alright, are we ready to see your little bundle today?"

"Yes," Bella answered.

"Are you Dad?" Karlie asked.

Dad? The word barreled over him. He didn't trust his voice, so he nodded.

Bella stiffened. A fissure of guilt swirled in his gut. His baby wasn't here yet and he was already fucking things up with her mama. Or his? It could be a boy.

"This might be a little cold. Sorry." Karlie lifted Bella's shirt and then tucked Bella's pants down lower. Bella's stomach still looked as soft and dimpled as it had that night, but now more of a bump protruded from her lower belly.

Bella cleared her throat, her cheeks flushing as she stared at the ceiling. Was she nervous?

"Okay, so we got your records from your previous doctors but they didn't include an ultrasound. Is this your first one?" Karlie asked.

"Yeah. I found out just before I moved and then everything was just so busy," Bella answered.

"Is that bad? Should we have come in earlier?" Nash asked.

Bella turned to him, brows drawn together, eyes narrowed.

"It's no problem. She's far enough along now that we can

probably skip the transvaginal part and try it on your belly. I'm sure Doctor Wright will want to get some bloodwork today too." Karlie answered as she squirted some clear jelly on Bella's stomach. Bella flinched.

Karlie picked up an attachment for the computer and pressed it against Bella's stomach, both women's eyes focusing on the grainy screen.

A moment later, a pulsing, whooshing sound filled the room. Chills raced up his spine, every hair standing on end.

Karlie smiled. "Baby has a strong heartbeat."

"That's the baby?"

"Yes."

The room shifted. *That's my baby. I'm really going to be a dad.* A burst of love like he'd never known flooded his chest. Tears burned the back of his eyes as the room tilted. That tiny little blob was his baby. So small and frail. Anxiety snaked around his rib cage, constricting more with every thought. *What if something happens to it? What if Bella gets hurt? What if I mess up? What if I'm not enough for them?*

A soft hand gripped his forearm. He turned to Bella's sympathetic smile.

"It'll be okay."

Could she read his mind?

The rest of the ultrasound went by in a blur. Before he knew it, he was sitting in an office with plain white walls next to Bella while Doctor Sebastian Wright explained everything.

"We'll give you a call if anything shows up in your bloodwork, but I don't expect there to be any problems. Make sure you take your prenatals, avoid the foods on that paper, and double-check with my office before taking any medications not on the pre-approved list. I know this isn't your first rodeo. Do either of you have any questions?" Sebastian asked.

Only a million. "What can I do?" Nash asked.

Sebastian smiled. "Be supportive. I'm sure she'd appreciate foot rubs and late-night runs for cravings. Anything you can do to help Mom feel more comfortable and ease stress will be appreciated. What's good for Mom is good for baby." Sebastian spun around in his chair, opening a cabinet and pulling out a piece of paper from a folder, then handing it to him. "Here's a list of reading I always recommend to partners. Should give you some peace of mind to learn exactly what's going on and what to expect."

Nash took the paper. "Thanks."

"If you have any other questions, feel free to reach out. It was good to see you again, Nash. And I look forward to getting to know you better, Isabella. Congratulations to the both of you." Sebastian stood offering his hand to shake.

Nash opened the door for Bella, doing his best to hold it together until they got outside. His heart raced. His mind spun. *What if . . . What if . . .* He couldn't shut it off.

If he'd learned anything, it was that when he was truly happy, something happened to take it away. He couldn't lose someone else. He wouldn't survive it.

"Nash?" Bella's voice pulled him out of his head. Her full lips pursed, lines appearing at the corner of her eyes. "You want to talk about it?"

He gritted his teeth, clenching his hands into fists, trying to hold the panic attack at bay just a little longer.

"It will be okay. We'll figure it out, step by step," she assured him.

He nodded curtly and spun around, running to his car, away from the woman who'd begun to haunt his dreams and carried his child. Away from the hurt that rose every time he looked at her, knowing he could never truly have her. He could never be what she needed because he was half a man—and a broken one at that.

26

———

ISABELLA

Isabella wiped the sweat from her forehead and sneezed. The dust in the storeroom was getting to her. She needed to take a break and get some fresh air, right after she finished this last count.

Another bout of nausea rolled through her. She braced herself against the shelf, closing her eyes and breathing through her mouth. Her parents sold fresh fish that the fishermen brought in, and usually, it didn't bother her. But it seemed her little donut hole wasn't a fan.

"Mom, this is the boat that's best and it's on sale. I already showed it to Nash and Abuelo. They both said it was a good investment. Please can we go look? Nash said he would come."

It seemed her son saw more of Nash than she had since the ultrasound earlier this month when he'd literally run from her afterwards. He still checked in, texting her to ask if she needed anything, and she'd seen him at Mama E's Sunday family dinners and get-togethers. But he hadn't tried to talk with her alone since then. He was pulling away when they were just beginning to get somewhere. Was this how it would be with him? Would he be there for their child but not for her?

So much for not being in this alone. But maybe he thought they didn't need to do anything more than go to the doctor visits together and wait for the baby? Her stupid heart just needed to get the memo and stop hoping for more. Not that she thought he would be more for her—just for the baby. All she wanted was to be friends with the father of her child. Was that too much to ask?

Although the dreams she'd been having lately were definitely not friendly. The man knew how to give her an orgasm, both in real life and in her fantasies. But she would blame that on her pregnancy. Hormones were making her libido skyrocket. Nash was a sexy mountain of a man, and it was only natural that she would crave his touch since he'd given her the best sex of her life. She needed to get him out of her head.

Her stomach seesawed. She clutched her belly and firmly pressed her lips together. She needed out of this store.

"Are you listening, Mom?" Eli asked.

"I am, sweetie. We can go look." She headed towards the main store.

"Today?" Eli followed her.

"No—"

"It's despicable, is what it is. How he took advantage of my daughter while she was grieving," her mother hissed.

Isabella froze. Anger and disgust roiled inside her until she saw red.

Nancy Plotts adjusted her purse over her shoulder. "Disgusting. And if I were you, I'd be terrified for her safety. You know what happened to his fiancée—"

"That is enough!" Isabella's frosty tone surprised even her.

Both women's heads whipped towards her. Her mother's

mouth opened, no doubt with admonishment for speaking that way to her. Isabella never raised her voice to her mother. But this wasn't right, and in front of Bella's son, no less.

"You two should be ashamed of yourselves. The man you are speaking of is the father of your grandchild, Mama. He's a good man who's been through a lot. You may not know what it's like to lose someone you love, but I do." Tears burned the back of her eyes, blurring her vision. Eli's hand gripped hers.

"Nash Emerson didn't take advantage of anyone. I was the one who asked him to spend the night with me—not that it's any of your business. So if you're going to spread gossip about someone, get your story straight."

"*Mija*—"

"No, Mama. I said enough!" She spun around and rushed outside, thumping into a hard body.

She pushed past, making her way to the dock just in time. She fell to her knees and vomited into the ocean. She spat, dizzy and fighting another bout of nausea as sweat beaded on her forehead.

A large palm rubbed her lower back in soothing circles as she stared into the water below.

"Can you get your mom a bottle of water, bud?" Nash asked.

She didn't know whether to be relived it was him or embarrassed he was seeing her losing what little breakfast she could hold down. Footsteps padded away, she assumed Eli doing as he asked.

Isabella wiped her mouth with her hand and then washed herself in the cleaner water of the ocean below. She scooped a handful of the seawater and pressed her cold hand on the back of her neck, sighing in relief.

Eli returned. Nash opened the water and handed it to her.

She pulled some in her mouth, swishing and then spitting it out a few times before taking a small sip.

"Thank you." She carefully stood.

Nash reached out to steady her as she walked back to the loading area of the marina.

"How can I help?"

She couldn't look him in the eyes. Had he heard the awful things her mother and Nancy had said about him? "I'll be fine."

He tucked his hands in his pockets. "At least let me get you something in your stomach. I read that it can help with the morning sickness. We can get some soup?"

He read? And where would they find soup in July except for a grocery store? She was grateful he was trying though.

"It's fine. I have some crackers in my purse and I don't want to spoil my dinner." She checked her phone for the time. Phillip should be here any second.

"You got dinner plans?" Something flashed in his dark gaze that looked a lot like jealousy. But that was a silly idea. Nash didn't want her like that; he'd made that clear from the beginning.

"Yeah."

"Uncle Phillip is here!" Eli announced.

She'd forgotten he was still standing nearby. He ran towards the Tesla parked by the marina entrance on the side of the building.

Phillip got out, a bright smile on his face as he raised his arm for a high five from Eli. "Hey, little man. How have you been?"

"Mom said we could go look at a boat I want to buy," Eli informed him.

Phillip's eyes widened before he glanced at her. "Really? I

mean, I knew she was the best mom ever, but wow. You are one lucky kid."

Phillip opened his arms to Isabella, and as she hugged him, she relished the familiarity in his touch. He'd been there for her every step of the way with Robert in the end. That had bonded them.

"Hey, beautiful. You look fantastic." He pulled away.

She laughed. "If you mean exhausted and sweaty, then I guess so."

"Nah." He tapped her nose. "You're gorgeous and you know it. But . . . if you wanted me to drop you off at home to get a quick shower and change before we go to dinner . . ." He laughed at the same time she did.

A throat clearing had her turning around. Nash stood there, glaring. His arms were crossed over his chest.

"Oh, I'm sorry. Nash, this is Phillip, he's a . . . friend." What he actually was to them was too complicated to explain and definitely not in front of Eli—not until he was older.

"You must be the father I've not heard hardly enough about." Phillip shook Nash's hand.

"And I've heard nothing about you," Nash grumbled, his gaze cutting to hers accusingly.

"Well, I guess we better go. Eli, stick with Abuelo, okay? He's in the office. We'll be back in a couple hours," Isabella said.

Phillip gave Eli another high five. "I'll take you out for ice cream later, and then you can show me this boat you want to buy. How does that sound?"

"Okay," Eli said before he waved goodbye and went inside the marina.

Isabella turned to Nash. "Thanks for . . . the water."

Nash didn't say anything. She sighed and climbed in

Phillip's car. They drove in silence back towards the main part of town.

"You know, I'm not really interested in dressing up and going out tonight. How about the diner for some burgers and fries?"

"A woman of my own heart," Phillip teased.

He pulled into the High Tide Diner's lot and soon they were at a window table with drinks on their way and menus in front of them.

"So, how is everything?" Phillip asked.

"It's . . . going." Phillip and Tessa were the two people she could be honest with about her situation. Neither of them would judge her—nor were they afraid to give her advice even though she may not like it.

"Eli seems like he's doing good. Must be wonderful for him to be so close to his passion. I'm sure your dad is happy for the extra help at the marina too."

She nodded. "Yeah, he is. Eli really wants this boat, but I'm not sure he's ready. He's only twelve."

"Ahh, getting him a boat doesn't mean he'll be going solo. It will give him something to work towards. You know him and Robert always talked about it. Eli getting to fulfill that dream will probably mean a lot more to him than either of us realize."

She sighed. "You're right."

"Is he still going to therapy?" Phillip asked.

She nodded. "Yes. Every week. Thankfully his therapist does online sessions, that's one less change he has to deal with with this move."

"That's good . . . So, that was your baby's dad? Damn. No wonder you got pregnant." He fanned his face as he smiled.

She bit back her smile. "He's sexy. Too sexy. That's probably why I lost my mind that night."

"You lucky woman."

She laughed. "Shouldn't this be weird?"

His brows drew together in question.

"You and I talking about a man I . . . a past lover, when we both . . ."

He chuckled. "I think nothing about our situation is normal. And society would deem us a very abnormal situation. But fuck them. Family, relationships—life is what we make it. Robert brought us together. We both loved him in our own ways, and now we're family. I loved your husband, and he was your best friend. Now, you've become like a sister to me, and Eli, my nephew. He would have been a stepson if Robert . . ." He swallowed, emotion flashing in his gaze.

Isabella reached out, covering his hand with hers. "I miss him too."

Phillip blinked the tears away before they could fall and flipped his hand over to hold hers with a smile. "Now, tell me you and Nash are a thing."

She burst out laughing and shook her head. "No. Not at all. I mean, we're trying to be friends, I think. It's hard to tell; he's so hot and cold."

"He looked pretty jealous when I got there to whisk you away."

So I'm not the only one who thought that? "Nash has made it clear he's not a relationship type of guy. He lost someone and I don't think he's over her, or know if he ever will be."

"And you won't play second fiddle again—and you shouldn't. But another roll in the hay with a man like that . . ." Phillip teased.

"You're terrible."

"Let me live vicariously through you."

Her gaze softened as she took in her friend. The love he and Robert had shared was brief, but stronger than anything she'd ever witnessed. It was like seeing two pieces of the same soul finding each other and becoming whole. Love like that wasn't something you could get over or replace. Had it been the same for Nash with his ex?

If so, no woman would ever stand a chance with him. It was better if she remembered that. All they had between them was sexual chemistry and a baby on the way. She couldn't compete with a ghost.

27

NASH

Nash closed the door to his truck, searching the Rye Marina. He'd been here a few times to fuel up; it was only a handful of nautical miles from the Noveas'. Bella's SUV was already there, sitting empty in the parking lot by the docks. A few people milled about with their vessels.

Nash headed for the first row of boats, scanning for Bella and Eli. He hadn't gotten to talk to her since she left with that guy, Phillip, a few days ago, because the fucker had been with them every waking moment. Who was he to her? A friend? A lover? And maybe it made Nash an asshole, but the thought of Bella with another man while she was carrying his child sent possession surging inside of him.

A flash of dark brown hair blowing in the wind caught his attention at the end of the dock. *Bella.* Heart racing, he moved forward with purpose, fists clenching and unclenching. Nash's stomach tipped, which had nothing to do with the bobbing dock. No, Bella's presence always had this effect on him.

She stood with her arms crossed in front of her, staring

across at the dated Boston Whaler Montauk. "It's smaller than I thought it would be."

The owner of the boat, a potbellied man with white hair, smiled as he kept an eye on Eli poring over the controls. "Seventeen feet. It's got a nine-inch draft."

"Draft?" Bella asked.

"The minimum depth your boat can go without the hull hitting bottom," Nash supplied.

Bella turned to him, surprise painting her expression. "Nash? What are you—"

"Nash! You came," Eli greeted him excitedly—or what he was coming to recognize as excitement in the boy. His hands flapped back and forth.

"Told you I would." Nash turned to the owner. "Mind if I come aboard?"

"Sure." The owner reached out his hand. "Mark."

Nash shook it. "Nash." He checked over the helm. An old rickety radio attached to the controls was missing a few buttons. "Does that work?"

Mark shook his head. "No, that will need to be replaced. Other than that, it's in fine condition for its age. And the emergency beacon has fresh batteries."

Nash checked the deck. There were no cracks or structural damage from what he could see, just some wear and tear and rust spots.

"You looked it over, Eli?" Nash asked.

The boy's eyes lit up. "Yeah."

"You check every compartment like we talked about?"

"Yes. I didn't see any water damage or animal nests," he answered.

Mark chuckled. "I told ya, I keep my boats in tip-top shape."

Nash ignored him, moving around the boat, checking the vinyl seams, testing the floor for soft spots, touching the different components to see if anything else was loose. Nothing seemed amiss—just well loved. Next up was the engine. There were no water lines suggesting the engine had been submerged at any point, and the hoses and wiring all looked relatively clean.

"You got a trailer to haul it out of the water?" Nash asked, closing the hatch and wiping his hands on his shorts.

Mark nodded reluctantly. "Yeah, I got a buddy's here we can use."

"We'll wait." Nash climbed out of the boat, helping Eli out after him.

"Why are we taking it out of the water? I'm not sure we're buying it yet," Bella said.

Mark started the boat and steered it towards the loading dock while they made their way through the marina.

"You never buy a boat unless you've inspected the whole thing. We need to check the hull for any damage," Nash explained.

"And the propeller," Eli added.

The corner of Nash's mouth turned up. "That's right, bud."

"Oh. Well, thanks for coming. I didn't know Eli asked you. My dad was going to come but he got tied up with an issue at the marina." Bella stopped by her SUV.

"It's not a problem. Phillip isn't coming?"

Bella shook her head. "No, he had to go back to Colorado."

So he wasn't sticking around? "It seemed you guys were close."

Bella flicked her attention to Eli and nodded. "Mm-hmm. So far, what do you think of the boat?"

So she didn't want to have this conversation in front of Eli. What did that mean?

It didn't matter. If he was back in Colorado, he obviously wasn't a problem right now. Nash didn't need to waste time worrying about him. "Looks like a great choice. It's clean and in good shape considering how old it is. I'll check the rest once they get it out of the water. How much is he asking for?"

She winced. "Twenty thousand."

It sure wasn't pennies to get into this business. But how was a single mom living with his sister going to afford it? "And you can handle that?" Nash asked.

Bella glanced at Eli and then back to him. "Robert set aside a separate fund for this. They'd been saving for years. It's not twenty thousand, but I can use some life insurance money to make up the difference. I know it seems like a huge purchase for a kid, and it is. But I think Eli needs this. It gives him something to look forward to, learn, and a place where he can be close to his dad's memory."

Nash nodded. It really wasn't his business, but it was a lot of money to drop on a kid's hobby. Although Nash didn't see Eli giving it up anytime soon. "Paying with a check or loan?"

"Check."

"I think we could get him lower if you're serious about it. But you have to be ready to walk away."

"Why would we walk away if we want it?" Eli asked. It was obvious he'd been listening in even though his focus darted around.

Nash turned to him, giving the kid all his attention. "Sometimes it's good to not seem too excited about some-thing, and you can usually get a better deal. Like for boats or cars. Hell, even furniture shopping."

Eli's brows drew down. "But we'll still get the boat even if we walk away?"

"If that's what you and your mom want."

"Can we, Mom?"

Bella's expression softened, her sympathetic smile lighting up her eyes. "If you're sure this is the one. And if Nash gives it his stamp of approval seeing as he's the expert."

"Do you trust me?" Nash asked Eli.

He hesitated as if deep in thought before he answered, "Mostly."

A burst of laughter left Nash's chest. The kid was brutally honest, and that was one thing he liked most about him. In a world full of fake individuals, having someone as steady and true as Eli was refreshing.

He straightened, meeting Bella's gaze. Nash sucked in a quick breath at the emotion that lit those whiskey eyes. She blinked and looked away, quickly ending the connection.

Mark approached them a few minutes later. Nash inspected the hull and the propeller, pointing out to Eli what he was doing so the boy would learn how to do it on his own next time. All in all, it was a good investment. After that, they returned the boat to the water and Nash, Eli, and Mark took it for an ocean test while Bella stayed behind.

After returning to the dock, Mark asked, "So, what do you think?"

"She's in pretty good condition. Few bits of wear and tear, and that radio will need to be replaced. Would you take fifteen?"

Mark scratched his head looking at the boat. "No. I could probably go down to eighteen. But that's it."

"She can write you a check for sixteen today," Nash countered.

Mark shook his head. "No can do."

Nash nodded and held out his hand to shake. "Thanks for your time."

Mark reluctantly shook his and then Nash placed his hand on Bella's lower back, guiding her towards the parking lot. He didn't want to risk her falling in the water from the swaying dock. It was concern that had him reaching for her, not the blistering need to touch her that battered his insides.

Eli followed behind, his fingers twisting nervously. Nash remembered what it was like to be a kid who really wanted something. It must be taking a lot for Eli to hold back.

Before they could get to the SUV, Mark's voice halted them. "Sixteen and we have a deal."

The corners of Nash's mouth turned up before he flattened his mouth. Eli turned to him, eyes meeting his for the briefest moments as a smile lit up his face and he clapped.

Nash turned towards Bella. "Well?"

She looked at her son, biting her lip before she nodded. "Okay."

"Yes! Thank you, Mom!" Eli's whole body shook as he waved his hands and moved his body in a circle.

Nash guided them through the paperwork, and before too long, Eli was holding the keys to his very first boat.

Mark held out his hand to shake Bella's. "Pleasure doing business with you."

Nash nudged Eli forward. "Shake his hand, bud. You made your first investment towards your future business."

Eli did as he said and Mark gave him a friendly smile.

"Good luck, captain." Mark waved goodbye, leaving the three of them alone in the parking lot.

"Do you want me to help Eli get it back to the marina?" Nash offered.

Bella's lips curled in a soft smile, gratitude shining in her brown orbs. "Would you mind?"

"Not at all." He didn't want a repeat of her last time at sea, even if her parents' marina was only five miles or so.

"Can I steer?" Eli asked.

Nash patted his shoulder. "Of course. You're the captain."

"And I get to name the boat, right?"

"We can look into that. First things first: let's get it to Abuelo's," Bella answered him. "I'll see you guys back there. Be safe. And don't forget to put your life jacket on."

"Always."

Nash waited until she drove away to get back in the boat with Eli.

"Okay. Give it a little gas—not too much."

"This is a no-wake zone," Eli said.

"Yup. So, let's go slow and get past the buoys."

Eli listened as Nash helped him navigate the boat into open water, following the coast towards the Noveas Marina.

"You know owning a boat is a huge responsibility."

Eli nodded. "Yes. I'll take care of it. I'll keep it clean. And perform maintenance checks every month. Or when there is a problem."

"And always keep your life vest on, okay, bud?"

"Yeah, Mom already told me that."

"You shouldn't take it out alone yet—not until you get some more experience under your belt and you're older."

"Like Anthony?" Eli asked.

"Eh, even Anthony isn't ready for some weather. The forecast out here can change on a dime. It's good practice to always keep an eye on the weather."

"How do I do that? Mom won't let me have a phone, and even if she did, I can only have screen time between certain hours. And when I sleep I have to close my eyes."

Right. Eli doesn't understand idioms. "I just mean, make sure you check the weather before you go out."

"Okay."

"Also, make sure you let someone know where you'll be going when you do go out. Just in case, for safety."

"Okay," Eli repeated.

The kid was probably sick of his safety talk, but the ocean could be the most beautiful thing Mother Nature had created one minute and the nastiest bitch the next.

"We'll have to get it fitted with a new radio," Eli said.

"Yes. You know, you can come out with me and Anthony more often if you want to learn the ropes of things."

"I already know how to tie eight types of knots."

Knots? What does that have to do with . . . oh. Ropes. "I meant you can come with us and learn how to manage a boat and how to fish these waters."

"Like an apprenticeship?" Eli asked, scanning the water ahead.

"Sure. I know you only have another month until school starts, but you're welcome to join us if your mom says it's okay."

Eli beamed, looking at his chest like he'd hung the moon. But that wasn't the case. If anything, Nash was the darkness that surrounded the light, trying to extinguish the brightness not because he was nefarious, but because it was his curse. He ruined everything he loved. Ana. His family had suffered from the accusations against him, losing contracts with some local stores because of Nash's reputation. His body tensed as a dark cloud of regrets loomed over him.

"My dad would be happy if he was alive." Eli's monotone voice pulled Nash from his depressing thoughts. It almost sounded like he was bored, but that was just how Eli spoke.

"Yeah?" Nash's voice came out hoarse.

Eli's gaze stayed on the horizon. "We looked at a Boston Whaler Montauk together. It was in his top-five choices of boats for us to get."

"Did you like going fishing together?"

"I did. I think my dad only went because I liked it. He wasn't really interested in outdoor things."

Nash couldn't help but be more curious about Bella's husband. "He wasn't?"

"No. He'd rather build model boats that fitted into the glass jars. And he read a lot."

"Sounds like he must have been smart if he liked books."

A few seagulls flew overhead, their shadows swooping across the boat.

"He was a professor of philosophy at the University of Colorado," Eli answered.

So Robert had been nothing like Nash. Why that bothered him, he wasn't sure.

Nash studied his calloused hands. They were usually covered in seawater and fish in the summer, and sawdust and manure in the winter. A working man's hands. Like everything else about Nash, they were hardened from life and rough.

Bella was nothing but soft curves and beaming light. Fire and resilience. He was just the monster that wanted what he couldn't have.

"Look, there's Mom." Eli pointed out as he shifted the boat to slow down, getting closer to the docks of the marina.

Bella stood with red Solo cups, a bottle of sparkling apple juice, and a smile that made his cock jerk and his chest ache. But those upturned lips weren't for him, and he needed to remember that.

He could take care of her from a distance. After all, the best way to avoid getting burnt was to stay away from the fire.

28

———

ISABELLA

Two Months Later

Isabella ran a hand over her five-month baby bump from the back of the marina as Eli expertly pulled the boat into Nash's spot. The crisp September air sent a shiver through her. She tugged her sweater over her shoulders a little tighter.

She smiled and waved as Eli helped Anthony unload a cooler from the boat and head her way with Nash trailing behind them. Eli went out with Nash as often as Isabella approved. Nash swore it wasn't a bother, but she didn't want to take advantage of his goodwill, so she tried to limit how often she said yes. She loved Eli, and he could require a lot of patience. But who better to talk to about an obsession with boats and fishing than a fisherman?

Nash had offered to take her out too, but she didn't want to risk getting seasick. This was his busy season, and the last thing she wanted to do was become a burden. So she settled for Sunday dinners, and weekend events with his family, and daily text check-ins from Nash.

Isabella kept herself busy at her parents' marina or helping at the Emersons' farm. She was happy to pitch in for Mama E, feeding some of the animals, or baking for the weekly farmers' market in Shattered Cove. She'd even whipped up a few batches of pot cookies with Nova.

"Mom! Look what we caught." Eli set down his end of the cooler and opened it. Isabella got a strong whiff of fish and covered her nose as she stepped away. The morning sickness had lessened now that she was in her second trimester, but the smell of fish was her biggest trigger.

Eli held up a huge striped bass that was nearly as big as he was. Nash reached out to steady her son's shoulder with a proud tilt of his lips. For a moment, Isabella couldn't speak. They almost looked like father and son. It was a bittersweet moment. A part of her heart ached for Robert missing this, but the other piece was so thankful that her son and Nash were getting along so well. Eli spent much more time with Nash than Isabella did. Nash came to every doctor visit, and spent time with her and the rest of his family during their weekend get-togethers. But other than that, he was out to sea, working before the sun rose and coming home after dark most days if the lights at his house were any indication.

"That's quite a fish," she remarked.

"I caught it. I almost fell into the water, it fought so strong." Eli beamed.

Her eyes widened and her heart raced as she looked to Nash. "What?"

"He was fine. Tugged him before we got it in the rod holder while we uncrossed lines. I had him the whole time. I wouldn't let anything happen to Eli," Nash promised, conviction soaking every word.

She breathed out a sigh of relief. Why couldn't her son take up a safer hobby?

"How about we head back to the farm. I'll cook some up for dinner?" Nash asked.

Adjusting her shirt, which was a bit too snug these days, Isabella shook her head. "As lovely as that sounds, we actually have somewhere to be." She turned to Eli. "Go up to Abuela's to shower and change, okay?"

Eli nodded and was off, Anthony leading the way into the marina with their catch. She turned back to Nash. His expression was stony and cold as ice. It was chilling how fast his emotions could change.

"What?"

"Are you seeing that guy again?"

That guy? "Who are you talking about?"

"Phillip," Nash ground out.

"No. He's still in Colorado. I have a meeting with a realtor."

That response melted some of the chill in his gaze. Nash replaced it with something else she couldn't quite put her finger on.

"Where's the house?" Nash asked.

"Right in town."

He grimaced.

"What?" she asked.

"Mind if I tag along?"

She blinked up at him. "You want to come with us?"

He nodded.

"Um, I mean . . . I guess."

* * *

An hour later, they were returning to the kitchen of the small house close to Main Street. Nash had been scowling the whole time and Eli walked around with a bored expression, opening doors and closets. A grumble came from Nash as he peered out the back door.

"I'll give you a moment to look around for yourselves. I'll be out front if you need me," the realtor, Sandra, said before leaving the room.

Isabella glanced around the room. Sunshine-yellow cabinets gleamed in the LED lighting. Could she really see herself living here with Eli and a baby?

A sigh came from Nash as he leaned against the counter, his massive arms flexing, showing off his veiny forearms. Heat rushed through her, flushing her cheeks. Stupid pregnancy hormones gave her an overactive libido. She couldn't help but be reminded of how those powerful limbs felt caging her in as he worshipped her body. How perfectly he'd fit inside her, stretching her and hitting all the right spots.

"You feeling okay?" Nash asked, pulling her from her salacious thoughts.

"Fine." Her answer came out breathless as she jerked around to stare at the granite countertop.

"Your cheeks are flushed. Are you hot in here?" Nash pressed.

"No, I'm great. So, what do you think?" she asked brightly, still unable to look him in the eye.

"Honestly, you can do better."

Her shoulders sunk in disappointment. "What's wrong with it?" It was one of the nicest ones she'd looked at in her price range. And honestly, she just needed a place to put down some roots long-term. She didn't want to wear out her welcome at Nova's.

"There's water damage on two of the ceilings. Could be

mold or mean a roof replacement or issues with the plumbing. The basement walls have a few cracks. The backyard is too small, and there isn't enough space to run around. It's too close to the road too. Wouldn't you prefer somewhere more rural, so Eli and the baby have space to explore and run 'round without worrying over cars?"

"I don't like it," Eli added.

Isabella ran a hand over her face, fighting tears of frustration. "Well, this is the tenth house I've looked at this month."

Nash's eyebrows rose. "It is?"

She nodded, crossing her arms in front of her. "A few sold before I could even make an offer. And none of the rest felt right. Honestly neither does this one, but I'm just so tired. We need our own space. I can't live with Nova forever, as awesome of a roommate that she is. And I want to be settled before the baby comes."

Isabella rubbed her tired eyes. What she wouldn't do for a cup of coffee right now.

"So move in with me."

She spun around. "What?" Maybe pregnancy brain also came with hallucinations?

"I've got the room. We can get to know each other better, figure out this co-parenting thing. There won't be a rush for you to move out. And I can be there after the baby is born to take turns, you know, feeding and changing diapers and stuff."

Isabella blinked. Her heart thrummed. The room tilted. This was the last thing she'd expected Nash to offer. He wanted to share midnight feedings with her? A warm sensation filled her chest as if her heart were melting.

"I'm not sure that's a good idea," she said.

"Why?"

"Because . . ." Because she already cared too much for him. How could she not with the way he treated Eli, and took care of her, even from a distance. His words might be stilted and gruff, but his actions spoke so much louder. Not to mention his starring roles in her pregnancy dreams—who knew you could orgasm in your sleep? She sure didn't until recently. That was part of the problem too. Her libido had gone into overdrive with the hormones. Living in the same quarters as him? That would turn into torture. It would be one thing if he wanted a relationship, if he was open to love. But he'd made it clear that that wasn't who he was anymore.

"I have Eli to think of. It's not fair to keep moving around and changing his routine."

"I'm fine living at Nash's," Eli said.

"Can I talk to you alone?" Isabella asked Nash, nodding towards the back door. "We'll be right back. Stay here, okay, Eli?"

"Okay."

She walked outside, Nash following her before he shut the door and then turned to her.

"Look, Eli is still dealing with a lot. And he's already gotten really attached to you. I don't want to do anything that could cause him harm."

"You think I'd hurt him?" he asked evenly.

"Not on purpose."

"I'm not going anywhere, Bella. You and I share a child now. That means Eli is also a part of my family too. Just think about it. If you guys live with me, I can take care of you."

His words soothed a place inside her that the light of day never saw. "That's not your job."

Nash stepped closer, getting into her space. His salty, masculine scent wrapped around her, intoxicating her. Arousal seeped into her pores, and her body ignited. *Fucking hormones.* "You became my business the moment I slid my cock into you."

She gasped. Lust burned her from the inside out at his words.

"And you solidified it when you told me you were carrying my child." He reached his hand towards her belly but stopped before he actually touched her. "Now, you're gonna go back into that house and tell the realtor you're gonna think about it."

Her brows drew together. She opened her mouth to give a retort, but he interrupted.

"Then I'm taking you and Eli back to Nova's to make you dinner. You can relax on the back deck, and I'll bring you some tea while you think over moving in with me—at least until the baby is a year old. I know from Roman how hard that first year can be with adjustments and struggles. Hell, the first few."

Over a year living with Nash?

His intense midnight eyes dropped to her lips before returning to hers. A beat of silence passed. "Let me help you. We're partners in this. Let me pick up the slack where I can. It's my responsibility as the father."

His responsibility? The word was like a bucket of ice water dropped on her. Right, that was how he saw her and this baby. A responsibility. Maybe he felt like he didn't have a choice? He was a good man, but not the man she needed, and it was best she remembered that.

29

NASH

Nash really hoped Bella took him up on the offer to move in with him. Was it too complicated? One hundred percent. But the thought of her and the baby and Eli living in town away from him didn't sit right. What if something happened and he couldn't get there in time? Sure, town was only a few miles from the farm, but anything could come up. Nash could watch over them at his house—make sure they were safe.

"How was school this week?" Nova asked Eli as he tossed the fish in a flour mixture.

"Fine." He handed the battered fish to Nash.

"You go ahead. Just like I showed you. Drop it in gently. Not too fast or it will splash," Nash directed.

Eli did as instructed.

"Good job. You can add chef to your resume soon," Nash encouraged.

The corners of Eli's mouth turned up. Nash's skin prickled with awareness. He glanced up and met Bella's attentive gaze from the small table in the attached dining area.

"I have a soccer game on Saturday," Eli supplied.

Nash didn't break their staring match as he replied, "Oh yeah?"

Bella's focus dropped to the mug of tea in her hands before she took a sip.

"Yes."

"Roman likes soccer. You should play him sometime." Nash scratched his chin, his fingers running over the coarse hairs of his beard. Or would she say no and buy a house in town with a shitty backyard by the street and have Phillip stay over? His gut churned at the thought.

"Okay," Eli said.

"I'll let him know." Nash turned back to the food as pain shot up his neck. He flinched, his hand going to the spot to squeeze it.

"You know there is a cute boutique in the city that sells maternity clothes. I was going to take a trip this weekend or next to Dark Cove," Nova said.

A puff of air left Bella's nose, like the beginning of a laugh not followed through. "Is that your way of telling me I resemble a beached whale?"

A whale? Bella was anything but. Her curves were just as delicious as they had been the first time he'd laid eyes on her —even more so now. She grew more beautiful by the day. It was one reason he limited how much time he spent with her —it was torture to be so close to her, to know what she felt like—tasted like—and not be able to touch her. He tried not to notice, but it was impossible, especially as her outfits grew tighter. Her breasts were fuller, and her belly rounder. And that ass. He bit his lip to stifle a groan and focused on the cooking food before he got a boner in front of everyone. *And somehow I'm supposed to live with her.* He'd have to jack off even more than he was now to keep his cock under control. But the alternative was her living alone, unprotected. *Not happening.*

"Girl, please. You know you're gorgeous. But I have noticed things seem a bit tight. I mean, what fun is being pregnant if you're not going to get a whole new wardrobe out of it?" Nova laughed.

Nash grabbed a plate for Eli to put the fish on, flicking his attention to Bella. She smiled at Nova, eyes bright. Fucking ray of sunshine. *I'm so fucked.*

"I guess I could use a few things," Bella conceded.

Nash plated dinner with Eli's help, bringing everyone's dishes to his sister's small table. They all took a seat.

"This looks amazing." Bella smiled.

"Eli did a great job." Nash patted the boy's shoulder, the muscle in his neck protesting with the movement.

The boy picked up his fork and dug in.

"Oh, I forgot to tell you guys, we have a yearly thing we do together when apples are in season as a family tradition. Apple picking, bonfire, hot cider, and donuts. It's actually a lot of fun. Do you think you'd be up for coming with us? It's next weekend." Nova took a bite of her sautéed broccoli.

"That sounds fun. What do you say, Eli? We can pick some apples and make apple crisp?" Bella lifted her fork to her lips. There was something about feeding a woman something he'd made—or helped make. Knowing he'd provided for her and the baby in some small way made him feel useful.

Eli nodded. "Yes."

Nash dug into his food, watching Bella out of the corner of his eye. His palm slid over the sore spot on his neck, squeezing and attempting to massage the kink out. That was the thing about his late thirties—all of a sudden, he had aches and pains from doing the most menial things. Turning his head or sleeping wrong could land him in pain. He felt nothing like the teen he'd been, sleeping under the stars with only a sleeping bag, bright eyed and bushy tailed in the morning.

"When do you find out if I'm getting a niece or nephew?" Nova asked.

Bella swallowed as Nova's gaze volleyed between the two of them. "Next month. There was an emergency with another patient when we went in for our last ultrasound and the tech was called away, so we didn't get to find out yet."

Less than thirty days and he'd know if he was having a son or a daughter. He'd seen that little profile on the ultrasound at the second to last visit and it had stolen his breath. He'd always thought love at first sight was bullshit. But all he'd glimpsed was a picture, and he was head over heels for that baby.

Bella laughed at something Nova said before her eyes widened and she gasped, grabbing her belly.

Nash stood so abruptly his chair toppled over. He darted over to her side of the table, every muscle tense. His heart pounded in his ears. "What is it? Is it the baby? Are you okay? Is something wrong?"

Bella looked over at him, a smile appearing on her gorgeous round face. "Yeah. Sorry. I just felt the baby move and it surprised me. It was a pretty big flutter. Must have liked your and Eli's cooking."

Nash blinked, staring at her belly. Relief that she was okay poured over him. But then the panic came with the reminder of just how powerless he was in this situation. What if something had been wrong? What could he have done except rush her to the hospital and hope for the best?

"Can you feel it?" Bella picked up his hand and pressed it against her warm stomach.

A steady thrum of energy hummed up his arm at her

touch. He met her whiskey orbs, so full of joy. Bella was lit up like she'd swallowed a thousand suns. She was breathtaking. This close, he could smell her sweet rose scent, filling his nose and bathing him in want.

Thud. Thud. Thud. He couldn't hear anything else except the pounding of his blood in his veins as the fire spread. Need. Lust. Desire.

And then the most amazing thing happened. A tiny flutter rippled under her skin. Nash sucked in a breath, falling to his knees, staggered by the tiny life that had just made his or her presence known. *That's my baby. My son or daughter.*

Warm, glowing joy burst in his chest, expanding his rib cage with unstoppable excitement. Happiness swelled so big he thought he'd explode. Instead, he found he had more room for it than he'd believed himself capable of having. A fullness crashed over him. Love grew and tangled for the unborn baby. His attention darted up to the woman who had made this moment possible. The mother of his child, Bella, smiling over at him.

Then, a sickening fear twisted inside him. All the warmth turned into something ugly and malicious, incinerating any goodness he'd felt. Love meant loss. It meant he was vulnerable to pain he never wanted to experience again. Only there was no escaping this. It was too late. He'd fucked up and created a life that now depended on him to keep it safe. *I'll fail her—him—all of them.*

Nash shot to his feet, stumbling out the door as the air evaporated from his lungs. Unable to draw breath, he clutched his chest and ran towards his house. Away from Nova's. Farther from Bella and their baby and Eli. If only he could run fast enough to go back in time and escape the inevitable. He'd fail them one day. He knew it in his marrow. Because Nash knew what they didn't—he really was a monster.

30

ISABELLA

Isabella adjusted the shopping bags on her arm as she carried her coffee to an empty table in the bustling café. It was within walking distance from the college campus in the city of Dark Cove. It was only twenty-five or so minutes from the farm but the atmosphere made the two towns seem like night and day. Tall buildings, honking cars, and crowded sidewalks made it feel like she was in Boston, not New Hampshire.

"Did you want a brownie? I got an extra one just in case," Nova said, taking the seat across from her.

Isabella shoved her bags under the table by her feet. "I guess we can't let it go to waste."

Nova smiled and passed it over on a napkin. "Of course not."

Their table jostled as a child-size blur ran into it. Both Nova and Isabella steadied their drinks.

A beautiful raven-haired woman turned around, her hand holding the little boy's who'd run into their table. "Oh no, I'm so sorry."

"That's alright," Isabella said.

"Elise?" Nova asked the woman, standing.

Elise blinked a few times, studying Nova before she nodded warily. "Yeah. Nova?"

Nova beamed. "How are you?"

Elise's attention flicked to Isabella and then back to Nova. "I'm good. This little guy keeps me busy. Right, Malaki?" She turned to the little boy with Down syndrome next to her and smiled affectionately.

"Oh, you're a mom? Wow!"

"Well—"

"Elise is my daddy's girlfriend. Elise and Daddy, sitting in a tree!" Malaki teased, his smile glowing.

Elise tucked a strand of hair behind her ear revealing a cochlear implant. "Well, you two enjoy your coffee. I'm gonna get this guy to story hour."

"Bye!" Nova waved. Elise nodded and left the café with the little boy in tow. She turned back to Isabella. "I'm sorry I totally didn't introduce you. She's an old friend from college."

"Ahh. Makes sense why I don't remember her." She sipped her coffee, savoring her limited caffeine indulgence.

"Did you get everything you needed from the maternity store?"

"I think so. Thanks for coming with me." She broke off a piece of a brownie before slipping it in her mouth. She moaned and closed her eyes, rich, dark chocolate exploding on her tongue. "Oh, this is good."

Nova laughed. "Isn't it? I always get one when I come into the city." She broke her own treat in half and ate it. "So, are we not gonna talk about the elephant in the room?"

Isabella stuffed another piece in her mouth, washing it down with more coffee before she replied, "What elephant?"

"Nash asking you to move in with him."

Isabella sighed, her thumb playing with the seam of the cardboard cup. "I'm not so sure that's a good idea."

"If you don't mind me asking, why?"

"Well, you saw how freaked out he got the other night." He'd looked disgusted after palming her belly. *Am I that awful to touch?* Why else would he have flinched away from her and run out the door?

"Besides, Eli needs something stable. Nash and I are not a couple, so I don't think it would be fair to Nash to move in. How weird would it be to live with your baby's mother and her child?" Technically, that was what she'd done with Robert.

Nova shrugged and picked up her tea. "Families look different for everyone. Who's to say what's weird or not? Personally, I think it should be taken on a case-by-case basis. What matters is what's right for you."

Sounds like what Phillip said. "Would it be easier in some respects? Absolutely. But it also brings up a lot more complications. Eli is already so attached to Nash. And it's like Nash can barely stand to be near me—and that's okay. I don't need him. However . . . it just makes things awkward."

Nova's lips turned up into a mischievous smile. "Well, obviously at one point he got extremely close to you."

Isabella rolled her eyes and laughed. "Well, that was *before.*" *When he thought he'd never have to see me again. Apparently, I'm good enough for a fuck, but not more.*

"Well, it's totally up to you, and as your friend, I will support whatever you decide. But you should know that Nash asking you to move in with him is a *huge* deal. Like, I thought hell would freeze over before he let anyone in like this."

"Asking me to share a living space isn't letting me in, Nova. Trust me. I know the difference between playing house and really connecting with a person."

Nova sat back in her chair, studying Isabella. "You don't

talk about your husband much. Is that what it was like with him? Playing house?"

Isabella bit her lip, Robert's face flashing in her mind. "Robert and I were better off as friends. I got pregnant in college and he proposed before Eli was born. Both our parents thought it best because of the pregnancy. We connected like I hadn't with any other guy, and I thought we had some sparks, but not . . ." *Not even close to what Nash and I shared.* "Not the lasting kind. No one here knows this but . . ." Could she trust Nova?

"I won't tell a soul." Nova crossed her finger over her heart in an X.

"We were filing for a divorce before he got sick."

"Wow. That must have been so hard. And yet you stayed with him?"

Isabella nodded, her eyes getting misty. "He was still my best friend. And Eli deserved as much time with his dad as possible before . . . before he passed."

Nova reached across the table, placing her hand on Isabella's. "You are an amazing woman, Bella. I mean it. Your strength and kindness are inspiring."

Isabella shook her head.

"Yes." Nova's voice was unyielding. "You are one of the strongest women I know, second to my mama. You deserve to find your happiness, and I truly believe you will."

"Thank you."

"Of course. You know you're welcome to stay with me even after you have the baby. You don't have to leave."

Isabella took a deep breath and exhaled. "I appreciate you saying so. But that isn't fair to anyone. It is going to be chaos for a little while as we adjust. Eli is going to need me more, and if the baby is half as fussy as he was, well, I'm exhausted just thinking about it."

"It sounds like you could use some help, then. I do know a certain man who's made it clear he's more than willing." She held up her hand. "And I know you think it would be awkward, but consider it this way: Nash is the baby's father. If anyone should lose sleep with a cranky baby, it's him. He may seem all gruff and made of stone, but I saw him with Ariel as an infant. That girl turned him into mush and wrapped him around her finger from the moment he met her. And I'm sure it will be the same for your baby."

Imagining Nash cupping a small baby in his giant arms sent enough heat to melt the polar ice caps swirling in her belly. There was something about a big brute being brought to his knees by such a vulnerable little human . . . Nash would be a good dad—at least, Nova seemed to think so. And Isabella's gut agreed.

So what was she really afraid of? Yes, it would be an adjustment living with someone else, sharing his space. But she'd managed with Nova. And it would be helpful to have another adult in the home to help her with the baby so Eli didn't feel like she was abandoning him. They would just be roommates.

"What is it that's really holding you back?" Nova asked, reading her mind.

"I need more. I've been his neighbor for months now and barely know him more than I did that night. And almost everything I know that matters has come from what you've told me or by observing him with my son. He's a good man. But I need to know he'll let me in enough to at least be friends. I don't want to have to walk on eggshells around him or worry he'll take off when I need him. I'd rather not have him to rely on at all than do so and have him not be there when it matters."

"You're afraid of being hurt. I get that."

"But that would only happen if I hoped, right? If I set my expectations correctly, then I can't be let down." She just needed to accept that she and Nash Emerson would never be anything other than co-parents. It wasn't like he'd given her any indication he wanted more.

So why was it so hard to accept?

"Have you talked to him about this? My brother has a lot of faults, but if you lay it out like it is, he'll listen and give you an honest answer. Actually, his answer will probably be more conservative than what he's really capable of, because behind all that bluster is a man who's just as afraid as you if not more." Nova took a sip of her drink.

"I can see that."

Nova spread her palms open. "All I'm asking is you give him a chance and let him know what you need. Give him the opportunity to respond without you making that decision for him. He needs someone to push him out of his comfort zone. I think you're just that person, Bella."

"I think that's fair." *This isn't just about me anymore. I have our baby to think of too.*

Nash would need to prove he was willing to go outside his comfort zone. He'd have to be open and honest with her so they were on the same page. But that meant opening herself up to possible heartbreak. No matter how much she wanted things to change, and for him to give them a chance, Nash had made his position perfectly clear. He was there to be a father—not a partner.

31

ISABELLA

Isabella held her belly as the wagon bounced over a pothole. The whole thing came to a stop in the middle of a small orchard still on the Emerson property, sending her leaning against the wooden wall. A brisk fall breeze blew against her skin, the scent of sweet apples in the air.

"Can we make apple crisp later?" Eli asked, his leg bouncing against hers as the rest of the Emerson family began filing off the wagon.

"Sure." Isabella stood, a twinge in her hips making her wince.

She was the last one off the wagon, gripping the edge of the stairs to jump down. Nash stepped in front of her before she could go, his hands reaching to her waist, picking her up and setting her down on the ground like she weighed nothing close to the two hundred and fifty pounds she was currently at. His palms burned against her, sending tendrils of arousal swirling through her.

The moment her feet touched the ground, he left, turning

abruptly and disappearing into the orchard. Her heart raced, her body reeling from that quick encounter. She hadn't even been able to utter a thank-you.

Isabella searched the rows of trees for Eli, tucking her sweater a little closer. She found him next to Ariel, pointing to an apple higher up and then to the little girl, and then to himself.

Ariel nodded and signed something with her hands. Eli picked her up, holding her so she could reach above his head to the apple. Ariel plucked it off, A triumphant smile lit her face as he set her back down and gave her a high five.

A burst of joy exploded in her heart. To see Eli connecting with another child was a rare occurrence, and when he did manage to do so, his friendships didn't last long. But after three months of weekly family dinners, he and Ariel seemed to connect so much so that she'd even caught him learning some basic signs and practicing them over and over.

"Remember that time Nash got Ricky to eat an apple with a worm in it?" Roman asked Nova who was busy picking up dropped fruit from under a tree and filling her bag with them.

"Yes." She snickered.

Ricky shrugged and bit into an apple. "Extra protein. Need it for all these muscles." He flexed his biceps.

Nash shoved him from behind playfully. "If only it worked for your brain, where you really need bulking up."

Ricky threw his apple at Nash's chest, the fruit exploding and falling to the ground. "You calling me stupid?"

"The fact that you even have to ask proves my point," Nash grumbled.

Ricky nodded. "Least I can communicate with sentences and not grunts and grumbles like a fu—" Ricky eyed the kids nearby. "*Freaking* caveman." Ricky pounded his chest. "Me Nash. Me like no one but fish."

Nova burst into laughter along with Roman, and Nash's eyes narrowed. "I do not sound like that."

Ricky smiled triumphantly, his gaze moving to Isabella. "Well, I guess it's not completely accurate. There is one person you liked so much you knocked her up."

Isabella stiffened as all eyes moved to her.

"You boys stop fooling around and pick apples. I need bushels to get my canning done. And leave Isabella alone," Renita interjected as she passed by to the next row.

"Of course, Ma." Ricky smacked his hand on Nash's back.

Nash didn't even flinch—he just turned his angry eyes onto his brother and wrapped his arm around Ricky's neck, pulling him against his body. "We'll just hug and make up."

Ricky's face turned red as he grabbed Nash's forearm.

"Nash, don't strangle your brother. I thought we'd been over this before?" Mama E said, exasperated, like this was just another day in the Emerson family.

The siblings were always poking each other, especially Ricky and Nash. Isabella had been an only child, so she'd missed out on this. But as much as the Emersons feuded, she could see the love they had for each other. Roman was the calm, mature one, seeming to mediate between the others and keep the peace. Nova was teased and gave it back tenfold. It must have been challenging to be the only girl and the youngest of all four of them. Ricky liked to push Nash's buttons the most. It was almost like he wasn't happy until he got a reaction from him.

"Boys, don't stress your mother out," James warned.

Nash shoved Ricky onto the ground.

Ricky stood, brushing bits of apple from his clothes. "You want a fair match? Come meet me in the gym sometime and we'll see who beats who in the ring."

"You wish," Nash grumbled, grabbing a bag and filling it with apples.

"Unless you're too chicken." Ricky squawked.

Nash ignored his brother, getting to work collecting apples for his mother.

Eli and Ariel wandered to the next row of trees. Isabella followed them, twisting apples off the branches as she went, filling her own bag.

Eli chatted about all the different apples and what his favorite things to eat with them were before he turned the conversation back to boats. Ariel plucked fruit, filling the bag her son held for her, smiling up at him from time to time. Maybe that was why they worked so well together as friends.

"I got it." Nash's deep voice beside her made her jump.

He pulled the handles of the apple bag from her hand.

"Oh, thanks. I can carry it though; it's not too heavy."

"I got it," he repeated.

She nodded and turned towards a tree, picking a few more apples and adding them to the bag. She repeated the process a few times until the bag was full, following the kids farther down the row. Voices of the rest of the Emerson family danced through the wind, getting farther and farther away as they scoured the orchard for apples.

"You look really nice. Is that one of the outfits you got with Nova yesterday?" Nash asked, his voice stilted.

She peeked out of the corner of her eye at him, a flush growing in her cheeks. He was complimenting her? "Yeah. They're cozy." Nothing like an elastic waistline for a growing belly. And the fabrics were all super soft. She might never return to buying normal clothing after this.

"You and Ricky make up?" she asked.

He grimaced. "We were just fooling around. He likes to get on my nerves."

"Oh, I can see that." She smiled. "He likes to get a rise out of you. I think it's the way he shows his love."

Nash turned to her, eyes focused before he looked away and shook his head. He winced and massaged his neck. "No. He just likes to be a pain in my ass."

They walked in silence for a few moments before Nash said, "Next weekend is my parents' last movie night of the year. We'll have a bonfire and food. Your parents are welcome if you want to ask them to come. My mom said they'd be happy to have them too."

She stopped. Nash took another step before he seemed to realize she was no longer with him. He turned, studying her.

"You want my parents to come?"

He shrugged. "I think it's important our families get to know each other. And . . ." He sighed. "That they get to know me and me them."

Nash was trying. Even after the mean things her mother had said about him, he was making an effort for their unborn child. He was going to be a great dad.

She blinked away the emotion that rose. Relief poured over her shoulders, lightening them of a burden she hadn't realized had weighed so heavily on her.

"I appreciate everything you're doing for us." She plucked a leaf off a nearby branch and smoothed it between her fingers.

His throat bobbed. "Same."

She shook her head. "I think I've brought you a lot of complications."

Nash cleared his throat. "You have."

Oh. Way to bring her down to reality. Her joy dimmed.

"But you've also given me a precious gift I never thought I'd have." His voice came out raw and ragged like it pained him to admit it.

His eyes darkened more. The tension between them was thick and heavy with so many unspoken confessions. The air was lit with combustible energy. His attention dropped to her lips. She licked them, the memory of his kiss so fresh her mouth tingled.

"Nash?" she asked.

"Yeah?"

"Why did you run away the other night?"

His jaw tensed, his gaze dropping to the grass.

"This is only going to work if we're honest with each other. I'd rather have a truth that hurts than a lie coated in sugar."

His swallow was audible.

"Is it me?"

He narrowed his focus on her once again. "What?"

"I just . . . The way you reacted, I thought maybe you were grossed out or something."

He ran a hand through his wild curls. The anger rolling off him was palpable. "Don't do this."

"Do what? I just . . . It's okay if that's the case. I just want to know the reason."

"You were so confident that night. That's one of the reasons I was so attracted to you. It's not every day a fucking gorgeous woman offers you everything you want for a night. I thought I made that clear when we were together, sweetness."

You're so fucking beautiful.

Has no one told you how fucking perfect you are?

These tits have me so spellbound I'm not sure whether or not to lick, bite, or fuck them.

God, you're so fucking sexy like this, laid out under me.

Heat rose to her cheeks at the reminder of the filthy things he'd said to her as he worshipped her body. But did he still see her that way? Now that her body was changing, getting bigger—rounder? Now that he was stuck with her as a co-parent?

She normally didn't have such insecurities, but loving herself was a work in progress. She had good days and bad. And when a godlike man flinched away from her and literally ran out the door, well, that was a blow to a girl's ego.

"Then why?" She stepped over a trio of fallen half-eaten brown apples in the grass.

He remained silent.

She huffed and shook her head. "I can't do this unless you're honest with me. You have to let me in enough to at least be friends." *Give me a reason to say yes to moving in with you.*

Nash remained stoic, his muscles tense. The pulse at his neck thumped wildly. Disappointment sunk in her belly like a lead weight. She sighed and headed towards the kids, giving up.

"Because I was scared." The confession sounded grated.

Isabella turned, tipping her head slightly. "What?"

"I was scared," he repeated.

"Of what?"

His jaw twitched. "Of not being able to protect the baby."

Isabella's chest deflated as she took two steps forward to the man who towered over her. "That's part of being a parent. It's scary knowing that you won't always be there to keep them from the dangers of this world. Having a child is the most terrifying thing because it's a piece of your heart manifested outside of your body. A living, breathing embodiment of everything you hold most precious in this world in the most vulnerable package." She turned to face the direction Eli and Ariel had wandered off in and found them snacking on apples at the end of one of the rows. "We won't always be there to save them, but that's why we do our best to make sure they have the tools to be capable of saving themselves one day."

Without debating it, she wrapped her arms around him and squeezed him into a hug. His salty musk blended with the sweet apples in the air.

Nash stiffened before his big arms wrapped around her too.

"You're not alone in this. We get to be terrified together."

Thick arms trembled slightly around her. Maybe Nova was right, and he really was much more terrified than Isabella had realized. Her heart tightened in sympathy as she pulled away, tipping her chin up to look at him.

Embers of want swirled in those dark eyes staring down at her. Her skin flushed. A steady, buzzing warmth pooled in her belly, spread to her limbs. God, it felt good to be in Nash's arms. She should probably back away now, but it had been so long since she'd been held like this. When he touched her, it was like every synapse in her body fired alive, spinning her up and making her want things she shouldn't.

"If you're serious about your offer and you're sure it won't be too much, I'll do it—move in with you, I mean. On the condition that we can keep being honest with each other."

Relief flashed in his gaze before his eyes shuttered with some sort of struggle. His arms dropped to his sides, ending their embrace. "I'm glad. I'll help you move in next weekend. Just tell me what day's best."

Nash turned and headed for the kids at the other end of the row.

At least he wasn't running this time. That was progress.

32

ISABELLA

Sparks drifted into the sky riding billows of grey smoke to the dark heavens from the fire. Stacks of old pallets reaching higher than Isabella's height flamed in the center of the meadow, giving off enough brightness that she could make out the faces of the people gathered around. Renita and James chatted with the Stone family, Mathew and Tilda. Remy, the Stones' daughter, and their daughter-in-law, Mia, stood by Isabella, making small talk. The ladies' husbands kept an eye on the younger kids watching the movie projected onto the side of the barn.

Ariel stayed close to her aunt Nova, sitting on her lap, her hands animatedly moving as Nova acted as translator between her and Eli. Her son sat beside them, attention locked on Ariel's movements. He tried a few signs of his own.

Roman kept his attention divided between Andre Stone, Mikel Evans, and his daughter. He was always the watchful father when Ariel was around. *How did he lose his wife?*

Isabella's skin bristled, her hair standing on end. She shivered, despite the massive heat the fire put out. Turning, she searched the field. Nash stood away from the others, beer in his hand as he stared at her. Flames reflected in his dark gaze. Shadows licked his skin, making him seem more like Hades than the god of the sea. Like gravity, his presence pulled her in. His arms were crossed, the bottle dangling from a few fingers. His expression was hard, his brow furrowed as if he were deep in thought. The urge to run her fingers over the lines and smooth them out like a sculptor, softening the ridges and finding the gentleness, lurched inside her.

"Where's Lyra?" Mia asked, bringing her attention back to the women beside her.

Remy smiled. "Oh, she's too cool to hang out with her parents on a Friday night. Sleepover at Jasmine's. She and Zoey wanted some cousin time."

"*Dios*, does it start that early? Ana's only three, and Matteo, five, but I can't imagine either one as a teenager." Mia shook her head.

"It goes faster than you think. At least Phoenix is still seven. He's a mama's boy through and through." Remy nodded towards the little boy running circles around his father.

"I think Lyra might be a little sad she missed this one, though, after I tell her how cute Eli is." Remy snickered.

Isabella smiled. Oh, boy. Was she ready for crushes? That hadn't been a bridge she and Eli had crossed yet.

"Speaking of crushes, you should tell Isabella how you got the bad boy of Shattered Cove to turn into such a family man," Mia motioned between Remy and Mikel.

Remy turned to her husband and beamed, her eyes lighting up with so much affection, it stole Isabella's breath. "It's a long story, and not an easy one to hear. We almost didn't make it. I think we need something a little stronger than cider to go over it." She lifted her drink and laughed. "You should come to our book club meetings. They're once a month and usually Pippa—she owns The Oyster Bookstore—hosts them. You don't have to actually read the book if you don't have time. Just come for the gossip and wine and sex toy samples."

Sex toy samples? Now that would be useful. She'd need a little battery-powered help to get through the rest of this pregnancy. "That sounds pretty nice actually. Let me know when the next one is."

"Who's your favorite uncle?" Ricky asked, arriving with several white bags and holding them up.

The kids raced towards him, jumping at his feet and holding grabby hands upwards.

"Who needs some cider donuts? They're still warm." Ricky set them on a folding table laid out with snacks and hot cider. "The blue bag is gluten-free for Remy and Lyra."

"Since your daughter isn't here, I guess you get extra." Mia laughed.

Remy snorted. "She already made me promise to bring her some home."

"I found these stragglers in the driveway." Ricky nodded towards the couple coming closer. Isabella's parents had come after all. Her mother's face was pinched, her arm locked around her father's.

"Hello, everyone. Thanks for inviting us," her papi said.

James and Renita greeted them as a heat stronger than the bonfire met her back.

Nash's arm brushed hers as he leaned in. "Do they know you're moving in tomorrow?"

She shook her head. "No. I was going to tell them tonight. That way, there are plenty of witnesses for when my mother murders me." She forced a laugh.

Nash stiffened. Obviously, her joke had missed the mark.

She patted his forearm, turning to face him. "You don't have to come with me."

His eyelids drooped as his attention dropped down her body to her round belly, his jaw hardening to granite before he returned his attention back to hers. "I told you, I'm in this."

Nash followed her lead as she greeted her parents. "Mama, Papi, thanks for coming."

Papi reached out, giving her a hug. "Of course, *mija*."

Her mother glanced at Nash, her expression souring even further.

"Catherine," her father prodded.

"We wouldn't have to be here if you'd learned your lesson the first time," she snapped.

Each of her mother's words were like a blow to the chest.

Nash slipped his pinky finger around hers. She sucked in a quick breath. Was he trying to comfort her?

Nash took a small step forward. "Mr. and Mrs. Noveas, I'm glad you could come. Help yourself to the snacks and drinks. I hope our families can get to know each other a little better—"

Her mother sniffed and walked away, ignoring Nash.

Mortification slammed into Isabella. "I'm sorry, Nash. You don't deserve that. I'll talk to her."

Her father spoke up. "No, I will." He released a heavy sigh.

"I'm sorry for causing you any more stress, Papi."

He shook his head and lifted his hand. "No, it's high time I spoke to her about her attitude. She loves you, sweetheart. She just wants you safe."

"I'm safe with Nash." She looped her hand in Nash's, squeezing. "And we've decided to move in together for a while. That way, he can help when the baby comes."

Her father studied them both. "You're together now?"

Nash flinched and pulled his hand out of hers. She tried not to take it personally, but she was only human.

"No, Papi. We're trying to find a way to co-parent that works for the both of us. It might be easier if we're in the same house for the beginning," she explained.

"Well, I don't understand it, but I trust you, *mija*." Her father turned to Nash. "You'll take care of my daughter and grandbabies? Make sure they're safe and have everything they need?"

"Papi—" She tried to argue. This wasn't the 1950s, after all. She didn't actually need a man.

"No, it's alright. I wouldn't expect anything less." Nash leveled his attention on her father. "I swear I'll do everything in my power to keep them safe."

Papi stared back at him, the men seemingly having a silent conversation with their eyes. Finally, her father gave a curt nod. "I'll hold you to that, young man."

Her father walked towards the table laden with goodies. Isabella let out a sigh. Thank God that was over. She turned to Nash, but he was gone. She searched the field, but he was nowhere to be seen.

"So much for that."

Isabella meandered around the field. The women tried to bring her into their conversations but her heart just wasn't in it. More than a dozen people surrounded her and yet she felt more alone than if she were here by herself. Eli was happily engrossed in the movie, so she took her leave. How was it possible to feel claustrophobic and lonely at the same time? She took the familiar footpath, heading up towards the bench she'd found months ago. This had become a special spot for her. A place to find peace when everything seemed so jumbled.

Sitting on the moonlit bench, she tilted her head up to the sky.

"Are you following me?" the gruff voice asked from behind her.

She jumped, clamping a hand over her racing heart. "You scared the *mierda* out of me!"

She spun around. Moonlight lit up his handsome face. The corners of his mouth quirked up before they flattened again. "Sorry."

"And no, I had no idea anyone was up here. I like to come here sometimes. It's . . . peaceful." She sat back down, crossing her arms over her chest. It was a lot colder away from the fire.

Nash took the space next to her. "They can be a lot to handle."

"Your family? Yeah, they can." She laughed. "But it's a good type of chaos."

An owl hooted in the trees behind them.

"Do you ever . . . never mind." She shook her head.

"What were you going to ask?"

"It's stupid."

"Say what you were gonna say." His voice was gruff.

She took a deep breath, focusing back on the constellations above. "Are you ever surrounded by people and yet still feel lonely?"

Nash focused on his hands in his lap.

She sighed. "Never—"

"All the damn time." His voice came out in a ragged whisper.

"Grief does that to a person," she said.

Black soul-piercing orbs cut to her, moonlight shining in them, making his eyes appear more grey than obsidian. Her heart thudded in her chest. The wind picked up, the trees creaking under the pressure. The soft pitter of crisp leaves falling to the forest floor behind them was the only other sound as Nash held her prisoner in his agonized inky gaze.

Maybe it was time she put herself out there. Let him know that if anyone could understand where he was coming from, it would be her. That he didn't have to suffer alone.

"It seems like everyone moves on, living their life, but you're still . . . stuck. You're not ready because it means leaving someone you love behind," she explained.

His hands fisted in his lap.

"Is that how you feel?" she asked.

A flash of vulnerability lit his eyes like a shooting star in their dark depths. But just as quickly as a wish, it disappeared, hidden behind stormy clouds of denial. His walls were back up. He snuffed out any sign of softness once again behind his stoic mask as he faced the meadow in front of them.

"If we're going to live together and become friends, we should know a little more about each other, don't you think?" she pressed.

"Drudging up the past never helped anyone." His voice was cold as ice.

"Neither did hanging on to it."

He stood abruptly, shoulders tensed to his ears. "You should get back to the fire. It's not safe to be out here alone at night."

Isabella got to her feet, casting one more look over the man who held so much locked behind reinforced walls. Did he know he was holding himself prisoner? She had a feeling that the monsters he was afraid of were not the shadows in this forest, but the ones inside him.

33

NASH

Nash carried the suitcase into the bedroom closest to his and set it down with a wince. His hand clasped his neck. That damn knot was only getting worse.

"So, this is my room?" Bella ran her eyes over the space. It was a far cry from Nova's meticulously decorated home.

He looked at the room, trying to see it through her eyes. It had bare white walls and a simple queen bed with a bright yellow-painted iron frame, the one pop of color in the room, and only because he'd gotten it half off at a yard sale.

"Yeah. I figured you should be closest to mine in case you need me."

She turned to him, full, fuckable lips parting as her eyes widened. *What did I say?*

"If something happens with the baby," he clarified.

A faint blush dusted her cheeks. Seemed he wasn't the only one who couldn't get that night out of their head.

"Come on. I'll show you the rest of the house." He turned, guiding her down the hall. "Behind us is my room. Here is the bathroom for you and Eli." He pointed to his left.

"Across the hall is a closet with sheets, extra towels, and blankets."

Her soft footsteps padded behind him. Her rose scent already clung to the air. Fuck, how was he going to survive living with her and not touching her again? *Because I have to.* He had to keep them safe.

"Wow, five rooms?" she noted, a question in her voice.

"And?" He stopped, turning towards her.

She shrugged. "Seems like a big house for one bachelor."

"Well, we'd already broken ground and started building when . . ." *When the woman I was supposed to marry and have a big family with was taken.*

"When?" she asked.

"I like my space," he gritted, turning back towards the other three bedrooms.

Eli popped his head out of the farthest doorway. "Can I have this room?"

Nash skipped the other two rooms and headed towards him. "Sure, bud. Whatever you want."

Bella filed in after him. A lonely twin bed sat in the corner next to a desk. A tall navy-blue dresser leaned against the far wall next to a closet that Eli would soon discover led to a secret crawl space connecting the other three rooms. Nash had designed it with kids in mind. What could be more fun than a secret tunnel?

"Should we go downstairs now?" Nash asked, leaving the room before he got an answer.

Bella caught up to him by the time he made it to the foyer. The front door was ahead of him. The urge to run away clawed through his veins. He shoved his hand in the air to the open-plan layout. "This is the rest." His living room to the left; the kitchen to the right. Farther down was a dining room, an office, and a laundry room and bathroom.

Bella scanned his mostly bare walls as she chewed on her lip.

"Is there anything we need to get out of your storage?" he asked.

"Uh, well, maybe some decor? This place is pretty bare." She tucked her hands into her pockets.

"Whatever you want."

"You don't mind?"

"No. Go for it."

"*Gracias.* I promise we'll try to stay out of your way as much as possible."

He exhaled. "Don't worry about it. You and Eli should make yourselves at home. If I need space, I'll deal with it."

She nodded. "You okay if I order pizza for dinner?"

"Sure. I gotta run into town anyways. You call it in and I'll pick it up." He grabbed his leather jacket off the hook by the door, patting his pocket for his keys before he left. He stepped outside and drew in a deep breath of fresh air. He'd needed to get out of the house before he did something he'd regret like kiss Bella.

Later that night, the house was quiet. But it didn't feel as empty as it usually did. Nash had locked himself in his bedroom after dinner and a very in-depth conversation with Eli over lobster fishing.

Eli had gone to bed hours ago, but Bella had curled up on his couch with a book. He was waiting for her to go to sleep before he locked the house up for the night—something he didn't usually do. But that was before.

Nash adjusted his reading glasses and focused on the book about pregnancy in front of him, the words blurring together as images of Bella played through his mind on a reel. The sexy vixen from their night together had blended with the fierce mama bear he'd come to know. The shy woman he'd caught sneaking caffeinated coffee earlier. And the person who'd seen through him on the bench, finding pieces of himself he wished didn't exist, shadows of regret and pain and loss. Bella was as captivating as a siren, and just as dangerous because she threatened his fragile existence. She made him want more.

Knock. Knock.

"Come in." Nash closed the book, set it on his bedside table, and sat up straighter.

Bella peeked in, stepping forward as her gaze flamed with heat, rolling up his bare feet to his charcoal sweatpants, past his abs. He sucked in a ragged breath, his skin burning under her perusal as she made her way up his bare chest to his face. Lust shone in those whiskey eyes, making him drunk on her need.

"I didn't know you wore glasses." Her voice was higher pitched than normal.

He pulled them off and set them on top of the stack of books. Below the pregnancy one were two of his favorites—by Robert Frost and Maya Angelou. "Just for reading."

"Oh." Her hand bunched the fabric to her sleep shirt, some sort of thin-strapped scrap of fabric that made her boobs look like fucking paradise. Her tan legs were bare but for a pair of shorts showing off those delicious strong thighs that had gripped his waist so good the last time he drove into her.

Clearing his throat, he tried to not make it obvious that he adjusted himself. "Did you need something?"

"Uh, yeah. I needed medication for my heartburn. I

checked the other bathrooms but didn't find anything. I must have left mine at Nova's."

Nash stood. "I think I have some in here."

Bella's eyes dropped to his semi, widening before her tongue darted out to lick her bottom lip.

He groaned and hurried to the bathroom. After opening the mirror, he grabbed the box of meds and brought it out to her. Bella scanned his room. He'd lost a bet with Nova, so this was the one room that was decorated more than the others with a navy-blue and grey theme, and nautical décor. His built-in bookshelf was so full, it was probably time to get another.

"Here you go." He reached out, handing her the medication. Pain sliced up his back to his neck. He hissed, gripping his nape to rub the most painful spot.

She took the box, studying him. "Are you in pain?"

"I slept wrong weeks ago. I thought it was better but then I tweaked it a few times."

She took out a couple tablets before handing him back the meds.

"You keep it." He waved her off.

"Thanks . . . Lie down."

"What?"

"Lie down. Let me help with your neck. Massage therapist, remember?" she asked, pointing to herself.

"Right. You don't have to—"

"Lie down, Nash. And stop arguing. No sense you being in pain when I can probably help."

Half his mouth turned up in a smile. "Yes, ma'am. Didn't realize you had a bossy side too."

"Oh, I have many sides. You just have to get to know me to learn them all," she teased.

He climbed on the bed, lying on his stomach as he moved the pillow out from under his head.

The sound of the bedside table being opened had him tensing and rolling over to grasp her hand, but it was too late. Her eyes widened, locked inside the drawer where the photograph of him and Ana lay for the nights when he really wanted to punish himself.

"What the fuck are you doing?" he snapped, slamming the drawer closed.

"L-lotion. I was looking for lotion."

All the easygoing energy was replaced with tension.

He sighed. "Bathroom sink."

She darted into the en suite, coming out a moment later, eyes downcast, body rigid, holding a bottle.

"You don't have to do this."

"No, it's fine. Just lie down."

He blew out a breath and closed his eyes as her hands smoothed over his back. The lotion was cool, but her hands were warm and soft. She kneaded his neck. He groaned as she found the spot that had caused him so much trouble.

"That's quite the knot." Her magic fingers worked deeper into the muscle. Pain mixed with relief. "You're really tense. Try to relax, okay?"

Nash attempted to do as she said, letting the tension leave his body with each swipe of her hand. Tingles raced from his skull to the base of his feet like she'd covered him with peppermint oil rather than regular lotion. Her touch soothed his muscles, turning him into a puddle of gratified groans and a firestorm of want. She worked his body over until every part of him was relaxed, except his cock, which was cutting into the bed.

"I wasn't trying to snoop." Her voice was soft.

"I know. I'm sorry." He should explain some things about Anastasia to her, clear up the rumors she'd no doubt heard. But he wasn't ready to broach that subject. Ana wasn't something he spoke about with anyone.

"What got you into massage?" he asked.

"Well, you know I originally wanted to be a nurse."

"Yeah, you told me." It was obvious she liked to help people. If she wasn't at her parents' marina these past few months, she was helping Nova or baking with his mom.

"I wanted something that would still be in the healing field." She got more lotion before continuing to work his lower back. "The classes were fun. And it got me out of the house. I feel terrible for saying that, but dealing with a toddler who screamed and cried eighty percent of his waking hours was a lot to handle—mostly by myself."

"Your husband wasn't around?"

Maybe he was a douche to her and that was why she was able to move on so quick?

"He was a student. So when he was at work, school, or staying late to study since it was too distracting at home with Eli, I was the only one there. I don't know how moms of multiples do it. I guess I'll find out soon, huh?"

Nash stayed quiet, enjoying the supple pressure from her fingers. The slight graze of her hair across his skin. Her sweet scent coated his space, like she was marking it as her own.

Fuck, he wanted her so bad it hurt.

"In the end, being a nurse might have been more useful." Her voice caught and it tore him up inside. What was her story? He wanted to know every part of her, but she'd want that in return. He wasn't ready to face his demons.

So instead, he closed his eyes and leveled out his breathing, pretending to be asleep as her soft hands slipped from his body. He didn't respond when she called his name. And he sure as fuck didn't go after her when she left the room to draw her into his arms and give in to the want rising in him like a rogue wave, unforeseen and devastating.

34

ISABELLA

Isabella shifted on the freezing cold metal bench, trying to get some circulation to her ass. Next time, she'd bring a cushion to Eli's game. But just getting out of the house and here on time had been a nightmare. Eli'd had a meltdown, not wanting to come and instead spend time searching eBay for a radio for his boat. After the cost of buying the thing, she really didn't want to put any more money into it, especially since the fishing season was pretty much over.

Eli stood on the field with his head lowered, his attention focused on the game playing out in front of him. She sighed. At least he was here. She had to take that as a win. He was the one who'd wanted to play soccer, and yes, she'd encouraged it. So what had changed?

"Here you go. It's loaded with sugar and hot." Nova handed her a paper cup with steaming hot chocolate before she sat beside her. Ariel scooted between them and sat too.

Isabella gladly wrapped her fingers around it, soaking in the warmth. "Thank you. And thanks for coming."

"Of course." Nova smiled, her attention focusing back on the field. "How's our boy doing?"

Eli turned around in that moment, his gaze searching the crowd of parents filling the bleachers until he landed on them. Ariel's hands moved and Eli's mouth turned up into a smile. He signed to her and then turned back to the game, running towards the opposing team kicking the ball his way.

"What did you say to him?" Isabella asked Ariel.

Ariel blinked shyly at her before her hands lifted, dancing sign language.

"She told him 'Go Eli,'" Nova replied.

That was all? Maybe her son's attitude change had something to do with who'd delivered the message rather than what it had said. She was glad he had a friend, even if she was half his age.

Isabella focused back on Eli as the ball flew towards him. He ran towards it, but he was too slow and it passed right by him.

"Come on! Coach, get this kid off the field and put someone in who knows their ass from their elbow!" a man shouted, pacing along the fence line that separated the spectators from the game.

Isabella was on her feet, her body thrumming with anger, marching towards the man to unleash hell on him.

"Hey, dickhead, shut your mouth." A razor-sharp deep voice cut through the noise of the crowd.

She froze. What was Nash doing here?

The man turned to Nash sitting on the bottom row of bleachers, his potbelly sticking out from his shirt as he got in his face. "What did you call me?"

Nash stood to his full height, towering over the other man, and leaned in, speaking too low for her to hear even as she made her way closer. The loudmouth's face went white as a sheet before he stumbled back. "S-sorry." He took off towards the other end of the bleachers and kept going.

"Shake it off, Eli. You'll get the next one!" Nash called onto the field, looping his fingers through the fence.

Eli nodded and focused back on the game.

"What did you say to him?" Isabella asked.

Nash stiffened, glancing at her and then back to Eli playing on the field. "What he needed to hear. To shut his mouth and grow some manners."

He'd stood up for Eli. That melting sensation warmed her heart again.

"Well, I appreciate it. Now I get to enjoy my hot chocolate instead of throwing it in his face." She laughed.

Half his mouth quirked up.

She took a sip. "I didn't realize you were coming to his game."

He shrugged. "Wanted to support him."

"I feel like I keep having things to thank you for."

"It's not a hardship to care about that boy. He's a good kid."

"So you've said. And you're a good man."

His lips flattened as he met her gaze. "I'm trying to be," he rasped, like the confession had cost him.

She blinked trying to get a hold of the gratitude and affection rising in her. *Oh, God. I'm falling for the father of my child.*

35

NASH

Later that week Nash lifted the massive fake bone as Roman put the last screw in. Ricky held the back of the giant skeleton up for stability.

"That's the last one." Roman stepped away, his feet crunching in the leaves that littered their parents' yard.

"Damn, these are almost as tall as the house." Ricky motioned to their parents' large home.

"We should convince Mom to do a haunted walk. We can use one of the fields. It would bring in a lot of money," Roman suggested.

"There's already one in Lee, the DeMeritt Hill Farm," Nash replied.

"Yeah, that's right. I haven't been in years. We should go." Ricky smiled.

"If you want to look at something truly horrific, all you have to do is check out a mirror," Nash grumbled.

Ricky punched his arm.

Nash swerved out of the way, but his brother still clipped him. "Ow, fucker."

"You started it."

"Okay, you two. Enough. Nash, you're the oldest. You're supposed to be the responsible one." Roman shook his head with a smile.

"What I want to know is how's having the mother of your future child living with you working out?" Roman asked.

"Fine."

"Come on, give me more than that. You've been alone for years. It's got to be an adjustment having not only one but two other people in your space."

"I heard she's a masseuse and looking for a few clients," Ricky added.

"Yeah. She got permission to use a room at Drift, the spa in town, part-time. At least until the baby comes," Nash answered.

Ricky's eyebrows moved up and down playfully, and Nash had a feeling he wasn't gonna like what came out of the bastard's mouth next.

"Does she give happy endings? If so, I might have to—"

Nash shoved his brother into the leaf-covered yard. "Don't you ever fucking talk about her like that."

Ricky held up his hands with a smirk. "I was just joking."

"You don't joke about shit like that."

"That was pretty low, Ricky," Roman agreed.

Ricky stood up, wiping his ass off. "You really like her."

"What's not to like?"

"No, I mean you care about her," Ricky said.

"Of course I do. She's the mother of my child."

"I'd say it's a little more than that," Ricky pressed.

"No." The part of Nash that was capable of loving someone, of taking that risk, had died when it was clear Ana wasn't coming back.

"I gotta go. Got an appointment to get to." Nash pushed

past them and headed towards the driveway where his truck was parked.

"Finding out if it's a girl or boy?" Roman asked.

"Yeah."

"I hope it's a girl and you turn as soft as Roman."

"Fuck you." Roman smacked Ricky's shoulder. "You're just jealous."

"Jesus, you two are so abusive." Ricky shook his head.

"But it would be cool to see him with a daughter," Roman agreed.

"I just hope the kid is healthy and safe, strong like their mama," Nash confessed, looking down at his boots.

His brothers remained silent. Nash glanced at the two idiots wearing identical smiles.

"What?"

"Bro, you're so gone, and you don't even know it," Ricky teased.

"Whatever." He turned around and headed towards his house. He needed a shower before they left for the appointment. He gave a weighted exhale, his muscles taut with tension and nerves. His brothers were right; he did care about Bella. And he was scared shitless about what that meant.

An hour later, he paced the pitiful length of the ultrasound room, eyes glued to the screen on the machine. The same tech they'd had the first time moved the wand over Bella's stomach, taking measurements and recording data.

"Okay, now, did you want to find out the sex?" Karlie asked.

"Yes," Bella answered.

Nash stepped beside her, taking the seat in the uncomfortable plastic chair. "Does the baby look okay? Healthy? No problems or concerns?"

Karlie gave him a sympathetic smile. "Yes. Everything looks great. Of course I'll have Doctor Wright look over the scans and you'll talk with him after." She focused back on the screen. "Now, let's see if the baby will cooperate with us. The baby's a little feisty today. I'm sure you feel that, Mom."

"Yes. It likes to jump on my bladder." Bella smiled.

Nash stared at Bella as she watched the monitor. A stray lock of hair fell against her cheek. Nash reached out to tuck it behind her ear. Bella turned to him, her eyes searching his for an answer he couldn't give. His heart drummed. His skin tingled, every hair standing on end. Adrenaline flooded his veins. This was it. A moment that would change his life forever. Beads of sweat broke out on his forehead.

Bella reached out, clasping his hand in hers and giving it a squeeze. Her comfort only made his chest cinch tighter. It was getting harder to breathe. The room shrunk with each second of anticipation that ticked by.

"Looks like you have yourselves a . . ."

One heartbeat.

Two.

Let me be strong enough for them.

"Girl. Congratulations," Karlie said.

Nash stared at the screen, blinking in disbelief. A girl? He had a daughter? Panic warred with the rush of affection that threatened to drown him.

"I'll just get these readings to Doctor Wright and call you into his office when he's ready. Here's some pictures." Karlie handed Bella the photos and left the room.

Bella snapped a picture of the ultrasound photo with her phone.

His brows drew together in question.

She smiled. "Sending it to my friend Tessa. She thought I was having another boy."

He nodded, and she tapped a message into her phone before tucking it back in her pocket.

"You okay?" Bella asked softly.

"A girl."

"Yeah."

He swallowed. Girls seemed so much more fragile than boys. Maybe that was sexist, but the shit women had to deal with, especially women of color, was unreal.

"How do you feel?" he asked her.

She smiled, her eyes growing watery. The sight of her tears tore at his chest. "I've always wanted a little girl."

"Why didn't you . . . I mean, it's none of my business, but if you wanted more kids, why is Eli an only child?"

Her smile dimmed and her attention dropped to her hands. "It just wasn't in the cards for us."

He hated that he'd been the one to bring her down in this joyous moment. "I hope she looks like you."

Surprise flared in Bella's gaze. Did this woman really not know how beautiful she was? He probably hadn't helped the situation with how he'd treated her. He would make it up to her—starting now.

He lifted their joined hands to his mouth and pressed a kiss to her silky skin. "Thank you for giving me this gift."

Tears dripped down her cheeks. She swiped them away with her free hand before she leaned in. "You're gonna be a great dad."

His chest lurched. "Let's go out and celebrate. Can I take you to dinner?"

She blinked, hope shining in her eyes. "Yeah. Eli is with my parents tonight after practice."

"Okay. I'll make a reservation for six."

36

ISABELLA

Isabella ran a hand over the silky fabric of her dress as Nash slipped his truck in park. The ride to Atlantis restaurant had been quiet, with nothing but the radio playing on low. He climbed out of the truck as she took a moment to compose herself. She gave her outfit one more once-over. The red fabric draped over her body, showing off her cleavage, but it wasn't too low. It cinched under her breasts in an empire cut and flowed loosely around her body. The length came to just above her knees, thanks to her belly. *Am I too dressed up?*

Her door opened and Nash held out his hand. *Is this a date?*

She slipped her palm into his and climbed down, adjusting her purse over her shoulder. "Thanks."

He nodded before the warmth of his hand met her lower back, ushering her towards the restaurant. She shivered, and it had nothing to do with the chilly evening air.

"Do you need a jacket?"

She shook her head as he reached for the entrance door. "I'll be fine. I tend to run hotter when I'm pregnant."

She walked in, scanning the room. This place used to be a fish market. But Atlantis looked nothing like she remembered. The pine floors shone. Pendant lighting hung over reclaimed wood tables scattered around the room, with almost every one filled with guests. Blown up black-and-white photographs hung on soft grey walls. Renita and James were in one image, holding up a bushel of apples and some vegetables with a few barnyard animals by their feet. The other photos also seemed familiar, with local farms or business names printed on the bottom of each one. Though one in particular stuck out. She could tell it was Nash from the hard set of his shoulders as he hauled in a huge fish. His corded arm was bulging with veins as his other hand reached for the hook. His dark curls seemed so wild and soft at the same time. Somehow the photographer had captured so much life in this one shot without even showing his face. She could feel the sun on her skin, taste the salt on her lips, and hear the seagulls flying overhead like she was in that moment with him.

"Bella?" Nash brought her attention back to him.

A hostess held a couple menus in her arms as she looked at Bella with a smile. "Are you ready to be seated?"

"Yeah. Sorry, just taking in the atmosphere. It's so much different than I remembered."

"Yes, Atlas and Jasmine have made this place into a destination for Shattered Cove. They have old pictures of the building's 'before' by the bathrooms, showing when it used to be a fish market. It's incredible," the hostess agreed. She led them to a table in the corner that was a little more private than the others.

"You'll have to check out the view of the bay from the deck before you go." The hostess pulled a small tablet device from her apron. "Is there anything I can get you started with to drink?"

"I'll have a non-alcoholic mulled cider, please," Isabella said, taking a seat. She hung her purse on the back of the chair facing the wall.

"Make it two," Nash agreed, taking the seat across from her.

"Okay, here are your menus. Your server, Will, will be right back with your drinks."

"Thanks," Nash said, picking up his menu.

Isabella glanced over the meals, her mouth watering. Everything looked so good—and all of it was locally sourced.

"I didn't realize your family supplied Atlantis with pork."

Nash set his menu down and shrugged. "Vegetables, fruit, pork, seafood, and honey."

"Did your brothers get a photo on the wall of their bees? Or just you and your fish because you're special?"

The corner of his mouth curved up, making her belly flip. What she wouldn't give to see this man smile again. "You caught that, huh?"

"It's a great shot, even though your face isn't in it."

"Ricky and Roman's is across the room that way." He pointed behind her.

She turned, taking in the photo of the brothers holding up a frame of honey as a few dozen bees flew around them without so much as a veil on their head.

Bella turned back around, wincing from the movement.

"You okay?" Nash asked, his alert gaze running over her as if scanning for injury.

She waved her hand hoping to set him at ease. "I'm fine. Just ligament pain. Something that's completely normal but not at all comfortable."

"Let me know if there's anything I can do."

"I appreciate that."

"You look beautiful tonight."

She smiled. "Thank you. You look pretty good yourself." Her attention dropped to the charcoal plaid button-up shirt he wore, rolled to his elbows and showing his veiny forearms that had become her weakness. Was arm porn a thing? Because she might just have to search that later.

His low chuckle speared her with want. Fuck, Nash was the only man who made her body react this way. She could blame the hormones, but she'd been this way since she spotted him at that wedding. She'd had no idea there could be so much chemistry between two people.

"Here's your drinks." Their server set the ciders in front of them before pulling out his tablet. "I'm Will. Can I get you started on some appetizers? Or would you like to hear our specials tonight?"

"Do you know what you want?" Nash asked her.

"Yeah. I'll have the lobster alfredo with a side salad."

"I'll have the filet, medium, with potatoes instead of rice, and broccolini. Also a side salad and the sweet and spicy wings sampler for an appetizer."

"Okay, that will—"

"And some of that warm sourdough, if you have it," Nash added.

Will tapped on his tablet. "I'll have that out shortly. Let me know if you need anything else."

"Thank you." Nash nodded as the server left.

"Do you think you ordered enough food?" she teased.

His brows drew together as if he were in thought. "Maybe I should have gotten the butternut squash bisque too."

"Are you serious?"

The corners of his mouth turned up, showing off his white teeth in a smile that stole her breath.

"I'm a big boy. I need my nutrients."

She laughed and shook her head. "I guess so."

"Don't worry. I'll share."

"Well, that bread does sound good," she agreed.

"Atlas is a magician in the kitchen. You haven't been here yet?"

"No. But if the remodel is any indication of what he can do as a chef, I'm sure I'll be more than satisfied." She sipped her cider, the warming spices teasing her tongue with the right ratio of tart to sweet.

His heated gaze dropped to her lips as she licked them. The stiffness in his shoulders from the car ride was gone. She much preferred this relaxed version of Nash.

"So, what were you thinking for names?" Isabella smoothed her napkin over her lap.

"For the baby?"

"Yeah. Do you have anything in mind?" she asked.

He blew out a breath. "I never . . ." His expression darkened.

She placed her hand on his, prepared this time for the thrum of energy at their connection. "It's okay. We have time."

His thumb lifted, pressing into her soft skin, rubbing back and forth. "Thank you for being patient with me. I know I'm not the easiest . . . that I'm definitely not who you wanted to have a baby with."

"I honestly didn't think I'd be able to have another child. I'd always wanted more. You've given me a gift too, even if it is unconventional. I'm grateful for this little girl."

"Me too." His voice shook.

"I think we can make this work for her. As long as we're open and honest with each other about our needs and where we stand. We can find a way to co-parent her in a way where she doesn't feel like she's missing out on a more traditional situation."

"You think so?"

"Absolutely. I've seen how much love your family has. They've taken me in and treated me better than my own mother in some ways."

"I'm sorry if I've caused a rift between you two." His thumb kept stroking.

She waved her free hand and shook her head. "You didn't. My mom and I haven't ever really been on the same page in life. We're very different. But she has this idea of how my life should look, and I ruined that freshman year in college. I went along with what she wanted then, and, well, I'm doing things my way this time and she just can't accept that." She sipped her cider. "Don't get me wrong. I know she loves me and her actions are coming from a place of that affection. She worries about me. But it doesn't make what she does or says right."

He swallowed, his prominent Adam's apple bobbing. "You stood up for me with her. I never got to thank you. But you know you don't have to."

"Why do you say that?"

His jaw tensed. Pulling his hand away, he grabbed the cider and took a few long gulps. The trio of women at a table nearby clinked their glasses together before laughing. Their joy was a complete contrast to the icy tension emanating from the man across from her.

"Nash, don't run away."

He set the cup down, his focus skimming over the other diners around them. "I'm sitting right here."

She shook her head. "But emotionally, you just took off like a sprint runner at the Olympics."

Somewhere in the restaurant, plates clinked together. A woman nearby laughed, loud and merry, but Nash was completely silent.

His chest rose and fell. "What do you want from me?"

"I've known you for months now, but this is the first time we've really gotten the chance to talk, besides the picnic on the mountain. We need to learn more about each other for this to work. I know you didn't want to have to see me again and definitely not have a baby with me, but this is where we are."

"It wasn't you."

"What?" she asked, confused.

"You were never the problem. I'm sorry if I ever made you feel like that was the case."

"It's not me, it's you?" She scoffed. "Can you get any more cliché?"

Long thick fingers wrapped around her wrist, pinning it to the table.

A small gasp left her mouth.

"Someone like you, Bella, deserves more than a man like me has to give. You should have someone who isn't as fucked up in his head. Someone who has a heart with love to give. A man who will worship that delicious pussy and make that smart mouth scream in pleasure every night. Someone who's whole and isn't ruined by his own mistakes. A partner to play ball with your son and be the role model he needs." His hand squeezed tighter, but it didn't hurt. "You want me to be real with you, but trust me, you won't like what you find."

She blinked, utterly stunned. What could she say to that? She'd wanted his honesty and she'd gotten it. Black eyes blazed, a tumultuous sea rising in their depths, promising her ruin. So why did it make her want to jump in with both feet? His words had clearly been intended to make her run the other way. But she was done making decisions out of fear. They never got her anywhere good. She was the new Isabella. And she wasn't afraid of the dark.

Will interrupted their stare-off, depositing their salads and appetizers on the table.

"Thank you," she said before pouring her dressing over the greens. She took a few bites and looked back at Nash.

His gaze was already locked on her as he cut a piece of bread, adding butter before handing it over to her.

She accepted it with a grateful turn of her lips. Biting into the warm, yeasty perfection, she moaned. God, was there anything more delicious than fresh bread?

"Told you you'd like it." Nash smirked, looking a little like Ricky in that moment.

She giggled. "I never disagreed. Carbs happen to be my weakness."

He buttered another piece and set it on her half-eaten salad plate before she even finished the one in her hand.

"I won't have any room left for dinner."

"So take it home. Besides, you're eating for two. We gotta keep you full."

"Oh, I think I'm plenty full enough," she joked.

His heated gaze scorched down the part of her body that wasn't hidden by the table like he was imagining her full of something else entirely—him.

Her skin tingled, like she was incinerating from the inside out. Phew. She needed to cool down. She reached for her cider, trying to get a hold of herself.

Nash started on the chicken wings next, placing a few on her plate. If she ate all this, she really wouldn't have any space for the pasta.

Thankfully, their conversation turned to lighter topics while he finished his appetizers. She tried a little of everything, saving room for her main course.

By the time their dinner was served, she'd learned more about his business operations and the clients he provided seafood for. She'd opened up and shared more about Eli's autism and how he was diagnosed as a child, and what that really meant in the day-to-day of their life.

She set her fork aside, not able to take another bite of her alfredo.

"So, what is it that you really want to do with your life?" Nash asked, dragging a piece of steak through the sauce on his plate before closing his mouth around it. Why was watching him eat so sexy?

"My ideal life?" she clarified.

"Yeah." He licked the bit of sauce from the corner of his full lips. God, the things that tongue could do were burned into her memory.

"Uh, well, it's nothing special. I want to be the best mom I can while also carving out something for me. I did that wrong the first time around. It's easy, when you become a mom, to get sucked into a role you think you're supposed to be based on some unattainable perfect mirage of motherhood. Somehow, you're supposed to meet your child's every waking need and maintain the patience of a saint while running on a few hours of broken sleep for months on end, on top of keeping a clean house, and somehow finding time to shave your legs and put on makeup, and work out to get rid of those extra baby pounds the day after you leave the hospital. But you're really screaming inside because you want just five minutes to pee alone or enjoy an actual hot cup of coffee that hasn't been reheated in the microwave five times." She took a deep breath, letting it out before meeting Nash's wide eyes. "I'm sorry."

"That's what it was like for you?"

"It was lonely. And I should have asked for help, but I felt so isolated. I was half a country away from my parents, and well, you know Eli wasn't a typical baby anyways. He needed more attention, and we didn't realize a big part of it was sensory issues."

"Your husband didn't help?" Nash's voice was tinged in anger.

"Robert did when he was home. He was a great dad. But he was going to college full-time and working to support us. There just weren't enough hours in the day."

Nash reached out his hand. This time, his palm rested over hers, that thumb stroking those delicate circles on her sensitive flesh. It was in complete contrast to the roughness of the man. Who knew the hand could be an erogenous zone?

"I'll be there for you. I won't let you drown in the rising stress of a new baby. I may not know exactly what I'm doing, but one thing about the Emersons is they're there for you whether you want them to be or not. You'll have a whole village this time 'round."

"I appreciate that more than you know."

"You better stop thanking me. I might get a complex," he teased.

Will approached their table and cleared away Nash's empty plate. "Can I interest you in dessert? And did you want a to-go box?"

"I would like the box, thank you. But I have no room for dessert."

"We'll take something home. Can't celebrate without dessert," Nash insisted, his voice rising to be heard over the table next to them erupting in laughter.

Flutters thudded against her belly—their daughter letting her presence be known, no doubt enjoying the dinner Isabella just ate. Or maybe it was the thick rumble of her baby's father's voice that made Isabella's whole body thrum.

Her libido had been on overdrive when she was pregnant with Eli too. But Robert had seemed less than enthusiastic. Isabella had killed herself trying to make her husband more attracted to her. She'd thought it was her body that had been the problem—and she'd been right. Just not in the way she'd assumed.

Those were some deep-seeded insecurities that liked to rear their ugly heads from time to time. But Nash didn't look at her the way Robert had. No, Nash's gaze threatened to devour her whole. And she might be just daring enough to let him.

37

NASH

Nash set their desserts in the fridge before grabbing a couple bottles of water. Bella sat on the couch, her dark hair cascading over the back of it, up off her neck. Her hands were spread over her growing belly. He thought she'd been a stunner the night they'd met, but now—with his child growing inside her—she looked like a goddess.

His breath hitched as he walked over to her, sat in the spot next to her, then handed Bella a water. Rain poured down outside, the pitter-patter hitting the roof in a heavy spray.

"Thanks." She smiled, lighting him up inside.

A peace settled over him. They'd had amazing conversation. He hadn't opened up like that with anyone since . . . "You're welcome."

She unscrewed the cap and took a few sips before setting it on the coffee table in front of them. Nash went ahead and guzzled half of his bottle, his head spinning. He hadn't been this at ease, felt this good except when he smoked some of his sister's weed. That was what Bella did to him—made him high on dreams of a brighter future.

"Tonight was fun." She rested her hand on her belly.

"It was. I can't remember the last time I did that," he agreed.

"Oh." She moved her palm over her stomach.

"Is something wrong?" Nash tensed.

She smiled and shook her head. "No. Your daughter must love the sound of your voice. She's doing somersaults."

She's moving because of me?

"She's kicking?"

"All through dinner, really."

"Must have been the lobster," he teased.

Her eyes widened and her mouth dropped opened. "Why, Nash Emerson, is that a joke?"

He blinked. "I joke."

"Never with me." She smiled, and damn, that small curve did things to the space in his chest where his heart should be.

He swallowed, getting lost in those light brown eyes. "Can I feel her?"

"Of course. You don't have to ask; I don't mind."

He slowly lifted his hand, smoothing it over her belly. Her soft fingers gripped his, moving his palm just above her belly button. The off-beat vibrations made his breath catch. Love pulsed, spearing through him for his unborn daughter. Emotion clogged his throat, burning the backs of his eyes.

They had created this life, together. He flicked his attention back to her, in awe that this good woman had given him this gift. That he was the lucky bastard who got to experience this.

"You're so beautiful," his voice came out in a hoarse whisper.

Her lips parted the smallest amount, her scent mingling with notes of rose hips in the thickening air between them. Tension snaked around him, tugging tighter and tighter. The woman was like a magnet, drawing him in, and he was powerless to fight it. He shouldn't do this . . . but he couldn't stop himself either.

He trailed his finger from her cheek over her jaw, mapping a line down the pulsing vein of her neck. She shivered, whiskey eyes growing dark with liquid need. He leaned in, the temptation too great. Just one taste. That was all he needed. Just one moment where nothing else mattered but this thing between them. His heart pounded, every muscle tense and on edge. *She deserves more.*

"Nash?" Her voice came out on a breath.

I should leave her alone.

Warm, soft lips slid against his, stealing his hesitation. Her mouth parted, wrapping around his lower lip, her teeth tugging, adding gasoline onto an already blazing fire. He kissed her back, his hand gently collaring her throat as he slid his tongue inside, stealing her taste like a thief.

This kiss wasn't the same as the kisses they'd shared the first time they were together. This was more than lust. It was different, somehow. Slow licks, sensual nips—he kissed her like she was his oxygen, because she was. The world could be falling apart and he wouldn't stop.

A tiny moan left her swollen lips. Her nails dug into his shoulders and he cursed the fabric between them. He should stop this before it went any further, but it was impossible to pull away from her. Not when kissing her made him feel free —whole.

She pulled back, her eyes glazed. Lips glistening. Chest heaving. "Nash?"

"I-I'm sorry." *Fuck!*

"I'm not," she whispered.

"What?" He was afraid to hope.

"I'm not sorry. I kissed you, after all."

"I can't give you more than this."

"I know."

"And can you do that—keep feelings out of it?"

Hesitation flashed in her gaze before she nodded and licked her lips. "I think so. I mean, I have so far, right?"

"This is probably the worst idea." But since when had Nash made the right decision when it really mattered?

38

ISABELLA

Isabella's body burned, yearning for his touch. She'd never craved someone as much as she did right now.

Having sex with Nash was probably not a good idea. But she knew the score. Nash had made it clear he'd never return the kind of affection she wanted in a partner someday. If she'd learned anything, it was that life was short. Nash made her happy. And he delivered multiple orgasms. Isabella deserved to find some joy for herself for however long it lasted.

His warm hand across her throat didn't budge as Nash stared at her like she held the secrets of the universe. There was something so arousing about that little bit of pressure on the sides of her neck, the display of dominance.

"You're okay with this being strictly physical," he confirmed.

"Friends with sexy benefits," she proposed. That was what most of her marriage had been like. This was the same thing, wasn't it?

His nose flared. Wordlessly, he stood, gently guiding her

up with him. Her knees trembled as his warm front brushed hers. Her nipples hardened, breasts aching.

Touch me. Please! Put me out of my misery.

"Are you sure?" he asked.

Relief and hope spun her up until she was dizzy. "I know the score, Nash. And I accept."

His mouth collided with hers, like whatever self-control he'd had snapped. He wrapped his arms around her, dark and possessive as the storm clouds blackening the sky outside. He held Isabella tight as his mouth plundered hers.

Thunder rumbled as the storm moved in. But something told her the real threat was inside, slipping his hands to the back of her dress.

The whoosh of the zipper cut through the air as lightning flashed. His mouth never left hers as his deft hands removed her bra, it, too, dropping to the growing pile of clothing on the floor.

He hooked his fingers in her already soaked panties, breaking the kiss to pull them down her legs. She stepped out of them, now completely naked in front of him. Nash's attention dragged up her body, scorching her skin. He looked at her as if she truly was the most beautiful woman he'd ever laid eyes on.

"Your turn." She reached for the buttons on his shirt, but his hand clamped over her wrist, halting her.

"No. I can't wait." He swiped the water bottles off the coffee table, and they landed on the floor with a thud. Nash guided her to sit on the table, pressing on her collarbone until she lay back on it like a sacrifice.

"Nash?"

"Do you know how long I've been craving another taste of this cunt?"

A fresh wave of desire crashed through her. "I haven't shaved—I can't reach—"

"You think I care? I just want you, however you are, creaming all over my face." He dropped to his knees, spreading her legs wide.

Nash kissed down her thigh, nipping gently. She whimpered in sweet agony.

"That's it, sweetness. Let me hear how much you like the way I eat this pussy." His tongue slipped between her folds, making her arch her back. She sucked in a breath through her teeth.

"Mmmm." His lips vibrated against her clit.

She was already so keyed up.

"Fuck, you taste better than I remembered."

"Nash!"

"You know how many times I got off to the memory of this?"

He'd fantasized about her too? That was hot, but oh God, his mouth, when he did that thing with his tongue—her whole body lit up. She was close, so fucking close to the edge. "Please, Nash, I can't take it. I just want you to fuck me. Fill me up."

"Not so fast. I've waited months for this cunt. I'm gonna take my time and enjoy every drop you give me. Even if you beg as pretty as last time."

She whimpered as another rumble of thunder sounded, much closer. She moved her hand to clutch his curls, holding on while he devoured her. His tongue swirled around her clit, diving inside her pussy and back. Building tension curled in her belly. He slipped two fingers inside her, crooking them as he sucked on her clit. She screamed in pleasure, white light flashing as her orgasm shattered her. A boom sounded as she fell apart.

His fingers slowed, matching the pace of his tongue as he lapped gently around that sensitive nub that still pulsed as she came down.

Nash sat up, his beard shiny with her release as he licked his lips. There was something so sexy about a man fucking you while he was fully clothed. But she wanted to see that gorgeous muscular chest. Feel his skin against hers.

"Take your shirt off."

He made quick work of removing the material. His dark brown skin glowed in the low light of the room. She reached for the button on his pants, undid it, and slid them down his legs, making his cock spring free. No underwear. He kicked out of the pants as she stared at his thick cock, eye level with her. Isabella wrapped her hand around his shaft. His stomach muscles contracted as he hissed, showing off those perfect abs.

She leaned in and licked his tip, lapping up the salty pre-cum with it.

Fingers wove in her hair, tugging just enough to show her who was in control. "Don't do that unless you want me to come all over your face. It's been too long."

She looked up at him, her pussy dripping wet with the image he'd painted for her. And then the second part of what he'd said caught up to her. "How long?"

"No one since you," he ground out, moving his hips forward and drawing them back, slowly fucking her hand. His eyes were half closed, his powerful legs trembling.

"I want you to fuck me. But you can come on me another time." She winked saucily at him.

He collared her throat once more, lifting so she had to stand.

"This won't hurt the baby?" he asked.

"Not at all."

"Then turn around. Bend over that table and let me fuck you so you come harder than ever before," he ordered.

She spun around, her hands braced against the table.

"Do you want me to wear a condom?"

"It's not like you can get me pregnant again," she teased.

A flash of hesitation streaked across his expression.

"If you're clean, then I'm fine without—"

He drove into her in one thrust, stealing her breath. His cock stretched her, hitting all the right spots. Firm hands gripped her waist, holding her in place so she didn't topple over.

"Fuck! You feel so good." She moaned as he withdrew and rocked back into her.

"You're so fucking tight," he gritted out.

She squeezed her inner muscles.

He groaned, his fingers diving into her soft flesh. "You bad girl. You want me to punish you, don't you?"

The crack of thunder was no match for the slap of his hand against her ass. Pain quickly morphed into pleasure, sending her rocketing into yet another orgasm.

"That's right, sweetness, you take this cock like a good girl."

His hips pistoned in and out of her. All she could do was take it. Moans escaped her as he thoroughly used her body. His hand fisted the hair at the base of her neck, tugging just enough to send prickles of pained arousal skittering from her neck down her spine.

"Yes. Fuck, yes." They were the only words she was capable of as he pounded into her.

"Look at that gorgeous ass, these hips. Fuck, Bella, you're beautiful. So sexy. Taking my cock like it was made for you."

"Nash!" Her eyes rolled up as the most intense pressure

erupted, sending an avalanche of ecstasy tumbling through her, burying each synapse in euphoria.

His breathing became more ragged. His movements jerky. "You ready for me to fill you with my cum?"

"*Si!*"

Nash thrust into her three more times until his cock pulsed, his hot release emptying inside her and sending another orgasm barreling into her.

The sound of the rain pounding the roof, the distant roll of thunder, and their heaving breaths filled the room. Nash slumped over her, releasing her hair to press his hands onto the coffee table, pinning her in place as he kissed up her neck.

He pulled away, sliding out of her.

She turned around, sitting on the table. "*Dios.*"

Would he react like last time, growing cold and distant? Would he run away?

His gaze flared. She looked down, trying to see what he was looking at when he knelt in front of her. He dragged two fingers over his release as it dripped down her thighs before pushing his cum back inside her like he was staking a claim.

Holy shit, that was hot.

He looked at her, eyes narrowing as if trying to gauge her reaction.

"That might have been the best sex of my life," she said. *There was no might about it.*

"Me too." Something dark flashed in his expression.

"Can we do it again?" Yes, she was putting herself out there.

"Tonight?"

However long you're willing to give me. "Yeah."

"Give me ten minutes."

39

NASH

Liquid pleasure flash flamed from the tip of Nash's cock to the base of his skull, incinerating him from the inside out with each drive of his hips into the silky heat of Bella's pussy. Fuck, she was so tight. Her plump lips glistened from his kisses and parted with her moans, each slipping out and shooting straight for his dick. His balls tightened with an impending release like a storm raging inside him gaining power with each of her cries of pleasure.

"That's it. You take my cock so good," he ground out, giving the illusion that he was the one in control here. But in reality, she'd stripped him naked of everything, body and soul. Bella consumed his desires, fueled his lust. After he'd taken her in the living room, he hadn't been able to stop until they'd somehow made it into her bed and had fallen asleep due to pure exhaustion. He'd woken her up by kissing her neck and then delivered two more orgasms with his mouth on her sweet pussy until she was begging for his cock again.

He couldn't help but take snapshots with each breath. Bella's hair splayed out over her pillow, messy and tangled from his hands. Her brown eyes rolling up in pleasure. The pebbles of her pointed nipples grazing his chest with each thrust before they bounced under him. Red marks from his mouth decorated each one. She'd done the same with the nail marks on his back and the half-moons dug into his biceps.

"Nash—"

He leaned down and kissed her, fucking her slow and hard. "I know, sweetness. Want you to wait and come with me. Can you do that?"

She gave a jerky nod, biting her lip, need painted on her cheeks. That blush always deepened right before she came.

He pulled back enough to meet her gaze as his hand collared her throat, squeezing the pressure points just enough so her eyes went hazy and her body relaxed, submitting to each grind of his hips.

His balls tingled with his impending release. Having someone like her trust him, giving him control, allowing him inside her body was . . . "Fuck, you're so perfect. Come with me, baby. Let go."

Her mouth dropped open in a scream. Her thighs locked around his waist. Her nails dug into his arms, the bite of pain sending his boiling cum shooting out of him. Pleasure flooded every cell, stealing his breath as her cunt took it all. Her inner walls squeezed around him, milking him for all he was worth. A feral groan left him as he gave three more shallow thrusts, not ready to leave the bliss of her pussy.

His chest heaved in lungfuls of air tainted with the scent of their shared arousal.

A satisfied smile curled her lips. Her eyes were glazed as she smoothed her hand over his cheek before gently tugging on his beard. "That was . . ."

"It was." He kissed her nose.

"I don't think I've ever felt so relaxed. That was better than I imagined."

He smirked. "You been fantasizing about this?"

Her eyes widened. "I mean. No. Sort of? I've had some pretty wild dreams. Pregnancy does that to me."

"I want to hear more about these dreams." He pulled out of her, catching her wince. "Are you in pain?" He hadn't exactly been gentle last night.

"In the best of ways. I'm gonna feel you for a few days." A puff of air left her in a pitiful laugh.

"Stay here." He got up, walking naked to the bathroom off his bedroom instead of hers.

Turning on the hot water, he ran a bath, throwing in a few cups of Epsom salt. He waited until the water was high enough before he went back for Bella.

She was exactly where he'd left her, only her eyes were closed. As he slid his arms under her, she stirred.

"Mmm, what are you—"

"Just relax. Have another one of those sexy dreams while I take care of you."

She clung tighter to him as he carried her and gently set her feet into the bath.

"Oh!"

"Is it too hot?" He pulled her out.

"No, no, it's perfect. I just didn't expect this."

He lowered her in and she got settled. The water enveloped her tan skin.

"I think I might fall asleep in here."

"That wouldn't be safe," he remarked, squatting down at the edge of the tub, dipping his hand in and splashing a small amount over her breasts as they bobbed at the surface.

"My hair is probably one big knot, but I'm too tired to do anything about it."

"I can help." *Should I though? Is this too much? I haven't ever washed a woman's hair.*

"Would you?"

The way Bella's eyes lit up made up for any discomfort he'd felt. "Why not? It's my fault anyways."

She moved forward in the bath, making room for him. But that would be too intimate. This was just sex. Taking a bath together was something people in a relationship would do.

As if sensing his hesitation, Bella spoke up. "It's easier if you're in here. Besides, you're dirty too. This way, we can multitask."

He let out a breath and nodded before standing. "Let me grab your shampoo."

He went to her bathroom, grabbing the conditioner too. Returning to her, he set the supplies on the side of the tub and climbed in behind her. The hot water felt good on his muscles, but the soft heat of Bella's body as she fit against his front brought an ease to his chest that he hadn't felt except when he'd been inside her. She brought him peace.

The bathtub was just big enough for them to fit in together with their legs stretched out. He'd had it custom built for his large frame and it was paying off.

"Scoot down to get your hair wet," he instructed.

Bella did as he said, her knees bending as her head lowered to his lap. Her long locks floated in the water around her face like a mermaid.

She giggled. "The water always tickles my ears when I go under."

Amused, he cupped more water, drizzling it carefully over the front of her hair, soaking it all before he tugged her back to sitting. Grabbing her shampoo, he squirted a small amount in his hand, lathering it between his palms before massaging it into her scalp.

"Mmm." Her moan had his cock coming to life again. But she was sore, and his dick needed to calm down. Maybe he'd take a cold shower after this.

"You're good at this."

"I'll take your word for it," he said.

After making sure she was thoroughly soaped up, he tapped her shoulder. She sunk below the water, her head hitting his cock on the way down. He ran his fingers through her hair, helping to wash the soap off, the bubbles floating on top of the bath. She sat back up and he repeated the process with the conditioner.

"This is like a trip to the spa, only sexier." He could hear the smile in her voice.

It sent a thrill through him to make her happy. To know he was taking care of her needs. It was addictive. He wanted to see what else would make those full lips curve up or that melodic laugh pour out.

"Glad I could be of service. But you're still really dirty." Nash grabbed his body wash. He probably should have gotten hers from the other bathroom, but the thought of her walking around, smelling like him, brought a possessive satisfaction rolling through him that he had no right to. He lathered it up in his hands and started with her breasts.

She whimpered and leaned her head against his chest.

"Are they sore?" He gently ran his thumbs over the dark nipples.

"No. Just sensitive—in a good way."

He dragged his nose down her nape, inhaling her scent before he nipped her ear. She shuddered, as he'd come to expect. It was just one of the places he'd discovered that turned her on.

"Well, we want to make sure we get every inch of you clean, Bella. After all, you've been a very dirty girl."

She giggled. God, he loved that sound.

"Wow, that was corny."

"Made you laugh, didn't it?" He kissed her shoulder and she leaned back against him. His hands roamed down her belly, cradling it in his hands.

"Whoever would have thought we'd end up here?" she mused out loud.

Who indeed. He'd never thought he would have this again. Someone to show him gentle touches. Someone he could share a bath with, kissing and laughing. But, for now at least, he had her. And he'd enjoy the time he could get. He wouldn't worry about the past or the future. He'd just be here with Bella in their own little bubble at home. For the first time in years, he'd let tomorrow worry about itself.

40

ISABELLA

"There's something different about you." Nova studied Isabella, her finger tapping her bottom lip.

Bella pulled out the old coffee can from the feed bag and tossed the contents into the pen with the chickens. "I don't know what you mean."

"You are absolutely glowing," Nova said.

A heat crept to Isabella's cheeks. "Well, I did hear that happens when you're pregnant." *Or it has to do with the fact that I had a sex marathon with your brother last weekend and it happened to be the most mind-blowing orgasms of my life.*

Nova picked up the pail of leftover food, snickering. "I have a feeling it has less to do with the baby inside you and more to do with the man who put it there."

"Nov—"

Her friend held up her hand and shook her head. "Nope. I don't want any details. I may joke, but I never want to know anything about my brother's sex life. Okay?"

Isabella laughed. "I wasn't going to give you any." *This is between him and me.*

"Good." Nova lugged the bucket over to the pigpen outside the barn and dumped the leftover scraps into the trough. Four fat pigs wandered over, snorting and going to town on their prize.

Isabella stepped back, waving her hand in front of her.

"Yeah, you get used to the smell after a while," Nova said.

"I don't think I will." Isabella held her breath until she moved farther inside the barn where the sweet smell of hay melded with the scent of horses.

Nova clucked her tongue, reaching into her pockets for two apples to hold out for the beautiful mares that greeted them.

Isabella petted the smaller one's soft nose as it chewed on the fruit.

"You guys coming to family dinner on Sunday?" Nova asked.

"I think so."

Nova turned towards her. "You know, I've never seen Nash this happy before."

"I thought we weren't talking about this."

"I said we won't talk about the dirty details. I mean in general. It's like I'm getting a glimpse of a whole new brother I didn't know existed."

"You mean since his ex?"

Nova shook her head. "No, I mean ever. Before Ana, he was still a very stoic guy. He worked hard on the farm and then played hard, but Nash has always been a bit of a loner."

So it wasn't just because of his ex?

"He took care of us when my parents worked long hours on the farm. He was more like a second parent. I'm not sure he ever really got the time to be one of us kids." Nova took a breath and sighed. "Then Ana came along. But she was just one more person for him to take care of."

Isabella's curiosity was piqued. "What do you mean?"

"Ana and Nash were up and down constantly. Ana had a way of self-sabotaging things. I think Nash's loyalty scared her because she wasn't used to it. Her childhood was no cup of tea. We were actually in a group home together for a little while, years ago, before the Emersons found me. That's how I met her."

"Oh, I see."

"Some would say she loved drama, but when someone is raised in an environment with constant stress and a roller coaster of ups and downs, you get used to it. It becomes the norm for you. So, when you're presented with something healthy and steady, it feels unsettling. You can do things, even subconsciously, to create that same rocky pattern. Ana and Nash were not healthy together. But I think he thought he could save her. I'm sure that's why he still blames himself."

Isabella's heart broke for Nash and for Ana.

Nova plucked a piece of hay from her shirt and dropped it into the grass. "He loved her in his own way, but I don't think she was the one for him long-term. They wanted different things out of life. I think he's a much better fit with you."

"Why do you think so?"

Nova smiled knowingly. "The way his eyes light up around you. The fact that he says more than two words and grunts at family dinner—hell, the fact that he's showing up regularly now. You're good for him."

Her heart skipped a beat, warm hope bubbling up inside her like a balloon. She gave a half-hearted attempt at tamping it down. "Nash has made it clear he isn't ready for anything resembling a relationship. We're just friends."

"You're living together," Nova sing-songed.

"Because of the baby. Once she's a year old, I'll start looking for a house of our own."

Nova chuckled. "You sure? Because from where I'm sitting, I don't see my overprotective, ultra-possessive big brother ever letting you, Eli, or that little girl out of his sight."

Nova walked farther into the barn, shaking her head.

Was she right? Nash had made it clear he didn't want a relationship, but maybe he meant right now? When they'd had sex the last time, it had felt different. He'd made love to her. And then he'd taken care of her, washed her the way a lover would. Still, the hesitation had been there, but he'd done it. And since then, he'd brushed his hand against hers and held it where Eli couldn't see. Massaged her feet on the couch while they watched a movie. Nipped her ear in passing, or squeezed her ass when he went to grab a plate in the cupboard above her. Little touches that had her ready to combust at the end of the day. Though he hadn't made a move to sleep with her again since Eli had been back. Maybe he thought she was still sore? Or this was strictly a Friday-night-while-her-son-was-away thing?

Maybe Nash just needed time and space. She would take this slow and see if things changed. Because if he did want to actually date her, if he saw a future with her and could love her, then Isabella would be all in. Nash was kind, and caring, and showed more through his actions than what he verbalized. He never seemed to say what he didn't mean. That honesty was something she needed in a partner.

But Isabella wouldn't settle for a man who didn't love her with every fiber of his being. She'd been down that road, and it only led to heartache—hers. As much as she wanted to believe Nash could be the one, she needed to face the fact that it might not happen. She wouldn't give herself false hope.

41

NASH

Nash opened the front door, the warmth of the home carrying a delicious savory smell that made his mouth water. He shrugged off his jacket, hanging it by the entrance, and toed off his boots, leaving them next to a pair of pink Converse and smaller Vans before he made his way into the house. All was quiet except for a few clanking sounds of dishes from the kitchen.

He scanned the couches where Eli was usually stationed with his iPad, but he wasn't there. Just a myriad of colorful throw pillows and a few impossibly soft blankets that had shown up one day. Kind of like the few knickknacks and plants spaced around the room that wasn't empty anymore. His house finally looked inhabited by more than a bachelor—like a family lived here.

He walked by the paintings he'd helped Bella hang last weekend and into the kitchen. She stood in front of the stove, stirring a pot. It was torture to be in the same house as her this week and not touch her like he truly wanted, settling for passing grazes to get enough of a fix to hold him over. His hands itched to wrap around her waist and kiss her neck, brushing his beard over it to make her shiver in his arms. But the young man sitting at the bar, staring at the marble countertop like it had angered him in some way, made him abandon those plans.

"Hey, guys."

Bella jumped, spinning around with her hand on her heart. "Oh, I didn't hear you come in."

"Just got home." Nash opened the fridge, grabbed an iced tea out, and shut it. A magnetic notepad with flowery designs stuck to the front and a list of groceries in cursive script on it was stuck there—just one more piece of decor that meshed their lives together. All these changes should have grated on his nerves, but they seemed to fit, like they'd always belonged here.

He turned to Eli. "How was your day, bud?"

Eli shrugged.

Nash glanced at Bella, who gave him a sympathetic tilt of her lips before saying, "Dinner is ready. Why don't you both go wash your hands and I'll plate it?"

Nash did as she said. Eli slid off the stool and did the same. By the time they were all seated at the table with a delicious-smelling meal of spaghetti with chunks of sausage and meatballs and a side of fresh garlic bread, Nash's stomach was rumbling.

"This looks fantastic. Thank you for cooking." Nash twisted some pasta around his fork.

"You're welcome."

Eli stirred his plain pasta on his plate absentmindedly.

"Eli has a game this weekend. Don't you, honey?" Bella asked.

Eli nodded. "Yeah, on Saturday at three if it doesn't rain."

"I look forward to it." Nash stuffed a bite of the food into his mouth. The rich, hearty sauce had a bit of spice to it, surprisingly.

Eli stared at his own plate, seemingly in his own world.

Nash cleared his throat. "I was going to schedule to get my boat taken out of the water in the next month or so. Gonna clean off the hull and then have it wrapped for the winter and stored. I'll have my guy wrap yours, too, unless your grandpa already had someone in mind?"

"Whatever," Eli answered without emotion. Usually when they talked boats his eyes lit up, but today they were dull and lifeless.

"Have you decided what to be for Halloween this year?" Nash asked, trying again.

"No."

"What do you do during the winter?" Bella asked Nash before eating her own food.

"This and that. I help my brothers build bee equipment when they need it. Or deliver for the farm. Plow the snow and maintain the farm equipment. Whatever's needed, really."

"I can't believe how many apples you guys get from that orchard. I feel like we've canned a thousand jars at this point." Bella laughed, but it sounded forced. She kept flicking concerned glances at Eli.

"Yeah, Mama's apple pie filling is a big seller in the city. We have one store that will buy up almost everything she makes—all but what she keeps for the farmers' market. And us, of course."

"Your farmland seems to have a bit of everything."

"Boredom was certainly not an option growing up," he agreed.

"I'm not hungry." Eli stood, carrying his barely touched plate to the counter before heading upstairs.

"Did something happen at school today?" Nash asked quietly.

Bella sighed and shook her head, worry lines appearing on her forehead as sadness crept into her expression. "No, tomorrow is the first anniversary of Robert's . . . passing."

Oh. A wave of sympathy crashed over him. He understood grief all too well. He'd been a mess the first anniversary of Anastasia being missing. He'd gotten so drunk, he'd woken to a destroyed room.

Bella set her fork down, getting to her feet as she held on to the table, her growing belly making it awkward for her to scoot back. "I'm going to go check on him."

Bella waddled away, her steps wider than they usually were. It was cute as hell.

Helplessness weighed down his shoulders. He wished he could make it better, have some of that light return to Eli's eyes and erase the worry in Bella's expression. But he was powerless. Grief never left—it only changed forms. This loss would be something they carried for the rest of their lives. Some days would be better, and others would be worse—like today. It wasn't like you could forget the person you loved and move on in a world without them, existing after they'd become a part of you. No, you just got used to dealing with the gaping hole and the pain until one day it didn't seem so big.

Nash got up from the table. He headed into his office, opened a drawer, and grabbed the brand-new composition notebook on top before picking out a pen and jogging upstairs. His heart thudded in his chest as he approached Eli's cracked door.

This is stupid. It probably won't work. But I have to try something. Eli's pain had somehow become his own. He wouldn't leave the boy to drown in it.

Nash knocked on the open door. Bella and Eli both looked up.

"Mind if I talk to Eli for a minute?" Nash asked.

Bella's eyes widened a fraction before she turned to Eli. "You okay with that, *mijo*?"

Eli shrugged. Bella stood, casting her worried expression towards Nash. "I'll be right down the hall if you need me."

He wanted to reach out and squeeze her hand in reassurance, but Eli was watching. The kid didn't need anything else to confuse him on such a trying day. He waited for Bella to clear out before he walked around the room, studying the way Eli had set things up. Boats in glass bottles of various sizes and shapes adorned his walls. Eli had mentioned his father had been into that. Robert must have done those.

"I like what you've done with the room." Nash hadn't been in here since they'd moved in, preferring to give him space.

When Eli didn't say anything, Nash turned around to find the boy holding his iPad, swiping left every few seconds. Nash sat on the side of the bed, peeking over his shoulder. Images of a man Nash assumed was Robert flashed on the screen. Eli looked a lot like his dad. They both had blue eyes, but his hair wasn't as light as his father's. Another swipe and there was another picture of Robert with his arm around a younger Eli as they stood on a boat, holding up their catch proudly. He swiped again, and this time Robert had his arm around Bella as she held a baby Eli. God, she looked like a kid. A sliver of jealousy stabbed through him that he had no right to.

Nash cleared his throat. "You know, I lost someone I loved too."

Eli set the iPad down on the bed.

Nash handed him the notebook and pen. Eli took it, his

fingers clasping the edges. "Sometimes it helps to write down what you would tell them if they were here."

"But he's not here," Eli argued.

"I know, bud. And it sucks that he isn't. But you'll always carry a piece of him with you."

"That's not possible—"

"I don't mean a physical piece. You have the memories you made together, right?"

Eli nodded.

"That's what you hold on to when you feel sad and when you're missing him. You remember all the good, and you work at being grateful for that time. And then with this . . ." Nash pointed to the notebook. "With this, you can talk to him. You can write letters to your dad to catch him up on what you've been up to. Tell him what makes you happy, sad, angry, and everything in between."

Eli squeezed the pen tighter, his knuckles whitening.

"And then when you're done, you can tear it out and throw it away or leave it in there. This is a special notebook for you to talk to your dad."

"What if I forget him?" Eli's voice was just above a whisper.

Nash slid his arm around him, giving him a sideways hug. Eli leaned against him. "Is that why you've been looking through pictures? You're afraid you'll forget?"

Eli nodded.

"I'll be honest—you may forget some of the details over time, but the core of who your dad was and how much he loved you will never be erased. And you have these pictures to help remind you, and I'm sure your mom will be able to tell you lots of stories of you all together."

"Did this work for you?" Eli asked, pointing to the notebook. "For the person you loved and lost?"

Nash sighed. He had stacks of them, mostly drunken apologies of failing Ana. Did it help? For one brief moment when the ink spread over the page he at least felt like he was doing something, and he wasn't so helpless. But it never lasted. His soul wouldn't settle without knowing where she was or what happened to her. But he couldn't explain that to a kid, especially a grieving one.

"Yeah, bud, it usually does." *For a little while at least.*

ISABELLA

Isabella sipped her tea in silence, taking in the view of Nash's backyard. The field was coated in frost and a dense fog had rolled in. She shivered in the cold shadows of the remaining darkness, enviously eyeing the golden sunlight peeking over the mountains in the distance. She tightened the blanket around her shoulders and sipped her drink for warmth. She wasn't ready to go inside just yet. The house was too quiet.

Her phone buzzed in her pocket. She pulled it out, squinting at the brightness of the screen.

Tessa: *Thinking of you today. I'm here if you want to talk.*

Isabella: *Thank you.*

Tessa: *Tell Eli to call his favorite auntie. I sent you guys a package with some goodies in it. Should be there by tomorrow.*

Isabella: *I will, and thanks.*

Tessa: *Of course! Love you lots.*

Isabella: *Love you too.*

She slid the phone back in her pocket and sighed. Eli would be happy to get a gift in the mail. Maybe that would cheer him up. Her belly twisted into knots. Eli's pain piled on top of her own. He'd opted to go to school today despite her offer to skip and spend time together. *It's just because he likes routine.* He probably needed that comfort.

The sliding door opened behind her before heavy footsteps walked up to her. Nash stuck his hands in his pockets, eyeing her from the side. "You want a distraction?"

She turned to him. "What did you have in mind?"

"Grab your coat and put your shoes on." Nash disappeared into the house again.

Curiosity had her following after him. After closing the door, she set her tea on the counter. "Where are we going?"

His palm rested on her lower back, ushering her towards the doorway. He reached down and grabbed her pink shoes, holding them out for her. It was a sweet gesture. Putting on shoes that required laces was next to impossible with her six-month pregnant belly.

The back of his hand clasped her calf as he eased her foot in the shoe. "It's a surprise."

"I-I like surprises." She smiled.

He finished tying her second shoe and stood, giving her a nod. "Good." He grabbed the keys from the hanger by the door and walked out, leaving her to put on her coat and catch up.

"Am I dressed right?" she asked, buckling in.

His gaze roamed over her, his eyes heating. "You're perfect."

The drive into town didn't take long. Nash opened her door and helped her out onto Main Street. He held her hand as they crossed the road, leading her to The Oyster Bookstore.

"We're getting books?" she asked excitedly.

"This is the first stop." He didn't let her hand go as they passed Pippa, the owner, with a wave.

"What kind of books do you like to read?" he asked.

"Uh, well, I'm a pretty big fan of romance and women's fiction. Also, mysteries."

"Let's start over here, then." He motioned to the far end of the store where half-naked men adorned most covers in the aisle.

She blushed. "You don't have to stay here. You can go to the boring literary section."

"How do you know what I read?"

"Because that's almost entirely what's on your bookshelf in the office, and from what I saw, your bedroom shelves too."

He nodded. "They're far from boring."

"Kind of like those documentaries you like to watch."

"Hey, you liked the one we watched last week about the bank heist."

She laughed. "Not falling asleep does not equate with *like*. I was just enjoying your foot massage too much to move."

He scoffed and shook his head. "I'll find one you love one of these days."

"Impossible."

"Is that a challenge?" His eyes lit up with mischief.

She shrugged, trying to not act affected. "No, it's a fact. Just like you probably won't read romance."

"Who says I haven't?" he asked, surprising her.

"Have you?"

"Nova made me watch *The Notebook*. Does that count?"

Isabella chuckled. "No, it does not. I'll make you a deal— for every documentary you put me through, you have to read one romance novel from now on."

He groaned, tipping back his head before he turned to her with a smirk on his edible lips. He leaned in, his voice coasting over the shell of her ear. "Fine, but only if you read them first and highlight your favorite parts so we can try them out later."

Her eyes widened as she looked around, afraid someone would hear him. No one was in this aisle except an older woman farther down, her face hidden between the pages of a book with a blue alien on the cover.

"It's cute how embarrassed you get when we both know you're far from innocent, Bella." Nash's dark gaze was full of heat, like he was replaying all the dirty things they'd done together in his mind.

She poked his chest with her finger. "You'd better watch it, Mr. Emerson. Or you'll find my red shirt has made it in with all your white clothes in the laundry. How do you feel about pink socks?"

He shrugged. "They feel the same as white ones."

She wasn't going to win with him, so she opted for a change in subject as she wandered down the aisle, picking up a few new releases from her favorite authors and one just because she liked the cover. "What book are you reading right now?"

"*The Whole-Brain Child.*"

She stopped and turned to him. "That one's about kids' brain development, isn't it?"

He rubbed the back of his head in a self-conscious gesture. "I finished the ones about pregnancy that Sebastian recommended."

"All of them?"

"Yeah."

"It means a lot that you're so committed to this—to her." She rubbed her belly.

Nash picked a book up, cracking it open and scanning the page before setting it back on the shelf. He stuffed his hands in his pockets. "I am here. For her, for Eli, and for you."

Was he saying . . .?

"Excuse me, dear."

Bella snapped out of her haze, moving out of the way for the older woman.

"I think this is a good start." Bella cradled the books she'd picked out.

"We might have to build a shelf in your bedroom." Nash took them out of her hands, carrying them towards the checkout counter.

"For five novels?"

He cut her a skeptical look. "You think I don't notice all the book-sized packages showing up on the porch?"

She shrugged, trying to act innocent. "I mean, who said they were books?"

"The fact that you have a different one in your hand every couple of days? Or the stack I nearly broke my leg tripping over when I dropped off the basket of your clothes?"

"Okay, fine. I won't say no to a shelf, but I mean, only if you think the room needs it. I won't be in there forever."

Something hard flashed in his dark eyes before he blinked it away, setting the books on the counter.

"Did you find everything you were looking for?" Pippa asked with a friendly smile.

"Yes, thank you."

He paid for her purchases despite her protest. Nash carried the paper bag as he held the door open for her. It was only a matter of time before they saw their first snowfall.

"Now, we need to grab a couple hot drinks and treats from The Stardust Café before we go to our next destination." Nash looked both ways before taking her hand and crossing the street.

"There's more to this surprise?" She stopped on the sidewalk.

He smoothed a piece of hair from her face, tucking it behind her ear. "Of course."

"Okay, fine, but I'm paying this time," she insisted.

He scowled. "But it's my surprise."

"Technically you told me what we're doing here, so it's preparation for the surprise."

He shook his head, grumbling. "Fine."

Satisfied, she stood on tiptoes and kissed his cheek. "Thank you."

43

ISABELLA

Thirty minutes later they sat in his truck, facing the crashing waves of the ocean as the wind whipped against the side of the vehicle with a vengeance. He had the heat on, keeping them snug and warm, protected from the elements.

"It's a cold one today." She shivered.

He wrapped his arm around her, pulling her closer to him. "You need the heat turned up?"

"No, I'm good." She reached for the decaf latte she'd picked out and wrapped her hands around the cup, savoring the warmth.

Her phone dinged. She pulled it out and swiped the message open.

Phillip: *Sending you and Eli all the love and light today. I'd love to come and visit sometime soon. Let me know when works for you. I'll call Eli later.*

Isabella typed out a quick reply and set her phone on the dashboard.

Nash didn't move his arm from around her. Instead, he

grabbed his own drink, taking a sip and gazing out at the wild waters crashing against the shoreline not more than ten yards in front of them.

"Thank you for today. I definitely needed this distraction."

He turned to her. "You're welcome."

The wind whistled, making the truck shudder.

"You want to talk about him? I mean, you don't have to, but you can . . . if you want." Nash's voice wavered, like he was unsure. It was endearing.

"Robert was my best friend."

Nash stiffened, but she pushed forward. "He was a great dad, and he really tried to be a good husband."

He cut her a questioning glance.

"Eli doesn't know this, but we were about to get a divorce before his ALS diagnosis."

"What?"

"We never should have been married in the first place. The only reason we did was because I was pregnant with Eli. Robert did what he thought was the right thing at the time. And I loved him—at least, what I thought was love. Both our parents pressured us to tie the knot before the baby came. We were young and went along with it." Isabella took a breath. This was the hard part. She'd only admitted the truth to two close friends. "I thought for the longest time the problems in our marriage were my fault. I wasn't good enough. I wasn't desirable."

Nash's grip on her shoulder tightened. His voice came out harsh. "That's why you asked me if you were good in bed that night? Did he make you feel that way?"

She cleared her throat, too afraid to look at him as she admitted this. "Robert was gay."

Nash was silent for so long that Isabella had no choice but

to peek up at him. She wasn't sure what she expected to find in his expression, but it wasn't anger.

His jaw ticced as rage blazed in his eyes. "He knew that and still married you? Put you through that?"

Oh, he's upset on my behalf.

"No. It wasn't like that. We were eighteen. So young, and fresh out of our parents' homes. Robert came from a very conservative upbringing. He'd repressed that part of himself. He'd never been with a man before. We were each other's firsts."

Nash's jaw clenched.

"He came out to me, and I felt this massive relief." Tears blurred her vision. "It all made sense. The reason he didn't initiate sex or why he'd rather stay up and talk together than make love."

"You blamed yourself for his lack of interest," Nash confirmed.

She nodded. "I was at the end of my rope. I was miserable, but I felt so guilty because he was such a good man and an amazing dad to Eli. But I knew I couldn't continue my life being that unhappy. So, I sat him down and told him, and he confessed to me he thought he was gay."

"Wow. I don't know what to say to that . . . but you stayed married?"

"Yes. We were getting everything in order to file and he was going to move out, and we were going to tell Eli, but then Robert got diagnosed with ALS." She wiped the tears that fell down her cheeks. "It's a death sentence. And we didn't know how long we'd have him for while his body slowly shut down. I couldn't be the one to take time away from Eli with his dad that he would never get back. And Robert needed me. His parents didn't want anything to do with him after they found out he was gay. I was all he had."

"So you stayed married to him and took care of him for years?" Nash asked.

"His disease progressed rather quickly. But once we'd accepted the news, Robert insisted on making lists. Things he wanted to do with Eli before he lost control of his muscles and couldn't move freely or talk. He even made me a list." She pulled out her phone. "So I would have something to guide me through the challenging months ahead. You were on that list."

"What?"

She handed him the phone, pointing to the section telling her to have a one-night stand.

Nash looked at her as she took the cell back and set it on the dashboard. "That's why you came up to me?"

"That's what gave me the confidence to talk to you. I hadn't planned for it to go all the way—or get knocked up again. But yeah, this is what set all this in motion."

"What does that part on the list mean? 'Stepping into tomorrow'?"

"It's something Robert used to say. When bad stuff happened or we were stressed about one thing or another, he'd tell me to focus on what I could control and take the first step. He shortened it by saying that. You keep taking one step, and before you know it, the sun will rise again."

"He sounds like a smart man."

She smiled. "He was."

"How does Phillip fit into this? Is he Robert's brother?"

A bark of laughter escaped her as she shook her head. "No, Phillip was Robert's boyfriend."

Nash's eyes rounded and his mouth dropped open. "What? He . . . he cheated on you while you were—fuck, Bella." His hand fisted as he brought it to his forehead and then back down, like he couldn't contain the angry energy pulsing in the cab of the truck.

Isabella turned her body to face him, placing her hand on his fist. "No, no. It's not like that. Our marriage ended the day he came out to me and we decided to file for a divorce. Probably long before that if I'm being honest. We stayed legally married, but we decided that we would stay friends and we'd both be free. One night when we were out celebrating him coming out, we ended up at a gay bar in the city, and this man approached Robert for a dance. The way they looked at each other—I've never been a believer in love at first sight, but I witnessed it with my own eyes. In the almost ten years of marriage we'd shared, Robert never looked at me like that— like I was everything. Was it bittersweet? Absolutely. Was I jealous? Surprisingly, no. When he was on the dance floor, I texted him to say I'd get home on my own and to have fun."

"He just left you?"

"We'd already discussed that being a possibility. He had a one-night stand of his own on his list. He didn't think it was fair to start a relationship with someone when he was dying. But Phillip was persistent, and he stuck by Robert and me until the end. I mean, he's still here for us. Checks in with us, keeps in contact with Eli. He's the one who came up with the idea of being called Uncle. We didn't want Eli to have to deal with the drama of our relationship status on top of the fact that his father was dying. That's too much for any kid to handle."

Two hands cupped her face as Nash leaned in, his breath mixing with hers.

"What—"

"I hate that you for one second thought you weren't good enough. That you took on his burden. That you put everyone else above your needs for so long. But that won't happen with me. I'm promising you right now, I'm here to take care of you, Eli, and our daughter. You don't have to carry the weight of the world on your shoulders alone anymore."

She swallowed the lump of emotion that had welled up in her throat. *Was he saying what she thought he was saying? Had Nova been right?*

"And you sure as fuck don't need to ever second-guess how goddamned gorgeous you are. Do you have any idea what you do to me? How many boners I have to hide throughout the day?"

She attempted to shake her head, but his hands held fast. Nash's forehead tipped against hers, his nose brushing her own. "You've got me addicted to your smiles and those little moans you let out when I touch your clit."

The temperature in the cab of the truck got significantly hotter. Coffee and saltwater filled her nose, along with the unique scent of Nash. His breaths whispered across her lips as he spoke, spinning her up until she was dizzy.

His thumb brushed over her cheek. "The way you scrunch your nose when you're concentrating. And the way your cheeks blush so red right before you come undone."

He slid his lips over hers, warm, soft, and torturously slow. She was burning up for him. Clutching his jacket, she slid her tongue against his lips. He sucked on it before biting her lower lip and tugging.

"And let's not forget the way you waddle around now. It's the cutest fucking thing."

She jerked back, smacking him on his chest while glaring. "*Cabrón*, I do not waddle!"

A loud laugh rumbled from his chest. "You do. It's adorable."

She crossed her arms. "See if I ever let you close enough to hear one of my moans you seem to like so much again."

"Aww, don't be like that." Nash pulled her against his chest.

She pushed against him, a pitiful half-attempt at getting away, but her heart wasn't in it. Nipping her neck playfully, he chuckled and slid his hands over her belly. Her back settled against his front, her legs lying over the truck seat.

Nash pressed a kiss to her temple. The gesture was so sweet it brought tears to her eyes. She hadn't felt this wanted or cared for by a man since . . . ever. That tiny seed of hope sprouted, growing roots, and inching towards the surface. How could she not wish for more with a man like Nash? Maybe they were exactly what each other needed—at least for now.

44

ISABELLA

Isabella flipped the corn tortilla in the pan and then peeked at her son. Eli bent over the table scribbling away in a notebook. She focused back on the veggies on the counter and began slicing the tomatoes.

"Can I help with anything?" Nash asked, leaning his hip against the counter.

"Can you grab the molcajete?"

His eyebrow quirked. "The what?"

"The bowl to make guacamole in. It's like a bigger mortar and pestle."

"I don't think I have one of those."

"I got it from storage. In the cupboard with the mixing bowls." She pointed across the room.

Nash turned his back, giving her one hell of a view. His plump ass looked ten times better in the dark-wash sweatpants he wore. It was hard as a rock, too—much like his abs. He reached into the cupboard, the snug T-shirt rising with the motion, giving her a glimpse of his lower back and the dark tattoo ink spreading up from his thigh.

She'd always had a thing for guys with tattoos. Even tried to convince Robert to get one. He hadn't been interested.

She focused back on the corn tortilla, now a little over-cooked. Quickly moving it off the pan, she shut the stove off.

"This is cool." Nash set the bowl by the wooden cutting board.

"You can't make proper guacamole without one of these." She smiled and turned to Eli once more. He hadn't moved from that spot since he'd gotten home from school thirty minutes ago.

"Put me to work," Nash said.

"Why don't you carry the dishes over to the table? I'll finish this up quick and meet you guys there."

Nash grabbed the bowl of pork in one hand and beans in the other before he was off.

Isabella got to work pitting the avocados and putting them in the molcajete. She mashed them before adding the chopped veggies. Next up was lime juice. She carried the whole container over, setting it in the open space on the table and sliding a spoon inside.

"I got you an iced tea." Nash motioned to the drink in front of her.

"Thanks." She turned to Eli. "Can you put that away? Dinner's ready and I know you don't like it when it gets cold."

Eli finished writing a sentence and then closed the book, tucking it away in his backpack.

The first few minutes of dinner went by with the clank of forks and a few satisfied groans from Nash.

Nash wiped his mouth with a napkin. "This is delicious. Thanks for cooking. I'll get tomorrow's dinner. How does homemade pizza sound?"

"That sounds good. Don't you think, Eli?"

Eli nodded. "Sure."

Nash finished off a third taco and wiped his hands. "I was thinking it might be fun to have a fire tonight out back. Maybe roast some s'mores for dessert?"

"Mmm, I won't say no to s'mores," Isabella agreed before grabbing her iced tea and taking a sip.

"Can I have two?" Eli perked up.

"I think we can make an exception this time." Isabella smiled.

"I also have another surprise." Nash dressed another two tacos on his plate.

"You do? What is it?"

Nash gave her a wink. "You'll have to wait and see, sweetness. Now eat up so you can have dessert after."

"I've eaten two tacos already," she argued.

"Great. Now have another two for the baby." He picked up a warm tortilla and dropped it on her plate.

She rolled her eyes. "Trust me, this baby is far from starving."

Eli went to town on his dinner; this was one of his favorites. Each ingredient was carefully separated on his plate without touching. Eli dug into the meat first, working his way clockwise around the plate with a spoon. Finger foods were not his favorite, but this way he could enjoy them. He didn't like the feeling of getting his hands dirty—even when fishing, he preferred to wear gloves.

After dinner, Nash cleaned up and did the dishes before he built a fire off the back porch. He carried a couple chairs down to the grass, a safe distance away from the flames.

"What can I do to help?" she asked.

"You can sit your pretty ass down and relax. I got this." Nash loaded a marshmallow onto a long bamboo stick.

"Well, okay, then." She took a seat, not needing to be told twice. Her feet were a little swollen and sore. Today would have been so much harder if it wasn't for the man sitting across from her.

Eli came out of the house, his sweatshirt zipped up and his hands in his pockets as he made his way to Nash.

Nash handed over the paper plate with all the fixings for a s'more to Eli. "Not sure if you like it all together or not?"

"No, I like it all separate. I got it." Eli went to work, preparing his confection while Nash did the same, making small talk about the art of roasting a marshmallow.

Isabella sat back in her chair, her hands staying warm as they wrapped around a mug of steaming tea. The bite of the chilly October air was staved off by the fire in front of her. A few dark storm clouds glowed in the sky, obscuring the moon. A smattering of stars broke through the nearly black heavens. A slight breeze blew, carrying the scent of dead leaves, pine, smoke from the fire, and a hint of rain. Orange and red flames reflected on her son and her . . . lover? Roommate with benefits? None of those seemed to fit Nash. She wasn't sure just what they were. He claimed to not be ready for a relationship and then he went and did such caring actions like he'd done today. He flirted. He said things to her that went beyond friendship. Things that made her wonder if he was ready for more—if there could be a future for them.

Nash walked over, his salty scent mixing with earth and fire, an elemental pull enticing her closer.

He handed over a s'more. "Here you go."

"Thank you." She smiled and licked her lips before taking a small bite. A few crumbs of Graham cracker fell onto her jacket. She brushed them away, chewing and swallowing before she looked to Nash, crouching before her. "It's perfect."

Eli had his back to them, bending over his plate of dessert at the small table Nash had dragged out. Nash turned back to her, blocking the light of the fire, eclipsing her in darkness, taking the warmth of the fire and replacing it with a heat of another kind. His warm tongue slipped along the corner of her mouth, sending a spiral of arousal twisting through her. He pressed a gentle kiss on her lips and pulled away, leaving her craving more.

Her chest rose and fell more rapidly as he backed away.

"You had a little marshmallow on your lip," he explained.

She blinked as he walked away, a faint smile etched on his face.

"Can we have the surprise now?" Eli asked, tossing his paper plate into the fire.

"Sure. Wait here." Nash disappeared returning to the house while she finished her dessert. He came out with two giant paper lightbulb-looking objects in his hands.

"What are they?" Eli asked.

Nash walked up to Isabella as Eli drew closer. "These are biodegradable paper lanterns. And this is a marker for you to write a message to your dad. We'll light them and the heat will make them rise into the sky and send your notes . . . well, up."

Dios, that is so thoughtful.

Nash shifted on his feet, as if he were feeling nervous. "You don't have to do it if you don't want to. I just thought . . ."

"That's cool." Eli grabbed the marker and went to work, using the light from the fire to write his message.

If Eli wasn't here, she would jump into Nash's arms and kiss him. Tears welled in her eyes. Nash had taken what was an extremely hard day for them and turned it into something memorable. Did he know just how much this meant to her? How could anyone not fall in love with this man? But could he love her back? Was that what he was telling her with how he'd taken care of her and her son today?

She choked up as she set her tea on the ground and stood. She interlaced her fingers with his. "Thank you."

Nash gave a curt nod. "It's not a big deal."

"Oh, it really is. And I think that's exactly why you did this. I'm so very grateful."

His gaze dropped to her lips. "I know what it's like to . . ."

To lose someone you love? To want to be close to them even after death?

"Have you done this . . . before?"

The light that had been in his eyes was snuffed out with her question, leaving only smoking grief swirling in their depths.

He stiffened and turned towards Eli. "Ready to light it, bud?"

"I think so."

Isabella stayed in place as Nash walked away. An invisible cord tugged her heart towards him. Somewhere along the way, she'd fallen for him. She was no longer approaching the cliff but plummeting off the edge. The question was, would he be there to catch her? Or would she crash?

45

NASH

Rain pelted the window beside the bed. Thankfully, it had held off until both lanterns had floated out of sight. Nash pressed a hand to his chest, shifting on the mattress, hoping to relieve some of the tightness that had been there all day. He'd known the anniversary was going to be tough for Bella and Eli, but it had also brought up a lot for him. He'd never been able to do that—let go—say goodbye for good, because his soul was still restless, not knowing what had happened to Ana. Logic told him she'd passed long ago. He'd kept hope for so long and been disappointed over and over; his heart had calcified. But lately, with Bella here, the fucker wanted to beat again. Could he move on? A part of him would always love Ana, but she was gone. And he'd carry that guilt forever. *I should have gone after her.* But she'd betrayed him.

He pulled in a deep breath, expelling the dark thoughts. Focusing back on his writing in the journal before him, he adjusted his glasses.

As I watched those lanterns floating up to the sky, I thought of you,

Ana. Of the weight of not knowing what happened to you. Are you out there living your life somewhere on the West Coast like you always talked about visiting? Or are you gone forever? I'll never know, will I? Maybe it's time I let you go. Stop writing to you. Leave your memories in peace. I have a baby on the way. A family I'm now responsible for. People I care about. They're relying on me. And I want to be what they need. But I feel so guilty as if I'm leaving you behind—

The floor outside his door creaked. Nash perked up. Should he go check on Bella? After they'd come in, she'd had a surprise of her own for her son. Apparently, Robert had left a series of videos for Eli to view on certain occasions. The first anniversary date of his death had been the first. Nash had left them alone, giving them privacy for their shared grief.

Knock. Knock.

He glanced at the clock—eleven thirty—and closed his book, shoving it in the bedside table, out of sight. "Come in."

Isabella walked in, shutting the door behind her. Her hair was slicked back, wet from her shower, her face, still a little puffy from crying, and her eyes, red. Everything inside him screamed to wrap her in his arms and do whatever he could to take the pain away.

Her plump lips quirked in a small smile. Some of the tension in his chest eased, replaced by an entirely different sensation—like he'd inhaled some of her radiance, had it lodged in his rib cage only to expand.

Bella stepped closer, her hands fisting the short pink nightdress. "Hey."

"Hey yourself." He set his glasses on the nightstand.

He moved over, making space for her beside him. She hadn't been in his bed since the night of the massage. Bella sat, her hand landing on his forearm.

"You okay?"

She nodded. "I am actually, because of you."

He focused on a loose thread on the comforter in his lap. He didn't deserve her gratitude. He'd just done what he could to ease her pain.

Her palm cupped his cheek, tipping his face towards hers. Two amber pools staring at him like he'd hung the fucking moon and crushed his self-doubt. The affection glowing from her overpowered the shadows of his guilt—wiping it away as if it had never existed. He'd do whatever he could to stay in her light, like she was the sun.

His hand pressed against hers, holding it in place as if he could actually keep her. Like this could be his life.

Her breathing hitched, her sweet, minty breath taking up the space between them as he leaned in. If he was a better man, he'd back away. End this before it got even more tangled. He'd do the right thing and leave her alone. A war raged inside him, his every muscle taut with tension. His self-restraint hung by a thread. Should he cross this line with her?

"Nash." His name fell from her lips in a warm whisper, deciding for him.

His lips crashed against hers, his hands fisting in her hair, tugging her closer. This felt so right. Like everything was exactly how it was supposed to be. His worries faded away, replaced by raging desire. Her light drowned out the darkness weighing him down. And he took from her like the greedy bastard he was, wanting more—everything she had to give.

He swallowed her small moan with his mouth, tugging her bottom lip, grazing his teeth over it. She raked her nails over his bare shoulders, like tiny daggers of pleasure urging him on.

"Tell me to stop," he warned her.

"More." She straddled his hips, grinding against his cock.

He groaned into her shoulder before sucking on her neck, his fingers inching the cotton fabric of her nightgown up.

She tipped her head back, exposing her neck to him. He bit her pulse point like the predator he was. She shuddered, a small gasp leaving her. Bella's body tensed around him, her thighs squeezing his.

"You like that?" he asked.

She nodded.

"Take this off. Let me see you."

She lifted the nightgown over her head. Her two full breasts bounced with the movement, his eyes drawn to the dark nipples. Leaning forward, he captured one in his mouth as he ran his thumb over the other.

"Nash!"

He pressed his hand over her mouth, locking in her screams. "Gotta be quiet. Can you be a good girl and not make a sound while I finger this pretty pussy and suck on these gorgeous tits?"

She nodded jerkily, her eyes rolling up.

Nash skimmed his hands over her thighs, squeezing as he gauged her reaction. Just how much pain could she handle? Enough to leave bruises of his prints? He dug his fingertips into her supple flesh. She whimpered, her eyes hazy with need as she bit her lip.

"You like a little pain, don't you, sweetness?"

"Yes."

"Gonna leave my marks all over you." He smoothed one hand down to the apex of her thighs, dragging two thick fingers through her slick lips and groaned. "Fuck, you're already so wet. No panties?"

She shook her head. "Not at bedtime."

"You're killing me." He pushed one finger inside her tight pussy. Fuck, she was so warm and slick. His cock throbbed under her, wanting a turn inside such sweet perfection.

Her back arched as she bit her bottom lip as if holding back her screams.

"Good girl." He cupped a breast, massaging it as he worked his finger in and out of her, curving it just so to hit that spongy spot inside. He added another, trying to memorize her pleasured expression. Long lashes fanned over half-closed whiskey eyes glazed in ecstasy.

Her cheeks were rosy, her lips swollen and shiny. Nipples peaked and pebbled. Goose bumps covered her arms and thighs, and her breath quickened with each thrust of his fingers.

"Please, Nash?"

"Please, what, baby? Tell me and I'll give it to you."

Her eyes flared, her pupils blown as dark as a whirlpool and just as powerful too. He was tumbling into their depths, lost to everything else but her.

"You. I want *you*." Her voice hitched with the weight of her request. Like she meant much more than his cock. Like she wanted to possess every piece of him that was left. She was like the sirens of old fishermen's stories—he was powerless to her.

Urgency roared. With his heart drumming against his chest, he slid his boxers down along with the blankets until his cock lined up with her pussy. She lowered herself on him, both of them groaning in unison. He gripped her hips, his fingers digging into her juicy ass as she bottomed out on his dick. His lips and tongue danced with hers as he held her in place, infusing everything he was into the kiss. He could give her himself—in this moment at least. She owned Nash, body and soul. His fucking heart flickered to life, powerless to her.

She gripped his shoulders as she rose on her knees, fucking him slowly. She was a fucking goddess, creator and nurturer of life. Her swollen belly brushed against his; her pussy squeezed around him.

"You're so beautiful. So fucking sexy, riding my cock like that. Taking what you need. That's it, sweetness. Use me."

Her whimpers increased as he guided her waist, slamming her down on him as he bucked his hips, meeting her thrust for thrust. Sweat beaded on his forehead as he did his best to hold back. One hand dropped between her thighs, his finger finding her clit with ease. She was so aroused. He swirled around the swollen nub, flicking it as she rose and fell. Tingling gathered at the base of his spine.

"I'm going to come," she moaned.

"Do it. Come all over my cock."

"Come with me," she pleaded.

Like he would refuse her anything. He drove his hips harder into her and pinched her clit. Her lips parted into an *0*, eyes widening as her cunt fluttered around him. His orgasm chased hers, roaring out of him. Nash's eyes locked on hers. His senses sharpened as time froze. Everything stopped, hanging in the balance as euphoria rammed into him and sent him spiraling into another plane of existence where nothing else existed except Bella and him, no longer bodies, but souls intertwined.

Soft lips captured his, drawing him back into his body as a glowing warmth radiated from his every cell. He kissed her back, cradling her face in his hands.

She slid off him and he tucked her against his side. Face-to-face, he stared at her, awed that this woman had given him this gift. That she chose to stay with him. Her lips curved into a tired, satisfied smile. Elation expanded in his chest, his ribs aching in the best of ways. Nash ran his thumb over her flushed cheeks. He'd do whatever it took to keep Bella, Eli, and their daughter safe. To take care of her.

She yawned and kissed his chest. "I'm so sleepy now."

God, she felt perfect against him like this. Too bad it had to end. "You should probably get back to your bed. Do you need me to carry you?"

She tipped her face to look at him. Vulnerability flashed in her gaze. "Or I could stay here?"

She wanted to sleep in his bed? Panic rose, contracting his airway. He had a choice to make. He could push her away and stay in his familiar solitary space with the guilt from his past mistakes. Or Nash could let her in and take the first step in moving on. His heart pounded like a war drum. For once, he would believe he deserved more. He wanted to be the man reflected in those golden-brown eyes that looked at him with so much hope and affection.

"It's okay. I didn't mean to push you." Bella sat up.

Nash gripped her arm, tugging her back down against him. She faced him, her gaze swimming with questions.

"Stay." His one whispered word held so much weight.

She slowly nodded. Her bottom lip slipped between her teeth before she snuggled against his chest.

Nash pulled the covers over them, making sure she was warm. He closed his eyes, reveling in her closeness. So much happiness swelled in his heart that it felt as if it had cracked open his chest. His eyes burned as her breathing evened out. He pressed his hand over her belly, growing their child. A thump against his palm caused the first tear to slip down his cheek.

"I'm falling in love with you. And it scares the shit out of me," he confessed in a whisper.

Bella didn't stir.

He kissed her temple and settled back into the pillow, adjusting her in his arms so he could hold her more securely. And, for the first time in forever, Nash was whole.

46

ISABELLA

A couple of weeks later, Isabella found herself covered in flour with dough stuck under her fingernails in Mama E's big kitchen. The smell of freshly baked pastry, apple, sweet potato, and pumpkin filled the warm air.

"That's the last one." Renita slid the pie into the oven.

Isabella wiped her forehead in the warm kitchen and took a drink of her ice water. "I can't believe you do this every week."

Dragging a cloth over the counter, Renita smiled. "It helps that I get orders ahead of time. I only bring about five extra."

"Still, fifteen pies this week, twenty last week. The holidays are right around the corner. I'm afraid to ask what those orders look like."

Renita walked over to the table, taking the seat opposite Isabella with a chuckle. "Oh, Lord, for that I usually enlist the assistance of a few more helpers. And I set a limit. Last year, it was a hundred apple, pumpkin, and sweet potato. I think we might do a little more this year—and that's just Thanksgiving."

"I'm exhausted simply thinking about it."

Renita patted her hand. "I appreciate your help, but you know you don't have to if it's too much."

Isabella waved her hand dismissively. "Oh, I'm just joking. It actually sounds like a lot of fun. Reminds me of holidays with my family. My *tías* and *tíos* and cousins would come over. We'd all pitch in and make tamales in my mother's tiny kitchen. The men would be sent out on some errand to keep them out of the house and my mother would break out her special tequila and make us all marguerites—virgin for those of us too young to indulge of course."

"It sounds like your family is close."

Isabella nodded. *We used to be.*

"I hope my son is making your life easier and not adding to the stress?" Renita sipped her coffee.

Isabella's heart fluttered. She couldn't contain her smile. "Nash has been wonderful. He's great with Eli." *And me.*

The morning after she'd stayed in his bed she'd woken early to sneak into her room before Eli woke, but Nash had pulled her back into his arms for a quick kiss before letting her go. Things had changed since last weekend. There was something new between them. He seemed more open.

"I think you moving in has been good for him. I worried for a long time that he wouldn't ever climb out of his grief."

He still hasn't, but he's getting there. Isabella wasn't going to say that out loud to his mother. She just nodded with a small smile.

Renita sighed knowingly. "I'm not sure how much my son has told you about Anastasia. And it isn't my place to say, but just know that Nash has been through a lot with that woman. And his previous relationships. He always seemed to attract users. I think it slowly chipped away at his self-esteem. And when everything happened with Ana, and she disappeared, the light in his eyes just went out."

"Losing someone you love is one of the hardest things to have to go through," Isabella said.

Renita's dark eyes reminded her of Nash's as she met her gaze. "Yes, it is. I thought we'd lost my boy for good. But lately, I've seen flickers of my son coming back to life—that spark he had for his future. And I think it's because of you."

Isabella closed her eyes and shook her head, holding back the tears. She couldn't help the bubble of hope that grew inside of her. "I think it just helps having someone who understands the pain of grief."

Renita patted her hand. "I wanted you to know I appreciate you being there for him, and I'm so grateful to have you as part of this family."

"I'm glad to be a part of it." Isabella took another sip of the cold water. Her head was starting to pound. She got to her feet. "I think I'm going to go lie down for a little while."

"Of course. Thanks for your help."

Isabella took her glass to the sink before she left the Emersons' home, walking down a worn path leading to Nash's. She carried her jacket on her arm, needing the chilly air after being in such a hot kitchen for hours. The sun shone. A few white puffs of clouds stuck out in the blue sky. The trees swayed in the light breeze, carrying the scent of dead leaves and burning firewood—no doubt from Mama Emerson's home nearby. Today was beautiful. Maybe she'd nap on the porch with some warm blankets.

Isabella approached the mailbox at the end of Nash's driveway. She pulled out the contents before heading into the house.

Her phone rang in her pocket. She pulled it out; Tessa's name flashed on the screen. "Hello, beautiful."

"Oh, someone is in a good mood. Tell me, does a certain fisherman have anything to do with it?" Tessa teased.

Isabella rolled her eyes as she approached the door, opened it, and walked in. She closed it behind her and set the mail on the table.

"He might." She went up the stairs.

"Tell me, does he have a decent rod?"

"You are terrible."

Tessa giggled. "Oh, come on, let me have my fun."

"Did you just call to harass me?" Isabella went into the bathroom and turned the shower on, letting the water warm up. A shower to wash the sweat off and cool her down might help with the headache too.

"Just checking in. I miss your beautiful face. And Eli. How's he doing?"

"Good. He's disappointed we're going to have to wrap his boat and put it in storage so soon after buying it. But there isn't one inch of that thing he hasn't cleaned or worked on. I'm glad he loves it so much."

Tessa sighed. "Boys and their boats. Tell me, do you let Nash park his in your dock?"

"Tessa, I swear—"

"Oh, come on. Give me some details, please?"

"All you're getting is I'm happy. Isn't that enough?" Isabella asked.

"Yes. That's more than enough. That's all I want for you, babe."

"I know. I love you."

"Me too."

"Talk to you later."

"Bye."

Isabella ended the call, slipping the phone into her pocket before she rubbed her temples. Her head throbbed now.

Steam rose from the shower. She just needed to get in, and hopefully she'd come out a little refreshed.

A noise sounded, like the slamming of a door. She shut the water off and walked out of the bathroom.

"I don't fucking need to hear it, Roman!" Nash growled.

"You should get that looked at. I think you need stitches," his brother argued.

Nash was hurt? She walked down the stairs, cradling her belly with each step and trying not to wince. Her hips and lower back ached the closer she got to the last trimester. *I don't remember the discomfort starting this early with Eli.*

"I said I'm fine. Just leave me alone."

"What happened?" Isabella asked, rounding the corner into the kitchen.

Nash held his hand under the sink. He turned the faucet on and flinched. "Nothing."

"My idiot brother cut his hand on a saw blade and is being a stubborn asshole, as usual. See if you can talk some sense into him." Roman shook his head, clearly frustrated.

Isabella walked over, gasping at the bloodred water filling the sink. She grabbed a few paper towels, folding them together as she reached for his hand.

He shut the sink off with his other arm as she pressed the makeshift bandage to the cut to stop the bleeding. "I'm fine."

"You're dripping blood," she argued.

"It's not big—just deep."

She pulled the paper towels away and peeked at his injury. The blood was already slowing. A gash about an inch and a half across sliced through the meat of his hand. She squeezed the bandage back on it.

Nash grimaced.

"Roman is right. You need stitches."

"No."

"Nash—"

"I said no," he snapped. Nash pulled his hand away from her, taking the bandage with him and holding it in place himself. He sighed and looked at her. "I'm sorry. I just don't want to go to the hospital for a scratch."

She crossed her arms over her chest. "It's a little more than a scratch."

"I've had worse. It'll be fine." He pulled a seat out from the table and sat, pushing around the pile of mail.

"I'm calling Ma," Roman said.

"What are you, fucking twelve?" Nash grumbled. "Don't you dare. I'm a grown man. I'll use some super glue and be good as new in a few days."

"At least clean it out with something first so you don't trap infection in." Roman opened the cupboard under the sink and pulled out a first-aid kit.

Isabella took the kit from Roman and got to work cleaning the wound. Nash hissed as she poured alcohol over it.

"Well, you could be numbed up if you went to the ER," Roman not-so-helpfully said.

Nash glared at him.

Isabella finished sealing the wound. Nash picked up an envelope as Roman returned the first-aid kit under the sink.

"You can go rest; you look a little tired. I can take care of him," Roman said.

"I'm right here, you know. You don't have to talk about me like I'm a child. And I can take care of myself." Nash ripped open one of the letters.

Roman walked around the table to face his brother. "You don't have to be an asshole. We only care about you—Nash? What's wrong? What is it?"

Isabella's attention snapped towards Nash. His eyes blazed with a mix of panic and grief. The hair on the back of her neck stood on end as he held a diamond ring in his trembling hand.

"What the fuck is that?" Roman asked, moving behind his brother and leaning in towards the letter.

"Nash?" Isabella whispered, afraid of the manic energy pulsing in the room. She could taste his fear; it was coming off him in such thick waves.

"How did this letter get here?" Nash's voice was cold as ice, his eyes not moving from the ring in his hand.

"How?!" he yelled.

She flinched. "Th-the mailbox. I got it on my way in."

"Holy shit. I'm calling the sheriff." Roman finished reading the letter and pulled out his phone before stepping into the other room.

"What's going on, Nash? You're scaring me." Her heart raced, a million scenarios spiraling through her mind.

Nash bolted upright so fast the chair turned over before he raced out the door. The four-wheeler engine roared a moment later, and then he was off.

Roman walked back into the room, his face ashen like he'd seen a ghost.

"What's going on? Where did Nash go?"

Roman's mouth opened and closed. He shook his head as if in disbelief. "To get Anastasia."

47

NASH

Nash gunned the gas as the four-wheeler climbed the path towards the clearing that he'd visited countless times. As soon as he reached the meadow, he forced himself to slow down enough to pull out the letter and map.

Nash,

I think it's about time you got some answers. You see, I know what it is like to be a casualty to these women. Anastasia is just the first. But she won't be the last.

It's time for you two to be reunited. So, follow my map and you'll find her in the grove where she took me five years ago to tell me all about what happened between you two. Only I know the truth.

I can't say I've ever felt sorry for someone before—it's just not an emotion I am capable of. But if I could be, I'd like to think it would be for you. For putting up with a lying, cheating, manipulator like Anastasia. She would have bled you dry like she did so many others before you.

She took something important from me that I couldn't get back. So I took her life for ruining mine.

And now, it's time to finish this.

The slashes across the paper tore his chest to ribbons as his mind continued to spin. Ana had been targeted by some psycho. He cut the engine and jumped off his ATV, grabbing the shovel tied to the back with one hand and scrutinizing the map with the other.

A symbol carved into the tree matched the one on the map. A line drawn in a circle. Below it was a pile of rocks covered in lichen and moss. He ripped them up one at a time, tossing them to the side until he reached bare earth. Worms and beetles scattered as he folded the letter and put it in his pocket. Nash heaved the shovel down, putting all his weight on it as his heartbeat drummed in his ears, making them ring.

Ana couldn't have been here the whole time. No. It's not possible. This is some sick joke.

Sweat poured down his forehead, mixing with dirt and grime. He didn't stop. He kept digging. Part of him begged the universe for her not to be there. But his exhausted soul just wanted answers.

A piece of dark fabric caught his eye as his vision darkened. His lungs refused to work, turning to solid stone.

No. Nonononono. It's not real.

He fell to his knees, gripping handfuls of cold dirt. The smell of musty, wet earth was stifling as he cleared it away. The pattern on the material was the final blow. As dark and mud-stained as it was, he could just make out the navy-blue flowers of the dress Ana had been wearing the night she disappeared.

A tortured sound scraped from his throat, pulled from the depths of his soul.

The events of that night flashing through his mind like a nightmare.

A line of shot glasses lined up in front of Ana. Her sweet perfume was tinged with something more masculine. It wasn't the first time. But when he confronted her about it, she'd blamed him of being a jealous asshole.

"I was thinking we could have the wedding at this place I found in Vermont. It's called The Orchard Inn. The pictures are nice. Maybe we can take a trip there next weekend when I get back from my trip to California and scout it out? Get away from everything for a weekend," Nash suggested, pulling the label from his beer.

Music from the live band made it hard to hear her response, so he leaned in.

"What's that?"

Finally, she looked at him. Her blue eyes were guarded as usual. "I don't think so. We're busy at work. I can't take more time off."

"We could just do an overnight. Saturday to Sunday."

"Why are you pushing this?" she snapped.

His brows furrowed. "Why are you avoiding it? Whenever I bring up the wedding or plans for the house, you shut me out or change the subject. What's going on, babe?"

Sadness seeped into her gaze seeming so bone-deep it caught him off guard. She blinked, and a moment later, the mask of indifference was back on her face. "Nothing. I'm just tired." She took one of the shots and then downed another without a chaser. The movement caused her hair to slip over her shoulder, revealing a hickey that he sure as hell hadn't put there.

"What the fuck is this?" he growled, pressing his finger to the offending mark.

Her eyes widened, panic flashing in them before her gaze averted to Charli, the bartender at the Shipwreck. She waved her down. "Another shot, please."

"Ana—"

"It's nothing."

"It's a fucking hickey."

"It's from you."

He leaned in, anger lighting his veins. He'd suspected for so long but never had proof until now. "Don't fucking lie to me. I think I'd know if I marked you."

She sighed and downed another shot. "Don't do this. Don't be the jealous asshole looking for ways to get mad at me. If you don't trust me, then maybe we shouldn't be getting married."

He gripped her arm, just firmly enough to make her look at him. He'd never hurt her. "I love you. I want to spend the rest of my life with you."

She laughed, shaking her head. "You don't even know me."

The liquor seemed to loosen her lips. It was rare she got this open with him. "What do you mean? Tell me. I want to know it all. I've begged you for years to show me every piece of you."

She scoffed. "You want this big house with five kids and the perfect family. You want monogamy and marriage."

He nodded. What was so wrong with that?

"I don't want that. I can't be with someone like you."

Her words hit him like a sledgehammer. "There's someone else?"

"Sometimes I need something . . . more," she admitted.

"And I'm not enough for you."

"You're a good man—too good, Nash. Someone like you doesn't belong with someone like me."

"What the fuck does that even mean?" he snarled, drawing the looks of the bartender and a few others around them.

Tears tracked down her face. She shook her head. "Nothing. Forget I said anything. It's just the liquor talking. I'm sure we can get through this. I can do this," she said as if trying to convince herself.

"Get through cheating on me?"

"You said you loved me." Tears welled in her eyes.

"And you said I wasn't enough."

Ana grabbed her purse and ran out of the bar. Nash turned back to his beer, his mind reeling as her words settled into his gut like lead.

This was the part in their arguments where he'd usually run after her. But not this time. This time, his heart was breaking into a million pieces.

He was tired of her games. There was no fixing this. Because he hadn't been enough for his last two girlfriends and he wasn't for Ana. Maybe it was time he gave up.

His phone buzzed in his pocket. A text from Ana.

Ana: *I'm sorry.*

Ana: *Please don't hate me.*

Ana: *You said you loved me. If you do, then you'll forgive me.*

Ana: *Meet me somewhere we can talk. Please?*

Nash swiped to reply.

Nash: *No. Nova's picking me up in a few minutes to go to the airport. I can't bail on her. She planned this conference trip months ago. I'll be back next weekend. Seems we both have some things to think about until then.*

He tucked the phone back in his pocket. If he wasn't enough for her now, he'd never be.

Nash pulled on his hair, pain pricking his skull. He deserved it. "I should have gone after her."

"Nash?" A solid hand landed on his shoulder, making him jerk.

His father frowned at him in worry. Roman and Sheriff Bently stood by his side.

"What the fuck are you doing, disturbing a possible crime scene?" Bently demanded.

"She's here," Nash confessed, his voice as hollow as he felt.

Bently moved around him, scanning the area. "I've got my deputy and a team coming with forensics. You really should have waited, Nash. This won't look good."

"You don't mean he's a suspect, do you?" his father asked.

"He's got an alibi," Roman argued. "He wasn't even in the state when she went missing."

Fuck. He was going to drag his family through this again. What if they lost contracts a second time around? The town gossips would have a field day with this. Oh, God, Bella and Eli. Shit. They were going to get tangled up in his mess.

"I know. Which is why he's not in cuffs right now. But this doesn't look good. The woman you were engaged to, who went missing, ends up found on your property. It means everything will be given another look," Bently explained.

"You gonna arrest me?" Nash asked.

"Did you do this to her?" Bently didn't mince words.

Rage burned so hot it clouded Nash's vision. "Of course not!"

"I'll probably need to question you again, but unless new evidence comes forward, there is no reason for me to suspect you on account of your alibi."

"Give him the letter, Nash," Roman urged him.

Nash dug into his pocket numbly, lifting the ring and the letter out. Bently pulled a glove from his pocket and slipped it on before taking a look. "Who else touched this?"

"Just me," Nash answered.

"Look, I know this is hard, but you gotta let me do my job so I can find out who did this to her, okay?"

Nash turned to the shallow hole he'd dug. He'd searched for years and Ana had been here all along. He'd wanted answers, believing that was the key to his torture. But he was even more lost than he'd been before.

Bently stepped forward. "I know it doesn't feel like it, but this will be a good thing. It will give us a wealth of new evidence, and we can figure out what sick fucker did this."

"She was here the whole time." Nash scanned the area. He'd brought Bella up here for a goddamned picnic. His house was visible from this view now that the trees had lost their leaves. Ana had been so close and yet so far.

Pain slashed at his chest. He barreled over from the force

of his emotions. Regret and grief. Guilt and anger. All of it slammed into him like an avalanche of boulders. He sucked in a jagged breath and shut it all out, detaching from everything and sinking into the numbness where only icy-cold darkness existed.

48

ISABELLA

Isabella stared at the stars above. Her breath came out in white puffs as she shivered. The creak of the trees and occasional hoot of an owl were the only other sounds out here as she sat on the front porch.

She checked her watch for what felt like the millionth time; it was after midnight and Nash still wasn't home . . . again. Ever since they'd discovered the remains on the property, Nash had shut everyone out. He'd turned into this version of himself that was barely recognizable. He didn't come near her or speak much at all. He only responded to Eli, but even that was only when Eli approached him.

Nash was a shell. She wanted to help him—if he'd only let her in. She'd been terrified the sheriff was going to arrest him, but thankfully, the Emersons were far more open than Nash and filled her in on the facts of the case, confirming that Nash was not a suspect.

Isabella placed a hand on her belly. "Where is your daddy? I wish he would let me be there for him."

The crack of a broken twig had her attention darting to

the side of the property and the woods that bordered it. Nash stumbled toward her along the same path he'd used every day since the discovery close to two weeks ago. The trail that led to where they'd found *her*.

"Nash?"

The crash of glass breaking had her darting to her feet and stepping through the dusting of snow covering the ground.

Nash walked unsteadily, swaying, cloaked in whiskey fumes that burned her nose up close. His eyes were bloodshot in the porch light. She reached out to help him into the house but he flinched away, stumbling onto his ass.

"Nash!"

"Leave me alone," he grumbled. "Don't want to get my filth on you."

She ignored him and slipped her hand in his. His skin was cold as ice.

She tugged but he pulled away like he'd been doing for days, rolling onto all fours and miraculously getting up on his own.

"Why are you doing this to yourself?"

He glared at her.

"Don't do this. *Please.*"

So much sadness and turmoil were reflected in his expression. Isabella backed up from the force of it. He turned away and walked up the porch.

Maybe he needed something to look forward to. Something to remind him that he had a brighter future despite all the ugly past that had been stirred up.

"We have an appointment tomorrow at two for the baby."

He didn't even slow, just walked in the front door, holding it open for her. "It's not safe to be out here alone."

They were the most words he'd spoken to her in so long.

Despite being lost in his grief, he still worried about her. But she couldn't help wondering if it was because he truly cared, or if it was from a sense of responsibility.

She wrapped her arms around herself and walked inside. He locked the door and disappeared into the kitchen. The clank of glass made it clear he was going to drink himself to sleep tonight once again.

Isabella didn't fight the tears as they streamed down her face. She walked up the stairs and crawled into her bed where she curled around her pillow and sobbed quietly, more alone than ever before.

She wanted to be there to support Nash. But you couldn't help someone who didn't want it, no matter how much you loved them. He wouldn't let her in. And she couldn't stand to be rejected night after night. She loved him with everything inside her, but it was unrequited. How had she gotten back where she started? Her life was coming full circle, repeating the same cycle. She'd fallen pregnant and fell for a man who couldn't love her back.

It was time she got off this merry-go-round once and for all.

* * *

The next afternoon, Isabella stared at the door, her hope extinguishing with every minute that Nash didn't step through it. He'd known about this appointment since they'd set it a month ago. It was on his phone calendar and the one on the wall in the kitchen. She'd left a sticky-note reminder on the coffee pot this morning. But Nash was a no-show.

"I'm a little concerned with your blood pressure, so we'll keep an eye on that. I'd like you to come in again in three days for a non-stress test just to be safe," Dr. Wright said.

Isabella pulled her attention to the doctor. "Is something wrong with the baby?"

The doctor's warm smile helped set her at ease. "No, nothing to be concerned about on that front. I'm more worried about you. Have you been under a lot of stress lately?"

She nodded hesitantly.

"It could be that. But I want to monitor you just in case. Especially with your medical history, it's better to be on the safe side."

"I appreciate that."

"Great. I'll walk you out, and you can schedule it with the front desk." Dr. Wright stood.

Isabella followed him out and made another appointment before heading to her car. Climbing in, she started the ignition and sat there. One more sweep of the parking lot told her all she needed to know. Nash was a no-show.

She backed up, pulling out of the parking lot onto the main road. Isabella's phone rang.

Was it Nash? Had something happened and that was why he couldn't be here?

She clicked the button to answer.

"Hello?" Tessa's voice greeted her on speaker.

Oh, not Nash. Disappointment settled in her chest, morphing into heartbreak. "Hey."

"What's wrong, sweetheart?"

Isabella's breath came out in a rush. "Why would you think something's wrong?"

"Because I know you, and your voice hitches when you're crying. Is it Nash? I swear I'll cut his balls off if he's hurt you."

"He hasn't done anything . . ." *That's the problem. He barely speaks to me.* She let out a defeated sigh, shoulders slumping as she turned into town. "I'm having an emotional day is all.

Nash is much the same as he has been since they discovered Anastasia's remains—he's pulled away emotionally. And he avoids us like the plague. He won't let me in."

"Oh, love, I'm sorry. Do they know for sure it's her?"

"The report isn't back, or at least that's what Bently said. But based on what she was wearing the night she disappeared and the letter from the killer, they are assuming it is."

"Oh, God. I can't imagine how awful that must be for him to relive."

"Yeah. I know. I'm trying to be understanding, but it's like he's just checked out. He's drunk whenever I manage to see him or well on his way to it. He spends all day and most of the night up on that hill. He missed our appointment today after I reminded him—" Isabella wiped the tears away and made another turn, a small blue car pulling out right behind her.

"I get that he's going through a hard time, but it's been two weeks and he seems to be slipping further away. He's not getting any better?" Tessa asked.

"No. I'm worried about him. But I don't want to burden you with my problems when you're supposed to be having fun in Ireland with your man."

"That's a tough situation to be in. And you're never a burden. I love you and always have your back," Tessa assured her. "So go ahead and lay it on me."

"Thank you." Isabella swallowed the emotion that rose in her throat. "I thought we were getting somewhere. I thought we had something . . . and then it all fell apart. I know it's selfish of me, but I'm jealous of a ghost."

"I don't think it's selfish to want love returned from a man who's become such a big part of your life. Is he willing to see someone? Maybe get some help navigating through his grief?" Tessa asked.

"No." Isabella sniffed. "I brought it up last week and he

stormed out of the house. I didn't see him again until the following night. His family have all tried to pull him out of this, but he's shut us all out. I'm afraid he's spiraling."

"Babe, that's it. I'm getting on a plane. I need to be there to hug you in person."

"No, Tessa. You're not leaving Ireland when you're supposed to be meeting Roy's family. I'll be fine. I promise. I just . . . I'd hoped the baby would be enough to pull him out of this. But he didn't show." Her voice broke.

"I think you know from experience that babies never solve the root of the problem. In fact, they can complicate things further," Tessa said, carefully.

"I don't mean she was going to magically heal him or make him fall in love with me. I just meant, I hoped that giving him something to look forward to would help pull him out of this dark place."

"The only one who can do that is him, sweetheart." Tessa's voice was full of sympathy.

"I know. I just don't know what to do. I can't keep going like this. But if he needs help—"

"Then he can ask for it. His family will be there for him. He has a whole bunch of people who care about him from what you've told me. It's not your job to save him."

Isabella nodded even though her friend couldn't see as she swallowed more tears. "Tessa? Is there something wrong with me that makes me so unlovable?"

"No. Don't you think that for one second, Bella! You are a smart, and sassy, gorgeous woman with a brilliant mind. You're the best mother and an amazing partner who bends over backwards for the men in her life—maybe too much sometimes."

The corners of Isabella's mouth turned up. Tessa always gave her the truth.

"Someday you'll find your Roy. I know I didn't believe that there were good men out there before him, especially ones who could truly love a woman like me . . . but—"

"But he worships the ground you walk on." Isabella chuckled, speeding up on the main road.

"He kinda does. What I'm trying to say is, I know there is someone out there for you too. If you want that, I mean, which you've said you do. So, just . . . don't settle. You deserve a man who will accept you as you are and love every part. Someone who's willing to be vulnerable and share their life, scars and all," Tessa said.

"You're right. And I won't settle. It's just hard because Nash is an amazing man. He doesn't let a lot of people in to see it, but he has this whole other side to him. He's kind and caring and so thoughtful. He treats me like I'm . . . like I'm special to him."

"But then he doesn't commit to you. He doesn't open up emotionally," Tessa argued, a voice of reason.

"Yeah. And his family keeps telling me he seems different with me, like he could care about me, and I want to believe it so much that maybe I'm just seeing things that aren't really there."

"Has he led you on to believe he could want more?"

"No. He's been very clear where we stand with his words. It's his actions that have me confused."

"What does your heart tell you?" her friend asked.

"That despite everything, I love him." Her voice hitched, emotion welling in her throat. "I didn't mean for it to happen. But it did. And now I'm right back where I started, like I was with Robert."

"My heart is breaking for you, babe. What does your brain tell you?"

"That this isn't going to work. That I'm setting myself up

for disaster. But I still have this small flicker of hope. Like if I just hold on a little longer and give him space and patience, he can get there."

"Oh, sweetheart. You shouldn't have to convince someone to love you. Either they do or they don't. And if this guy is too scared to be vulnerable with you, he isn't worth it. Real love isn't conditional. It's not based on a perfect set of circumstances. If he can't love you back today, he doesn't deserve you tomorrow."

"I hear you." It didn't make her heart any less tangled or her chest ache any less. But the support of her friend meant everything to her.

"I can come and visit. Just say the word and I'll be on a plane if you need me."

"I appreciate it, Tessa. I'm just . . . I need to really think this through and make some decisions."

"I love you."

"Me too."

The line cut and Isabella flicked a glance in her rearview mirror. The same blue car was riding her ass. She was going as fast as she dared on the slick roads. Maybe she should pull over and let them pass. She put on her blinker and slowed, maneuvering towards the side of the road. The car behind her didn't reduce its speed though.

She didn't have time to scream as the car jolted and a flash of blue zoomed by. Her car fishtailed and spun. She instinctively hit the brakes, which only made things worse as she coasted over black ice. The crash of glass and creak of metal boomed in her ears. The world spun as the car veered off the road out of her control, heading for a ditch.

Her son's face flashed through her mind before everything went black.

49

NASH

Nash's fingers were numb from the cold, but he didn't do anything to warm them. He sat on the frozen stone, his pants damp with snow as he stared towards the tree line where they'd discovered Ana's body.

He lifted the bottle of whiskey to his mouth and drank another mouthful. It didn't even burn going down anymore. His thumb brushed against the clear bottle, the amber liquid reminding him of Bella's eyes, so full of hurt last night.

She was better off without him. Everyone was. If it wasn't for the baby, he might just leave. Go out on his boat and never look back. Get as far away from his pain as he could. Maybe then he could outrun this guilt over not being there when Ana needed him most. If he'd agreed to meet with her, she might still be alive.

The hum of an engine cut through his thoughts as another four-wheeler broke through the trees from the trail, his father driving. Nash stiffened and set the whiskey down beside him. His dad parked nearby and climbed off. Nash's skin prickled under his scrutiny before his father approached and sat on the snow-covered stone beside him. They both stared out at the view in silence as minutes passed. Fat snowflakes drifted down from the grey overcast sky.

"She wouldn't want you to blame yourself."

Nash scoffed. "It's my fault she's fucking dead."

"That's not true—"

"It is!" Nash bolted to his feet, facing his father. Chest heaving, he confessed what he'd held in for so long. "I found out she'd been cheating on me. And I blew up at her. She left because of me—because I wasn't enough."

"Bullshit."

"That's what happened! And then she texted me to meet her and talk. And I said no. If I had met her, she'd still be alive! It's my fault. I wasn't there to protect her." Nash's voice broke as he sunk to his knees, the cold, frozen earth biting harshly through his thin denim pants.

His father walked over, his feet crunching the snow until he was right by Nash. A warm arm wrapped around Nash's shoulders, pulling him against his father's chest.

"You've always been enough, son. Those women you were with, Ana included, took advantage of your kind heart."

Nash shook his head.

"Yes. You can pretend all you like that you're some emotionless bear, but your ma and I know the truth. You're the same sensitive kid who nursed a half-dead kitten back to life after the barn cat wouldn't tend to the runt of her litter. You're the same boy who worked all summer to buy your high school girlfriend a plane ticket to Greece so she could visit her dream destination only to find out she was seeing a college guy—and you still gave her the tickets. You're the man who fell in love with a woman who wasn't capable of loving you back because she hadn't learned yet how to love herself."

Tears dripped down Nash's cheeks, landing on his father's Carhartt jacket.

"Ana, God love her, was a mess. It's a horrible tragedy, what happened to her. But it wasn't anyone's fault except the person who took her life."

"She asked me to meet her—"

"The note that was left made it clear this was personal. The sick fucker who did this would have waited for another opportunity. You couldn't be with her twenty-four/seven," his dad argued.

Nash's chest ached, his shoulders tense. "All this time I swore I couldn't let her go because I didn't know where she was. I know it's next to impossible, but I held out hope that maybe she'd just left me and was living it up somewhere else."

His dad patted his back and pulled away enough to look him in the eyes. "You were afraid to let go because you didn't want to get hurt again. You've had shit luck when it comes to women."

"I loved Ana . . . I mean, I thought I did. But what I felt for her doesn't feel like what I feel for . . ."

"For Isabella?"

Nash nodded. "I don't know, Dad. Everything is so mixed up in my head right now. I can't help feeling like what happened to Ana is my fault. I'd wanted answers for five fucking years and now I have them . . . I feel even more hopeless than before."

"You've just gotta take it one day at a time, son. Start by quitting the drinking and shutting out the people who love you."

Nash swallowed, his eye sockets dry and burning from all the tears he'd cried in the last few weeks. "I can't let her go."

"Why?"

"Because I'm all she had."

His father sighed. "Son, I don't know why someone would do this—we might never know. What I do know is you've been stuck, living like you're the one in the ground. But you've got a daughter on the way, and a good woman who cares a lot more than you realize, and her boy who looks up to you. And if you don't stop beating yourself up for things you can't control or change, you're gonna lose the best thing that's ever happened to you."

Nash took a breath while his father's words sunk in, the truth of them settling into his bones. "I let her down."

"Ana let you down too."

"No, not her. Bella."

"It's not too late for you to do something about it."

"What if it is? I've been a mess since we found Ana. I tried to push her away so she wouldn't get pulled into my shit and get hurt, but, fuck." Bella's pain-filled expression from last night flashed in his mind. He ran a palm over his beard and sighed. "I hurt her because I was too much of a coward to face her."

"If anyone understands the loss of someone they love, it's her . . . and Roman or even Nova. You're not alone in this. And it's time you pulled your head out of your ass and saw that. I didn't raise my son to be a coward. Nor for you to be a martyr. What's done is done. You're still alive. And you can move forward. You have a real chance at happiness and a family with Bella. You say you have feelings for her? Well, it's high time you did something about it."

His father's phone rang as Nash reeled. He'd been so concerned with how this affected him that he hadn't once thought of how his family must have felt about him withdrawing.

"Hello? . . . Yes, he's here with me. What—" Panic flashed in his dad's eyes as he looked at his son.

Nash's guts twisted. What now?

"Is she okay? . . . And the baby?"

Nash shot to his feet.

"We'll be right there." His dad hung up.

"What happened? Are they okay?" Nash held his breath, pleading with the universe that it wasn't too late to make this right.

"Isabella was in an accident on her way home from the appointment."

I was supposed to be there with her! He ran his hand through his hair and tugged hard, needing the bite of pain to stay grounded.

His father held up his hands. "She's okay. The baby is fine. She's just got a couple bumps and bruises. She went to the hospital and got cleared. She's at home."

"I need to go." Nash ran to his ATV.

"Nash!"

"What?"

"She said someone hit her—"

"Someone intentionally hit her car? Was she followed? Fuck!" The blood drained from Nash's face as he started the engine and raced off without a backwards glance to his dad.

He sped down the trail, his heart racing as he zoomed next to his house. He cut the engine before he hopped off and burst through the door.

Catherine Noveas was seated at his table with Eli. They both looked up at his abrupt entrance.

"Where's Bella?"

Catherine scowled and got to her feet. "None of this would have happened if it wasn't for you—"

Nash ducked out of the kitchen, scanning the house for any sign of Bella. He took the stairs two at a time until he reached her room. His shoulders relaxed the moment she came into view. She folded a shirt over her belly and set it in a pile before reaching for another.

"Bella!" He wrapped his arms around her, tugging her against his chest, careful not to hold her too tight in case she was in pain. "Fuck, sweetness, I was so worried when my dad got the call. Are you okay?" He kissed her forehead and pulled her away enough to look her over for injuries. There was slight bruising by her neck in a line that suggested it was from the seat belt. A small cut on her cheek was a stark contrast to her smooth skin. But her eyes, usually so full of warmth and light, were dull and hollow.

"Baby? Where are you hurt?"

"I'm fine." Her tone was even, cold. Her body stiffened in his hold as she pulled away.

"I'm so sorry I missed the appointment."

She shrugged and picked up a pile of folded clothes before placing them in an open suitcase on the bed. "It's fine."

"No, it's not. I should have been there. I let you down."

"I'm spending the night at my parents'. I'll be back for our stuff at some point. My mom knows someone who has a duplex for rent in town. I think that might be for the best."

"What?" His ears rang as her words hit him like a battering ram. "You can't go. It's not safe for you to be alone."

"I'm alone here too!" Her chest heaved.

The pain in her gaze sliced him into ribbons. He'd caused this.

"So I don't think it really matters where I am." She shoved a sweatshirt into the bag and zipped it up.

Nash pressed his hand over hers to stop her. "Baby, please. You can't go." *I can't lose you too.*

"I need some space, Nash . . . and it's obvious you do too." She tugged the suitcase, but he held it in place. Panic bound his chest. Fear soaked his cells. If she walked out that door, that sick fuck could get to her too. What if it was someone close to Nash? What if Bella was next? Was that who'd run her off the road?

"I can keep you safe. Please, just stay here."

"Let me go, Nash."

"Someone was after you. Dad said someone followed you and hit your car."

She sighed as if she carried the weight of the world on her shoulders. Tears shone in her eyes. Bella swallowed and looked up to him. "No one followed me. They just rode my ass and then clipped me and I hit a patch of black ice. They probably left so they didn't get caught."

"I can't take any chances with you and our baby." He placed a gentle hand on her belly.

"You know, I kept waiting for you to show up today at the appointment. You haven't missed one. And after I was in the accident, I tried to call you. Over and over. But I kept getting your voicemail."

"I didn't have my phone on me—a stupid mistake on my part." He'd been so consumed with running away from everything.

"I think it's better if we take some time apart."

No. She couldn't leave him. She would be out there, unprotected. If she stayed here, he could be with her or make sure someone else was. If she left—anything could happen.

"Marry me."

She gasped. "What?"

He cupped her face in his hands, her sweet scent wrapping around him, easing some of the ache in his chest. "Marry me. I can protect you. I swear I won't let anything else happen to you or Eli or this baby. Just marry me and stay."

"Why?" She searched his eyes as if looking for something specific.

His brows drew together. He hadn't expected that question. "Why . . . because I have to keep you safe. I can't lose you and the baby—or Eli."

"You have to?"

"Yes! I can take care of you. Protect you, provide everything you need." *Let me give you everything.*

Fat tears dripped down her cheeks over his fingers, soaking into his skin as the last bit of hope sparking in her eyes was snuffed out. "I can't believe you'd ask me that. I told you about Robert—about what it did to me. I'll never be in that situation again." She shook her head and straightened, leveling him with a glare that made him realize he'd royally fucked up somehow. "I won't be your wife because I'm having your baby. I won't marry someone incapable of loving me back. I deserve better." Her voice broke with a sob.

He reached out to hold her, but she held up her hand and backed up. "No. Don't make this harder than it has to be. Just . . . I'll let you know when the next appointment is. You can come or not. It's up to you."

She pulled the suitcase but he stopped her, picking it up himself and carrying it wordlessly out of the room and down the stairs on leaden feet while his heart shattered into a million pieces.

Her mother took it from him and wheeled it out to her waiting car. Eli hiked a bag over his shoulder, head down and shoulders slumped.

Nash walked over, barely holding it together himself, and placed his hand on the boy's shoulder. "Hey, bud. You have everything?"

Eli nodded.

"You need me, you call me, okay? Anything at all. And I'll see you soon."

"Let's go, Eli," his grandmother called, glaring at Nash.

Eli followed his grandmother obediently. Bella unplugged a charger from the kitchen wall and walked past him.

Nash reached out, tangling his fingers with hers. "This is what you really want?"

Her gaze was filled with so much pain and sorrow, Nash stumbled back a step.

"What I want doesn't matter—it never does." She turned and left, closing the door behind her. The quiet click was just as powerful as if she'd slammed it.

Nash fell to his knees, his face in his hands. The most heartbreaking pain and devastation slammed into him as the woman he'd fallen in love with left him for good.

50

NASH

"God damn, he stinks." Nova's voice grated on Nash's nerves. His skull throbbed. Why was she in his bedroom?

"I'd get the hose if the water wasn't frozen," Ricky's obnoxious self was quick to offer. He's here too?

"I don't think waking him up like that will make him any more receptive, guys," Roman admonished, always the voice of reason. Why were his siblings in his bedroom?

"You should have brought Ariel. He couldn't attempt to murder us that way." Nova again.

"Why the fuck are you three in my bedroom at the fucking butt-crack of dawn? Don't you have better things to do?" Nash growled, sitting up and rubbing his eyes.

"Oh, God! I can smell your morning breath from here. That may be why Bella left." Ricky snickered.

Rage boiled in Nash's veins as he jumped out of bed, hands fisted. Nova and Roman jumped between him and Ricky.

"Whoa, calm down, asshole. It was just a joke . . . well, except your breath really does stink," Ricky said.

"And it's noon, by the way," Nova added.

"Just calm down." Roman patted his stiff shoulder.

Nash ran both hands over his eyes, attempting to rub the remaining sleepiness away. "I was calm until you three broke into my house."

"Your door wasn't locked, so technically, we didn't break anything," Nova supplied with a smirk.

Nash sat on the edge of his bed and ran a hand through his hair. "What the fuck do you want?"

Nova stepped forward, her arms crossed. "I want to know what you did to make my friend run away from here like she did."

A fresh bout of pain sliced through his chest at the reminder of what he'd lost. "I asked her to marry me."

His siblings were silent.

"Is he still drunk?" Roman asked.

"I haven't drunk at all."

"You proposed and she turned you down?" Ricky asked, none of his usual chiding in his voice.

"Yup."

"How did you do it?" Nova asked.

"You really want to make me relive it and further humiliate myself? Fine. I went to see her after I found out she'd been in the accident only to find her packing. Dad said someone hit her—what if it was intentional? I can't protect her when she's not with me. If we were married, then she'd be here all the time, she'd never move away, and I could provide for her and the kids and keep them safe."

His siblings shared a glance.

"What?"

Nova shook her head and sighed. "You're an idiot, that's what."

"Please, enlighten me, oh wise-ass one."

"Bro, you didn't even tell her you love her? Even I know better." Ricky chuckled.

"But I . . ." Fuck. He'd never told Bella how he felt about her. He hadn't even been able to acknowledge his feelings for her were much deeper than he'd ever experienced until his dad had pulled it out of him.

"I do love her."

"Wondering when you'd finally realize that, you stubborn man." Nova rolled her eyes. "And you basically insulted her like she was some helpless woman from the fifties who needed her reputation saved for having a baby out of wedlock and offered her money and a house in exchange for marrying your sorry ass. You realize she'd been in this situation before with her ex, right?"

"I didn't look at it like that. But it wouldn't be the same—I love her. I want to be with her and have a family together. Is it so bad I want to give her things? Protect her?"

"No, it isn't, Nash. But you made it sound like those were the only reasons. You forgot the most important piece of the proposal—telling her how you feel," Nova answered.

"But I screwed it all up. I abandoned her and I wasn't there when she needed me. And there's no way she could love me back—not now."

"Oh my God, you're an idiot." Roman sighed.

Nash glared at him. "How so?"

"Blind as a bat," Ricky agreed.

"You're saying she loves me too?"

"Man, you're a little slow on the uptake. Must have been from Ma dropping you on your head as a baby so much," Ricky teased.

"Who else would put up with your grumpy self for so long? She defended you even when none of us knew you were the supposed baby daddy who'd left her high and dry. And she moved in with you—God knows that takes a special kind of woman, to put up with you that much," Roman said.

"And I know there was a lot more to her glow than just pregnancy—not that we need to go into those details." Nova held up her hand as she grimaced.

"Nash, don't be a dumbass and waste your second chance." Roman's voice wavered with emotion. He was no doubt thinking of his own situation with his wife.

"Would you do it?" Nash asked.

Pain flashed in Roman's dark eyes before he nodded. "I'd like to think so. But I don't have just me to think about. Ariel is my number one priority—besides, we're not talking about me here. We're talking about you."

"What's holding you back?" Nova asked, her eyes narrowing on him.

Nash took a deep breath and then let it out. "What if I'm not enough? What if something happens and I lose her too after I get even more attached?"

Roman clapped a hand on his back. "What if you stay stubborn and carry on like you have been, keeping everyone at arm's length and being miserable? Is that a life you want? Yes, something could happen tomorrow and you could lose her. So why not make the best out of today? No regrets."

Nash rubbed the back of his neck and sighed. "You're right."

"I'm sorry, I didn't quite hear you. Can you say that again?" Roman smirked.

Nash chuckled. "You're right. You're all obnoxiously right. Happy?"

Nova sat beside him on the other side of the bed, leaning

on his shoulder. "We'll be happy when you are, big brother. That's what we've always wanted for you."

He kissed her temple and hugged her close. "Thank you, guys, for sticking with me even though I've been a total asshole."

"You can always make it up to us . . ." Ricky's eyes flashed with mischief.

"How so?"

"Tell us how you plan on winning our girl back," Nova answered.

"I think it's time I told her the truth about everything . . . my past and how I feel about her."

"Not to knock on your plan, but I mean, you've been a complete egghead for the past week. You might need to do something else, you know, to prove to her she's your lobster," Nova said.

Nash flicked a questioning glance to his brothers who looked just as stumped as he was. "Uh, I doubt calling her a crustacean is the way to go if I want to win her over."

Nova rolled her eyes again. "You know what? Never mind. Just . . . good luck."

"I have something I need to do first." Nash got up and headed for his office.

"Yeah, definitely shower and brush your teeth before you go," Ricky agreed.

Nash ignored him and found the stacks of notebooks, all letters to Ana. His pain had been poured into hundreds and hundreds of pages. He carried them over to his fireplace, setting them on the stone before lighting them. He drew out his wallet, plucking out the worn and weathered missing poster with Ana's face on it.

I'm sorry I wasn't what you needed. He tossed the image into the burning pile.

Footsteps from his siblings padded down the stairs as he sat back and watched years of guilt and pain being devoured by the flames. He needed to let go of his past to move forward into a future. As his first love, Ana would always carry a piece of his heart. But she was gone. And he could only hope she was finally at peace. "Goodbye, Ana."

Nothing was holding him back from moving forward with Bella except the things left unsaid between them.

"What's the plan now?" Roman asked.

Nash stood, hope flickering to life in his chest. "Now, I'm going to get my girl."

51

ISABELLA

Isabella stared out at the sea beyond the small window in her parents' flat. Greenish-grey waves rose and fell, tossing the few boats left at the marina. She hugged her arms around her chest, wishing it was Nash holding her. She'd felt so safe in his arms. But that feeling hadn't been real. She needed to remember that.

"I'm ready to go home," Eli said, shrugging his backpack over his shoulder.

She turned towards her son. "Honey, I told you that we aren't going back today. I'm going to go check out a house that Abuelo's friend has for rent."

He shook his head. "No. I don't want to move again. I want to go back home—to Nash's."

"Eli." She sighed. "We can't stay there any longer."

"Why? Did Nash kick us out?"

"No—"

"Then why? My room is there. All my boats from Dad."

"We'll get them, sweetheart." She reached for him but he jerked away.

"No! I'm not moving again." He twisted his fingers over and over, getting more agitated by the second as his eyes raced back and forth.

I'm the worst mother in the world, putting my son through this. Dragging him from place to place like a bag of luggage.

"Eli, I promise this will be the last move for a while, okay? I know it isn't easy, but we don't have another choice—"

"So Nash wanted us to leave? Was it me? Did I do something?"

Just when Isabella thought her heart couldn't possibly break anymore, the jagged pieces shattered into smithereens. "No, baby. You did nothing wrong. Do you hear me?"

"Then why?" His voice broke, his hands fisted and his small chest heaving.

"Things . . . just . . ." She sighed, rubbing her hand over her tired eyes. "It just isn't working anymore—Eli! Where are you going? Eli!"

He stormed out of the room, the front door opening and slamming closed.

Isabella moved to follow but her mother gripped her shoulder. "Let him go. Your papi is down there. Eli will cool off and understand."

Isabella shook her head, slumping into a chair at the kitchen table completely drained both mentally and physically. With her head in her hands, too exhausted to try to stop the tears.

Her mother's soft, warm hand smoothed over Isabella's forehead, removing the hair from her eyes.

Isabella sniffled. "I'm sorry, Mama. I don't know how, but I always seem to make a mess of things."

Her mother took the seat next to her. "Oh, sweetheart, you have definitely chosen a much more difficult path in life. But you wouldn't be who you are if you took the easy road.

You've always done things your own way. And just as you have every single time before, you'll find your way through this challenge."

"I love him, Mama."

Her mother's cheek twitched.

"I know you hate him—but he's a good man. He never lied to me or led me on. He made it clear to me what he was capable of and what he could offer me."

"He shouldn't have touched you. What kind of man gets a woman pregnant, has her move in and play house, but won't commit?" She shook her head, disgusted.

"I wasn't taken advantage of."

"Why? Why would you give him the *leche* for free? He should buy the cow!"

Isabella shook her head at the way her mother jumbled the saying. "I am not livestock. I'm a woman. An adult who made decisions. Why do you hate him so much? You disliked him even before you knew he was the father."

She shook her head. "That man's fiancée disappeared and he went and bought a boat six months later. Nancy said she heard he and his ex got into a huge fight at the bar the last night she was seen. Even if there was only a small chance he was a killer—I didn't want that for you, *mija*. I was scared for you."

"Nash isn't like that. He's never laid a finger on me or come close. Even when he was angry and upset, he took care of me."

"I still don't like it. I don't trust him," she argued.

"You're basing all this on rumors. You know what your friend says about me behind your back?"

Her mother stood abruptly. "Nancy is a friend. She would never badmouth my family."

"You're wrong, Mama. That woman spreads misinformation like it's her job. According to her, I was cheating on my husband and this baby is a love child. I just convinced Nash it was his because he's only one of my many lovers."

"No—"

"Overheard her at the grocery store telling the baker."

Her mother's face pinched.

"What?"

"I—never mind. It's none of my business." Her mother went to the sink, poured water into a kettle, and set it on the stove.

"No, tell me, Mama."

Her mother sighed and turned around, staring at her daughter. "It did seem awfully fast after . . . Robert's passing that you . . . moved on."

"That's what this is really about, isn't it?"

Her mother's eyes darted to the colorful rug on the floor.

"Robert and I agreed to divorce before he was diagnosed."

Her mother gasped.

"Robert was gay, Mama. He didn't love me—not the way a husband should. I stayed with him until the end, but we were no longer married in any way that mattered."

Her mother's face was white as a sheet as she opened and closed her mouth like a fish. "What do you mean he was gay? He made a child with you—he married you."

"He wasn't sexually attracted to me, or any woman for that matter. Our first time was an experiment for both of us. We were friends, and I wanted to know what it would be like. Everyone was talking about sex at school. And I felt like the odd one out for not experiencing it yet. Later, I found out he was struggling with his attraction to men and thought that he could stop it if he slept with me."

Her mother swallowed and shook her head. "But he . . . Robert never seemed . . ."

"Gay?"

Her mom nodded.

"He came out to me right before his diagnosis and we agreed to get divorced, but then we found out about the ALS and I couldn't leave him."

"That was years ago."

"Yes."

"That's around the same time that man Phillip started showing up in the pictures you posted online," her mom pointed out, and Isabella could almost see the cogs turning in her mind.

Isabella exhaled. "Phillip and Robert fell in love."

Her mother opened her arms, stepping forward and wrapping Isabella in a hug. "I'm so sorry, *mija*. Why didn't you tell me? You dealt with so much all on your own."

"Robert's parents turned their backs on him after he came out to them. I couldn't deal with how you'd react too. It was better just to pretend things were the same."

"I thought you and he were happy."

"He was my best friend."

"Oh, my sweet girl. You've carried so much on your shoulders alone." Her mother squeezed Isabella tighter. "For the record, I would have loved him the same, but I would have been upset that he hurt you in the process."

Tears fell from Isabella's eyes. She couldn't seem to stop them these days.

Her mother pulled back, framing Isabella's face in her hands. "You listen to me. You deserve to have someone who loves you enough to put you first like your papi does to me. Someone who puts up with your temper and gives you your way most of the time."

Isabella laughed.

"I don't know if I've said it nearly enough, but I'm proud of you, *mija*."

Her vision blurred with more tears before she blinked them away.

"I may not agree with all your choices, but you're right—they are yours to make. I've only ever wanted to keep you safe. Robert might not have been the man for you, but he was a good man. So, as much as it pains me, I will try to give Nash the benefit of the doubt. But if I see one thing that I don't like—"

"I know. Although I don't think that's going to be an issue now."

"Then it's his loss."

"Thank you, Mama—"

"*Cariño*, have you seen Eli? I was going to see if he wanted to wrap his boat with me for the winter. Storm's rolling in—wanted to get it out before it hits. I've procrastinated long enough." Her dad interrupted them, opening the door and letting in a blustery cold November wind.

"He wasn't with you?" Isabella asked, her stomach pitching as the hair on her neck and arms stood on end. A knowing twisting her guts.

She grabbed her coat and rushed outside, slipping it on as she made it down the steps, her father and mother hot on her heels.

"I'll check the shop." Her mother darted inside.

"I'll check out back in the storage yard." Her dad disappeared as Isabella raced towards the docks.

Her lungs froze as fear pierced her chest like icy spears. "Papi! His boat's gone!"

She turned and ran into the shop.

Her mother came out of the back room. "He's not here."

Her father's footsteps thudded inside as she pulled up the app on her phone. She'd bought a special monitor for her son since he'd wandered off from school one day back in Colorado. Robert had insisted on using it since his diagnosis. They'd been worried, considering he was so trusting. It was a safety measure that stuck.

A small green dot appeared on her screen in the middle of the blue ocean. "He's out there! I need the keys to Papi's boat." She reached behind the counter, grabbing the ring with the orange mini buoy.

"What's wrong?" Nash's deep voice cut through the room, lashing her chest in part relief, part pain.

"Eli is missing," her father answered.

Nash's eyes widened, fear splintering his usual stoic mask.

"He took off in a boat," Isabella added.

"He went out in this?" Nash asked.

"He's not in the storage yard." Her dad shook his head.

"He's at sea." Isabella held up her phone.

Nash grabbed it from her, studying it intently. "I told him never to go out alone."

"He was upset," her mother added.

"I have to go after him. Papi, do you still have the emergency kit in the boat?" Isabella asked.

She turned but Nash and her father were gone. Where were they? Would Nash really abandon her at a moment like this?

Isabella ran outside as the wind picked up. "Papi?"

Nash was in her father's boat, tossing the ropes off the dock as her father got behind the helm. Isabella raced down the docks as quickly as possible, being careful of the slippery surface.

"Wait! I'm coming with you."

Nash held up her phone and shook his head. He aimed a fierce, determined look her way. "No, baby. You stay here where it's safe. We'll bring Eli back. Promise." After that, her dad gunned the engine, ignoring the no-wake zone.

"Nash!" She stood at the edge of the dock as he moved farther and farther away. The waves got bigger and bigger, and this was just the bay. *Oh Dios, the sea will be so much worse.* "I can't lose him!"

Icy wind whipped against her skin, unforgiving even through her coat. She waited until the boat was out of view before she turned back towards the marina.

Her mother came out with a blanket to wrap around her. "Come inside, *mija*. There is nothing we can do right now. I've called the coast guard."

"I just want him back—both of them."

"I know. But Nash and your father know these waters well. Come on." She led her inside.

She stood by the window, staring out at the churning sea. The tea in her hand was incapable of chasing the chill from her bones. Three of the people she loved most were out there at the mercy of Mother Nature.

52

NASH

Nash's body trembled from a mixture of adrenaline and the cold. His eyes flicked between the green dot on the phone screen and the dangerous giant waves crashing against the boat. Tomas was careful to angle his vessel the right way so as not to be capsized, however it was slowing down their progress. But it looked like Eli was taking a familiar route that Nash had shown him when fishing on countless occasions. They were almost to Eli's favorite spot by the sandbar. *It's gonna be hard to control the boat. What if he hits it? His much smaller boat is no match for these waves—especially with a kid at the helm.*

Nash searched the green water. The buoy signaling to boats a warning of the sandbar should be there—there it was.

"Where is he?" Tomas asked.

Nash glanced down at the screen once more, but the green dot was gone.

His heart stuttered in his chest. His eyes were glued to the raging ocean. "Where are you, bud?"

A flicker of orange capped a wave and then disappeared.

"There he is!" Nash pointed to the break only yards away.

Tomas gunned the engine, heading towards it. The orange life vest poked through the water once more.

Tomas murmured a prayer in Spanish as he sped as close as was safe.

"Fuck!" Nash swore.

Eli bobbed in the icy water, the red light of his emergency beacon flashing on his life vest.

"I'll get him." Nash grabbed a life vest and jumped into the dark waters.

A thousand pinpricks like frigid knives pierced his nerve endings. His lungs were just as frozen as the rest of his body as he floated. One second stretched into eternity before his fight-or-flight mode kicked in. He needed to grab Eli and get him out of the water before they both died of hypothermia.

Nash's legs kicked and his arms shot out through the dark depths, forcing his sluggish limbs to move. His life vest helped carry him to the surface as he attempted to suck in a breath. Eli bobbed in the water only a few feet ahead. Nash swam towards him and grabbed his vest.

"I got you, bud. You're gonna be okay."

"I'm-m-m s-c-c-cared."

"I know." Nash kicked and swam as hard as he could, dragging the boy with him. As soon as they approached the boat, Tomas was there, reaching for his grandson. Nash gripped the ladder and shoved Eli out of the water, pushing him on board. The boat lurched. Nash's hand slipped, knocking him back. Pain sliced across his side as his body hit something hard under the water.

Nash sunk beneath the surface. Lungs burning, darkness encroached his vision as everything quieted under the water. He struggled with lead-filled limbs; everything hurt. If he didn't get through this, he'd never get to apologize to Bella.

He'd never see his daughter be born. Nash gathered what was left of his strength and swam to the surface, heading back towards the ladder. Each breath was like swallowing shards of ice. He heaved himself on board. Eli lay on the deck, shaking uncontrollably in his grandpa's arms, his lips blue.

Nash snapped into action, helping to lift Eli and take him out of the wind towards the helm. He stripped Eli's clothes off down to his boxers, and then Tomas piled all the blankets he could find over the small boy. Nash picked him up and bundled him in his arms as Tomas headed back to the captain's chair.

"Stay awake. You hear me? Stay awake. We'll get you home." Nash shook Eli just a bit, trying to get him to keep his eyes open.

Tomas gunned the engine, driving the boat back towards the marina as Nash's eyes grew heavy. His body shook uncontrollably. He gripped the boy in his lap, trying to infuse whatever heat he had remaining into Eli as Tomas fought to get them home safe.

Tomas handed him the radio, keeping his solemn voice low. "Tell them where we are. We need the coast guard. I'm not sure we can make it back in this. We're fighting the current and the wind. These waves are too big for this boat."

Nash relayed their coordinates. "If you're listening, Bella, I got him. He's gonna need m-m-medical attention. He went in . . ."

The radio crackled, voices cutting through with too much white noise to understand.

"Bella?"

"N . . . sh, ah . . . you . . . re." Her panic was palpable even through the shitty connection.

He shook Eli a little. The boy looked up at him with eyes

that were heavy with sleep. "Stay with me, bud. Tell me about boats."

"I'm-m-m s-s-sorry."

"It's okay. I'm the one who's sorry." Nash's gaze caught on the red droplets spreading into a small puddle by his feet. He reached for his side and jerked from the pain. Fuck, he was injured. Judging by the growing crimson pool, it was bad.

"N . . . sh? Are y . . . kay?" Bella's voice cut through the speaker again.

His heart slowly thumped in his chest. The chill was so deep in his bones, he was sure slush was pumping through his veins. The wind sliced through the wet clothes hanging frozen off his body. All his remaining strength was used to hold Eli against him as Nash shared what little body warmth he had left. He might not make it out of this. He picked up the radio, his thumb sluggishly moving over the button. His heart rate slowed with every shallow breath he took. He leaned against the window on the opposite side of the captain's chair.

"Bella, I don't know if you can hear mmme." He relayed the coordinates again. "You always wanted my honesty. I don't think I'm gonna make it back, baby. Send the coast guard to our location to get Eli and your dad. I don't know how much longer I can stay awake." He shook his head, eyes burning as regret stabbed him. "I love you, Bella. That's the one truth I kept from you. I'm so fucking sorry I can't be there to tell you to your face like you deserve."

The radio crackled, but nothing came through. Minutes or hours ticked by—he wasn't sure. Tomas steered the boat as best as he could. Nash's body locked up, his movements slow and painful. His head was foggy like he'd been drugged. Waves crashed against the boat, making them bob dramatically through the water. Cold seawater splashed over his back, the salt stinging his wound. He held on to Eli, shielding him as much as possible.

"Sss okay, b-b-ud. Almost there."

Eli's shivering had calmed down. He peeked his head out of the blankets as a light shone over them.

"There's a helicopter!" Tomas pulled out a flare, ignited it, and waved it in the air.

Thank fuck.

"They're here to save us," Eli said before another wave rose, its shadow darkening the boat before everything went black.

53

ISABELLA

Isabella sat in the uncomfortable hospital chair. Machines beeped and the tang of cleaning solution clung to the sterile air. Nash's chest moved up and down, but his eyes remained closed. They said he'd woken a few times, coming in and out of consciousness since he, Eli, and her dad had been brought in yesterday evening. Eli was now safe at her parents', resting with his abuelo and happily playing on his tablet, while his abuela spoiled him with treats. Isabella still needed to have a stern talking to him, but the loss of his boat had hit him hard.

Nash stirred, his eyes blinking open.

"Nash?" Isabella inched closer, taking his hand in hers.

He turned his head towards her and grimaced as if in pain. His eyelids drooped half closed. "Is Eli okay? Or did I dream it?"

"He's fine. You and Papi saved him."

She stood, grabbing the cup of water from the tray and offering him the straw. He sucked down a few sips and she put it back.

"Thank you, Nash. You risked your life for my son. I can never repay you."

He shook his head, obsidian eyes falling on her with such weight she couldn't breathe. "I made you a promise."

"You did."

He picked up her hand, rubbing his thumb over her flesh. "I'm sorry I shut you out. That I was an asshole, so stuck in my self-loathing that I took you for granted."

"Nash—"

"No. I need to say this." He cleared his throat. "I was on my way to the marina to tell you all this. And when I was on the boat, my biggest regret was I never got to look you in the eyes and tell you how I feel about you."

His voice had come garbled through the radio, but she'd heard the confession. The truth through the white noise.

"I love you, sweetness. I didn't think I was capable. Thought that part of me died a long time ago. Believed my heart was destroyed, and had nothing left to give. But you— you captured my soul. Somehow, without me realizing it, you'd caused my heart to beat again."

She swallowed the emotion bubbling up in her throat.

"When you walked out the door, it broke me. It took me some time, but I realized that I'd just let the best thing that ever happened to me go because I was too caught up in my head to do something about it."

"You're grieving."

"Yeah, but mostly I'm just blaming myself for things I can't control. I decided I'm going to let the past go. I want a future with you. I know I fucked it all up. I never meant to hurt you with my proposal."

She snorted and shook her head. "Is that what you call it?"

The corner of his mouth turned up. "No. I promise when I do it again, I'll do it right."

Her eyebrows rose. "Oh, you think you'll get the chance to try it a second time?"

"I fucking hope so," he grated. "But I'll wait until I've earned your forgiveness."

"I don't need marriage, Nash."

"I know. But I want you forever, sweetness. Whether that means a white dress someday or a promise."

"I forgive you for being lost in your grief. But I can't be with someone who turns to alcohol when they are hurting. That isn't healthy."

"I know. You're right. And I won't do it again."

That was something only time would tell. But Nash had never gone back on his word.

"And I can't be in a partnership with someone who won't let me in. I love you, Nash, scars and all. In the same way that I hope you love me."

He nodded solemnly. "That brings me to my next confession. Take a seat."

She settled back in the chair, still clasping his hand.

"The night that Ana disappeared, I found out she was cheating on me. And it wasn't the first time."

She'd cheated on him? She couldn't help the ache in her heart for Nash.

"We argued, and then she left. I got texts from her a little while later, asking me to meet her and telling me she was sorry. I told her no. I had already made plans with Nova to fly to California for a weed convention."

He stared down at the blanket in his lap. "Ana didn't contact me again, and I didn't reach out. I half expected her stuff to be gone from the apartment when I got back. But everything was exactly how we'd left it before the bar. I thought maybe she was with the guy she'd cheated on me with. So I messaged her, and didn't hear back."

He sighed. "Nova couldn't get a hold of her either. By the time I went to the police a couple days later, she'd already been missing for over a week . . . I blamed myself because I was the only person she'd had to count on. If I had reported her missing earlier, maybe they would have found her sooner."

"How did they know when she went missing? You had an alibi for the first night, but what about after that?"

"After I reported it, Bently pulled the camera footage from the Shipwreck. She was seen getting into a car with another driver. Too blurry to make out plates, or who it was, but that was the last time she was seen alive. I was on that footage getting into Nova's car and then at the airport. I was out of the state for a week, but by then she'd already not been to work, and no one had heard from her. So unless they have some proof—which they won't because I didn't do it—I won't be held accountable."

"I'm sorry. I can understand why you'd blame yourself, but I hope you know it wasn't your fault."

He nodded. "I do now. At least, I'm trying to believe it. I shut myself off after that for years until you showed up. That first night we were together at the wedding, I felt something spark in me. I couldn't walk away from you even though I tried. And when we had sex—it all felt so real. I was too vulnerable. That's why I left you the way I did and shut down."

She nodded. "I appreciate you explaining that. After everything with Robert, I blamed myself for not being . . . enough in the bedroom. And when you reacted that way, I thought . . ."

He squeezed her hand. "No way, sweetness. You're a fucking goddess in and out of bed."

She smiled shyly. Nash tugged her hand, moving over on the mattress.

She pulled away. "I don't think that's a good idea."

"Please? Just let me hold you, sweetness." His hoarse voice dipped with his plea.

She moved to sit beside him, careful of the wires and his stitches from his injury. He wrapped her up in his arm, pulling her against his chest and kissing her temple.

She turned to face him. Affection shimmered in his dark irises, aimed at her.

"Isabella Noveas, I love you more than I'd thought possible. And I swear if you give me the chance, I'm going to remind you every day just how much you mean to me."

She closed her eyes. It seemed too good to be true.

"I love your smile." He traced her lips with his finger. "Your fire. And the way you don't let my grumpy attitude push you around."

She laughed, meeting his eyes, needing to see the honesty in them.

"I love that you stay true to who you are and stand up for what you need. You push me to be a better man—challenge me in the best of ways." He palmed her belly. "I love our daughter and hope she's just like you. And I love Eli like he was my own. Even if you decide you can't trust me with your heart, I want you to know I'll respect your decision and I'll be there for you, him, and our daughter no matter what."

She tucked her head against his chest. "Where do we go from here?"

He kissed the top of her head. "I think we take a play from your book, and start by stepping into tomorrow."

54

NASH

Three Weeks Later

Bella pulled out her phone as they walked from the main barn back to their house. She swiped open the screen and tapped a reply before returning the device to her pocket.

She looked adorable with his oversized hoodie snug over her belly. She'd taken to wearing his sweatshirts because hers didn't fit anymore. It brought him an embarrassing amount of possessive satisfaction to see her in his clothes.

"Was that Phillip?" Nash asked.

She nodded, her nose reddening in the chilly air. "Yeah, he wants to schedule a time to visit when the baby's here."

"Mom and Dad have extra rooms in the main house if he needs a place to stay," Nash offered.

"You sure they wouldn't mind?"

"Have you met my mother? She basically adopts anyone who comes for dinner." He chuckled.

Bella laughed, her teeth chattering. They strode another few moments in the beautiful peace of the snow. "My fingers are so cold I can't feel them anymore."

Nash stepped in front of her, pulling her thin-gloved hands into his before blowing warm air on them. "You're the one who wanted to walk. I told you it would be too chilly."

She rolled her eyes, surveying the fresh blanket of snow covering the fields and woods around them. Only a few spots of greenery were left in the trees lining the property. "I was hot when we left, but I didn't account for the wind."

"I guess you'll just have to let me carry you the rest of the way."

"Nash—"

He hooked one arm under her knees and one under her upper back, lifting Bella against his chest where she'd be warm.

"I'm too heavy and you're gonna drop me on this ice and reinjure your side!" she screeched.

"I'm not gonna drop you." He headed for the house. "And you sure as fuck aren't too heavy, so stop saying that."

The house wasn't too much further. She clung to his neck, her eyes closed. He loved having her so close.

"You trust me, don't you?" he asked, a little afraid of the answer.

There was no sound but the crunch-swoosh of his feet wading through the snow-covered road and a few crows overhead.

His chest squeezed tight as his steps slowed. "I'll put you down."

"No." She gripped his jacket. "Sorry, I was just lost in thought. You asked if I trusted you and . . . and I really want to. I don't mean about you carrying me—I know you wouldn't drop me on purpose. And if we fell, you'd make sure you took the brunt of it, because that's who you are—a protector."

Nash flicked her a glance as they rounded to the bottom of his driveway. He kept his attention on the slippery ground after that, nervously waiting and hoping as she mused aloud.

"You risked your life for my son. So in the physical sense, I trust you one hundred percent. But when it comes to . . . other matters . . ."

"Like your heart?" he clarified.

"I want to trust you, if that makes sense? I just . . . need some more time."

He gave a stiff nod. "I understand."

"I'm sorry," she apologized.

"You have nothing to be sorry for. If you don't feel completely safe with me, that's on me. I know it's gonna take a while." He kissed her forehead. "Thing is, sweetness, I've already decided you're it for me. So I have all the time in the world to wait and earn your faith. I'll wait forever if I have to."

Her stare at the side of his face made his skin prickle as he carried her up the porch. The rumble of an engine bounding up the driveway had him turning as he set her on her feet. The tan sheriff's truck parked next to Bella's new SUV.

Bently got out and gave them a wave as he walked to the bottom of the steps. "Hey, Nash, Isabella. Do you have a minute to talk about the case?"

Nash swallowed, dread sinking into his veins. "Sure, come on in where it's warm."

Bella walked in first, stripping off her winter jacket and boots before slipping into the kitchen. Nash followed suit. Bently toed off his boots and shut the door behind him.

"Hot chocolate, anyone?" Isabella asked.

"That would be lovely," Bently answered.

Nash rounded the counter and grabbed the kettle from her hands. "I got this."

Hurt flashed in her eyes. "Oh, okay. I'll just, um, go upstairs, then."

She moved to step around him, but he gently gripped her shoulder, holding her in place. "Stay. Please?"

Big whiskey eyes looked up at him. "You sure?"

He slipped his fingers in between hers, linking them together before he brought them up to his lips for a kiss. "Absolutely. You go sit down and put your feet up. I'll handle this."

"Okay." Her lips curved in a small smile, her eyes glittering with a mix of joy and hope.

He'd do anything he had to in order to keep that mix of emotions there.

Nash prepared the drinks and brought them over to everyone.

"Thanks." Bently took his.

He set Bella's in front of her and kissed her temple before sitting between her and Bently. His heart thudded. "What did you find?"

Bently took a sip and set his drink down. "We got the autopsy report. And we can confirm the remains are Anastasia's."

His body tensed. His muscles contracted until he was rigid stone. He'd had no doubt it would be her, but the confirmation released something in him.

Bella's warm hand landed on his thigh, bringing him a sense of comfort. Relief trickled through Nash, along with a sigh. His shoulders lowered a fraction.

"Are there any leads? Any idea who could have done this?" His voice came out hoarse.

Bently cleared his throat. "They're still processing evidence."

The sheriff was holding something back. Nash could feel it in his bones. "How did it happen?"

"The answers to that will only cause more pain. It's better to remember her—"

"How?" Nash insisted.

Bently glanced at Bella and then met his gaze head-on. "We believe she was strangled due to the broken hyoid bone."

Nash nodded and pulled his hands off the table, allowing them to fall by his sides as he sat back in the chair.

Images of Ana all alone up on the hill with her attacker flashed in his mind. Did she call out for him? She'd have been terrified in her last moments.

Bently's voice droned on, but Nash couldn't bring himself to tune in while his thoughts were spiraling.

I should have been there for her.

I should have—

"Nash?" Bella's voice pulled him back to reality.

"Is that all?" Nash asked Bently.

There was still a killer out there. Someone who had targeted someone he cared about and buried her body on his land.

"For now. I'll let you know if we get any leads, but I'll be honest—it's a cold case. The killer was likely feeling some guilt and reached out. It's not probable they've stuck around to get caught. I want you to know my team is doing all we can to try and figure out who did this, no matter how impossible it seems, but we may never get answers. That's unfortunately the way a lot of crime goes," Bently assured him.

"I appreciate that."

Bently gave a nod and stood. "Thanks for the hot chocolate. Have yourselves a good day."

Bella saw him to the door. Nash's lungs felt stiff. He shot to his feet, anxious energy pulsing inside him. He needed to move, to escape. To forget. Fuck!

He walked over to the cupboard above the fridge and pulled out the bottle of whiskey, setting it on the counter with shaking hands.

"Nash?" Bella's sweet voice reached out to him like a lifeline, and he wanted to go to her but what was the point? He'd just hurt her more. She needed to stay away from him.

No. I can't push her from me again.

He picked up the bottle and slammed it down into the sink. It cracked, the bottom breaking off entirely as the amber liquid spilled down the drain.

He ran both hands over his face, his shoulders hunched over. With his eyes burning, he turned to her, palms held out. "I wasn't there for her when she needed me."

Bella's lips turned into a frown and her expression filled with sympathy he didn't deserve. "You think it was your fault still?"

He nodded and then shook his head. "Fuck. I don't know anymore. All I know is I don't want to ever fail you when you need me." Nash stepped closer and cupped her face in his hands like he was holding the most precious thing in the universe—because he was. "I've made so many mistakes in my life. I have a lot to make up for, with you especially. And I'm trying." His voice broke.

Bella's arms surrounded him as she pulled him into a hug so tight he wasn't sure who was holding who. "I see that. I know you are. You're a good man, Nash Emerson. And you will get through this—*we* will. Together."

He looked down at her, tipping her chin to look her in the eyes. "What did I do to deserve you?"

She offered him a smile. "You were brave enough to take a

chance and do something different, remember? You took the steps that would lead you someplace different. We just found each other along the way."

"I really want to kiss you right now," he said.

"So do it." She lifted on tiptoes. His arms dropped to her waist as he leaned in and brought his lips to hers. She smelled so sweet, roses and hot chocolate with a hint of snow. Her warm mouth melded against his and his cock hardened. But this moment wasn't about lust. She brought him comfort and hope for a better future. With Bella, all his dreams and then some were possible. Life meant more when it was shared with her.

They would get through this day by day, together. And he'd earn her complete trust, mind, body, and soul. Only then would he ask Bella for her forever too. Because he'd become the man she deserved if it was the last thing he did. And he'd spend every day being worthy of her love.

55

ISABELLA

One Month Later

"Thank you for coming." Isabella smiled and gave her mother a hug in the crowded kitchen of the home she and Nash shared. The rest of his family gathered around to show their support.

"Of course." Her mother turned to Nash, not quite meeting his eyes. "My condolences."

Nash leaned against the kitchen counter, sliding his arm around Isabella's waist, his large hand resting on her belly as it did most days. Like he subconsciously needed to reassure himself everything was alright. She got the feeling that today of all days, at the official funeral for Anastasia, he needed something to ground him.

Isabella was happy to be there for him. True to his word, Nash hadn't turned back to alcohol.

"Thanks," Nash said.

Her father cleared his throat, flicking a look to her mother.

"And I wanted to let you know that I appreciate all you've

341

done for my daughter and grandson. I'm . . . glad they have someone else watching over them," her mother said.

That was as close to an apology from Catherine Noveas as anyone would get.

Nash nodded. "I will do everything in my power to keep them safe."

Her dad patted Eli's shoulder. "Well, I'll see you on Friday for our sleepover."

"Okay, Abuelo." Eli walked to the living room and organized the chess board as Roman sat across from him with Ariel in his lap.

Her father helped her mom get her coat on before they left.

"I think she might be warming up to me," Nash whispered in her ear.

Isabella smiled and turned to face him, looping her arms around his neck. "I think saving her grandson's life has won you some good grace."

Nash chuckled and kissed her chastely on the mouth. "I'm just glad Eli promised never to do it again."

Isabella's chest tightened. It didn't matter how much time passed. The fear of losing her son would stick with her forever. "I'm certainly not going to replace the boat anytime soon."

"He'll just have to go out with me until he's old enough to handle it on his own." Nash smoothed his thumb over her cheek.

"I know he was hurting, and the sea is a place of calm for him—where he feels connected to his dad. I just wish he'd find a safer hobby."

Nash kissed her forehead. "I'll teach him everything he needs to know, including respect for the unyielding power of Mother Nature. Though I think she taught him that herself."

Nova plucked a cookie from the platter on the table under

the bouquet of lilies that had been delivered earlier. "Would you two lovebirds give it a rest? You know you don't have to touch her every minute out of every day, big brother."

"I'm pretty sure that's what got them into this mess—Nash's inability to keep his hands, and *other* parts, to himself." Ricky snickered, motioning towards her nine-month belly from his seat at the table.

"When is the little princess going to make an appearance?" Nova asked.

"Alba is due Friday," Nash answered.

Ricky winced. "You sure that's the name you're going with?"

"It's Latin for sunrise. And don't you dare start, Ricardo Andrew Emerson." Isabella pointed her finger at him.

"Ooh, she used your full name. You're in trouble, Uncle Ricky." Nova laughed, wiping what was left of the cookie crumbs off her chest.

Ricky held up his hands. "I'm just saying, a niece named after her favorite tío might be better."

"Keep dreaming." Nash chuckled.

"I don't need anyone else," Roman said, walking into the dining area a few steps ahead of his mother.

Renita already had her coat on, as if she were ready to take her leave.

"Don't need anyone for what?" Nova asked.

Renita looked around the room. "I suppose now that you're all here, it's as good a time as any to tell you the news. Your father and I decided to take that trip we've always talked about later this summer. And with the weddings already booked, I know I won't have enough time to keep an eye on Ariel every day like I have been doing."

"I can help some days," Nova offered.

"No, your brother needs to hire a nanny. Someone who

can give her consistent care so she doesn't have to be shuffled from place to place every other day. And someone who can prepare her for starting school next fall," Renita argued.

Roman sighed. "She hasn't been around anyone else but her family—"

"And that's exactly why you should do this. It will ease her into being social with more people and break her out of that protective little shell she's stuck inside. Otherwise school is going to be much more of a shock to her." Mama Emerson wasn't backing down.

"Maybe I'll homeschool her again." Roman wiped a hand over the back of his neck.

Renita placed her hand on her son's shoulder. "You can't keep her in a bubble forever, son. It will do more harm than good. Trust me. We'll find someone who can sign, and be the perfect fit."

Roman waited a beat, then nodded. "Fine." Turning towards Nash, he said, "I'm gonna head out with Ariel and get her ready for bed. You good?"

Nash nodded. "Yeah. Thanks for being here."

"Of course."

"I don't just mean today." His gaze moved from one sibling to the next until he landed on his mother. "I mean the whole time. You never gave up on me, and I can't say how much I appreciate that."

His brothers and sister looked at each other before they moved as one, surrounding Nash and pulling him into a group hug.

"They can push each other's buttons like nobody else, but then there are these moments that make all the stress they put me through worth it," Renita said as she stepped to Isabella's side.

"You have a wonderful family."

"And it's about to get a little bigger." She winked and rubbed Isabella's belly. "Thank you. You've given me my son back and a grandchild."

Isabella's stomach fluttered. She wasn't sure if it was the baby or the nerves.

Renita turned towards her children who were now joking and teasing each other in the center of the kitchen.

"Alright, I'm heading out. Love you all." Renita turned and made her way to the door, Roman carrying a sleepy Ariel behind her soon after.

"That's my cue too." Ricky grabbed his coat and wrapped a scarf around his neck. "I'm going to hit the gym before I head home."

"Drive safe." Isabella waved.

"Well, now that they caught the guy that hit your car and left you in a ditch, the roads should be safer," Ricky remarked on his way out the door.

It seems the man hadn't learned his lesson and had done the same thing a few weeks later in another town after one too many drinks. This time, there were witnesses and he couldn't escape. It was the same description as the car that had hit Isabella's and the paint was a match. He was now serving time in jail for the hit and runs.

"Where's Eli?" Nova asked, glancing around the corner where Eli was busy flicking through TV channels until he landed on reruns of a fishing show he was obsessed with. Nova cut a glance at Isabella, a smile on her lips. "I think I'll spend some time with my nephew before I leave."

Nash wrapped his arms around Isabella's waist, pulling her back to his front and inhaling at her neck. "Have I ever told you, you smell like rose hips? You know, the sweet pink flower that grows in bushes around the edges of the coast?"

"It's my body wash."

"Well, whatever it is, I like it." As if to further prove his point, he nuzzled her neck.

"Come with me." She took his hand, leading him upstairs.

"Sweetness, are you trying to take advantage of me while my sister is in the house?" His low chuckle made her pussy clench. They hadn't crossed that line since she came back home. She couldn't risk her heart without knowing for sure it would be taken care of this time. Nash had been so patient. But her vibrator was sure getting a workout.

"Maybe." She led him towards his bedroom. "I know today was hard for you. And I didn't want to take away from that. But I hoped I could also turn it around and make it a good memory for you too." She opened the door and walked in.

Nash followed her to the bed where a biodegradable lantern lay with a marker. He stopped and turned to her.

She tucked a few strands of loose hair behind her ear nervously. "It seemed to help Eli when you did this for us, so I thought . . ."

Nash stepped into her space, cupped her face with his warm, calloused hands. "This was so thoughtful, but you see . . . I've already said my goodbyes. Ana will always be with me, much like I assume Robert will stay with you. They are people we've loved and lost." His voice broke, and he cleared his throat. "I'm glad we could lay her to rest today. That she isn't missing anymore. But—" His lips pressed together in a grim line, his eyes glassy with unshed tears.

The emotion radiating off him made her chest ache. She wished she could do something to ease his sorrow. "But?"

He opened his mouth and closed it, pulling away. Her heart sunk. He still couldn't let her in when things got hard. Tears welled in her own eyes. He couldn't—

Nash knelt in front of her, his face pressed against her very pregnant belly as his hands wrapped around her waist. She placed her hand on his head.

"But she's gone. And I'm here with the most amazing woman I've had the privilege of knowing and loving, and have love me. Maybe it makes me a heartless asshole, but today wasn't an end for me. It's the beginning of a new phase of my life. One that I'm actively choosing."

He tipped his head back to look at her, tear tracks glistening down his cheeks. "I've never loved anyone the way I love you. Never thought I'd experience this or have the family that I'd wanted for so long. But I stopped feeling sorry for myself and realized that if I wanted a woman like you, I'd have to be the man you needed."

"Is that why you finally agreed to go to therapy?" she asked.

"Yeah. Enough was enough. I wasn't getting anywhere on my own. And I didn't want to keep hurtin' you."

She was just grateful he'd finally reached out for help.

Nash got to his feet, his hands dropping to his sides. "Do you . . . I mean . . ." He blew out a breath, his body trembling like he was nervous. "Do you think you can forgive me? Even if you're not ready today—I'll wait as long as it takes."

She pressed her hand to the side of his face. "I've already forgiven you. And more than that—I trust you. If you want to do this . . ."

His chest stopped moving as if he were holding his breath. His eyes glittered with hope.

"I'll need you to be all in. I'll need your vulnerability as well as your truths. You gotta let me take care of you too sometimes," she finished.

"I can do that," Nash agreed, wrapping his arms around her.

She leaned forward, capturing his mouth in a kiss of hope

and promise. His lips glided over hers, soft and sweet, torturously gentle. Her heart burst with love and happiness. Could she really have it all? A man as good as Nash who loved her and her son? A partner in life through all its ups and downs? *Yes!*

He gripped the back of her neck, tugging her closer, like he couldn't get enough of her. She moaned into his mouth and dragged her teeth over his lip.

He froze. "Are you sure you're ready for this? We don't have to have sex right now if—"

"Nash?"

"Yeah, sweetness?"

"Shut up and make love to me."

The corner of his mouth quirked up. "Yes, my love."

Nash picked her up and she squealed.

"Shhh. Don't want my sister or Eli coming up to investigate the noise." Nash's voice rumbled as he set her gently on the bed.

He climbed next to her and tugged down her leggings. "No panties again?"

She shrugged. "Underwear lines."

After licking his lips, he bit the bottom one, his eyes growing hazy with lust. "What am I gonna do with you?"

"I can think of a few things," she said playfully.

"Fuck, baby. You're killing me here." He pulled the bottom of her sweater up and over her head, exposing her ginormous stomach and breasts that were barely contained by her bra. A blush rose to her cheeks, self-conscious of how different her body looked now compared to the last time they'd been together two months ago.

"Fuck, sweetness. Gonna come just from looking at you. You're so damn sexy, round with my child," he rasped like he truly was barely holding on.

"Then you better get inside me, because I want to feel you when you come," she confessed.

He lay on the bed, still fully clothed. "Sit on my face and hold the headboard."

"What? You can't be serious."

One of his eyebrows quirked. "Why not?"

"I'll smother you. Don't know if you've noticed, but I've gained quite a bit of extra weight due to the baby currently taking residence in my entire abdomen."

He smacked her ass and gripped her hips, picking her up like she weighed nothing and setting her on his chest. "Don't know if you've noticed, but I'm not some young boy who can't handle a real woman. Now sit on my face and let me make you come like a good girl."

Fuck, why was it so hot when he got all growly and demanding? She gripped the headboard, putting her weight on her knees as she moved to straddle his face. A sharp smack landed on her ass.

"Ow!"

"Stop fucking hovering. Sit your pretty ass——"

She sat just to shut him up. He groaned, the noise vibrating through her pussy as his tongue slicked through her folds. Oh good God, of all things holy! Her eyes rolled back in her head. Somehow, despite the aches and pains of being nine months pregnant and feeling like a whale, Nash made her feel beautiful. His fingers dug into her hips, tugging her down on his face as his beard scratched her thighs. His hot tongue slid into her pussy, fucking her before moving up to tease her clit. She sucked in a breath as pressure gathered in her center, threatening to explode.

"Nash." Her voice was a breathless plea.

He hummed as he sucked her clit into his mouth. Her back arched, eyes rolling back as she rocked her hips, fucking his face with reckless abandon. She was so close. Her orgasm just within reach—

Nash clamped one hand over her mouth and then pinched her nipple with the other as she ground down on him, unabashedly seeking her pleasure.

Her mouth opened, his hand muffling her keening cry as her orgasm hit. She tensed, her thighs locking around his head, his tongue never changing the rhythm as he drew out her climax until it rolled into another wave. Warm euphoria rushed through her, drowning her every synapse in an eruption of ecstasy. She rolled off Nash, lying next to him. He pulled her into his arms before his lips were on hers. She tasted herself on his kiss, which only made them seem that much closer.

She caught her breath as he drew lazy swirls down her body and around her belly with his fingers.

"Good girl. Damn, I missed this—watching you come apart." He laid his palm on her chest.

"I missed this too."

He gently kissed her before pulling back. "Never again. That's another promise I intend on keeping. Whatever you need or want, I'll be the one to give it to you." His fingers swirled over her clit causing her muscles to contract as a gush of fluid spread over the bed.

He sat up. "Fuck, you're soaked. I've never seen you squirt like that."

"Nash—"

"Fuck, that's hot." He swirled her clit again as a dull throb expanded around her lower back.

"Nash, stop, that's not—my water just broke."

His eyes widened as he stared at her like he was frozen.

"Nash?"

"That means . . ."

She placed a hand on his forearm. "It means we're gonna have this baby."

"Fuck!" He shot up, heading for the door. "We need your bag. And to call Sebastian. And Eli needs someone to watch him—and I have to tell my mom—and your mom!"

"Nash!"

He paused, looking at her. She'd never seen him so disorientated.

"It's gonna be okay. Grab our hospital bags, and ask Nova to stay with Eli until my mom can get here. I'll text her and your mom while you're getting our things into the car."

"Right, yeah, okay. I can do that." He grabbed the bags and raced out of the room.

"Just don't forget me!" She chuckled and then hissed as a contraction barreled through her.

"Fuck, that hurt." She held her belly and slowly got to her feet after it passed. She needed to change and clean up. Soon enough, she'd have her legs spread in front of who knew how many medical staff with no dignity whatsoever. But she had some pride, and she really didn't want to have her doctor's hand inside her while she stunk of sex.

She hobbled to the bathroom, having to breathe through another contraction on the toilet. "Looks like you'll be coming a few days sooner than I thought, love bug."

* * *

Four hours later, Alba Catherine Emerson was born at eight pounds, and with the darkest brown eyes. Matted curly black hair stuck to her head as she screamed her little lungs out. Nash was the first to hold her, with so much awe and love shining from his eyes that it stole Isabella's breath.

"She's perfect." He handed her to Isabella.

She studied her daughter's angry little face as Alba rooted around Isabella's bare chest. Isabella lifted her breast to her mouth, wincing at the strength of Alba's little latch. Eager sucking sounds replaced her cries as Isabella looked adoringly at her daughter. Tears blurred the snapshot she was trying to memorize.

Nash kissed her cheek, leaning his forehead against her temple. "Thank you for giving me this gift."

"I love you so much."

He kissed her, soft and sweet, before leaning down to kiss their daughter's forehead. Isabella stayed like that, her daughter suckling, the man she loved holding them both with his back to the door, like he could shield them.

But life was full of unexpected things. Both good and bad. And as much as Isabella wanted to perceive him as the god of the sea, he was human.

She let out a deep breath. She wouldn't let the worry of what could happen taint this joyous moment. She'd continue doing what she'd promised and step into tomorrow.

EPILOGUE - ISABELLA

"Watch your step," Nash warned, holding her hand and guiding her onto his boat.

Rays of warm sunshine danced over the mostly calm ocean waters. The scent of salt and sea melded with a hint of cedar from the captain himself. She buried her face in his chest and wrapped her arms around him. It was nice to be able to do that without a basketball between them anymore.

"Do you think Alba will have enough to eat? Maybe I should pump one more time—"

He hooked his arm around her and held her tightly against him. "She's got plenty of milk. We won't be gone long at all. My mother's raised four kids; I think she can handle a five-month-old for a couple hours. Besides . . ." He kissed her neck, making her shiver. "Daddy needs some alone time with Mommy."

She giggled. "And we had to come out to the boat for that? In my parents' marina?"

"Of course not. Just sit your pretty ass in that seat right

there and enjoy the ride." He pulled away and pointed to the spot next to the captain's chair.

"Hmm. What if I want to drive this time?"

A low chuckle rumbled in his chest. "Sweetness, you can drive my boat anytime you like."

"Are we talking your actual boat or is this a euphemism? Because I have to tell you, the first time you told me you had rods to go fishin', I wasn't sure."

Mirth sparkled in his eyes. "Guess you'll have to wait and see. Now go get settled."

She obeyed, taking in the view as he untied the boat and started the engine.

It was smooth waters as they chugged out of the bay. She kept her attention ahead on the white caps of the waves towards the horizon. The sea birds flew overhead, and the lighthouse was in the distance. Waves lapped at the boat as a warm, salty breeze blew over them. She turned, taking in the man beside her. His black riot of curls were tousled from the wind. His beard had grown out a little longer. It was a little messy from the weather and her own fingers. His dark umber skin shone in the sun with tints of gold. She'd seen this man in many lights: co-parent, boyfriend, father, son, brother, and lover. But her favorite was like this, when he was in his element. Her Poseidon.

The engine slowed before it cut. Nash turned towards her and smiled. His white teeth were a contrast to his full brown lips. "What are you thinking about?"

She bit her lip. "How you would look shirtless with a trident."

His eyes rounded and his brows drew together. "What?"

"The first time I saw you, I thought you looked like Poseidon, god of the sea."

He tipped his head to the side. "Well, I guess we know what I'll be for next Halloween." He winked.

A burst of laughter escaped her as she looked around. "Where are we?"

"You don't remember?"

"Should I?" she asked.

"This is where I took you fishing that night."

"Well, that explains it. I didn't really get to see much of the top deck while we were here," she teased.

"That's right. I guess you better go below to see if it jogs any memories." He motioned to the door.

She gave him a cursory glance as she did just that, opening the door and sucking in a breath. She was met with the flickering of dozens of flameless candles bathing the room in a warm glow.

"Nash. What . . . how . . .?"

"Go on in." He spoke in her ear.

She stepped down into the space. The table on her left was littered with battery-powered tea lights. The bed where they'd conceived Alba was farthest to her right.

In the center of the mattress was an envelope.

She picked it up and turned towards Nash. "What is this?"

"Open it and find out."

She took a deep breath, slid her shaky fingers inside, and pulled out a handwritten note. The script was slanted and masculine, and surprisingly neat. She recognized it immediately as Nash's.

She flicked a glance to him.

"Read it."

Bella,

The day you walked into my life changed me forever. From the moment I met you, you inspired me to be better. To take a chance and seek a better future. Little did I know just how much that one decision would change my life forever.

Everything good in my life now is because of you.

Tears welled in Isabella's eyes. She had to wipe them to see the rest of the words. Her heart was so full of incandescent happiness—it was like she'd swallowed a piece of the sun.

Because of you, I found out that I'm not as broken as I thought. That I have a lot more to offer. You made me a father—a gift I will cherish forever. You made my heart beat again after I'd thought it had died.

And still, I want more. I want all your tomorrows so I can wrap you in my arms and cherish each and every moment with you. I want your sick days and your happy days. I want the rain and the sun. But more than anything, I just want you.

My last request, because I'm a selfish bastard who won't ever be satisfied with just pieces, is that you make me a husband.

In exchange for your forever, I swear to you I'll lay down my life for you and for the kids if needed. I'll be your lighthouse in the dark. And your shelter in the storms that are bound to come our way.

I'll do my best every day to show you just how much I appreciate and love you with my words and my actions.

You want the moon? It's yours. You want the sun and stars? Just say the word.

I promise you my heart, my mind, and my soul. I'll bare it all to you in the hope that you will agree and make me the happiest man in the world by saying yes.

She wiped her eyes again and lowered the letter, meeting Nash's shiny gaze as he got to his knees and pulled out a blue velvet box with a gold-embossed trident on it. It was from Poseidon's Treasure, the high-end artisan jewelry store in town. He opened it to reveal a stunning raw blue apatite stone like someone had captured a piece of the sea in the stone and encased it with rose gold.

Nash gripped her hand, still holding out the gorgeous ring

to her. "My beautiful, fierce, sweet Bella, I've never been a man of many words—at least spoken aloud. But everything I do have is yours. My body, my heart, and my soul no longer belong to me alone. Will you do me the honor of being my wife and letting me hold your hand for the rest of my life? Let me be the arms you run to when you're happy or upset. The man who provides you with everything you need or want—but above all, my truths?"

Happy tears dripped down her cheeks as she nodded. "Yes!"

He removed the ring from the box and slid it onto her finger before rising to his feet to slam his lips against hers. This kiss was fire and love. A promise and hope for a brighter tomorrow. She dug her nails into the back of his neck, squeezing him closer as his big hands slipped beneath her dress.

She gasped as he swiped his fingers between her slick folds.

"You're fucking soaked."

"I need you inside me."

"I want a taste first," he grated, dropping to his knees as his hands firmly spun her around. Pressure on her lower back had her bending onto the bed on all fours. Cool air rushed over her exposed backside as he lifted her sundress.

"What did I tell you about not wearing panties?" A firm slap on her ass had her hissing through her teeth as hot arousal dripped down her thighs.

"That you loved it?" She tried to sound innocent.

His tongue lapped between her lower lips, drawing a moan from her.

"I told you that if you did it again, you'd be punished. Is that what you want, sweetness?"

Yes! "Maybe." Her voice was all breath.

"I'm going to fuck your pussy and make you cream all

over me. You're gonna scream for me like a good girl, aren't you?"

"Yes."

"You can't come until I tell you—is that clear?"

Her response was cut off by the sensation of his cock dragging her arousal from her tight hole down to her clit over and over, making her whimper with need.

"What's that? Tell me what you need, baby."

"You. I need you inside me."

He plunged his cock inside all the way to the hilt as his hand cupped around her mouth, imprisoning her attempted screams.

"Fuck, you feel so good. Like this cunt was made for me. It's all mine, isn't it, Bella? Forever mine."

She nodded, her eyes rolling up as he thrust slowly and forcefully in a steady rhythm, just the way she liked it.

One hand gripped her ass, tucking a few fingers around her hip bone to pull her harder against him. He moved his palm from her mouth. "You like that?"

"Yes." Pressure swirled, gathering tighter and tighter in her core. Liquid heat spread out to her limbs, and she burned with the fire of a thousand suns—all in delicious need. "I'm going to come."

"Not until you beg me."

"Please. Nash, please. Let me come."

"I want to hear my name from your sexy lips when you do."

She closed her eyes, her muscles tensing as he drove into her harder and harder.

She was lost in a cloud of bliss, climbing higher and higher on a rising flood of pleasure. Her toes curled, her nails digging into the comforter as he reached around and swirled his thumb over her clit. His voice vibrated in his chest against her back, his lips nipping the shell of her ear as he commanded, "Come for me, sweetness."

And just like that, like her ecstasy was dependent on his permission, she broke apart in a sunburst. Bright light flashed in her gaze as warm euphoria exploded inside her, flooding every synapse with a high she'd never known.

Three more thrusts kept her strung along like an addict, riding the high of decadent, dark pleasure until his cock pulsed inside her, tipping her over the edge yet again. Nash yelled her name as he came, and it reverberated softly like a caress sent straight to her clit.

Nash slid out of her, lying on the bed, his chest rising and falling with each deep breath. She rolled over and snuggled against him, basking in the afterglow.

His hand smoothed up and down her arm. "I love you."

"I can't wait to start the rest of my life with you." She smiled.

"Think we could plan a wedding before my parents leave for their vacation?" he asked.

"That soon?"

"Don't want to wait another minute to make you officially mine."

"And you'll be mine," she reminded him.

He curled a lock of her hair around his finger as he rose on his elbow to look at her. His gaze was adoring and full of heat despite having just come inside her. "I'm already yours."

She smiled, her belly tumbling with butterflies.

"I have one more surprise." He reached into the cabinet by the bed and pulled out another envelope.

"What's this? Another love letter?" she asked.

"No, it's the official name change for the boat."

She blinked up at him. "For this one? Nash, you didn't have to—"

"I wanted to. I needed to let go of my guilt, and admittedly, I'd be pretty pissed if you had a boat named after your ex even if I understood it."

"What did you name it?" she asked.

He set the paperwork back in the cabinet. "Renamed her *El Amanecer.*"

She swallowed the fresh bout of emotion rising in her throat. "You named your boat The Sunrise?"

He nuzzled her neck and kissed the corner of her mouth. "Sure did, sweetness. After our daughter, but also because I plan on spending the rest of my sunrises with you."

She placed her hand on his cheek. "Who would have thought that the grumpy man I went fishing with who could barely string a few sentences together was this romantic, sentimental, and poetic guy deep down?"

He gave a snort and shook his head. "You're the only one who knows, so don't ruin my rep and tell everyone."

She laughed and took his mouth in a slow, sensual kiss. He licked her bottom lip and pulled back.

"One thing we haven't discussed is how many more kids do you want," he said, his hand splayed over her stomach, tracing the lines of her newest stretch marks. It seemed to be his favorite thing to do lately when they snuggled.

"Well, I've always wanted a big family. I would like a few years in between getting pregnant again. But I am open to adoption."

His eyes lit up. "Really?"

"What about you?"

"I didn't build my house with five rooms for nothing." He smirked and lowered his mouth to her belly, kissing along the red marks the creation of their daughter had left behind. "God, you're so beautiful."

She relaxed against him, savoring the tender kisses he placed on her body.

The shrill ring of her cell phone had her tensing. "Where's my phone?"

He reached down to his pants and pulled it out. "I told them not to disturb us. It's Roman."

"It could be about Eli or Alba. Answer it."

"What do you want?" His brows drew together in a concerned line as he tensed. "Someone broke in?"

Isabella sat up, placing her hand on Nash's forearm.

"Christ, man. You could have led with that." He breathed a sigh of relief, and it brought a sliver of comfort to her as he traced his thumb up and down her bare thigh. "Yeah, well, I was in the middle of it when you interrupted me. Yeah, it's today." He smiled. "She said yes, by the way . . . I will . . . Yup." Nash ended the call and tossed the phone onto the pile of clothes.

"What happened?"

"Apparently Roman thought he had an intruder in his house, and he acted accordingly. Thing is . . ." He chuckled. "It's not a thief but his new live-in nanny. Apparently, Mom didn't give him a heads-up and, well, he made a mess of things."

"Is everyone okay?"

"Yeah. Guess she has a strong right hook." He laughed.

"She punched Roman?"

He nodded. "I'd like to know how that happened."

"Now that's quite the first impression."

His arms tightened around her. "Not as good as ours though, right?"

She smiled and kissed his pec. "Ours will forever be my favorite."

He gripped the back of her neck. "Mine too.

The End.

Now, turn the page for a sneak peek of Book 2 of The Emerson Family Series, ***Risking Forever***, (featuring Roman and Elise's story), right away!

Or visit the website below to order Book 2 in The Emerson Family of Shattered Cove Series right now.

WWW.AMKUSI.COM/RISKINGFOREVER

SNEAK PEEK OF RISKING FOREVER
CHAPTER 1

Elise

"You can do this," Elise said aloud to herself in the rearview mirror.

Ding!

Her gaze focused on the gauges in front of her. Shit! The tire-pressure icon was lit up red. She had so many of those little colored lights, you'd think she was collecting them like Girl Scout badges.

"Just one more reason you need this job. So go in there and convince this family you're their best choice for a nanny." *At least it's a step above free babysitting for my slimy two-timing ex.*

Elise blew out a breath and squeezed the back of her neck. A tension headache was pinching her nerves.

Before she could overthink it anymore, she shut off the engine and climbed out of the piece of junk that needed more work than it was worth. It seemed so out of place here next to the neatly trimmed yard, rolling green hills, and tidy garage. The gravel driveway was huge and rounded, lined with trees on one side. A white van parked by the edge of the house had an *Emerson Farms* logo on the sliding door. Colorful flowers adorned the walkway up to a massive wraparound porch. Planters with purple, pink, and blue flowers hung from the edge of the porch roof above the railings.

The sound of a screen door shutting drew her focus to the older Black woman smiling from the entryway with a wave.

Her brown, purple-tipped dreadlocks swayed with her motion. "You must be Elise Aki."

"Yes, ma'am. And you must be Mrs. Emerson."

"Oh, please call me Renita or Mama E." She waved her hand as if dismissing the formality.

Elise scanned the property once more. Lush green grass with wildflowers poking through it covered the fields to her right. There was a barn and pasture down the hill, and another larger barn that seemed newer farther along with a gravel parking lot she'd passed on her way up the long tree-lined driveway. "You have a beautiful home."

"Thank you. Come on in. Ariel is excited to meet you, and I've got a cup of coffee with your name on it or tea if you prefer?"

"Tea would be lovely. Thank you." Elise followed the woman inside.

The home was spacious and bright. Colorful rugs scattered the pine floors. Pictures adorned the walls of the hall and the living room she passed which contained a mishmash of furniture.

Renita led her past some smaller rooms and a shut door before they entered a large kitchen that chefs' dreams were made of.

"Have a seat." Mrs. Emerson motioned to a stool at the large kitchen island.

Elise did as she said. A little girl with puff buns in her hair peeked into the room. Elise smiled and waved to her, but she hid behind the wall once again.

"Ariel Daisy Emerson, you get your butt out here and greet our guest," Renita chided while setting a plate of cookies on the table between them.

Elise's stomach grumbled embarrassingly loudly. She'd skipped breakfast and lunch—again. Her savings were down to almost nothing and her credit card was maxed. If her best friends Sam and Jack knew she'd been skipping meals, they'd be furious with her, but she didn't want to be a drain on them any more than she had these last few weeks.

Renita pushed the cookies towards her. "Help yourself. Your tea will be ready in a moment. I have peppermint or chamomile, and I think black mango."

"Black mango, please, but I'm more than happy to get it." Elise rose.

Renita shook her head as the little girl walked into the room. "No way. You sit right there and get started on those cookies."

Ariel climbed onto the stool across from her. Her head was bowed, but her eyes were definitely aimed at Elise.

Elise gave the girl her most friendly smile and signed as she spoke. "Hello. You must be Ariel; I've heard so much about you. But I have one question. Are you a mermaid, like the Ariel in the movie?"

The little girl bit back a smile, her eyes lighting up as she signed back to Elise. "*No, I'm not. But I want to meet a mermaid.*"

"Maybe we'll be lucky enough to spot one sometime." Elise winked.

Ariel reached across the counter and grabbed a cookie. She bit into it as Renita set a cup of tea and jar of honey in front of Elise before taking a seat beside them.

Elise stirred a spoonful of sweetener into her tea. "Thank you."

"You're welcome. I don't believe we should waste each other's time. Let's get down to brass tacks, shall we?" Renita asked.

Elise's stomach clenched. Had she messed this up already? "Of course."

"I went over your references, and you seem more than qualified to take care of my granddaughter this summer. But what I'd like to know is why a young woman like you with your degree wants to nanny?" Renita didn't pull any punches.

"I'm actually teaching this fall at Shattered Cove Grade School, so this was perfect as I needed something to do during the summer. I've double-checked the date, and I would need to report to school a week before my work officially ends for Ariel. Will that be a problem?"

Renita shook her head. "It shouldn't be. I'll be back by then, and we can make necessary arrangements for her care. Are you new to the area?"

"No, my family is from Dark Cove, so just the next city over."

Renita's eyes widened. "Oh, well then, that's great. You already know your way around."

"Yes."

"And you're okay with the live-in position? You'd be staying in my son Roman's house. You passed the turn-off on your way in. You'll have a bedroom to yourself, but share a bathroom with this little one." Renita motioned to her granddaughter.

"Yeah, that's fine."

Ariel reached for another cookie, eyeing her grandma. Renita glanced at the little girl. "Don't tell your daddy I let you eat cookies so close to dinner."

Ariel smiled and shook her head, holding out her pinky finger. Renita looped her smallest digit with her granddaughter's in a pinky promise.

"Your resume didn't list your employment for the last two years." Renita's attention was back on Elise.

"I, uh, well, I was . . ." Sweat dotted her forehead as the newly scabbed wounds over her heart opened wide again. "I had a family situation that needed my attention." Vague but hopefully professional. Elise was pretty sure if she spilled the whole sordid tale of her shitty judgment in men, Renita would show her the door. But she needed this job. She'd searched and there was nothing else that would allow her to make enough money in the two months before school started to save for a down payment on an apartment, and this was a live-in position. She wouldn't have to force Sam and Jack to put up with her in their guest bedroom any longer than the two weeks she'd already commandeered it for.

Renita's eyes crinkled, her keen gaze studying Elise for a beat. "Well, I'm pretty satisfied with our phone interview, your background checks out, and you obviously know American Sign Language well." She turned to Ariel. "What do you think, pumpkin? Would you like to spend the summer playing with Elise?"

Ariel licked a few crumbs off her lips and signed, *"Will you take me to the beach to look for mermaids?"*

Elise laughed. "If your parents say it's okay."

"And will you give me cookies like Gramma?"

"Well, I do love to bake."

"Okay." Ariel nodded.

"She drives a hard bargain," Renita joked. "Ariel, why don't you go clean up your toys? Your dad will be home soon."

Ariel hopped off the stool and gave Elise a wave before disappearing out of the room.

Renita got up and grabbed a framed photo from the kitchen wall, handing it over to Elise. "It's just my son. His wife—Ariel's mom—passed almost five years ago. Since then, Ariel hasn't said a word."

"I see." Elise's heart broke for the little girl. A smiling Ariel beamed at the camera, holding a line with a small fish out in front of her. The man next to her smiled down at her like the little girl was his whole world—and he was one of the sexiest men she'd ever laid eyes on. He could have been a model with his toned body and six-pack like she'd only ever seen on magazines and book covers. Damn, he was fine. And that was the dad she would be living with? Her skin heated.

But the last thing I need is another single dad taking advantage of me —no matter how hot he is.

"Roman is really busy in the summers unless it's bad weather. He's up before the sun most days and home after it sometimes. You'd have to be able to make dinner too. Is that a problem?"

"No. I can cook. I enjoy it actually," Elise assured her. It would make things easier if she didn't have too many run-ins with the hottie from the picture.

Renita smiled. "Great. Ariel has therapy every other Monday. And she's been homeschooled up until now. She's going to school this fall, so if you don't mind working with her on the things she may need to know?"

"Absolutely."

"And the salary is alright with you?"

"Yes, ma'am," she quickly agreed, handing the photo back.

Renita stood again and walked over to the counter to grab a piece of paper and pen and return the frame. She slid a legal-looking document over to Elise. "Then I'd like to officially offer you the job. This is a contract with everything we agreed to over the phone. You go ahead and read through it and make sure it's agreeable to you."

Elise skimmed the particulars. At this point, it didn't matter if Mrs. Emerson required a kidney; she needed this job. She'd nannied during college but she'd never been presented with a contract before.

As if sensing her question, Renita explained, "There's a part in there about not speaking to the press or anyone outside the family except the authorities about the open investigation regarding the murder of my son's ex. I hope you understand the sensitive manner of this request?"

Murder? Oh, God. How much had Ariel lost? Had she seen her mother be attacked? Was that why she didn't speak? How strange Elise hadn't heard about the case. She'd been gone a long time from Dark Cove, but this kind of news usually traveled.

"Of course. I understand." She signed her name on the line and dated it.

Renita did the same and produced another copy for Elise to keep.

"Great. Now, let's show you where you'll be staying this summer. Did you need a few days to move in?"

Elise shifted on her feet, tucking her hair behind her ear anxiously. "I actually have everything with me." *Because I'm kinda without an address at the moment.*

"I like a woman who comes prepared. Perfect. Ariel?"

The little girl came bounding around the corner.

"Let's go show Elise her room in your house."

Elise followed them outside. Renita didn't bother locking the door. Elise had forgotten what it was like living in a small town.

"Why don't you drive back down the driveway, take a left at the first turn-off. Around the corner, you'll see Roman's house."

Elise stumbled over her feet, quickly catching herself as the pulsing in her head got worse. "Sure."

"My son Nash lives on the other side of the property with his fiancée, Isabella, her son, Eli, and my grandbaby, Alba." Renita pointed to the other side of the property. "Ricky lives on the south side. And Nova's up on the hill. I'm lucky enough to have all my children so close." Renita's lips turned up, the mother's love evident in her warm expression.

Elise gave a polite smile and tried not to be envious of people she didn't even know. But the affection with which Renita spoke about her children, the way she wanted them near, drew attention to the ache inside Elise. She'd never had that—her parents had dumped her at a boarding school as soon as they'd found what they assumed was an imperfection in her. That was one reason she couldn't go to them with her problems. It would prove them right—that she was incapable and not good enough. *They never wanted me before. Now that I'm a grown woman, I don't see them taking me back in.* She blew out a long breath and climbed into her junker, praying that it started and didn't embarrass her in front of her new employer.

The engine cranked and then puttered. All those blinking icons flashed on.

She gritted her teeth, sending a fresh wave of pain slicing through her head. She wanted to tear off her cochlear implant and hit the gas, driving as far away from here as she could— but Elise didn't have that luxury. She needed this job and had nowhere else to go.

"Suck it up, buttercup. No one's got your back but you," Elise chastised herself in the mirror.

The fresh burn of tears had her blinking to clear them as she shifted the car in reverse. A pit formed in her stomach. Anxiety snaked up her limbs and constricted around her chest.

Elise pulled out of the driveway and headed toward the next beautiful family home. She would be the best nanny. She would get enough money to rent an apartment before school started. And she would survive the next two months under this hot stranger's roof. Then she could start over. And no one would take advantage of her again. She wouldn't fall for another handsome smile and empty words. No—she'd learned her lesson and had the scars to prove it.

She peeked at herself in the rearview mirror. "You got this, Elise. Show them you are good enough. You can do anything."

No one would stop her from rising from the ashes—especially not another hot single dad.

To continue reading Elise and Roman's story, visit the website below to get your copy of *Risking Forever* today.

WWW.AMKUSI.COM/RISKINGFOREVER

ACKNOWLEDGMENTS

It's always super intimidating to start a new series. Without our team, these books would not be what they are today.

Our editor and writing coach, Lauren, you are amazing. Thank you so much for all you do to inspire us to grow and be the best version of our author selves as we can.

To our sensitivity editors, Renita and Curtis, you guys are such an integral part of our books and our lives. You're always happy to help and answer messages or chat and share your wisdom and honest opinion. We are so grateful to you both.

Our beta readers, Valina, Holly, Chantique, and everyone at CREATING ink, who shared their culture and honest feedback to help make this story the best it can be—you guys ROCK! Betas are such an invaluable part of this process and we can't thank you enough.

Thanks to our loyal and enthusiastic ARC readers—we just love how much you love these stories and look forward to our release week Zooms that go all night.

To our readers—you are the reason we're able to do what we do and provide you with steamy, diverse, and emotional stories that rip your heart out and put it back together just a little different than before. Thank you for your support in buying our books and leaving reviews.

JOIN OUR NEWSLETTER

The best way to get updates about new releases, sneak peeks, pre-orders, giveaways, and more is by joining our newsletter.

You'll also receive a **FREE** short novel that's not available on any retailer to read.

Visit the website below to join now.

WWW.AMKUSI.COM/NEWSLETTER

THANK YOU

Thank you for reading *Stepping Into Tomorrow*. We hope you are emotionally satisfied with Nash and Isabella's love story. If you enjoyed this novel, please consider leaving a review on your favorite retailer and sharing it with your friends and family.

Want to read Remy and Mikel's story? Check out ***A Fallen Star*** (Book 1 in The Shattered Cove Series). The eBook is free on all retailers.

Lastly, if you haven't read all the books in ***The Shattered Cove Series***, make sure you get your copy so you don't miss out any of the eight amazing romances.

Thank you again for reading *Stepping Into Tomorrow!*

Cheers,

Ash & Marcus

ABOUT A. M. KUSI

A. M. Kusi is the pen name of a wife-and-husband team, Ash and Marcus Kusi. We enjoy writing romance novels that are inspired by our experiences as an interracial/multicultural couple.

Our novels are about strong women and the sexy heroes they fall in love with, are emotionally satisfying, and always have a happy ending.

Discover more about us at:

WWW.AMKUSI.COM

To receive updates about new releases, preorders, give-aways, and more, visit the website below to join our newsletter today:

WWW.AMKUSI.COM/NEWSLETTER

After you join the newsletter, we will send you a FREE story to read.

To contact us, use this email address: amkusinovels@gmail.com.

Happy reading!

Ash and Marcus

tiktok.com/@amkusi.romanceauthor

instagram.com/amkusinovels

facebook.com/amkusi

pinterest.com/amkusinovels

ALSO BY A. M. KUSI

A Fallen Star (eBook FREE on all retailers)

(Book 1 in The Shattered Cove Series)

Glass Secrets

(Book 2 in The Shattered Cove Series)

Defying Gravity

(Book 3 in The Shattered Cove Series)

The Lighthouse Inn

(Book 4 in The Shattered Cove series)

His True North

(Book 5 in The Shattered Cove series)

In The Grey

(Book 6 in The Shattered Cove series)

Brave Love

(Book 7 in The Shattered Cove series)

Hope Between Us

(Book 8 in The Shattered Cove series)